Also by Sheneska Jackson

Caught Up in the Rapture

Li'l Mama's Rules

Sheneska Jackson

Simon & Schuster

SIMON & SCHUSTER
Rockefeller Center
1230 Avenue of the Americas
New York, NY 10020

SIMON & SCHUSTER and colophon are registered trademarks
of Simon & Schuster Inc.

Designed by Elina Nudelman

Manufactured in the United States of America

10   9   8   7   6   5   4   3   2   1

Library of Congress Cataloging-in-Publication Data

Jackson, Sheneska.
Li'l Mama's Rules / Sheneska Jackson.
p.   cm.
1. Afro-American women—Fiction.   I. Title.
PS3560.A245S76   1997
813'.54—dc21   96-29735
                                                   CIP

ISBN 0-684-81842-6

This one's dedicated to the one I love—I always wanted to say that. But seriously folks . . . There is but one man in my life whom I can depend on without a doubt. To him, all praises are due. From him, all blessings flow. Because of him, I know who I am. I am so dedicated. I am so grateful. I am so fortunate to be a child of God.

Acknowledgments

One person believed even before I did. Without her, this novel and its message would never be. So . . .

I wrote a song about her. Wanna hear it? Here it goes.

■

Mary Ann, Mary Ann, Mary Ann . . . Mary Ann, Mary Ann, Mary Ann . . . Oh! *Mary Ann, Mary Ann, Mary Ann. Everybody should have a Mary Ann.*

■

Repeat chorus till blue in the face.
Peace.

—Sheneska

1

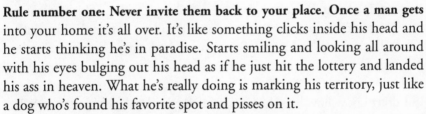

Rule number one: Never invite them back to your place. Once a man gets into your home it's all over. It's like something clicks inside his head and he starts thinking he's in paradise. Starts smiling and looking all around with his eyes bulging out his head as if he just hit the lottery and landed his ass in heaven. What he's really doing is marking his territory, just like a dog who's found his favorite spot and pisses on it.

I'm usually a stickler about my dating rules, but for some reason I slipped up this evening and allowed Terrence, with his pretty self, to come up to my condo, and now I'm sitting here on the edge of the sofa wondering when, if ever, he's gonna get out. I knew something was up when he pulled his car in front of my building and turned off the engine. I should've just said good-bye and jumped out, but I sat for a second too long, which gave Terrence just enough time to ask me if he could come in and use my bathroom. Damn. I rolled my eyes as I reached for the door handle, thinking, Can't you hold it till you get back to your own apartment? But Terrence got to squirming and squenching his knees together like some three-year-old toddler who was about to burst, so I decided to cut the brother a break and let him come in.

Big mistake.

Once we got up to my condo it was plain to see that Terrence didn't really have to use the bathroom at all. That was just a lie he made up so he could get his narrow behind into my house, where he's been now for the past hour, and from the looks of things he's not going to be leaving any-time too soon.

And to think, for a second there I thought Terrence might be my secret admirer. *Not.* He's too stupid to be that romantic, I thought to myself as I stared down at the sterling silver bracelet on my wrist. My secret admirer sent it to me on Monday and I still can't believe it. I've actually got a *secret admirer.* I thought this kind of thing only happened in the movies, or bad romance novels. Guess I thought wrong. *Any*way, my secret admirer has been romancing me all month long. Every day, a new anonymous package arrives for me at my office, and for the life of me, I cannot figure out who has been sending them. Like I said, I thought it might have been Terrence, but I showed him my bracelet over dinner and he barely blinked an eye. Besides, being a secret admirer would be out of character for Terrence with his pretty ass. He's too into himself to flatter anyone else. To tell the truth, I don't have a clue about who's sending me all these gifts. I've called every guy I've ever known and asked him if he's the one, but they all say no. Somebody's lying. But every day, the gifts keep coming. This week alone, my secret admirer has sent me this bracelet, a box of Mrs. Fields cookies, a red silk camisole, and a fern. But never is there a card or a return address or anything to tip me in the direction of finding out who is sending me all these things.

I don't know how long I can stand being in the dark about this. When I think about it, it's really kind of weird. I'm starting to think that maybe I don't even know the person who's doing this at all. I mean, I know a lot of guys, but none of them have this much flair about themselves, or at least I don't think they do. Maybe my secret admirer doesn't even know who *I* am. Maybe I'm just someone he saw walking down the street. Maybe he's a rich oil baron who has decided to sweep me off my feet by sending endless gifts. Or maybe he's a psychotic killer. I mean, this is L.A. The guy could be some deranged freakazoid who's been watching me for years. Maybe he's trying to set me up or something. He'll send me gifts un-til he goes broke, then one day he'll show up at my office door with a bunch of receipts and a sawed-off shotgun and demand his money and threaten to kill me . . . Okay, okay. That probably won't happen, but I'm just saying, in L.A. you never know.

*Any*way, one thing is for damn sure. My secret admirer is not pretty boy Terrence. Just look at him. Done made himself right at home. The first thing he did when he walked through the door was head for the refrigerator. I hadn't even turned on the lights and already he had his big, hairy hands wrapped around my last diet Coke. Well I'll be damned, I said to myself as I watched him from the doorway. I was planning on taking that Coke with me to work tomorrow, and here he was popping it open and putting his fat lips around it like he was the one who'd clipped out the coupon from the Sunday *Times* and gone to the store and bought the case of soda and lugged it back home up three flights of stairs because the elevator was out. Well, I thought to myself, I'll just be damned.

"Nice place you got here, Madison," he said, walking through the living room and looking at everything as if he was casing the joint. Then his beady eyes spotted my new leather recliner, where he proceeded to plop his sloppy ass down. He tossed his leg over the arm of the chair, grabbed the remote control off the table next to him, turned on the television set, and made himself really comfortable. Too comfortable. As if he was the one who'd spent two weekends in a row going from mall to mall looking for the perfect recliner and big-screen TV that would fit just perfectly in the living room while not taking up too much space and looking too gaudy. How dare he? I thought and squinted my eyes. No really, how dare he?

I stood in the doorway watching as he flipped through all one hundred and twenty channels of my cable system, and thought to myself, This fool must be crazy. Who did he think he was, barging into my place and taking over? This was my damn condo, that was my damn recliner, my remote control, my TV, and that was my last damn diet Coke! I was pissed and I wanted Terrence to be gone and this whole date to be over with. I don't even know why I went out with him in the first place. He's not my type. He's one of those damn pretty boys. Handsome, wavy hair, manicured nails, uses more skin products than I do—just pretty. Prettier than me. Terrence is definitely fine, and if I'm honest with myself, which I try never to be, I'll have to admit that Terrence's fineness is the reason why I accepted his date in the first place. When I first saw him jogging on the trail at Cheviot Hills Park I knew I had to meet him. He was jogging about ten feet in front of me and all I did for about twenty minutes was watch his butt bounce and wonder what it might take for a little woman like me to get my hands around a piece of meat like that. I couldn't catch up to him so I did the next best thing, the only thing an intelligent woman who hadn't had sex in a while could do—I faked an ankle sprain, screamed, and hit the dirt. It was overly dramatic, but it worked, and Terrence stopped jogging and ran back to help me up. "Ooch, ooch, hurt, hurt," I whimpered as he bent over my ankle, giving me ample opportunity to check out his perfectly perfect body. He was wearing a pair of biker shorts with a pair of running shorts over them and no shirt. The butt was tight, the abs were tighter, and the pecs were popping straight out at me like they knew me personally. I swear I thought his chest was calling my name—*Madison, Madison. Touch me, Madison*—and I almost did, until I remembered that I was supposed to be hurt and went back to faking pain. "It hurts *so* bad," I cooed.

Terrence was kind enough to help me back to my car, and by the time we'd gotten there he'd asked me out. I've always been a sucker for a good body, so I let the fact that Terrence was a pretty boy slide, even though after further examination I could swear it looked like he'd had a nose job, and the more I looked at his perfect pecs, the more I suspected they might be implants too. But anyway, he was fine and I wanted to get to *know* him, so I accepted his invitation for a date.

Big mistake.

He took me out to my favorite Mexican restaurant, which was a plus, but all he did all night long was talk about himself—a big negative. By the time our food arrived at our table, Terrence had gone on and on about how he was a model slash actor who was up for a big part in one of Spike Lee's new joints. But after dinner and about three strawberry margaritas, the real truth came out, which was that he'd only posed for one picture in his whole entire life, and the big part in the film he was up for was as an extra in a mall scene. Whoever said liquor will bring out the truth did not lie. I hardly talked at all during dinner, not because I didn't have anything to say, but because Terrence wouldn't give me a chance. Even after he confessed the truth about his bullshit career, he wouldn't shut his mouth long enough for me to get a word in edgewise. He talked nonstop about all the celebrities he'd met on auditions he'd gone to over the years, as if that would make up for the fact that he was still just another wanna-be actor who couldn't get a part in a film even if it was the autobiography of his own life.

He did shut up long enough to gaze into my eyes for a few minutes between stories. He was so fine that even though he was boring me to death, I couldn't help but smile and gaze back at his beautiful almond-shaped eyes and fantasize about how he'd look in a leopard skin G-string. Until, that is, he frowned up his nose and asked, "Is that a pimple or a blackhead on your cheek?"

I almost choked on the tortilla chip I'd just put in my mouth. It's a pimple, you little punk, I thought and tried to smile my embarrassment away. I'd thought putting a little black eyeliner over it would make it look like a beauty mark, but leave it to Mr. Pretty Boy to see through my Cindy Crawford impersonation and call me on it. Asshole. He even had the nerve to reach into his coat pocket and pull out a business card from his dermatologist.

"You might consider getting a chemical peel," he said and placed the card next to my balled-up fist on the table. "He also specializes in liposuction," he said and ever so slightly glanced around the table at my thighs.

I was speechless and embarrassed and mad as hell. He looked so perfect that I couldn't come back with an insult for him, so I just gritted my teeth, called over the waiter, and ordered another Midori margarita, an extra order of chips and guacamole, a side of beans and rice, and a shot of Triple Sec. By the time I got finished with Terrence I'd run the bill up to over eighty dollars and had eaten so much that I felt like I was going to pop clear out of my DKNY tailored suit. That'll teach Terrence to insult me, I thought and watched him squirm when it came time to pay the waiter. Needless to say, by the time we left the restaurant I was ready for the date to be over. I didn't want to see Terrence's perfect face ever again, and although I'd dreamt for a week about getting him in bed, I didn't want him anywhere near me anymore and I sure as hell didn't want him in my home, making himself comfy and invading my private sanctuary and drinking my last damn diet Coke. I hated to be rude, but I wanted him out and I wanted him out right now.

"Excuse me," I said, strolling through the living room like everything was peachy keen. "The bathroom is right down the hall," I said, pointing over my shoulder.

"Oh thanks, Madison," he said without even looking in my direction. "I just wanna catch this last couple minutes of *ER*. I was up for the role of the black doctor, you know. I coulda had that role, man. I shoulda had that role."

Yeah right, I thought, walking closer to him. "But I thought you had to go to the bathroom *so* badly," I said and watched this no-mannered SOB set his dripping wet soda can on the arm of my brand-new recliner.

"Ssh," he said and waved me off as he stared at the television.

Ssh, I thought to myself and eyed Terrence with a look that, if he had been paying me any attention, would have made him jump up and run for his life. *Ssh?* No, I didn't just get shushed in my own damn condo, I thought to myself as I felt an overwhelming urge to slap him on the back of his peanut-shaped head. I walked over to the coffee table, picked up a coaster, and threw it at him. "That's for the soda," I said and sat on the sofa across from him, wishing I'd aimed the coaster at his head.

"Thanks, babe."

Babe? Did he just call me babe? Whatever, Terrence, I thought and tried to keep calm. I crossed my legs and folded my arms across my chest and silently cursed myself out for not sticking to my dating rules and allowing this goon into my home. If I'd just stuck to my rules Terrence would not be here and I could be in my own damn recliner, flipping my own damn remote and sipping my own damn diet Coke—the diet Coke thing was really pissing me off. Instead I'm stuck here staring at the side of Terrence's big head and wishing I'd had this condo booby-trapped with hidden doors so I could push a button and make him disappear. But it's all my fault. See, I made up the dating rules for my own protection, which is why rule number one is: Never invite them back to your place. I'm a single woman living by myself in Los Angeles, California. A girl can never be too careful in a place like this, where every man you meet is a potential serial killer. I've never had a date nut up and turn psycho on me, but you never know. I mean, Terrence could suddenly get pissed off because he didn't get that part on *ER* and go crazy. He could pull out a gun, blow the TV away, then grab me and lock me in a closet and torture me for weeks with boring stories of how he and Gary Coleman used to kick it together, until I'd beg for him to blow my brains out. Okay, okay, that probably won't happen, but I'm just saying, in L.A. you never know.

My dating rules are mainly for my own peace of mind, so I don't have to put up with shit that I don't like. Take rule number fifteen, for instance: Never date a man who wears white dress shoes or white belts. Ugh! That means he has no sense of style whatsoever and may show up for a date wearing a light blue checkered suit or a bow tie or some other out-of-date shit like that. Then there's rule number six: Never date a man who's shorter than you. I don't care what anyone says, but to me when a woman is taller than her man it looks crazy. It's okay for some people, but it always makes me feel like I'm the guy's mother instead of his date, and I for one find it hard to get in a romantic mood when every time the guy asks me for a kiss he has to stand up on his tippy toes. And too tall guys are out of the question as well. To me, anybody over six foot five is a freak. It's unnatural to be that damn big. I've never understood why people make fun of dwarfs but somebody like Shaquille O'Neal is a sex symbol. The guy's a giant. What's so cute about that? That's why dating rule number six point five is: Never go out with anyone who has to bend over to get through a door. Those guys may be attractive to some women, but to me it's just not natural.

But what I don't like the most is dealing with company when what I truly want to do is be alone. That's why "Never invite them back to your place" is at the top of my dating rules list. I like my solitude. I don't like people around me. I like balance and order. I'm an organized person and I believe there is a proper way to do everything, including dating. I've found over the years that men are ornery, dangerous creatures, and unless you have precise methods for dealing with them, they can turn your life upside down. Now, I don't mean to male-bash, but I just gotta tell it like it is. Men are bozos basically, and it takes an intelligent woman with an equally intelligent plan of action to navigate through the swamp of the male species and stay above water. And when done properly, dating can be a pleasant, harmless experience. But tonight is my own damn fault.

I thought my prayer that Terrence would find it in his heart to cut a sister a break and get his peanut head up and out of my damn house had been answered when the closing credits to *ER* popped up on the screen. I felt like jumping for joy when I saw him stretch out his legs and prepare to get up. Finally, I thought, I can have my home all to myself. Oh what joy, oh what splendor—oh what is this fool doing? Just as Terrence was about to get up, he grabbed the remote control again and started flipping through the channels. I could've screamed. I thought he was gone, bye-bye, adios, au revoir, arrivederci, see ya when I see ya. But no, apparently Terrence had found his new home in my recliner and he wasn't about to give it up. It was all I could do to keep myself from getting ugly and jumping in his face and yelling, "Get out!" I'm usually not this nice with men I can't stand, but for some reason I didn't go off on Terrence, though it was taking every ounce of self-restraint I had in me not to. I don't know if it was because I was feeling bad for running up the dinner bill so high when I knew that Terrence didn't have a steady job, or if it was because I'd had one too many margaritas and my reflexes were numb. Whatever it was,

Terrence had lucked out, but if he had any brains, he'd realize that my niceness wouldn't last for too long. But Terrence wasn't that smart. He just continued flipping the channels until he found a show he liked, then put down the remote and sank back into the cushions of the recliner.

"*Twilight Zone,* babe," he said as the theme music came blasting through the speakers.

"You're telling me," I said and got up from the sofa and stomped out the room.

I stormed into the bathroom and slammed the door behind me, promising myself that I would never break my dating rules again. The next time a man drops me off and starts talking that shit about using my bathroom I'm gonna direct his stupid ass to the nearest gas station and run for my life. No, better yet, I thought as I opened the bathroom door and ran to my bedroom. I opened my top dresser drawer and pulled out my little pink book. It was time to make some additions to my dating rules list. I grabbed a pen, then headed back to the bathroom and closed the door. I opened my little pink book to the back and began writing. Rule number thirty-two: Always take separate cars. That's a good one. That way the guy won't have to pick me up or drop me off and he'll never know where I live and never be able to invite himself into my private sanctuary, unless *I* decide that *I* want him here. And while I'm at it, let me add yet another rule. Rule number thirty-three: No more dating pretty boys. I like my men to look good, but when they look too good, most times they know it, which means they're conceited, and I simply don't have time to deal with men like Terrence who think it kosher to remind a woman that she has a pimple on her cheek. What kind of mess is that? And further-more, I'm gonna add rule number thirty-four: No more staying out past ten o'clock on a weeknight. I'm getting too old for this shit. It's only a few minutes after midnight, but I'm tired as hell. I'm a working woman and I've got to be up at the crack of dawn. Staying out late was cool when I was in my twenties. I could stay out till the sun came up, come home, take a quick catnap, and be up and out the door to work without a bag under my eye or a yawn in my mouth. But now that I've reached the big three-0, I can't do that anymore. If I'm not in the bed by ten-thirty and asleep by eleven, I can forget about being a productive member of society the next day. Right about now I'm feeling like I could just fall out, and if it wasn't for the knucklehead in the other room I would be flanked in flannel and dreaming in the comfort of my brass bed and satin sheets. But no. I'm up and agitated, and as I look at myself in the mirror I get even more upset because the eyeliner I'd put on top of my pimple has rubbed off to reveal a big, red, swollen lump with just a touch of white gooky stuff in the center. Damn, I thought as I went on ahead and popped the darn thing. "Do I really need a chemical peel?" I mumbled and ran my hand across my face and checked myself out from every angle. "Hell no," I finally said and blew myself a kiss. I don't care what Terrence says, I know I look good for my age. Hell, I'm in my prime. And I don't need any liposuction either. Shit, I jog every weekend and take three step classes during the week, so whatever fat is still on my body after all that is meant to be there. Fuck Terrence with his pretty ass and his dermatology suggestions, I thought and turned on the faucet. I balled a piece of soap in my hands and began washing my face, until that is, I got some of the soap in my eyes and almost threw my arms out of their sockets as I flung them around in search of a towel. It was only fitting, considering the type of night I was having, that I couldn't find a towel because I'd taken them all out earlier to be washed, so I stuck my head in the sink and let the water run over my eyes until the burning stopped. Of course the water got in my ears and my mouth and ran up my nose and I couldn't breathe, and for a second there I was sure I was going to drown myself, which I figured would be the perfect ending to this mess of a night. Luckily for me, I was able to pull myself out of the death trap I'd gotten into, and after banging my head on all sides of the sink and knocking over the soap dish, I fell to the floor, gasping for air. Well I'll be damned, I said to myself as I grabbed ahold of the counter and pulled myself back up. Can this night get any worse?

When I looked into the mirror again, I almost screamed. My shoulder-length braids were soaking wet, the collar of my DKNY suit was dripping, and my eyes were swollen and looking as red as the big-ass pimple on my cheek. "Damn it all to heck," I said and tore myself out of my suit. I stepped out of my black patent DKNY pumps and picked up the bottle of DKNY perfume that had fallen to the floor in my tussle to free my head from the sink. I bent over and wrung out my braids and wrapped one of those squooshy hair bands around them. "This night has been a disaster," I said to myself as I closed the lid on the toilet and sat down. A big, fat disaster. The only good thing about tonight is that I got to eat at my favorite Mexican restaurant, but even that was starting to turn on me because now I've got gas like a diesel truck and it's stinking up this little bathroom so badly that I can't even sit in here any longer.

I got up and opened the door and headed for my bedroom, but before I got there, I stuck my head around the corner to peep into the living room at Terrence. Still there. Hadn't even changed his position. Damn. I hurried into my room and slammed the door behind me and threw my suit and shoes into a pile in the corner. Since I had on Calvin Klein underwear, I opened my dresser drawer and pulled out a CK T-shirt and a pair of CK boxer shorts and fell across my bed wondering when or if this date from the dark side would end.

It's nights like this that make me think that maybe I should just give up dating altogether. "Yeah right, Madison," I mumbled and stared up at the ceiling. That will never happen. I wouldn't know how to act if I didn't have a man on my arm at least two times a week. That's my damn problem. I like men too much. Even the ones that get on my nerves, like Terrence. As bad as this date has been with him, I know that if he were to ask me out again, I'd say yes. I know I should be pickier about the men I date, but I figure if the man is offering me a free meal and I don't have anything else to do, why not say yes? Hell, it beats sitting at home in front of the cable all by myself and nibbling on popcorn. My mother is always telling me that I should find myself one good man and stick with him, but for some reason I just can't do that. To be honest, I really don't want just one man. I don't want to be tied down and fall into some boring domestic routine, and I sure as hell don't want to be married. Fuck that. I don't believe in marriage. I don't care what anyone says; the whole institution of marriage is a joke. It's played out. Everyone I know who's gotten married has ended up getting a divorce, except for my aunt Farcie and uncle Frank, but they don't count 'cause they don't even screw anymore. They're only fifty years old and they sleep in separate beds, and whenever the family gets together they end up arguing over silly shit like who's gonna drive home. I swear, the last time we all had dinner at my mother's house they stood outside on the curb for fifteen minutes throwing the car keys back and forth at each other. I just stood in the window watching and laughing though it really wasn't funny. When I thought about it, it was actually sad. I can't figure out why anyone would stay married to someone they can't stand. Doesn't make any sense to me. I've never seen one totally blissful marriage in all my days, and I figure if I can't be happy with someone for the rest of my life, then I might as well stay on my own. Contrary to popular belief, there is no shortage of eligible black men, at least not that I can see. Women are always bitching about how hard it is to find a good man, but for me it's no problem at all. The only reason women have problems with men is because women are liars. They aren't looking for good men, they're looking for *husbands.* They don't want to go out on nice, fun dates, they want to set dates—wedding dates. If women would just chill and accept men for who they are instead of all the time trying to lock themselves into serious relationships, they'd have no problem. Women only have trouble dating because every man they see is a man they want to marry. But not me. When I go out with a man all I want is a good time. I don't want to tie him down, I don't want commitments, and I damn sure don't want a husband. I'm quite content to be thirty and single, and regardless of what my mother says, I do not need a steady man in my life. What for? So he can come in and start ruling every damn thing? That's how men are. They're selfish by nature, and again, I don't mean to bash the male species as a whole, but I've got to tell it like it is. I've dated every kind of man there is and I have yet to find one who is willing to have a totally honest fifty-fifty relationship. Seventy-thirty, yes. Sixty-forty, yes. But fifty-fifty? Please. In all my years of dating, I've never found one man who I'd even halfway consider marrying. . . . Okay, okay. . . . I'm lying. There was this one guy, a long time ago. A very, very long time ago. But it was nothing serious. . . . Okay, okay, I'm lying again. It was very serious. In fact we were engaged to be married. We were in love, and I was happy. Oh what joy, oh what splendor—oh what a big, fucking joke.

■

His name was Christopher Anzel, and although it sickens me to admit it now, he was my first and only love. He was a beautiful man. Intelligent, thoughtful, hardworking, caring, and, oh yes, the brother was fine. Not pretty boy fine like Terrence out there, but chiseled, steak-eating, rugged, pass me a beer fine. But I didn't fall in love with Chris because of his fineness. It was the man underneath the chocolate skin, sexy eyes, and rock hard chest that got me hooked. Chris was . . . he was . . . Well, to tell the truth, the brother was a bit strange. We met when I was in my junior year at Loyola Marymount University and Chris had just transferred there from Chicago to complete his last year of medical residency at the university's Emergency Center. Neither one of us had much time for dating, but every time we saw each other zipping through the hallways at school we'd take a second to stop and chat. We'd barely talk for more than five minutes at a time, but somehow I knew Chris was something special. Maybe it was the way he always looked me dead in the eyes when we spoke, or maybe it was the way he always asked how I was doing and waited for my response like he really cared what my answer would be. Or maybe it was the strange way he spoke. He didn't have a lisp or anything like that. It was just his words. They were odd. I'd never heard a man use words the way Chris did. He'd say things like, "Hello, Madison. Isn't this a glorious day?" *Glorious?* How many brothers have you heard use that word before? Think about it. Not too many. But Chris was always saying kind things like that. He wasn't afraid to speak softly or from his heart. Chris was an eternal optimist. He often talked about things like faith and believing and miracles. I remember one afternoon when I ran into him as I was walking to class and freaking out over this big exam I was about to take. Chris stopped me, put his hand on my shoulder, and looked into my eyes as if he could plainly see every ounce of frustration that was brewing through my body. "Faith is the evidence of things not seen," he said. "Relax. Let the energy of the universe enter your soul. Close your eyes and inhale. Claim your right to succeed and the universe will do the rest."

So I'm standing there, right. I'm listening. I've got my eyes closed, I'm inhaling, and I'm thinking, Either this guy is higher than a helicopter, working overtime for the Psychic Friends Network, or just plain nuts. Or maybe I was the one who was nuts for standing in the middle of the hallway trying to snort a piece of the universe up my nose. "This is silly," I said and opened my eyes, but when I did I realized Chris was gone. I looked both ways down the hall, but he was nowhere to be seen, and for a second there I thought my mind was playing tricks on me. But since I didn't have the time or the brainpower to unravel the mysteries of the unknown, I went on to class and took my test and—drum roll, please—I aced it. It was a miracle. No really, it was. I'd gotten A's on tests before, but I hadn't even studied for that test, which was why I was so nervous and freaked out about taking it. Still, I pulled down an A, and the only logical explanation for it was that cosmic, metaphysical pep talk I'd had with Chris. I'm telling you, it was a miracle. Plain and simple.

After my exam was over, I ran over to the university's Emergency Center to hunt Chris down. I wanted to let him know the good news and to thank him for calming my nerves enough so that I could go into that classroom and ace that test. But when I found him sitting all alone in the Medical Center cafeteria, a bolder thought popped into my mind. I walked straight over to his table, leaned down, and planted two fat lips on his mouth. When I pulled away from him and waited for his response, I expected to hear more beautiful words. Something like, "Your kiss has sent chills through my soul," or, "The tantalizing taste of your lips is one that will never be forgotten." But much to my surprise, for once, Chris was tongue-tied. He swallowed hard and the only word he was able to muster was, "*Damn.*" He pulled me back to him and kissed me again, and when it was all over he whispered, "It would bring me great pleasure if you would allow me to escort you on a date tonight."

Now, any other girl in her right mind would have said yes immediately, but I was reserved. It's not that I didn't like Chris, because I really did. It's just that when I first started college at Loyola, I'd made myself one promise, and that's that I would let nothing or no one distract me from getting my degree. In other words, that meant no dating. No dating. It was a hard promise to keep, but it was necessary. If there was one thing that could distract me from my goal, it was men, which is why I promised myself that until I was done with my higher learning, men were off-limits. School was my top priority. I was there on a scholarship and I didn't want to blow it. I considered myself privileged. Mother had been on welfare ever since I was born. And as I grew up watching her struggle, watching her do without, watching her trying to make ends meet when there was obviously a barrier in the path, I swore that I would never go through that. I promised myself I'd never be on welfare. It wasn't something that my mother instilled in me; I made the decision on my own. I could see how we lived and it wasn't good. So I vowed that I was going to do something with myself. I was not going to end up on welfare. I was not going to struggle for everything I needed.

I had my life and future all planned out. I figured I'd take four years off from men and focus on getting my degree in liberal arts and child development, then it was on to a permanent teaching position at Mighty Avalon Preparatory School, where I was already working part-time as a teacher's assistant. Mighty Avalon was the only private school for black kids in L.A., and at the time the list for prospective teachers ran longer than the waiting list for student enrollment. Landing a guaranteed position there was no small feat. Everyone wanted to teach at Mighty Avalon. The school's reputation in the black community rivaled that of the NAACP, thanks in no small part to the school's founder, Tommy Thompson. I swear that man could be the first black president if he wanted to be. He had it all. The charisma of Jesse Jackson, the style of Quincy Jones, and the bank account of Michael Jordan. But the reason everyone admired Tommy Thompson was because of his vision. In a world where little black boys are told that their ability to dunk a basketball will make them millionaires, Tommy Thompson disagreed. "The only way to set a child's future is to nourish their minds. All else is fantasy," he always says. That's why he founded Mighty Avalon Prep School, a place where black students come to *learn,* not fantasize. Ever since the school's opening day it has been a pillar in the community. I was totally blown away when Mr. Thompson hired me as a part-time teacher's assistant and even more astonished when after less than a month on the job he offered me a permanent spot upon receiving my degree. Tommy Thompson was a good man—sorta. But that's a whole 'nother story.

Anyway, I was determined to finish school. That was my one and only goal. And that's why I was hesitant about accepting Chris's invitation for a date. My future was set, but like I said, if there was one thing that could trip me up, it would be the distraction of a man. Men are and have always been my major weakness and I knew that if I accepted Chris's invitation I'd be setting myself up for disaster. So what did I do? The only thing an intelligent, goal-oriented woman who believed in keeping promises to herself could do—I told Chris to pick me up at seven.

I have to admit that breaking my promise to keep away from men till I was finished with my education was one of the best things I'd ever done because it afforded me the opportunity to do something I'd never done before—fall in love. Ten minutes into my date with Christopher, I knew I was in love. I knew it the second he opened up and told me about his dreams. He said that his ultimate goal in life was to open a free clinic for underprivileged children and their parents. Chris wasn't concerned about becoming a doctor so he could go to work for some fancy hospital where he could charge outrageous fees and rake in the money. He wanted to give. He wanted his life and his work to have meaning. And as I listened to him talk, I knew he was sincere and I knew that Chris was the ultimate man for me.

I fell in love with Chris so fast that it scared me. Love was a state I'd never visited before, and being there for the first time excited and frightened me at the same time. Love changed me. I went from being a single-minded visionary to a love-struck, sprung chicken. I had it bad for Chris. So bad that I could hardly sleep at night. So bad that I rescheduled all my college courses just so I could be free at night when Chris was on leave from the Emergency Center. So bad that I started doing stupid shit, like making homemade cards out of contact paper and lace and sending them to Chris with big, fat lipstick imprints on the cover. I was out of my mind. And so was Chris. He was in love with me too and he didn't mind showing it or saying it. Most guys say they love you in private, but get them out in public and they have to walk two steps ahead of you just to prove they are men. Chris's love wasn't like that. It was constant and tight. It was real love from a real man, and each day it got stronger, until . . .

"Madison," Chris said one night as we laid in his bed at his campus apartment.

"Yes," I said and sat up next to him. There was a moment of silence as I gazed into his eyes and realized he had something serious to say. I wondered what it could be as I watched the man I loved search his mind for just the right words to say. Then he broke out in a sly grin, and after another second I knew what was going on. "You farted," I said and jumped out of bed.

He laughed and shook the sheets, exposing even more obnoxious fumes, and I swear I could have choked to death. "Sorry, babe," he said, giggling uncontrollably. "I couldn't hold it in."

"You could have given me a warning," I said as I stood in the corner of the room, cupping my hand over my nose.

"I'm sorry," he said and patted the bed. "Come on back."

"Hell no," I said as I left the room. I came back with a can of Lysol. I stood in the doorway and threw it at him and waited for him to fumigate.

"Okay," he called to me, stifling a giggle. "Smell's all gone."

I came back in cautiously, sniffing ever so lightly until I was sure the coast was clear. Then I jumped back in bed and popped him on his forehead. "Nasty dog," I said and rolled my eyes. "How would you like it if I started pooting all over the place?"

"You fart all the time in your sleep," he said as my mouth dropped open from embarrassment. "It's okay," he said and grabbed my hand. "It's natural, honey."

"I do not fart in my sleep," I said and folded my arms across my chest.

"And it stinks really bad too," he said and twitched his nose.

"Shut up," I whined. I sat pouting until Chris stopped cracking up and put his arm around my shoulder. "Don't touch me," I whimpered, and squirmed until Chris soothed my embarrassment away with a kiss.

"You can fart, belch, scratch your butt. It doesn't bother me, baby," he said with a seriousness that was too strong for the topic of conversation. "I love you, Madison," he said and stared at me, and when I looked into his eyes again I saw that *look*. A look that told me he wanted to say something but couldn't find the right words. I thought he'd given up when he pulled away from me and stared straight ahead at the wall in front of him. Then, out of nowhere, he said it. He turned to me slowly and said the words, "Will you marry me?"

Huh? I almost fell out. I didn't know what to say or what to do. I stuttered, I looked around the room, I looked at Chris, and before I knew it, I was fixing my mouth to say the only thing I could say, "Hell yes."

Chris cried that night. I'd never seen a man cry before. I held him and kissed his face as tears fell down his cheeks, and all I could think was, This man really loves me and I really love this man. I'd found him. Mr. Right. There he was in my arms. My man. My love.

Looking back on it now, I have to admit that Chris, more than any other man I've known, has shaped my life and made me the woman I am today. He taught me to love, to be open, to care outside myself, and most of all he taught me that when a man really loves you wholeheartedly and wants to spend the rest of his life with you, making you happy, sharing, caring, giving . . . when a man loves you deeper than you've ever been loved before and welcomes you into his heart and soul—*watch out,* because the bastard is really a selfish, conniving son of a bitch who will turn on you so fast that by the time you realize just what type of asshole you're dealing with, it's too late to save your heart from breaking into a million tiny pieces. Christopher squashed my heart like a fly on the wall, like a mosquito on his leg, like a wad of bubble gum in the middle of the sidewalk—he hurt my feelings. Badly. And since Christopher, I've never been quite the same.

Oh sure, Christopher loved me and I loved him. He was a good man. He was everything I thought I was supposed to want or need in a man, and for a while after we were engaged, everything went well. We'd decided we were going to get married that following summer, just after Chris finished his residency at the Emergency Center and just before I started my senior year at the university. We'd made all the plans, sent out invitations, bought a dress, the cake—our wedding was set. Until, that is, Christopher took me to dinner one evening so we could *talk*. Chris changed my whole life that night . . .

We held hands across the dinner table and did nothing but gaze out the window at the hypnotic beach of Marina del Rey. I could tell we were both getting it. The fact that we would soon be man and wife was sinking into both our hearts. It was an idea that we both cherished, an idea that sat well with us. We laughed at our absentmindedness when the waiter stopped by our table for the third time to take our order. But we were too consumed with each other to concern ourselves with the menu and once again the waiter breezed away leaving us to our idleness. When I finally did pick up the menu my eyes nearly popped out my head as I scanned the prices. "Twenty-five dollars for chicken?" I gagged and looked over at Chris. "Unless you've hit the lottery I suggest we head on over to Kentucky Fried Chicken. I've got coupons, you know."

Chris smiled and glided his hand through the air. "Just relax," he said and gave me a wink. "Tonight is special. We're celebrating."

"Celebrating?" I repeated and cracked a smile. "Celebrating what?"

"Well," he said and clasped his hands together. "You know how it's always been my dream to open up a free clinic for underprivileged kids, right?"

"Of course," I said, feeling myself getting caught up in Chris's excitement.

"And you know how it's always been my goal to give back to the black community, right?"

"Yes, yes," I said as I noticed the passion rising in Chris's voice.

"Well, it's all coming together, Madison. I've got the best news ever," he said and paused for a second too long.

"What!"

"We're moving to Chicago, honey," he told me and smiled from ear to ear.

I was so taken aback by his words that I had to look around the room to make sure he was talking to me. Moving to Chicago, I thought as my face froze.

"What do you mean we're moving to Chicago?"

"Well, I figure if I'm gonna give back to the community it might as well be the community where I grew up. So I've had my parents look around at a few buildings for me in Chicago and they say they've found the per-

fect little two-flat building on the South Side. Now, that's a rough neighborhood, but those kids out there deserve quality medical attention just
like everybody else."

Moving to Chicago? I thought again as I sat across from Chris and listened to him babble about returning to his homeland. But what about
me? What about my education? What about the teaching job I had waiting for me when I graduated? What about my dreams? The clinic was
Christopher's dream. Mine was right here in L.A. Why do we have to
move to Chicago? There were underprivileged children everywhere. If
helping out kids was all Chris wanted to do, he could open up a clinic
right here in L.A., or South Central or Pacoima or Watts. Children needed
help everywhere, not just in Chicago.

"Madison," Chris called to me, noticing that my mind had drifted else-
where. "What do you think?"

"About what?"

"About moving to Chicago, honey. I figure we could leave right after
the wedding, rent a car, take a couple of weeks, and drive all the way."

"Excuse me?"

"Or we could fly. No problem."

"Christopher," I said and slammed my hand on the table.

"Madison?"

I breathed deeply and held my breath for a long time, trying to keep
myself calm. When I finally spoke, the words came slowly and intently.
"Have you forgotten about *me*?" I asked as a helpless look of confusion
washed over his face. "I am on scholarship at Loyola. I can't leave now. I
still have another year of school to finish."

"Yes, but there are fine schools in Chic—"

"Christopher," I grunted, and frowned. "Do you understand how hard
it was for me to line up that job at Mighty Avalon? Do you realize that
moving to Chicago would ruin all my plans? I've worked hard, Chris. I'm
still working hard. And you want me to give it all up? You think I'm just
gonna jump to attention and change all my plans, change my future? Are
you out of your everlasting mind?" I said as my voice got more and more
loud with every sentence. "Why should I give up the life I've created here
in L.A. for you? Huh? Don't my goals and dreams mean anything?"

We sat in silence for what seemed an eternity. Not even the waiter's
fourth appearance at our table could pull us out of the funk we'd fallen
into. Finally Chris dropped his head into the palms of his hands and spoke

in a whisper. "I don't know what to say, Madison. I guess I was just so wrapped up in my world that I forgot you had a life too. You're absolutely right. I can't expect you to give up everything you've worked for to follow me to Chicago. I'm an idiot. A stupid, selfish idiot."

Damn right you are, I thought as I folded my arms across my chest and gloated. I'd won, and the sweet cloud of victory had engulfed me. But as I sat listening to Chris go on about what a jerk he'd been I had to stop and check myself. There across from me sat the man who loved me. A good man. A man with a passion about his career. A man who wanted to make a difference in the world. The more I sat there thinking, the more I realized that maybe I was the selfish idiot. Was Chris really asking too much of me? Weren't there schools in Chicago? I mean, I'm sure I could find another teaching job, right? It's not like Chris was asking me to give up my life and move to Alaska so he could open up a tanning salon. He was asking me to love him, to support him, to be his wife. Yes, my life was here, but what kind of life would I have without Chris? Could I sacrifice it all? Oh, the decisions, decisions, decisions, I thought as I looked into Chris's eyes. And that's all it took. I looked at Chris and melted. I was sprung. In love. Out my mind—I was moving to Chicago.

Tears came to my eyes as I opened my mouth to tell Chris I'd follow him wherever he'd lead. But before I could get the words out, Chris was already speaking.

"I'm a real jerk, Madison," he said as tears seemed to well up in his eyes too. "Why would you want to marry an idiot like me?"

"No, Chris. I'm the jerk," I said and took a deep breath. Chris was a wonderful man. How could I be so stupid? Of course I'd move to Chicago. I'd do anything for Chris.

"No, Madison. I'm not the man you think I am. I'm stupid, I'm selfish, I'm not good enough for you. I'm a liar, a cheat, I'm—"

Excuse me? "What are you talking about?" I asked, not understanding why Chris was being so hard on himself. "It's okay, Chris. I've changed my mind. I'll go."

"No, no, Madison. I can't continue on like this. You know how important honesty is to me. I've got to come clean."

"What are you talking about?" I asked as anxiety flushed over me. Somehow I got the feeling we weren't just talking about moving to Chicago anymore.

"I've been taking you for granted too long."

"What are you talking about?"

"I cheated on you," he said softly. "Twice."

There was a long, devastating silence. I was frozen. Had I heard him correctly? I wondered as I peered across the table at the man I was about to marry. Then suddenly I broke out laughing. "Oh Chris," I said and slapped his hand. "Stop playing, boy."

"Actually I cheated on you three times."

"Stop playing, Chris," I chuckled.

"I can't lie to you anymore," he said, too seriously. "You know that med student with the jet black hair?"

"Stop it, Chris."

"And Anne? The girl at the student store who's always giving me a discount on books?"

"Chris."

"And Cherise."

"Please."

"I had to tell you, Madison. My mind has been too heavy for too long. I had to come clean. What I did was wrong. I know that. But I swear, my cheating days are in the past. I love you and I still want you to marry me. I promise you from the depth of my soul that I will never cheat on you again, especially not after we're married."

For a second there, Chris looked relieved. As if a huge weight had been lifted from his shoulders. I wondered how long he'd been keeping this from me. I wondered how he could talk about honesty and faith and doing the right thing when all the while he was doing wrong. I should have known Chris was too good to be true, I thought as a tear slipped out of my eye. I should have known. Chris saw my tear and grabbed my hand, desperately. "I love you," he said in the most sincere tone I'd ever heard. "Please say you'll still marry me."

That's all Chris had to say that night. That's all he could say, considering the way I'd lodged my fist into his mouth and sent him tumbling out his chair and onto the floor. I walked out the restaurant and never looked back. Devastated, betrayed, mocked—none of those words could encompass the way I felt at that moment. I had been ready to give up everything for Chris, only to find out that he had never been the man I'd thought he was. I'd almost made a huge mistake, but I promised myself it would never happen again.

He called me day and night from then on, all the way up to the day he was to be leaving for Chicago. He begged. He pleaded. Asked for my forgiveness. Said I was making a big mistake if I didn't marry him. Said he was just being honest with me. Said he was being a real man by telling me what he'd done. That a lesser man would have just kept silent. Said that he'd never cheat on me after we were wed. But I said, "Bullshit." How was a marriage license and a piece of paper supposed to change things? If a man cheats before the wedding, he'll cheat after. It doesn't take a genius to figure that out. Hell no, I wasn't going to marry Christopher. Not this black woman and not in this lifetime.

In Chris's final call to me before he left for Chicago, he told me that he would always love me and asked if I still loved him. I told him yes, but that was beside the point. Love didn't have a damn thing to do with this. Women love men all the time who they know they shouldn't. They even marry men they know they shouldn't. They hope that somehow, magically, marriage will change a man. But it can't. And marriage couldn't change me either. Even though I still loved Chris I couldn't trust him. And what's a marriage without trust? If I went ahead with the marriage, I'd be forever looking over my shoulder, peeping around corners, trying to keep an eye on Chris and follow his every move. I didn't have time for that kind of life. I refused to put myself through that. So I told Chris to go fuck himself and hung up the phone in his face. I never heard from him again. I never trusted a man again.

My mother got on my nerves for weeks after Christopher left. The two of them had gotten really close since the first time I introduced them. Actually Chris became like a son to my mother, and after he left, it seemed every time I turned around she was on my heels nagging me. I guess she thought I had been bluffing about refusing to marry Christopher, but after he left, she found out I was serious about my convictions, and that's when she let me have it.

"You've got to be the silliest girl I know, Li'l Mama," she said one night as she followed me around the kitchen like a pit bull. I'd gotten home late from school with a headache and I really didn't want to hear none of her shit, but I couldn't very well tell her that, though I wanted to. I really wanted to. "That man loved you, Li'l Mama," she nagged. "He told me so. He called me every day and told me so."

"So?"

"Why are you so silly and stubborn?"

"Why don't you shut up?" I wanted to say, but didn't. No, what I really wanted to say was, "Stop calling me Li'l Mama!" I hate that damn nickname. My family had been calling me that ever since I was a baby and I hate it. Aunt Farcie started that mess. She said she made up the name because I was always so grown. I always acted like I was the lady of the house even when I was nothing but a snot-nosed three-year-old. It was a cute nickname for a while, but now I can't stand to be called that and my mother knew it, which is probably why she kept doing it. Mother does a lot of shit just to bug me, and that night she really got under my skin. "You girls today are so silly. You think you know so damn much and don't know shit," she said as my head pounded like a heavy metal band was locked inside my skull. "Christopher was a good man, Li'l Mama. And you should've taken your ass to Chicago. The boy knew he did wrong, but how can you blame him? He was young."

"And he still would have been young after we married. Marriage couldn't make Chris be faithful, Mother. A man's gotta start out that way."

"Silly girl."

I swear I wanted to slap her a couple times. I wanted to tell her I was sad, that I hurt. But I couldn't. I had to be strong or else I'd fall apart. I couldn't do that. Besides, who was Mother to talk, anyway? Here she was giving me advice on men and the only man she'd ever dealt with was my sorry-ass daddy, who has never been man enough to accept more than two cents' worth of responsibility in his whole exhausted life. "Christopher was a good man," my mother scolded at me. "You ought to be smart enough to know a good man when you see one," she said. And that was the last straw.

"And who was my example?" I shouted back at her. "Your husband?—Oh excuse me. Daddy never wanted you enough to marry you, did he, Mother? No, Daddy just fucked you and ran off, right?"

Smack! I should've seen it coming. Mother knocked me right in the face for saying that. I was twenty-two at the time, but that didn't stop her from putting me in my place. She looked like she could have body-slammed me for what I'd said, but instead she started crying, and I started feeling sorry, but I still didn't apologize for what I'd said. I didn't care if it hurt her feelings. I was telling the truth. My daddy was a low-down, mangy, flea-infested dog. He got my mother pregnant with me and after I was born he wouldn't even claim me. Said he didn't know if I was really his or not. Said he wanted to take a blood test, but he never did. It wasn't necessary after I turned four years old and became his spitting image. This overbite I got—

his. These big-ass ears that prevent me from cutting my hair too short—his. This mole on my left thigh—all his. After a while it was too obvious who my daddy was, but even after all that, he never really claimed me. Oh, he said I was his daughter and all, but he never became my father. Never moved in with my mother and helped her raise me. Never came over to visit except on special occasions, and even then he might show up drunk or not all. My daddy was a true motherfucker. That's all he did, was fuck my mother, and Mother was so strung out for affection that she let him whenever he wanted. That's how come sixteen years after I was born, I wound up with a baby sister. Daddy got to talking that same old shit about the baby not being his, but this time he said he wanted to take DNA tests. Stupid fool. He talked that shit for months until he learned how expensive DNA tests were and decided that claiming my sister was a whole lot cheaper. For him it was cheap as it could get. Daddy never shelled out any money for either one of his kids. Not that spending money on us would have made him more like a father. He could never be that. I just don't understand how a man can sit back and watch the mother of his children go on welfare. How could he watch a woman struggle with two kids that belong to him and not try to help out? What kind of mess is that? Even to this day, Daddy doesn't do shit for Serena, my sister. I'm more her daddy than anyone else. Hell, the family ought to be calling me Li'l Daddy instead of Li'l Mama.

Serena just turned fourteen and I think she's seen her daddy maybe ten times since she was born, and ever since she's been diagnosed with that damn disease, her daddy hardly ever comes around anymore. He practically acts like he doesn't even know her. Son of a bitch. The bastard only lives a few blocks away from my mother, but does he ever stop by to see Serena? Hell no. I haven't even seen him in six years myself, and to be honest I don't really know if he's dead or alive. That's why I check the obituaries in the paper every day to see if his name is in there. Hoping his name is in there. Serena, on the other hand, is younger, thus less bitter about the man than I am, but give her a few years and she'll come to see what an asshole of a man her daddy is and always will be.

It's no coincidence that Daddy hasn't seen her in the past few years. I know it's because of her disease. He, just like everybody else, is embarrassed of Serena. I've never understood why she had to get stuck with Tourette's syndrome. That's a fucked-up condition if I've ever seen one. It's a neurological disease and there's no cure and they don't even know what causes the shit. I'd never even heard of it before Serena got it. All I know is one evening when I was still in college and still living with my mother, Serena just suddenly flipped out. She must have been around six or seven, and as always she was running behind me trying to help me get ready for church, but really just getting in the way. She was always up under me, trying to see what her big sister was getting into. She was so cute, even though she looked like me, which meant she looked like our ugly daddy— but she was still the cutest little thing in the world to me. Anyway, she was sitting next to me on Mother's plastic-wrapped sofa when all of a sudden her body just started moving. I told her to stop and be still, but Serena wouldn't listen. She'd be still for a minute, then suddenly her head would tic to the side or her leg would kick up or she'd bite her teeth together like a dog. I thought she was just being a normal, weirdo, seven-year-old child, so I didn't trip. I just told her to cut it out and sit still and be a good little girl. I should've known something was wrong because Serena got really quiet. I thought she was just mad because I wouldn't let her fool around, so I didn't bother her. I just sat sipping on my diet Coke, until the next thing I knew Serena flung out her arm and knocked my soda all over my dress. I was mad as hell. I grabbed her by the arm and stood her up. "Look what you did to my dress," I screamed at her. Serena snapped her teeth together and grunted. "Stop it, Serena," I said and shook her. But all she did was tic her head to the side three times and kick her foot at me. "I'm gonna spank your little behind, girl," I said and turned her around and prepared to give her a good smack on the butt. That's when I knew something was wrong. Whenever Serena had been a bad little girl and was about to get her butt spanked, she'd start running and crying out, "No, no, Li'l Ma. I'm sorry. Don't pop my booty." But this time she was silent. She didn't say a word and she wouldn't stop jerking her head. I turned her back around to face me and stared into her eyes. She couldn't say a word. She was too stunned. Her body had taken over her mind and she didn't know what was going on inside herself. She was so scared. She was seven years old and scared. She couldn't stop the tics. She just couldn't control it. And there I was, yelling at her and about to give her a spanking. I felt so bad as I looked into my baby sister's eyes. She was moving around like she was possessed and I could tell she was so frightened, but she didn't cry. She was too scared to cry. I got down on my knees in front of her and held her tightly in my arms as she continued to grunt and tic. I screamed for Mother and she came running out her bedroom, and when she reached the front and saw Serena standing in the middle of the floor moving her body involuntarily, Mother started to cry. No, she stared at Serena for a long time, then she started to cry.

The next couple of weeks were frantic as we took Serena around from clinic to clinic and specialist to specialist getting first, second, and third opinions. They all said the same thing, though. Tourette's syndrome. No cause, no cure. The only way to control the disease was for Serena to take this high-priced medication, but there was only so far Mother could stretch her welfare checks. I was still in college with no job except for my teacher's assistant position, which didn't pay shit, so I couldn't afford it either. It was all fucked up. And it got worse. As Serena got older her symptoms worsened, and for a while when she was in the third grade, Serena gave up on school altogether. It was too hard for her. Every day she was coming home in tears because someone had made fun of her or someone had mimicked her or hit her or laughed too hard or yelled at her. I had just graduated from college and had yet to start my permanent teaching position at Mighty Avalon Prep. School, so I had enough free time on my hands to tutor her at home, which I did for a whole year until Mother finally started working part-time at the grocery store and earned enough money to pay for Serena's high-priced medication. And thank God for that. Once Serena started taking the meds she was able to control a lot of her symptoms, though not completely. Still, the change in Serena was like night and day. Her tics lessened and her grunts were cut down to a minimum, and within days she was able to control her movements a lot better. Every now and then she has a really bad spell, where she just totally loses it. But if she stays on her meds like she is supposed to and like I always remind her to, she hardly has any trouble at all. When she went back to school in the fourth grade no one hardly recognized she had a problem. Most of the kids thought she was just being a wiseass whenever she suddenly grunted or kicked out her leg uncontrollably. In fact she was voted the school's class clown that year. But with that year of personal tutoring I gave her she had also become a straight-A student and she's been so ever since.

If I'm honest with myself, which I'm not, I'll admit that Serena is the main reason why at age thirty I'm not tripping about the fact that I don't have kids. Most women get my age and lose their fucking minds because they haven't yet procreated. Not me. I've been a parent to my sister since the day she was born which is more than I can say for her sorry-ass daddy.

If I'm honest with myself again, which of course I'm not going to be, I'll have to admit that Daddy is the reason why I never want to get married. You'd think the fact that he didn't marry my mother would make me insistent on finding a man I love and falling into holy matrimony, but it's just the other way around. Because of him, I don't think I can ever truly trust a man. Chris has a lot to do with that too. Still, I could never believe in a man blindly and give my all to him like my mother has done for my daddy. I don't believe my mother has ever been with any other man but him. She just sits around waiting on him to one day come to his senses and be the man she's always hoped he could be. I swear sometimes I wanna knock my mother upside the head. It's sad. Really sad. I know one thing for sure, though, and that's that I will never allow myself to be used like my mother. Hell no. Not this black woman. Not in this life. And I'll never allow myself to fall so completely for a man to where he becomes my everything, my all in all, my salvation. Fuck that. It ain't worth it. No, I'm content to stay by myself. Just give me a couple of dates a week so I can continue to prove to myself that I am a woman, and I'll be just fine. I'm happy with my life just the way it is—happy enough.

■

Actually, what I am right now is tired and irritated, I thought to myself and got up off my bed. I checked the clock on the nightstand and found it was going on one o'clock now. Okay, Terrence. I've tried to be nice since you did take me to my favorite Mexican restaurant, but enough is enough. Your black ass has got to go. And I mean right now, I thought to myself as I opened my bedroom door and walked down the hall toward the living room. Instead of hearing the television along the way, I heard the stereo and I frowned as I tried to figure out what the hell Terrence was up to now. I turned the corner into the living room and this time I found my recliner empty. Terrence had moved his private party to the sofa, where he had his long legs stretched out and his huge head resting on the arm. The lights were out and Chanté Moore's "Love Supreme" was purring through the speakers. All I could do was shake my head as I stopped in the middle of the floor and stared at Terrence. Was this some kind of *mood* he was trying to set? I thought, and eyed him as he flashed a smile my way. Don't even think about it, you selfish bastard, I said to myself and turned on the lights. To a less cohesive woman this atmosphere would send chills up her spine, but not me. No, no. There will be no sex jumping off in this condo tonight. I was hoping there would be, but now that I've gotten to know Terrence I'll gladly take the zero. Besides, I've already broken enough of my dating rules and I sure wasn't gonna add to it by breaking rule number two: Never sleep with anyone, no matter how fine they are, if the thought of getting pregnant by them would cause you to want to stick an iron hanger between your legs.

"Hey, babe," he said, still smiling. Smiling too damn much. "What's up with the lights?"

"Okay, Terrence," I said as nicely as I could. "It's been a wonderful evening, but—"

"But nothing," he said and raised up from the sofa and grabbed my arm. "Come here, girl," he said and pulled me down to the sofa with him. "The night's just getting started," he said, blowing his onion-and-cilantro breath with just a hint of diet Coke flavor all in my face.

"No, Terrence," I said calmly and wiggled out of his grasp. "It's getting late and I have to get up for work in the morning."

"Work? What kind of work do you do?"

If you had let me get a word in over dinner you would have known that already.

"So where do you spend your eight hours a day?" he asked.

So now he wants to have a conversation? Please.

"No really, where do you work?"

"I'm a teacher at Mighty Avalon Prep."

"That's that private school for black kids, right?" he asked and sat up. "I know your students must love you," he said as his eyes drifted down to my chest.

"I love my students."

"Damn. If I had a teacher that looked like you, I might have finished school."

Oh please. Stop the drama, I thought as I yawned, hoping he'd get the hint. Then I thought maybe I too had leftover Mexican food breath and waved my hand in front of my face in case any odor came out.

"So, teacher," he said, steadily making his way closer to my corner of the sofa. "What lesson are you gonna teach me tonight?"

Okay, I've had enough. "It's time for you to step. Bounce. Go!"

"Ah, come on now," he said and put his face right in front of mine, and suddenly, time stopped. I took one look into Terrence's luscious eyes and completely forgot that less than two seconds ago, I'd wanted his ass out my house. I hate when that happens to me. I hate it when the lustfulness of my loins overrides the intelligence of my brain and I become a sappy, romantic sex kitten. But like I said before, men have always been my weakness, and here is my dilemma: Terrence is fine. This is a fact. But Terrence is an asshole. This too is a fact. Then again, I haven't had sex in, oh, two, three weeks. Major fact. So, what do I do? Stick to my dating rules or get my freak on? Decisions, decisions. Okay, let's see what Terrence says next before I decide.

"I like you, Madison," he said, practically drooling. "I really like you."

You barely know me, dork. I smiled.

"I know we barely know each other . . ."

We've known each other for four hours. Would have been two, but I couldn't get your ass out of here. I smiled harder.

"We're both adults . . ."

I know I am, but you? All smiles.

"What do you say we do a little bump and grind?" he said and proceeded to kiss my neck.

Bump and grind? No, he didn't just say "bump and grind." I ought to throw his ass out right now, I thought to myself. Until, that is, he started kissing my ear. Then my face. Eyelids, nose. Mouth . . . No, no, no, I said to myself and pushed him off me. I've got my rules.

"What's the matter, baby?" he said, stunned.

"I don't think I'm ready for this," I said and tried not to look into his beautiful eyes.

"Oh, I think you're ready. I know I am."

"Well, good for you," I said and got halfway off the sofa until he grabbed my arm and pulled me back to him.

"I know you like me," he said, shaking his finger at me and taunting me like a child.

"And? Does that mean just because I like you I've got to screw you?"

"No, but a woman like you ought not deprive herself of the pleasures in life," he said and leaned back on the sofa so the big bulge in his pants became the center of attention.

I stared at it. I didn't give a fuck. It was my house. I could look wherever I wanted. I popped out of my stare when he reached for me again and pulled me on top of him. I leaned my head back so he couldn't kiss me and propped myself up on my elbows. "Alright, Terrence," I said sternly. "Check this out. I am a working woman. I don't have the luxury of lounging around the house all day long. I have to get up early in the morning and I simply don't have time to play these kissy-kissy, lovey-dovey games with you. Now if you would be so kind," I said and sat back up. "I would like you to lea—."

"Okay," he said and sat up next to me. "I know I've overstayed my welcome."

You got that right. Now hit the road.

He hesitated a bit, then turned toward me one last time. "Can I at least have a good-bye hug?" he asked and held out his arms.

I paused for a second, then shrugged my shoulders. What the hey, I thought and fell into his grasp.

Big mistake.

I swear, I've been fucking up all night long. Just as I was about to let him go, he whispered in my ear. "I know you're tired," he said softly. "But it only takes me five minutes."

"Five minutes?" I said, not even trying to spare his feelings. "Baby, if all you can give me is five minutes, then you sho nuff need to get to stepping," I said and pointed to the door.

"No, baby," he said and looked me in the eyes. "It'll only take five minutes to get you off."

Say what? "Yeah, right. You men have always got a gimmick. I don't care how good you guys *think* you are, you always take forever and a day to do what takes me forty-five seconds." I've timed myself before.

"I'm telling you, Madison," he said with too much confidence. "Five minutes."

Oh please. Come on. "Five minutes?"

"Five minutes."

Damn. Five minutes, I thought to myself. I've never had a partner induced orgasm in less than fourteen point six. The clock on my nightstand has a second hand. Damn, I thought as time seemed to stop again. What to do, what to do? I glanced over at the VCR for the time. One-fifteen A.M. Gotta get up at six. Terrence is fine. Haven't had sex in three weeks. Possible implants? Five minutes. Gets on my nerves. Five minutes. Bulge in pants. Five minutes. Terrence. Cute. Five minutes. Decisions, decisions . . . Oh fuck it. I'm grown. I've got needs. And I damn sure got five minutes.

2

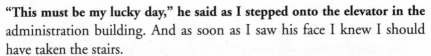

"This must be my lucky day," he said as I stepped onto the elevator in the administration building. And as soon as I saw his face I knew I should have taken the stairs.

"Morning," I mumbled and turned my back to him. I pressed the button for the third floor and prayed the elevator would make like a spaceship and zoom me up to my office like a bolt of lightning, because the thought of being all alone in a tiny elevator with this slimy snake in a three-piece suit was not my idea of starting the day off right.

"You look lovely today as usual," he said, standing directly behind me and leaning over my shoulder.

"Would you like a Tic Tac?" I asked and waved his breath away from me.

"Funny," he said and chuckled, though I wasn't joking. His breath smelled like green eggs and Spam, but obviously he didn't give a damn about his oral hygiene or he would have swallowed a pack of gum a long time ago.

I moved to the corner of the elevator, opened up my purse, and pretended to be searching for something so I wouldn't have to hold a conversation with this jackass, but as usual, he always had something to say. He slid back the sleeve of his jacket and peered closely at his watch.

"Eight-fifteen," he said and moved beside me. "Just getting in?"

"No," I lied as he brushed up against me and stared into my face. "For your information, I forgot something in my car and I had to go back and get it. Not that it's any of your business."

"Yeah right," he said, getting too close to me for comfort. "And what was so important that you had to get?"

"My stun gun," I said and nudged him away from me. "Don't make me have to use it."

"Stun gun?" he said and laughed. "I've got a stun gun for you," he said and slid his hand down his leg.

"Nasty dog," I said and rolled my eyes.

"Now, Madison," he said, eyeing me from head to toe. "After all these years we still can't be friends?"

"Hell no."

"And why is that?" he asked, edging his way back to me.

"Because you don't want to be *just* friends."

"Why be friends when we can be lovers?" he asked and reached out toward me. "Remember how it used to be?"

"You son of a bitch," I said and slapped his hand away from my breast.

"What?" he said, wincing. "You had some lint on your shirt."

"I'll handle my own damn lint, thank you."

"Come on, Madison. Why don't you come up to my office?" he asked, pinning me in the corner. "We can talk, clear off the desk . . . Have a little fun."

"I swear. One of these days I'm gonna slap the shit out of you."

"On the ass, I hope."

"You make me sick," I said as the elevator chimed, reaching my floor. "Get out of my way," I said and pushed my elbow into his stomach.

"How 'bout lunch?" he said, as the door opened.

"Fuck you."

"Please do."

"Ugh!" I grunted and stepped off the elevator.

"I'll call you later," he said as I watched the doors close in front of his face.

Some guys just don't get it, I thought to myself as I walked down the hallway to my office. You try to be nice and spare their feelings by telling them that the two of you can only be friends, but for some reason, they just won't accept it. The more you tell them no, the more they want you. It's like they have a chip missing in their brains and they just can't compute the words "I don't like you." For those guys there are no rules. You can't be nice, you can't be sweet—you've got to be a bitch. Mr. Smooth back there on the elevator is one of those guys. His name is Tommy Thompson. He's my boss—the principal and founder of Mighty Avalon Prep. But anyway . . .

By the time I got down to my office, I was convinced it was going to be a very long day. The phone was ringing off the hook, the receptionist was nowhere to be found, and lying on the floor outside my office door was a pile of unopened mail, my newspaper, and a yellow sheet of paper marked *Urgent* with my name on it in big red letters. "Damn," I said to myself as I rushed around the receptionist's desk and picked up the phone, "I knew I should have called in sick today."

I got to the phone too late and all I heard on the other end was a dial tone so I replaced the receiver and headed for my office door, yawning all the way and cursing Terrence for putting me in this tired state of mind. He was right when he said it would only take five minutes to get me to ecstasy's peak, but he failed to mention that it would take a whole hour and seventeen minutes for him to meet me there. I'm not complaining, though. The sex was great and if it hadn't been for dating rule number eight, I would have invited Terrence to spend the night with me so we could wake up together and do it one more time before I came in to work. But rule number eight—No sleepovers—is a rule that I never, ever break. The reason is very simple—I don't want any man I'm dating to see how I look first thing in the morning. To say that I wake up looking like a Booger Wolf would be an understatement. I don't know what kind of mysterious freak occurrence takes place while I'm sleeping, but every morning when I look at myself in the mirror I could swear that someone snuck into my bedroom during the night and beat me with an ugly stick. My eyes get all puffy, my nose runs, my lips get crusty, and my whole face looks like it's been run over with a set of brick tires. And what makes it so bad is that morning ugliness is not the kind of ugliness that disappears when you put on makeup. It doesn't fade in the shower and you can't clean it away with soap and water. Morning ugliness needs time to wear off on its own, which is why I never sleep over at a man's house or allow anyone to sleep over with me. I'd much rather wake up alone and deal with my morning ugliness all by myself. Plus, sleeping with a man can cause confusion. It blurs the senses. You spend all night wrapped in a man's arms and before long you start to get too comfortable. I don't want to be that comfortable with a man. You never know, one of us might start to get attached, and being attached is something that I never want to be.

Still, Terrence didn't leave my condo until four o'clock this morning, which is the reason why I overslept and got to work so late. School doesn't actually start until eight-forty-five, but Principal Thompson likes all the teachers to be in their offices by eight o'clock. We don't do shit but sit around twiddling our thumbs and drinking coffee; still, eight o'clock arrival is the rule around here, per Thompson. I usually use this time to catch up on my lesson plan or grade papers, but I'd rather be in bed. All I'm doing here is wasting time, and if you ask me, it would be better for the teachers to spend an extra forty-five minutes *after* school. That way, if our students needed counseling or to come in for tutoring, we'd be available. I told Thompson about my little idea about a month ago, but all he did was stare at my breast and tell me to put my idea in writing and maybe he'd consider it. I did, but he's never gotten back to me on it. I know it's a good idea, but Thompson just doesn't want to admit it. He's probably just mad because he didn't come up with it. That's the only thing I hate about working at a private school. Thompson makes the rules and we follow them, and if we don't like them, we follow them anyway or else find ourselves out of a job. At least in public schools, the teachers have a bit of say-so. If they don't like the way things are being done they can take their grievances up with the Board of Education and get things changed. But not at Mighty Avalon. It's all about dictatorship around here, and Thompson is the King Dick. Sometimes I wish I'd gone to work for a public school. At least that way I'd feel like I had a tiny bit of control over my teaching. The only thing is that public school teachers don't make any money. Here at Mighty Avalon, we may not get treated like much, but at least we get paid. I don't envy those public school teachers. It takes heart and dedication to do what they do. Those teachers only get half of what I make, yet every day their lives are put on the line. Teaching in a public school in L.A. is like teaching in Alcatraz. Not only are the classes overcrowded, but you never know which one of your students may be the designated gun carrier for the day. Last year alone, the public school system confiscated one hundred and twenty-three guns, seventy-nine knives, and sixty-two box cutters. It's getting so bad that teachers are afraid to take any authority in the classroom, and I don't blame them. Ever try to tell a thirteen-year-old gangbanger that he has to stay after school for detention when you know that the little fucker has got a six-shooter stuck down between his balls? Scary thought. One that I don't ever want to face. And that's why I put up with this shit at Mighty Avalon.

It may be a dictatorship around here, but it's better than teaching in a battlefield.

I picked up the bundle of junk outside my office door, went inside, and flipped on the lights. I plopped everything down on my desk and sat in front of my computer, staring straight ahead like a zombie and hoping that I could just have ten minutes of complete silence so that I could get my head together and transform my brain from sleep mode to work mode, but I wasn't so lucky. The phone rang out before I could even get comfortable in my chair, and since the receptionist was still nowhere to be found, I picked up the phone myself and put on my best teacher's voice.

"Mighty Avalon Prep, Madison McGuire speaking. How may I help you?"

"Morning again."

Speaking of King Dick . . . "What do you want?"

"You."

"I'm hanging up," I said and pulled the phone away from my ear until I heard him yell out.

"Wait. This is serious."

"Uh-huh."

"I need to see you in my office."

"Get a life, Tommy."

"I'm serious," he said forcefully. "In my office. Before class," he said and hung up the phone.

"You can kiss my dimpled ass," I said as I hung up the phone and put my head down on my desk. "I am not in the mood to deal with Tommy Thompson today," I mumbled and closed my eyes. Although I hate to use the word "hate," there are a few people in this world for whom there is no other verb to describe the way I feel. There's my daddy, who I really do hate and have every right to; Christopher, because I allowed myself to love him and he wound up breaking my heart; and last but not least, good old Tommy Thompson, the ultimate pussy prowler. Tommy and I have an unusual relationship. I know I should probably be afraid of him like all the other teachers. I mean, he is my boss, the principal, King Dick, etcetera. If any of the other teachers had spoken to him the way I just had, they'd be fired on the spot. But not me. I've got it like that where Principal Thompson is concerned, and as long as I don't disrespect him in front of any of the other teachers, Tommy puts up with my bitchy attitude. The only reason he does is because he's the one who made me this way. Tommy

Thompson has been trying to get a piece of my ass ever since the first day I started working here, and every year he seems to get bolder and more obnoxious with his come-ons. That scene in the elevator awhile ago was tame compared to his usual antics, like cornering me in the mail room and lifting up my skirt, or following me out to my car and refusing to let me get inside until I give him a kiss, complete with tongue. The man is a little off, and to be honest, I should have given him my resignation letter a long time ago. But I didn't and I doubt I ever will. See, it's partly my fault that this whole mess got started between us in the first place. Although I hate to admit it, I used to be quite taken with Tommy Thompson. Okay, okay, I might as well be totally honest. When I first started working here I thought Tommy Thompson was the be-all end-all. I don't know if it was because he was rich, or handsome, or drove a convertible 500 SEL—I don't know what it was, but Tommy Thompson had me sniffing behind him like I was a poodle in heat, and what excited me even more was that he was actually interested in me too. I was young at the time and it didn't take much to impress me. So when Tommy started giving me the eye, inviting me out for lunch and making special trips down to my seventh-grade classroom just so he could "check on the new hire," as he put it, I accepted all his flattery one hundred percent. I couldn't believe that a man like him, the founder of his own school, could be interested in a young, fresh-out-the-box teacher who'd just graduated from college. But he was interested and I was interested right back, so we got together. Okay, okay, I knew he was my boss and that getting involved with a man I worked with was worse than begging for trouble, but at the time I was just getting started on my dating rules list and I hadn't yet come up with rule number ten: Never date coworkers. Besides, even if I had gotten to rule number ten, I probably would have ignored it because for a while there, Tommy Thompson had my nose wide open. He was nice to me, he was older, more mature; and even though we worked right underneath each other's noses, he never tried to smother me. I was younger at the time, but I had already reached the conclusion that I didn't want to be attached to any one man, and my relationship with Tommy gave me all the freedom I needed. He never called me at home or bugged me on the weekends when I was busy with the other men in my life. For the most part, our relationship only consisted of a couple of lunches per week and a few late nights up in his office making out like teenagers on his sofa . . . or the desk, whichever one wasn't piled high with papers. Our relationship lasted for a good six months, until, that is, I found out Tommy was in violation of dating rule number three, the strictest rule of all. The son of a bitch was married.

I couldn't believe it took me six months to figure that out, but when I did I immediately called it quits. I don't play that shit. I think women who knowingly date married men are low-down, trampy sluts, and that's a clique that I definitely don't want to be a part of. Those kind of women are so desperate to have a man in their lives and a steady dick between their legs that they can't see through the fog and realize that there's another woman out there whose life they are destroying. If they took one minute to think about the wife and put themselves in her position, they'd give up those married men in a hot second. But most of those women don't give a damn about anything more than creating a fantasy world where they can parade around like they actually have a man who cares about them, until, that is, Christmas rolls around and reality sets in. December twenty-fifth is the day most mistresses get their fantasy worlds blown away. That's the most special day of the year. The day they just *know* that married man is gonna be all theirs. Yeah right. I don't give a damn how many times that man says he loves you, on Christmas Day, guess where he's gonna be? Not with you. He'll be with his wife and his kids, where he belongs, and it doesn't make a difference if he's made plans with you or not. Mistresses are always alone on holidays, especially Christmas. And New Year's? Psych. You'll be all alone again. Easter? Fourth of July? Please. The only holiday you'll be spending with that man is Groundhog Day, and you better hope his wife doesn't barbecue or he'll be standing you up again.

Though I never plan on being a wife, I do know this: If I ever found out my husband was cheating, I'd pull a Lorena Bobbit on his ass and cut off his dick so fast that he'd think he'd never even had one. And I wouldn't stop there. I'd go hunt down the whore he'd been screwing around with and open up a can of kick-ass on her too. I feel like this: A man can't cheat unless there's a bitch out there who'll let him. And a woman who know-ingly fucks around with another woman's husband deserves to get her face backslapped. That's why rule number three—Stay away from married men—is so strict. I couldn't live with myself knowing that I was wrecking another woman's world by bedding down her man. So when I found out Tommy was not the eligible bachelor I thought he was I backed off him like he was a poisonous snake and promised myself that I would never be with him again. I didn't even get mad or go off on him, which I had every right to do since he'd conned me into thinking he was available. I just took our six-month fling as a learning experience and added a few footnotes to my dating rules list, like, Never believe a man when he says the woman he's hugging in the picture on his desk is just his sister. I know, I know, I was stupid. But that was years ago, when I was young and naive. I should have never gotten involved with Tommy in the first place, and believe me, if I had it to do all over again, I would have never given him a second look. The only good thing that has come out of our relationship is the fact that he allows my little sister to attend school here free of charge. Tommy can be nice when he wants to be. Too bad he doesn't want to be more often.

Still, the fact remains that I *did* have a relationship with Tommy and although I told him a long time ago that it was over between us, he doesn't quite seem to get it. He's always making up some stupid excuse to get me upstairs in his office so he can be alone with me and figure out some way to get me undressed and on top of his desk. It's become a game to him. A game that I'm getting tired of. If I had any sense, I'd slap a sexual harassment suit on his ass and take the man for everything he's got, including this school, and to be honest I don't know why I haven't done that yet. I guess it's because although I'm tired of all his shit, I still feel like I can handle him. Oh sure, he may get too close to me at times, put his hand down too low on my back, or stare for too long at the wrong part of my anatomy, but those are all things I can handle. If Tommy gets too out of line with me, I just threaten to call up his wife and he backs off—for a while. That's why I say this is all a game to him. He wants to see how far he can push me before I finally give in and give him what he wants—me, butt naked on a platter. But he's never gonna get it. Try as he might, I'm too strong a woman to give in to his silly game. Hell will freeze over before Tommy Thompson gets a piece of me again.

And today I don't even feel like going through the motions with him, which is why I'm hardly worried about rushing up to his office to meet with him before class. All I want to do, what I'm gonna do, is close my office door and sit and stare straight ahead until eight-forty-five comes calling. But as soon as I got up from my seat to close my door, the phone rang again. I poked my head out front to see if the receptionist had decided to show her face yet, but her chair was still empty. "Dammit," I moaned, as I closed my door and came back to my desk. I picked up line one and tried not to sound too agitated.

"Mighty Avalon Prep, Madison McGuire, please hold," I said as another line rang out.

"Mighty Avalon, Ms. McGuire, please hold, please," I said, as still another line lit up.

"M. A. McGuire—help you?"

"Good loving, body rocking, knocking boots all night long," a familiar voice sang through the receiver.

"Excuse me?" I said and frowned, wondering who in the world. "This is Mighty Avalon Preparatory School, not amateur night at the Apollo," I said strictly.

"Girl, don't be so mean," the voice said, laughing. "Don't you know who this is?"

"No. Is this Milli or Vanilli?" I snapped.

"It's Terrence, babe," he said, sounding slightly offended.

"Terrence?" I said, trying to remember when I'd given him my work number.

"The one and only, babe," he said, trying to turn me on with a low, sexy voice. It wasn't working. I'd gotten my fill of Terrence last night, and right now I just didn't feel like being bothered. "I've been thinking about you ever since I left your place."

"Oh, is that right?" I said, realizing I should be flattered but wasn't. "Can you hold on a second? I've got another call."

"Don't take too long."

Yeah right, I thought and put him on hold, wondering why I wasn't the least bit excited to hear from him. But I guess good sex can't make up for a fucked up personality, and I still hadn't quite forgotten about that sly reference he made about my thighs and the chemical peel. No, Terrence may be good in bed, but he's not the type of man I want to spend more than one night a month with. I picked up line two. "Ms. McGuire, may I help you?"

"Hi, Li'l Ma."

"Hey, baby," I said, happy to hear my little sister's voice. Then I realized the time and panicked. "What's wrong? Why aren't you on your way to school?"

" 'Cause it be like dat sometimes," she said in that exaggerated street slur she knew I hated.

"Speak like a lady, little girl."

"Big Mama's car is tripping and I gotta take the bus."

"Dammit. Why didn't you call me last night so I could pick you up on my way in?"

"The car wasn't broke last night."

"Alright, uh, I guess I gotta come get you," I said, peeking at the clock on my desk.

"That's okay. I'm just gonna be a little late. Will you tell Mr. Tate so I won't get detention?"

"You sure you're gonna be okay on the bus?"

"Yeah, but you're gonna have to give me a ride home 'cause I ain't catching the bus two times in one day."

"Okay, little girl. You just make sure you go straight to the bus stop. Don't talk to nobody, don't look at nobody, don't—"

"*Okay*, Li'l Ma. I know the routine," she whined. "Can I straight kick it at your house tonight?"

"Excuse me?"

"Can I spend the night with you?"

"We'll see."

"Please."

"I said we will see, okay? I've gotta go. Kiss-kiss," I said and smiled.

"Kiss-kiss," she said and hung up.

I didn't particularly like the thought of Serena catching the bus to school. Too many damn fools out there on the streets. But I was sure Mother was going to walk with her to the bus stop and wait there until she saw Serena off. That's how she used to do me when I was a kid and she didn't have a car. I wished Mother had gone on ahead and bought a new car while she was working at the grocery store, but now it's too late. When she finally got off welfare and went to work at Ralph's, Mother just plain went crazy. Disposable income was a new one for her. Besides being able to buy Serena's medication, I don't know what she did with all the money she was making, but I know it never went to buying a decent ride. And I guess she'll never have a decent car now that she fell down on the job and broke her hip. Her disability checks can only cover so much. I try to help her out, when she'll accept my help—which is hardly ever. That's Mother for you. So proud, so stubborn. If she'd just let me buy her a little used Pacer or something, she'd be good to go and Serena wouldn't have to catch the bus. But it'll never happen. Not Mother. I sighed as I picked up line one and said, "Ms. McGuire, how may I be of service to you?"

"You can give me a repeat of last night?"

"Terrence?" I said, realizing I'd pressed the wrong button.

"How 'bout it?" he asked and started singing again. *"Some body rocking, knocking the boots."*

"Please hold," I said and put the phone down. Terrence was really getting on my nerves, I thought, and picked up line one. "Ms. McGuire here."

"Where the hell have you been?" a voice yelled at me.

"Malik?"

"Didn't you get the note I left outside your door?"

"Oh, that yellow sheet of paper? I thought it was work so I didn't look at it," I said as I searched through the pile of junk on my desk, trying to find it. "What's up?"

"Never mind. I'm gonna shoot down to the cafeteria and I'll stop by your office on my way back," he said and hung up the phone on me.

I pulled the phone away from my ear and stared at it, wondering what could it be that had Malik so jumpy this morning. That's not his style. Malik is the most laid-back person I know, and I know him well. Malik and I are best friends. That's right, *friends,* just friends. Unlike what most people think, it is possible for a man and a woman to have a completely platonic relationship. I didn't think it was possible myself until Malik started teaching here six years ago, and ever since we've been tighter than shoe laces. I don't get along with women too well, which is why I don't have any female friends. Me and women just don't mix. Even when I was a kid in school I never had girlfriends. For some reason women see me as their competition. All I have to do is walk into a room and women instantly hate me. Malik says it's a jealousy thang. "Your hair is always jamming. Your outfits are meticulous. And look at your face," he said to me once. "You don't have female friends because they all know you could snatch their men away from them anytime you got good and ready."

"I'd never do that to a friend," I told him.

"I know you wouldn't, but you know how you women are. Anyone threatens to take your man away and you go on tactical alert."

"*Some* women are like that, Malik," I corrected him. "Personally, I don't give a damn. If a man is out with me and he sees someone else he wants, he can go for it. Be my guest. Ain't no man worth fighting over."

"I heard that," he said and gave me a high five. "Just stop tripping, girl. You don't need any female friends anyway. You've got me."

And that was the truth. Malik and I have each other. As a matter of fact, Malik and I spend so much time together that the rumor mill around school has it that we're an item. Last year there was a rumor that we were engaged, and the year before that it was that I was pregnant by him—twins. I don't know who started that mess, but it's actually quite funny to me.

Malik and I are just very good friends and we could never be more than that because we have too much in common, including the fact that we both love men. Oh yes, Malik is gay. None of the other teachers know it, but it's the truth. I didn't even know it until last year, when we went to the annual Christmas party together that Thompson throws for all the teachers as his way of saying, Thanks for letting me stick in your ass for one more year. Anyway, Malik had a little too much to drink and so did I, so we just sat by ourselves most of the night in a corner of the room, too scared to get up and walk around for fear that we'd do something stupid, like fall down. We just sat and drank and drank and got drunk and more drunk. Until, that is, Malik kissed me on the mouth and told me he loved me. I was drunk, but I hadn't lost my mind. And even though I'd caught myself fantasizing about Malik on more than one occasion, I pushed him away from me and slurred out rule number ten. "I don't date men I work with, so you can just forget it," I said, barely able to keep my head in an upright position.

"I don't wanna date you," he said and laughed as he bent over and took a sip out of the champagne bottle we'd taken from the buffet and hidden in our corner for our own private use.

"Well, we can't be bed buddies either," I said and took the bottle from him and gulped down a mouthful.

"No, no, no, no, no, no, no," he said as drunk as he could be. "I just love you. That's it," he said, slurring.

"Oh, you mean like a brover, I mean a broder, loves a sista?" I said and hid our bottle of champagne underneath my seat.

"Like a gay brother loves his sister," he said and stared at me until I got it and when I did, I almost passed out.

"You're gay?" I said, shocked. "Get out of here. You're gay? You don't look gay."

"And how does gay look, Madison?" he said and chuckled.

I was so drunk that that question really confused me and I had to think about it to come up with an answer, but all I came up with was, "You're gay?"

"True that," he said and snickered. I didn't know why he was laughing, but he looked so funny sitting there drunk out of his mind and snorkeling like a pig that I couldn't help but join in. We laughed so hard that we could barely keep ourselves in our seats. Until, that is, I realized that I'd known Malik for six years, and got mad as hell.

"You little fucker," I said and hit him hard on the arm.

"What?" he said, grabbing his arm and still laughing.

"Fucking asshole," I said and hit him again, almost making him tumble over.

"What?" he said, looking like a confused wino.

"You're supposed to be my friend."

"I am your friend."

"Then why are you just now telling me this?"

"Ah, Madison, please," he said and reached under my seat for the bottle. "This isn't something you tell just anybody."

That's when I started crying. Big, fat drunken tears. "I'm not just anybody," I cried. "I'm your homie. Aren't you my homie? I thought we were homies, homie."

"Ssh," he said and patted my back. "People are beginning to stare."

"I hate you," I slurred, spitting all over myself.

"Okay," he said and gripped me by the arm. "It's time to get your drunk ass out of here."

We stumbled our way out the banquet hall and somehow got down to the lobby, where Malik sat me down on the floor outside the elevator while he went to call a cab to pick us up. By that time I was a sloppy, crying, shit-faced mess, but I was still mad as hell because Malik hadn't trusted me enough to confide in me.

"Fonky fucker," I said as he sat down on the floor next to me and rested his head against the wall.

"I just couldn't tell you, Madison," he said, closing his eyes.

"Why come? I tell you stuff all the time," I said, nudging him till he reopened his eyes. "Don't I always tell you my business?"

"Yes, Madison."

"Didn't I tell you I hate my daddy and want to cut him into a million pieces? 'Member that time I told you that?"

"Yes, Madison."

"And, and, didn't I tell you that sometimes when I'm out in public with my sister and she has one of her spells and starts ticing her head and mumbling that I sometimes wanna pretend like I don't know her? Didn't I tell you that?"

"Yes, Madison."

"And didn't I tell you about me and Tommy?"

"Yes, Madison."

"See, I tell you all my secrets, Malik. I tell you all my deep dark shit. But see how you do me? I thought we were friends and stuff," I said and started crying really hard.

"I couldn't tell you, Li'l Mama. I—"

"Didn't I tell you I hate that nickname?"

"Yes, Madison."

"See, I tell you everything."

"You don't understand what I go through, Madison," he said, banging his head against the wall. "Every time I think I can trust someone enough to tell them about me, they end up turning on me. Even my own family turned on me, Madison. I told them and they . . . Man, you just don't understand," he said and closed his eyes. "It's so hard being who I am. I couldn't tell you because I love you and I didn't wanna lose our friendship," he said and began to cry even harder than I was.

"Ooo," I slurred, watching him slobber all over himself. "Ooo, Malik. Don't cry," I said, wanting to give him a hug, but in the state I was in all I could do was reach out my hand and pat him on the head. "Don't cry, Malik," I said as he leaned over and rested his head in my lap. "I love you, okay? I'm your friend."

"You promise?"

"Cross my heart and hope to die," I said and wiped his tears away.

■

Now that I think about it, Malik is the only man I've ever really loved. Okay, okay, there was Christopher, but he's a natural born asshole so he doesn't count. I sure never loved my daddy. As a matter of fact, I doubt I even loved him as a baby. I searched through the pile of junk on my desk for my newspaper and quickly turned to the obituaries and looked for my daddy's sorry name. "Cleophus McGuire," I said as I searched and soon found it was not my lucky day. "Maybe tomorrow," I said and tossed the paper in the trash.

I stared at the pile of mail on top of my desk for the longest time, until I finally decided to pick up an envelope and open it. But before I could get halfway through the first memo, the phone rang out again and I suddenly remembered . . . Terrence.

"How you gonna leave me on hold for ten minutes?" he asked with an attitude.

"Sorry. It's just so hectic around here this morning. Do you mind if I call you back later?"

"What about tonight?"

Damn, I knew he was gonna ask that. "Tonight? Well, uh . . . I'm sorry, Terrence. Tonight's not good for me."

"What? You already got a date or something?"

"No. As a matter of fact, I think I'm gonna spend some time with my little sister tonight," I said, wondering why I was explaining myself to him.

"You'd rather spend a romantic Friday night with your sister than with me?" he asked as time seemed to stop completely. And here again was my dilemma. It's Friday night and I haven't been dateless on a Friday night since, since . . . I've never been dateless on a Friday night. But I haven't spent any quality time with Serena lately either. But last night's sexcapade was great. But I don't really like Terrence. Sexcapade. Serena. Friday night. Terrence. Decisions, decisions . . .

"Sorry, Terrence. Can't make it tonight."

"But what about the *good loving, body rocking, knock—*"

"Good-bye, Terrence," I said and hung up the phone.

I'll take Serena over Terrence any day, I thought as I picked up another piece of mail. Besides, I've already got a date lined up for Saturday night. Two dates a week is enough for me, I thought as I stopped fiddling with my mail and gazed over to the corner of my office.

"How did I miss that?" I said aloud and eyed the small blue box on the floor. I giggled like a happy baby as I rose up from my chair and went over to pick up the box. I smiled from ear to ear as I struggled to open it, and after a while of tugging and pulling and ripping the box to shreds, I found a stack of CDs. "My favorites," I said as I pulled them out one by one. There was Me'Shell Ndegéocello, D'Angelo, Maxwell, Dionne Farris, and a triple set of Teena Marie's greatest hits. But as usual, there was no card, no note, no hint of who, what, or where they came from. "Secret admirer strikes again," I said as I took the stack of CDs back to my desk.

I browsed through my new collection of CDs again as I racked my brain trying to figure out who my secret admirer could be, but when I heard a faint hum and the clicking of heels outside my doorway, I put everything aside. That could only be one person—Malik.

He stood in front of the door for a second while he gripped a cup of coffee with one hand and unbuttoned his jacket with the other. I couldn't help but notice how fine my friend was. Malik had things popping. He was smart, had fat pockets, and that *GQ* kind of style that would make a sister swear he was some kind of superstar instead of an eighth-grade teacher. Malik could have any woman he wanted, only he didn't want it. Every time we go out together he gets women breaking their necks to get a glimpse of his goodness. But all he does is grip my arm and whisper in my ear, "Would you tell these hoes I already got a man?" I just smile and squeeze him around the waist to let all the looky-loos know he's taken. But every now and again a bold woman will step to him and let him know she's got a thang for him. But Malik is straight up. He'll tell a woman in a minute that he's gay and keep right on walking. The woman usually stands there with her mouth hanging open like she'd just been told a dirty secret. But Malik isn't stressed by shock. There's no shame in his game. He knows who he is and he's not afraid to admit it. Now that doesn't mean Malik is out the closet completely, especially not here at school. Nobody knows Malik is gay around here except me, and until he's ready, that's the way it has to be.

"Serena just called," I told him as he sat down in front of my desk looking like he was about to explode. "She wanted me to tell you she's going to be late. Mom's car is on the blink and—"

"Yeah, yeah, yeah," he said anxiously and sat his cup down on my desk.

"What the hell is wrong with you?" I asked and raised a brow.

"You haven't heard yet?" he asked quickly.

Oh no. More rumors, I thought and rolled my eyes. "Alright, who's screwing who?" I asked and rested my head on my hand.

"This is serious, Madison," he said, leaning forward in his chair.

"What, what?" I asked, suddenly getting concerned.

"We're gonna get fired."

"What?"

"You heard me. We're outta here. Jobless. Fired."

"Shut it down, Malik," I said and rolled my eyes. "Now really. What's up?"

"It's true, Madison. I heard it from a very reliable source."

"Malik," I said, and sighed, "your reliable source is Junior, the second-floor janitor. I don't call that a reliable source."

"Hey. Junior has given me some great gossip over the years," he said defensively. "But Junior didn't tell me this. I got this gossip practically from the horse's mouth."

"Who?"

"Thompson's secretary."

"Please. I just talked to Cynthia yesterday and she didn't say anything about anybody getting fired, especially not me."

"Well she's not just gonna come right out and tell you. You gotta be cool about it. Like me."

"You're cool?"

"The coolest," he said, flashing a smile, then quickly taking it away. He gripped his face in his hand and shook his head. "I knew we should have never tried to change things around here," he said, then looked up at me. "What were we thinking?"

"Wait a minute," I said and leaned across my desk. "Back up. Are you telling me that Cynthia told you we both were being fired?"

"Well," he said and hesitated. "Not exactly."

I sucked my teeth and leaned back in my chair. "What exactly did Cynthia say?"

Malik crossed his legs and took a deep breath. "Cynthia said that somebody was being let go. Then she looked at me like this," he said and squinted his eyes.

"Is that all?" I asked and threw up my hands. "I swear, Malik. You are too damn paranoid."

"Come on, Madison," he said and fidgeted in his seat. "You know what you and I have been up to lately. Thompson probably got wind of it and decided to kick our asses to the curb. You know he doesn't play that shit."

"Nobody knows what we're doing but us," I said and stood up from my seat. "And I'll prove it to you," I said as I straightened out my skirt and began walking toward the door.

"Where are you going?" he asked and stood up with me.

"Thompson called. He wants to see me in his office."

"Oh shit. Oh shit," he said and sank back down in his chair. "I knew it. He knows. We're goners."

"Take a pill," I said and stopped in front of him and watched as he panted like a dog.

"I need this job. I can't get fired. A brother's got bills, Madison."

"Listen," I said and cupped his face with my hands, but Malik was past the point of listening. He was already on the road to hysteria.

"I got rent. I got car note. I haven't even paid off this damn suit. I need my job."

"Shut it down," I said and squeezed his cheeks. "We are not going to get fired. Do you hear me?" I said and squeezed harder to capture his full attention. "Now repeat after me. We are not going to get fired."

"We gonna get fired."

"*Malik.*"

"Alright, alright," he said, trying to pull himself together. "We are not going to get fired."

"Good boy," I said and let him go. "Now, I'm going to see King Dick and I'll meet you later in the teachers' lounge at recess," I said and hustled out the door.

I had ten minutes to get up to Thompson's office before my class started and since I didn't have five to spend waiting for the elevator, I took the stairs.

As I walked up the two flights to the fifth floor, I couldn't help thinking about Malik and the frenzy he'd worked himself into over what I was sure would turn out to be nothing. Malik was always overreacting. There was no way we were going to get fired, I thought to myself as I climbed the final step. Unless . . . Naw. There was no way Thompson could know about what Malik and I were up to. Still, the way rumors fly around this place, it wouldn't be a surprise if someone slipped up and spilled the beans. And if they did, Thompson would surely go on a rampage.

∎

See, it all started last semester when one of the girls in Malik's eighth grade class wound up pregnant. In public schools a pregnant teen is a common part of the scene, but here at Mighty Avalon it was a scandal. The little girl's name was Tameka. She was fourteen years old, a straight-A student, a member of the Science Society—a brainiac. The girl was a wiz when it came to the books, but dumb as a moth when it came to boys. She got conned into lifting her skirt for some sly-talking boy who lived around the corner from her house. She got pregnant her first time out and of course she panicked. She was afraid to tell her parents so she told the only adult she could talk to—her teacher, Malik. Well, Malik didn't know what to do so he came to me and asked me for help.

I did all I could for Tameka. I became her friend, gave her a shoulder to cry on, but most important, I convinced her to tell her parents because the girl was already three months along and still hadn't gotten any kind of prenatal treatment. One morning before class I invited her and her parents to my office. Her parents knew something was up since I was calling them in for a conference and I wasn't even Tameka's teacher. Still, they showed up, and I stood next to Tameka, holding her hand as she told her parents that their baby was carrying a baby. Tameka left with her parents after the conference, but she was back the next day. She told me she and her parents talked and though they were disappointed in her, they'd worked everything out. Tameka was going to have her baby.

Everything was cool for the next couple months. Tameka got her prenatal care, she stopped stressing, and her mom even called to thank me for being there for her daughter when she couldn't be. But then Tameka started showing and the school started talking. Kids were laughing and pointing fingers, and teachers were glaring at her and shaking their heads. And then Thompson got wind of Tameka's pregnancy and it was all over. He called Tameka and her parents in for a meeting and the next day Tameka was gone. Kicked out of school just like that. When Malik went to Thompson to find out what had happened, Thompson told him he'd expelled Tameka because she was a bad influence on the other students. Said he didn't want any pregnant teenagers parading around his campus and setting a bad example. Malik tried to go to bat for Tameka, telling Thompson that she was a good kid who had just gotten herself caught up in a bad situation. But Thompson wasn't trying to hear all that. It was his school, he made the rules, and everybody else hailed the king. I don't think I'd ever seen Malik so angry before. In fact he was all set to go back to Thompson's office and resign. Until that is, he thought about those monthly payments he had to make on that new Lexus he's been sporting. Still, Malik was on fire and so was I. What happened to Tameka was not right.

On one hand, I've got to commend Thompson on the way he runs his school. Avalon is the only private school for black students in L.A., and the students we turn out are exemplary. The parents of Mighty Avalon pay big dollars to ensure that their children get the best education, and that's what we provide. We take special precautions to ensure that the students are provided with a safe learning environment, free from all distractions, so that the only thing that goes on when they walk through the school gates is learning. But on the other hand Mighty Avalon is way behind the times. It's like a military academy around here. We have no extracurricular activities like football, cheerleading, or even drill team. Those are only distractions, Thompson says. He won't even let the kids have dances or year-end parties. According to Thompson, the only agenda going on at Mighty Avalon is education. If kids want to shake their booties and throw balls they can go to public school, but here at Mighty Avalon they're going to learn and nothing else.

Well that's all good in theory, but children are children. They want to have fun too, or at least that's my opinion. But then again, who asked me?

Anyway, after Tameka got expelled, Malik and I got to talking and, though no one ever asked us for our opinions, we decided Mighty Avalon Prep needed a change. The situation Tameka found herself in was one that no fourteen-year-old girl should ever have to face. In the first place, no fourteen-year-old girl should be having sex at all. That's a given. But the simple fact is that they do. It didn't take a genius to understand that. Malik and I are teachers. We're around teenagers every day. We hear what they whisper about, we see how they look at each other. And the bottom line is that these kids are doing it. Tameka wasn't the only one; she was just the one who got caught. And the way Malik and I figured it, it was high time we did something to make sure no other student had to face what Tameka faced. The students needed guidance, they needed counseling, they needed education—sex education.

In most public schools, sex education classes are a normal part of the curriculum. But here at Avalon, Thompson says no-no. According to him sex education is nothing more than a distraction, and there was no need to teach students about sex. Sex couldn't land them a job and it wouldn't get them through college. I say that's bull. I mean, I see where Thompson is coming from, but don't we owe it to our students to teach them about all aspects of life? I can almost understand Thompson's ambivalence about not having any distractions like sports and cheerleading and all. Black students need to understand that education is the most important thing in their lives. But come on. If we don't start teaching these kids how to survive in the real world, we won't be doing anything but turning out a bunch of brainiacs who have no idea what life is all about. Malik and I figure that teaching the kids about their own sexuality—how to be responsible and, most important, how to say no—could save them from going through what Tameka had to go through.

I'm not saying that teaching sex education will stop teens from having sex. I'm just saying that when kids know what could happen when they lay down together they may think twice. They need all the info they can get to make the right choices for themselves, and if we teach them correctly, hopefully their choice will be to just say no.

Anyway, Malik and I came up with a plan. We knew if we simply went to Thompson and asked him about adding a sex education class to the curriculum, his answer would be a big, fat "Get out of my office." So we decided to put together a petition of sorts. For the last two months we've been secretly contacting parents and asking their opinion about a sex education course. If they were for the idea, we'd have them sign a petition. So far, much to my surprise, the majority of the parents have been yea. They'd all heard about Tameka and most of them were willing to do whatever it took so that their child wouldn't "turn out like her."

So far, Malik and I have gotten over a hundred names, and we figure that in another month or so we'll have over two hundred, and when we do, we plan on taking the petition and our proposal to Thompson and demanding that a sex education class be added to the curriculum. We figure Thompson may refuse two teachers, but he could hardly afford to refuse two hundred tuition-paying parents.

Just this week I racked up two more parents for the proposal without even trying. I was walking out of the aerobics room at my gym, looking and smelling quite funky, when I saw two familiar faces sitting in the new members' area. As I passed by, one of them shouted out. "Hey, Ms. McGuire."

I smiled and slowed down, trying to figure out where I'd seen this woman before.

"I'm Carmen Drew's mom," she said, rushing over to me with her hand out. "My daughter was in your class last year."

"Yeah," I said and shook her hand. I took a step back so my odor wouldn't make her pass out. "How are you?"

"Just fine," she said, beaming. "You know my daughter still talks about you. She just loved you as a teacher."

"Well, I love my students," I said and smiled, thinking this was a perfect opportunity. Mrs. Drew may have been at the gym to sign up for aerobics, but little did she know she was about to sign up for my team as well.

I walked her back over to her friend, who she introduced as Vicki Brown, mother of a fifth-grader named Monique. We chatted lively about the gym and the aerobics classes for a hot second and then I let them have it. I jumped right in like I always do and got right down to business. "How would you two like to become grandmothers?"

Mrs. Drew curled up her lip and Vicki raised an eyebrow. "Honey, I am too young for that. Why you think I'm in this gym? I'm trying to look and feel younger, not older, baby."

Perfect answer, I thought and grinned. It was on. By the time I walked out that gym I had two more parents backing me up. This job is too easy. At first I thought getting the parents behind me would be hard. But these parents care about their children. That's why they send them to Mighty Avalon in the first place. It doesn't take much to convince them that what Malik and I are doing is right. The only hard part will be making Tommy Thompson see that.

■

Like I said before, this school is a dictatorship and Thompson is the King Dick, and if word got out about what Malik and I were up to before we could get our plan fully together there is no doubt that we could find ourselves out of a job. That's just the way things are around here.

But if Thompson had heard about what we were up to he would have said something to me by now, I thought to myself as I opened the door to the fifth floor and walked down the hall to his office. When I stepped through the door the first person I saw was Cynthia, and when she saw me coming, she turned her head and looked away. That made me curious. That made me nervous. I started to really wonder if maybe someone had dropped a dime on me and Malik. Did Cynthia know that we were sneaking around and trying to change the school's curriculum? No—more important—did Thompson know?

"Hey, Cynthia. Is the boss man in?" I asked as I stopped at her desk.

"Go right in," she said without looking at me.

No, no, Cynthia. You're holding out on me, I thought as I leaned over her desk and whispered, "What's the four-one-one, Cynth? Who's getting fired?"

"I don't know nothing, I don't know nothing," she said and put her hands over her head.

"Come on, Cynthia. Give up the knowledge," I whispered until an ugly voice called out behind me.

"Madison. I've been waiting for you," Tommy said as I turned around to face him.

"I bet you have," I said as I walked into his office and sat down.

He closed the door and walked over to me, smiling that smile that used to get me so hot but now only made me notice that his two front teeth were crooked. "Did I tell you how nice you looked yet?" he asked and sat down behind his desk. "And you smell nice too."

"Chanel No. 5. I'm sure your wife would love it."

"Oh Madison," he said and chuckled.

"Oh Tommy," I said and faked a grin.

"Let me get right to the point," he said and took a deep breath. "I've been hearing rumors," he said, leaning back in his chair.

Oh shit, I thought and wondered if I should just go ahead and tell him the whole story. Maybe if I tried to reason with him he'd recognize the necessity for a sex education class and cut me a break. But as I looked more closely at Thompson, I knew there was no reasoning with him. He was an asshole through and through, and he liked it like that.

"I fired Mrs. Morris," he said too quickly for me to comprehend.

"What?"

"Mrs. Morris. Your third-floor receptionist. I fired her," he said and folded his hands on his desk. "So now you know. That should put an end to all the rumors."

I almost smiled. I was off the hook. I knew Malik had gotten his information wrong. But after a second, it hit me. "You fired Mrs. Morris? But why?"

"Incompetent."

"Incompetent? She was a receptionist. She answered phones, filed papers. She was good at her job."

"Well I let her go anyway. Didn't like her attitude."

"Didn't like her attitude?"

"Is there an echo in here?"

"Whatever, Tommy. Why are you telling me all this?"

"Because you will be in charge of phones in the morning until I find a replacement for her."

"And that's it. That's why you called me to your office? To tell me I had to answer phones?"

"Correct."

"Yeah right. Now let's get down to the real reason you summoned me to your bat cave."

"What do you mean, *real* reason? I just wanted you to know about your phone duty."

"And?"

"And nothing," he said and grinned.

"And that's it?"

"That's it."

"So I can leave now?"

"You may mosey on out the door."

"Okay," I said and rose up from my seat, and paused. "I'm going."

"Go on."

"Alrighty," I said and headed for the door, and as soon as I was almost home free . . .

"Oh, Madison," he sang.

"What?" I said and closed my eyes without turning around.

"How about dinner?"

"Don't you ever give up?"

"Nope. How 'bout lunch?"

"You know what? I'm gonna call your wife."

"Go right ahead. She filed for divorce last month," he said and stood up and walked directly in front of me. "Can I have a kiss?" he said and grabbed me by the waist.

"You asshole," I said as I pushed him away and slapped the shit out of him. I slapped him so hard that my hand stung, but all he did was smile. Damn, I thought. I forgot he liked it rough. "So this is the real reason you called me up here? Look, Tommy, I don't have time for your shit this morning."

"What? I'm a free man now. You broke up with me because I was married, right? Well I'm going to be divorced in a few months. Can't we give it another shot?"

"Hell no."

"Why not?"

"Because I said so."

"Okay," he said and walked back to his desk. "Have it your way."

Tommy was up to his old games again, but I couldn't blame him. I was a part of the game too. I allowed myself to be. I should have quit a long time ago, but I didn't. I couldn't. My job was my life. It was my security and Tommy knew that. He gave me a sly wink and blew me a fake kiss as I walked out the door and slammed it behind me.

Damn, I hate that man, I thought as I headed to the elevator. I really, really hate that man.

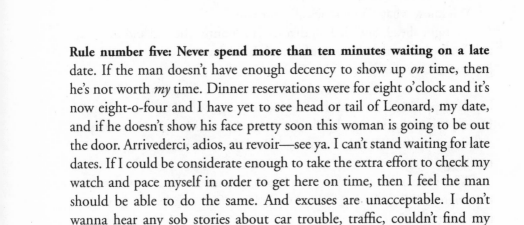

3

Rule number five: Never spend more than ten minutes waiting on a late date. If the man doesn't have enough decency to show up *on* time, then he's not worth *my* time. Dinner reservations were for eight o'clock and it's now eight-o-four and I have yet to see head or tail of Leonard, my date, and if he doesn't show his face pretty soon this woman is going to be out the door. Arrivederci, adios, au revoir—see ya. I can't stand waiting for late dates. If I could be considerate enough to take the extra effort to check my watch and pace myself in order to get here on time, then I feel the man should be able to do the same. And excuses are unacceptable. I don't wanna hear any sob stories about car trouble, traffic, couldn't find my keys, wrong directions, dog ate my homework—none of that. There are no excuses for keeping a woman waiting. It's rude, it's thoughtless, it's unkind, inconsiderate, impolite, selfish, it's neglectful, it's, it's—did I say rude? What I hate most about waiting is this eerie, helpless feeling that comes over me. It's a feeling that makes my heart race and my head pound. It's a feeling of abandonment. A feeling like the one I always felt when I was a little girl and my daddy would promise to come see me.

I never heard much from my daddy when I was a child, but on the occasional blue moon when he'd take the time to pick up the phone and let me know he was still alive, I'd instantly become the happiest little girl in the world. Just hearing my daddy's voice would send me into a wonderful frenzy. All at once I'd become perky and nervous and amazed. My eyes would light up and my mouth would start moving so fast that I could barely get out a complete sentence. There was always so much I wanted to tell Daddy about me and about school and about the tooth fairy and Santa Claus. And I wanted to ask him questions too. Questions like "Why is the sky blue?" and "How do birds fly?" and "Why come the roaches in the kitchen only come out when the lights are off?" Mother had already answered most of these questions for me, but I still wanted to hear what Daddy had to say about them. I just wanted to talk to my Daddy about everything, and for me talking would have been enough, but Daddy would always take things an extra step.

"I'm gonna come over and see you, baby," he'd say, and as soon as the words came out his mouth, I'd jump all over him.

"When, Daddy? Today? You coming to see me today?" I'd ask, thrilled to the bone.

"Uh, yeah," he'd stutter. Daddy always stuttered when he got excited.

"When? What time, Daddy? *Daddy?* Can you come now? Huh? Daddy, can you come see me right now?"

"Uh, yeah, baby," he'd stutter again. "I'm on my way over to see you right now."

And that's all I needed to hear. I'd hang up the phone and go running to Mother. "Mama," I'd scream.

"Stop yelling in the house," she'd scream back, but I couldn't help myself.

"Mama, Daddy say he gon' come over to see me. Right now."

"Uh-huh," she'd say, not even bothering to fake a smile or get excited with me. I'd stand there in front of her as she laid on her bed watching TV and I'd be tingling with delight and waiting for my mother to join in the merriment, but she wouldn't even raise a brow.

"Mama," I'd say and pull on her mattress. "I said Daddy is coming over."

"I heard you, Madison," she'd say and turn to look at me. She'd get really happy then. So happy that her eyes would water and she'd stroke the side of my face and look so deeply into my eyes that I'd almost get scared. But I didn't have time for all that sentimental stuff. I had to get ready for my daddy.

I'd rush off to my room and get all dolled up in my finest and frilliest dress. I'd put on my white opaque tights and my white patent Mary Jane shoes with the buckles on the sides. Then I'd go back to Mama's room and beg her to let me put on some of her pink Chantilly perfume. Mother would be so happy by that time that she'd be crying, which made it easy for me to persuade her to let me use her perfume. After I doused myself in pink Chantilly and primped for a few minutes in front of the bathroom mirror, I'd be set. I'd go into the living room, pull back the curtains, and sit down on the plastic-covered sofa and wait. Wait for my daddy to come see me.

Whenever I heard movement outside on the street, I'd run to the window and look out for Daddy. Usually the only thing I'd see was a group of my neighborhood friends, and when they saw me they'd wave and come over to the window and beg me to come out and play. If I knew how to curse at the time, I would have said, "Hell no." Instead, I just shook my head and smiled like a queen addressing her subjects. "I can't come out and play 'cause my daddy's coming over," I'd say as my subjects eyed me with amazement. "My daddy's coming and he's gonna take me to Mc-Donald's and we gonna get some ice cream and he, and he, he gon' take me to the movies and the park and the circus and we gon' have popcorn and candy and, and he gon' let me spend the night with him, 'cause, um, 'cause he live in a upstairs-downstairs house like the one on *The Brady Bunch* and he got a maid and a backyard, and when we get up in the morning the maid is gonna cook us brefiss."

"The maid gon' cook y'all brefiss?" my subjects would say in unison.

"That's right. Pancakes and toast," I'd say with a grin.

I'd boast all day long about my daddy and all the wonderful things I'd dreamt up for us to do together. And after I'd had enough boasting, I'd shoo all my friends away from the window and I'd go back to the sofa and wait. And I would wait. Nothing could stop me from waiting. I'd sit on that sofa and I would wait, wait, wait. Mother would come into the living room every so often and check on me, and after a couple of hours she'd ask if I was hungry. But no. I couldn't eat. Didn't want to spoil my appetite cause I was going to McDonald's or maybe Pizza Kingdom as soon as Daddy got there, I'd tell Mother. She'd shake her head and go back to her room for a while, then she'd come check on me a bit later and ask if I wanted to change into some more comfortable clothes. But no. I wanted to look good for my daddy. Daddy and I were going special places, doing special things, and I had to look nice, I'd tell Mother, and send her away again. Again she'd shake her head and leave the room, but she'd be back soon asking if I wanted to watch television or color or do something else besides waiting. That's when I'd get mad at her. "No, Mama. Don't you understand? I have to wait for Daddy. He said he was coming and I know he's coming and I've got to wait right here because I have to be ready when he comes," I'd say as my head started to pound and my heart began to race. She'd leave me alone for the last time and I'd wait. And I would wait. And nighttime would come. And I'd still wait. And then I'd fall asleep.

When I woke up I'd be in my room in my pajamas. My heart would still be racing and my head would still be pounding and I'd be confused and hurt and I'd feel so alone. I'd walk to my mother's room, crying all the way and rubbing my eyes.

"Did Daddy come?" I'd ask and climb into bed with her. She wouldn't answer me. She'd just shake her head and stroke the side of my face, but I didn't have time for all that sentimental stuff. I wanted answers. "Why didn't he come? Did he call? What happened?" I'd ask. But all Mother would do was give me this pitiful look, like the one you give someone when you know a secret but are afraid to let them in on it because the truth would hurt their feelings. It took me a while to know what that pitiful look was all about, and when I figured it out, I came to the realization that my daddy was a bitch. I was about eight when I realized that, and that's when I figured out that men were unreliable, lying scoundrels, and ever since then, no man has ever been able to make a fool out of me. Well, there was Chris, but everyone's entitled to at least one mistake.

I still wish my daddy was dead, though, but I checked the obits today and found that my wishes had yet to come true. But I'll keep checking. Justice has to be served someday.

■

I glanced at my watch and noticed that Leonard had exactly four minutes and forty-five seconds to walk through the door or I was going to be walking out of it. I flagged down the bartender and ordered a vodka collins with a splash of grenadine and chomped on a couple of peanuts, wondering if Leonard would even bother to show at all. I knew he was only five minutes late so far, but for me that was an eternity. If he didn't show, this weekend will go down in history as the only weekend since I finished college that I didn't have a date on a Friday or Saturday night. But I'm not complaining. Actually, I'm glad I didn't have a date last night because it gave me a chance to spend some time with my little sister, which I hadn't done in about a month.

I didn't realize how much I missed Serena until yesterday, when I was sitting in my car after school, waiting for her to come out. Although I see her every day walking through the halls, I never get to spend much quality time with her. Actually, Malik sees her more than I do since he's her teacher. I felt like a proud mother when I finally spotted her and watched as she laughed and waved good-bye to all her friends. She looked calm and at ease with herself, which meant more to me than I could say.

I eyed Serena like a hawk until I heard a thud that nearly scared me out my skin. I turned to my window to find Mr. Thyme, the father of one of my students. I'd tried to catch up with him last week when I saw him picking up little Conroy after school. But he had to rush off that day and I didn't get a chance to talk up my proposal. I rolled my window down and stuck out my hand. "Got a minute today?" I asked as we shook.

"Only a minute," he said and looked across the street to his car, where Conroy sat waiting. "Gotta get to work," he said and checked his watch. "So what's this all about? You did say Conroy wasn't in any kind of trouble the last time we talked."

"Well, he's not in any kind of trouble now," I said coyly.

"Alright. What'd he do?"

"Nothing yet. I'm just wondering how you'd feel if one day Conroy walked in the house and said, ''Skuse me, Dad. I got little Suzy Q pregnant.' What would you do, Mr. Thyme?"

The startled look on his face let me know that I'd gotten to him. I quickly told him about the proposal for the sex education class, but first I had to assure him that Conroy had not gotten any girl in a family way. At least not that I knew of. But anyway, after a good five-minute lecture Mr. Thyme was on my side. I pulled out my attaché and handed Mr. Thyme a sheet of paper to fill out.

"You're a good saleswoman," he said as he took the paper and began writing. "I hear you're a good teacher too. Conroy has never been excited about a teacher until you."

"I just enjoy my job. I love kids."

"It shows," he said and handed me back the paper with a grin on his face that let me know something was up. "You wouldn't happen to be married, would you?" he asked with a sly "hee-hee."

Rule number twenty-five: Never date the parents of your students. Been there, done that—disaster.

"I'm engaged," I lied.

"Lucky man," he said and reached out for my hand. "You take it easy, now."

"I will," I said and shook his hand. "And I'll keep you posted on how things are going."

"Please do," he said as he crossed the street to his car and jumped in.

Men. Never can pass up an opportunity, I thought as I watched him drive off.

I closed my attaché and returned my attention to the front of the school and Serena. I don't know why I couldn't keep myself from smiling. Just looking at her seemed to bring me joy. It was like I could see myself in her and I liked what I saw. Even though Serena was fourteen now, I couldn't help but remember how she used to be as a child. A child with Tourette's syndrome. A child who couldn't control her speech or her movements. It amazed me to see how well she had learned to cope with her disease since she's been on her medication. She barely tics or jerks her body at all now, at least not enough for anybody to notice she has a problem. She looks and acts like a regular, normal fourteen-year-old girl now, and as I watched her from my car I couldn't help noticing how beautiful she was becoming. Apparently I wasn't the only one who'd noticed, because just as Serena was about to walk out the school gates, some big-head boy stopped her in her tracks and pulled her to the side. Serena turned to him and started grinning from ear to ear as the big-head boy stared her up and down and tried to look cool. My first instinct was to honk my horn and bust up their little tête-à-tête, but I decided to hold off since Serena seemed so pleased with her big-head friend, and besides, I was curious to see how Serena handled herself with the boys. Like I said, Serena was a beauty and I knew it was only a matter of time before she would begin to catch the attention of the little boys at school. I just prayed that she'd know what to do when that finally happened, and from what I could see, she did. She batted her eyes and flipped her hair back just as I'd taught her. She looked the big-head boy dead in the eyes as she spoke, and she even touched him on the hand. I taught her that too. I guess the little boy asked for her phone number because she opened up her spiral notebook and scribbled something down and handed it to him. That was good. That's right, Serena, I thought as I watched the transaction. Give him your number and don't take his. That way he has to make the first move and call you. I was so proud that she'd taken to heart all the advice I'd given her over the years. But then it happened. I saw it coming. The big-head boy got that look in his eyes. He was going in for the kill—the kiss. No, no, I thought and eased my hand up to honk my horn, but Serena beat me to the punch. She put her hand to his chest as he leaned toward her and pushed him away. Good girl, I thought as I watched her smile and shake her head no. Make the bonehead wait. Make him beg. That's when she looked out to the parking lot and saw my car. I looked away quickly so she wouldn't know I was spying on her, and in a couple seconds, she was knocking at the passenger window. I looked over at the window with fake surprise and unlocked the door. She eyed me suspiciously, obviously wanting to know if I'd seen her teenybop scenario with big-head, so I played it off.

"You ought to know better than to keep me waiting, missy."

"It's only three-thirty-five."

"Well next time you hustle that little body out that class more quickly," I said and faked a frown.

"Sorry Li'l Ma," she said and peered out the window at big-head. I caught her smiling at him out the corner of my eye and chuckled to myself. Puppy love, I thought and drove off. How cute.

"So can I spend the night?" she asked as I bent the corner at the end of the block. "Please," she whined and smiled my way. How could I resist my little sister?

"Did you ask Mama?"

"No, but I'll call her when I get to your place."

"You know my bathroom needs cleaning."

"I'll clean it."

"And my kitchen's a mess too."

"I'll handle it."

Ah, the joys of having a younger sister. Who needs maid service when you've got a sister who loves you? "Yeah, I guess you can spend the night," I said and zoomed down the street.

As soon as we got to my place, she went directly to the television and turned on BET. She sat down on the floor in front of the screen and bopped her head along to the tunes. I sat down with her and watched as a group of girls gyrated and bounced around the screen. The song was loud and had too much bass, but it was catchy, and soon I found myself snapping my fingers and singing the lyrics.

"Do the fast track. Do the fast track," I sang, until Serena turned around and gave me a stupid look.

"What are you talking about?"

"I'm singing the song," I said and swayed to the beat of the music.

"It's not, *'Do the fast track,'*" Serena scolded. "It's, *'Dip and fall back,'*" she said and started singing. *"Dip and fall back. Dip and fall back."*

"Oh," I said and decided to shut up and just watch. "Is that some new dance?" I asked and winced at all the girls on the screen.

"That's the Tootsie Roll," she said and got up from the floor.

The Tootsie Roll? Looked more like a pussy roll to me, but I guess I was too old to understand.

"See," Serena said and started moving in front of me. "You open your legs and roll," she said, demonstrating. "Come on, Li'l Ma," she said and pulled me by the arm.

I got up and stood next to her and opened my legs and tried to follow her moves. "This is nasty," I said and stopped. "You don't do this dance out in public, do you?"

"Everybody does it," she said and kept going. I raised my eyebrow as I watched her, and for the first time I realized my little sister wasn't so little anymore. She was fourteen and already five foot seven, and if I wasn't mistaken, those were hips I saw forming at her sides and as I looked closer—oh my goodness—boobies! I took a step back and watched her dance around the living room, and I knew then we were going to have to have a talk. A long, long talk. Ever since Malik and I have been on this sex education kick, I'd been schooling Serena about her sexuality. Well actually what I'd told her is that I'd kick her ass if she had sex before she was twenty-five years old. But by the way she's standing there shaking her groove thang, I realize I should probably do a bit more talking. Not necessarily about sex, because I've already told her all she needs to know about that. But after seeing her with that big-head boy today, I think she needs to know a little more about men. Real men and how they *really* are.

"Serena—" I said as the phone rang out.

She stopped dancing and looked at me.

"Hold on a second," I said and picked up the phone. "Mighty Avalon Prep—I mean, hello?"

"Still in work mode?" Malik's voice asked.

"Yeah. Hold on a sec," I said and turned to Serena, and for some reason all I could see were her boobies. "We're going to have a little talk."

"What?"

"What nothing," I said and switched the television channel from BET to Nickelodeon. "You sit right here and don't touch that remote control," I said as my favorite Schoolhouse Rock song blasted. *"Conjunction junction. What's your function?"*

"What's wrong with you?"

"Sit," I said and gripped the phone between my ear and my shoulder.

"I'm hungry."

"Sit," I told her, then I said into the phone, "You still there?" I walked into the bathroom and closed the door. "Malik?"

"Who are you ordering around?"

"I've got Serena for the night."

"Make sure she does her homework."

"Oh, she will," I said and propped myself up on the sink. "But first I'm gonna have a little talk with her. She's getting too big for her britches."

"What do you mean? Serena's a good girl."

"Yeah right. Who's the little guy with the big head?"

"You must mean Anthony Anderson. I've seen him cutting his eyes at Serena in class. He's a good kid."

"He'd better be."

Malik laughed, but I didn't think anything was funny. Serena looked more like eighteen than fourteen and it was time somebody talked to her about the facts of life before she Tootsie Rolled herself into a bad situation. "Take it easy on her. It's just puppy love," Malik said as he stopped laughing. "Anyway, I'm just calling to let you know I've added a few more names to our petition."

"Oh yeah?"

"Three," he said and cleared his throat. "I've been thinking. Maybe we should take our proposal to Thompson next week. I think we're ready."

"I don't know, Malik. We wanted two hundred names."

"Yeah, but I'm ready to get this over with. I don't want Thompson finding out what's up before we approach him with our idea. You know how he is about people doing things behind his back."

"You're just being paranoid again."

"Call it what you want. I'm just ready to move on with this."

"Okay, Malik. Next week. We'll do it."

"Good," he said and sighed. "By the way, a package came for you after you left."

"My secret admirer?"

"I guess," he said coyly. "I went to my office after school and saw it laying outside your door."

"Secret admirer strikes again," I said and smiled to myself. "What did he send this time?" I asked, surprised, since my admirer had already sent me the box of CDs this morning. He usually only sends one gift a day, but I guess he was in the mood for splurging.

"Excuse me, but are you implying that I would be so bold as to open a package that didn't belong to me?"

"Exactly."

"Chocolate turtles," he said and sucked his teeth. "I'm eating them right now."

"Thanks," I said as I pulled off my stockings. "If I eat one more box of candy from him, I'll be big as a house by the time I meet him."

"*If* you meet him," Malik corrected me. "I still think it's Thompson who's been sending you all this stuff. Maybe he's doing it so you won't be so mad when he finally fires you."

"I asked Tommy about the gifts last week and he got all jealous. He's definitely not the one," I said and moaned. "And by the way, I am not getting fired, Malik, and neither are you. We've been through this once today," I said, trying to ease his mind.

"Alright," he said as if he still didn't believe me. "So you're not going out tonight?"

"Nope. It's just me and Serena."

"That's a first. You must be losing your touch in your old age."

"Forget you," I said and grabbed my robe off the door. "What about you?"

"Tyrone is coming over tonight and you know what that means."

"I thought you were going to break up with him."

"I was until he got down on his knees."

"He begged you not to dump him?"

"No, he just got down on his knees, if you know what I mean."

"Good-bye, Malik," I said and laughed.

"Bye, Madison."

I clicked off the phone and shook my head. So Malik is back with Tyrone, I thought. Big mistake. Those two break up at least twice a month. They act like an old married couple, always arguing, throwing fits, cursing each other out. If that's what a relationship is all about, then I'm glad I'm not in one. Actually, their troubles are mostly Malik's fault. He's always being paranoid and overreacting. If his boyfriend doesn't call him or stop by to see him every day, Malik swears he's seeing somebody else. I told him he should just give up and break things off with Tyrone for good. Ain't no relationship worth suffering through if you can't trust the person you're involved with. But Malik swears he's in love. He's a hopeless romantic. Believes love can conquer all, and all that bullshit. Yeah right. All I know is that if you're constantly worrying that your man is doing dirt behind your back, then he probably is. If I told Malik once, I told him a million times—dump Tyrone and just play the field. But will he listen to me? Hell no.

I washed off my makeup and tried to decide if I was ready to have my little talk with Serena, but I figured I'd let her relax a bit more before I started with my big sister lecture. I walked over to my spa tub and turned on the water and decided to take a long, hot bath and wind down. I added a capful of bubble bath to the water and took off my robe and got in. As soon as I got comfortable, I felt like going to sleep. Oh what joy, oh what splendor, oh what relaxation—"Oh, Serena," I said as I heard her knocking outside the door. "What do you want?"

"Can I come in?"

"No."

"Please."

When I didn't answer, she took that as an okay and opened the door. "What you doing?"

"*Hello*? What does it look like I'm doing?"

"I'm hungry."

"You know where the kitchen is."

"I want pizza, Li'l Ma."

Pizza, I thought and looked at her older-than-fourteen body, and again, all I could focus on were her boobies. It was time for the lecture. "You know, Serena, since you're getting older you're going to have to start watching what you eat if you want to keep your figure looking nice," I said, staring at her behind as she leaned over the counter and looked in the mirror.

"I don't have a problem with my figure."

That was for sure. Her body was perfectly proportioned, and for a second there I felt a tinge of jealousy as I noticed her behind was tighter than mine. But that was the problem. Serena looked too damn good and she was only fourteen. "Who was that little knucklehead boy you were talking to after school?"

"You saw us?"

"Yes, I saw you," I said, sitting straight up in the tub. "Does he make good grades? Does he have a job? Who are his parents?"

"Dang," she said, rolling her eyes and sitting down on top of the commode.

"You watch your mouth, little girl."

"I said 'dang,' not 'da—'"

"What, what, what? Go ahead and say it."

"I don't use foul language, Li'l Ma. You told me it was unladylike."
Good girl.

"Even though you curse all the time."

"Excuse me. I'm grown, and don't try and change the subject. We're talking about you and that big-head boy you gave your number to today."

"How you know I gave him my number?"

"I know everything. Now, what's this child's name?"

"Anthony Anderson."

"Is he a player?"

"What's a player?" she asked and frowned. "Oh, you mean, is he a Mack?"

"Whatever," I said and grabbed the soap. "Is he a nice boy?"

"Yes, and he's cute."

Oh my goodness. The girl is sprung. "Alright, let me lay down the rules."

"You already taught me the rules. Smile, look them in the eyes, throw my hair over my shoulders, compliment them—"

"Well now it's time to get down to the serious rules," I said and slid around the tub so I could face her head-on. Now, how should I put this? I thought as I looked into her innocent eyes. Should I sugarcoat it, or be straight? Should I tell her all men are mangy mutts that are not to be trusted? Or should I be nice about it and say *almost* all men are mangy mutts that are not to be trusted? Decisions, decisions.

"I'll get it," Serena said as the phone rang, and she jumped up to grab the cordless from the sink counter. "Hello," she said, trying to sound like me. "Oh hi, Mama," she said and sat back down on the commode. "Yeah . . . yeah . . . okay," she said and handed me the phone.

I shook the water off my hand and grabbed the phone with two fingers. "What's up, Mama?"

"You could at least have the decency to call and let me know you were taking Serena. I was sitting here worrying myself half to death when she didn't show up from school on time."

"Sorry, Mama," I said as Serena pointed at me, laughing and mouthing the words "You're in trouble." I squinted my eyes at Serena as she continued to laugh. Then I grinned and began speaking to Mother again. "I told Serena to call you, as soon as we walked in the door, but she just wouldn't listen to me. She's so hardheaded. I'm sorry, Mama, I thought she called you."

"I'm gonna skin her little behind," Mama said, viciously. "Put her back on the phone."

"Who's in trouble now?" I asked as I passed the phone back to Serena.

"Sorry, Mama," she said. "Uh-huh . . . Yes, okay, Mama," she said and gave me back the phone and licked her tongue out at me.

I splashed water on her and put the phone to my ear. "I need you to take me to church on Sunday," Mother said, sounding disgusted.

"What's wrong with your car anyway?" I asked.

"I don't know. Just as soon as I get one thing fixed on it, something else breaks down."

"Don't worry about it," I said and sighed. "I'll call up James and have him go over and look at it next week."

"You're still dating James?"

"Every once in a while," I said and repositioned myself in the tub. That's the beauty of dating a lot of men. You never have to worry when things break down. Whenever something goes wrong, I call up one of my old boyfriends. There's James, the mechanic, for car problems. Dennis, the plumber, for when my sink backs up. Then there's Oscar, the electrician, Dr. Bailey and Dr. Nortant, dentist and dermatologist, respectively. Tony, the gardener. Rodney, the painter. And the list goes on and on. Of course, there was Christopher, the doctor, but he's a natural born asshole so he doesn't count.

"When are you bringing Serena home?" Mother asked.

"Tomorrow afternoon."

"Alright. And don't forget, I need a ride to church on Sunday."

"Good-bye, Mother."

"Give Serena a kiss."

"Mother says kiss-kiss," I told Serena as I clicked off the phone and handed it to her. "Now back to you, Miss I Got A Boyfriend," I said and resumed my head-on position.

"I don't have a boyfriend yet."

"I saw the way big-head was looking at you today. You'll have one soon enough and there are some things that you need to know."

"I already know what you're going to tell me."

"Excuse me?" I said as I smoothed out the bubbles in the tub. "How do you know what I'm gonna say before I say it?"

"Because you've said it before. No sex, no sex, no sex," she said and rolled her eyes. "I'm only fourteen years old, Li'l Ma. I don't get down like that."

"Well Tameka was only fourteen years old too, and you see what happened to her."

"Well that won't happen to me. Me and Anthony are just friends."

"Well you two had better stay just friends, and if you ever think about having sex—"

"I know, I know. You'll kick my ass."

"Watch your mouth."

She paused for a minute and stared at me as if she wanted to say something but didn't know how to put it. "What?" I asked as I lathered myself up with soap.

"How come you're not married?"

Where did that come from? I thought and dropped the soap.

"Never mind, I already know," she said satisfied.

"You already know what?"

"Big Mama told me," she said and rested her head on the wall behind her.

"Excuse me?"

"She said that you're not married because you don't like men."

"What?"

"I asked her why come you were so pretty but you weren't married. And she said that you could have any man you want, but you're not married 'cause you don't like men. She said you don't let nobody get close to you, so you're always gonna be by yourself."

How dare she? I thought and frowned. How can she talk about me when she's sitting up single her damn self? "And did Mother offer any explanations as to why she was not married?"

"I didn't ask her. Besides, Big Mama's too old to be married. But she did say that if *you* don't start acting right, you're gonna end up just like her. Do you really wanna end up like Big Mama?" she asked and winced like the thought of that turned her stomach.

"Alright, listen up," I said seriously. "I'm gonna talk to you like a grown-up 'cause there are some things you need to know. Can you handle it?"

"Yep," she said and sat up tall.

"Now. All I can tell you is what I know for myself to be true, okay?" I said as she nodded her head in agreement. "It's not that I don't like men, it's just that I know from experience that they are . . ." I wanted to say "assholes," but I thought that would be too grown-up for our grown-up conversation. I paused and tried to figure out how I could tell Serena what I knew to be true without ruining her innocent mind.

"What, what?" she asked, staring at me. "Men are what?"

I shook my hands in the air as if that motion would help me come up with just the right way to tell Serena that all men were dogs, without turning her into a man hater. I definitely didn't want to do that. Serena was young and I didn't want to shape her future experiences with men by telling her something that may not hold true for her. Just because I haven't found the right man or even want to find the right man doesn't mean that she'll never meet him. Hell, for all I know this Anthony Anderson guy may be her knight in shining armor. Or even if he's not, that doesn't mean she won't meet that one special man who'll love her and be true to her some day. It doesn't matter that I know there are no Mr. Rights. Why blow her fantasy at such a young age?

"What, Li'l Ma?" she asked again, impatiently.

"All I can say, Serena, is that you have to be careful. You're at that age when boys are starting to look good to you and I know that you're starting to look good to them," I said as I eyed her boobies and wondered if she was a B or C cup. "Anyway, you're just going to have to be careful. You can't believe everything these little boys tell you. You've got to be smart. Every little boy that looks your way and smiles is not a little boy that you want to associate with. Whether the guy is cute or not doesn't matter. It's all about his mind, not his behind. Be picky about the guys you let into your world."

"In other words, don't be no sucka."

This girl's too smart. "Exactly. Don't be no sucka," I said and relaxed. "And whatever you do, don't have sex or you know what will happen."

"You'll kick my ass."

"That's right," I said and splashed water on her. "And watch your mouth."

"Can I order the pizza now?"

"Go ahead."

"Stuffed crust?"

"Alright," I said and lathered up. "The number's on the refrigerator," I said and watched her as she leapt to attention and ran out the bathroom.

That went well, I thought and scrubbed my arms. I gave Serena just enough information to start her out on her adventures with the opposite sex, and I didn't turn her off to men in the process. I was sort of pissed off about the things she said Mama had told her about me, though. I don't like men? Please. Just because I don't want to tie myself up with one man doesn't mean I don't like men. I love men, I just don't want to be *in* love with them anymore. I've learned my lesson in that department and believe me, that's a mistake that I will not make again.

There is one thing that I didn't get into with Serena about her new adventures with the opposite sex, and I guess the reason that I didn't say anything is because I don't know exactly how to put it. The thing is that I can't help but wonder what would happen if she ever had a Tourette's spell in front of her friends. She's made it a point not to tell any of her friends that she has the disease, and she hides it so well now that telling them wouldn't even make a difference. Still I sometimes wonder what would happen if Serena were with a boy and suddenly had an attack. She'd be devastated. The doctors said that the next few years could be tough on Serena. Though she's been handling her disorder with no problem, they say the adolescent years could worsen her symptoms. For some reason, and they don't know why—they never know why—the symptoms of Tourette's seem to heighten during the age of twelve to sixteen. And that's why I'm so concerned. I can't help but wonder what would happen if she ever had a spell or started flipping out at school. Luckily for her, the only spell she had recently was last year. It was a minor one and it happened on the weekend, when she was at home and away from her friends. But what worries me is the thought that one of these days she may lose it at school. I could just see her in the midst of all her friends and all of a sudden she loses control of her body and starts ticcing and jerking and uttering words she has no control over. And if it happens in front of one of her little boyfriends, I know she'll be mortified. She'll be a laughingstock. I know how cruel little kids can be about things they don't understand. I remember when I was in middle school and Harvey J. Causewall would have seizures. We'd be playing on the school grounds at recess and all of a sudden he'd flip out and stop cold. The right side of his body seemed like it was paralyzed and he'd drop to the ground. The poor guy was seizing and could have died, but what did us kids do? Laugh. We'd laugh and point and crowd around Harvey until the seizing stopped or until a teacher found out what was going on and came over to help Harvey up. I knew what we were doing was wrong. Harvey could have died. But I was young and I didn't know what else to do, so I laughed right along with everybody else. Last year while I was looking through the obituaries for my daddy's name, I saw Harvey's. He died at the age of thirty-two of a massive seizure and heart attack. I cried when I read that. Harvey was a nice guy; he just had a disease that he couldn't help. I shouldn't have laughed at him. I was wrong, but it was too late for apologies.

That's why I worry so much about Serena. She's a beautiful girl. She's nice, outgoing, lovable, but she's got a disease that she can't help. I never want her to have to experience what Harvey had to go through. I don't want anyone like me laughing and pointing and crowding around my baby sister. She wouldn't be able to take that. She shouldn't have to take that.

■

What I *can't take is waiting for a late date, I thought as I checked my* watch and found that Leonard had exactly one minute and four seconds to arrive before I left. I drank down the last of my vodka collins and looked over toward the entrance. No sign of him. I scanned the bar area and put down my drink, as I made a mental note to add another rule to my list. Rule number thirty-five: Never wait for dates in the bar area of a restaurant. Ever since I got here, all the men have been eyeing me like a piece of T-bone steak, and if the guy at the end of the bar winks at me one more time, I swear I'm going to chunk a piece of ice at him.

Come on, Leonard, I silently begged, and when I heard my name called out, I thought he'd arrived. Until, that is, I turned around to find . . .

"Mitchell," I said as he hurried over to me and kissed my cheek. "Long time no see."

"Too long," he said and stood back to get a better look at me. "You haven't changed a bit."

"Neither have you," I said. He was still white.

"Waiting on a date?"

"Not for much longer," I said and checked my watch again. Leonard had forty-eight seconds. "Who's the bubblicious blond babe?" I asked and peeked over his shoulder at his date.

"Just a substitute for you," he said and smiled. "I'd much rather be out with you, but you won't return my calls," he said and grabbed his chest like he was so heartbroken. "Must be because I'm white."

"Shut up, Mitch," I said and nudged his arm. "You only called me once since we went out last month."

"And why didn't you call me back?"

"I was *busy*."

"What's that? Code for 'I don't date white boys no more'?"

"Mitchell," I cooed and batted my eyelashes. "I promise. I'll call you next week and we'll get together, okay?"

"Okay," he agreed and kissed my cheek. "And I promise. Next time will be better," he said as he shuffled off back to his date.

Until I met Mitchell, I always thought that I could tell if a person was white or black just by listening to their voice over the phone. Wrong. We met one morning when he called up my extension at school looking for someone by the name of Glen Matthews. He had the wrong number, but his voice sounded so good that I just had to strike up a conversation with him. I guess my voice must have sounded good to him too, because he kept me on the phone for half an hour and by the end of our conversation we'd made plans to meet for dinner at Georgia's on Melrose.

I'd almost backed out of meeting him for dinner after I had time to think about what I was doing. I couldn't believe that I'd made a date with a man I met over the phone and barely knew, and as I drove to the restaurant, all I could think about was, What if this man is a serial killer or a rapist or what if he was just plain ugly? But I knew he had to be attractive because of his deep, sexy voice. I pictured him to be tall and muscular and dark, with a big juicy butt, and the more I thought about him, the more I knew I had to go meet him.

When I got to the restaurant, I was a nervous wreck. I sat down at a table and waited for him to walk through the door. He told me he would be wearing a tan suit with a gold tie, and as I waited for someone to walk in with that wardrobe, I couldn't help thinking I was crazy. I didn't know this man from Adam, but I was having dinner with him? Was I getting desperate or what? Well maybe I was desperate, but I wasn't stupid, which is why I picked out a table in the rear of the restaurant, near the exit. That way I could get a good look at the man in the tan suit and gold tie before he got to me, and if he seemed the least bit odd, I was going to be out the door.

And that's when I saw Mitchell. He was handsome, he was tall, muscular, and walking in my direction, but I didn't pay him any attention. Not even when I noticed he was wearing a tan suit and a gold tie. Not even when he stopped in front of my table and smiled.

"Madison?" he asked, eyeing the red silk blouse I told him I'd be wearing.

How did this white boy know my name? I thought, staring at him as he offered his hand to me. He shook it for a second then put it to his mouth and bam! That's when I got it.

"Mitchell?" I said and stared into his light blue eyes. "Nice tie."

We sat across the table from one another and bullshitted about the weather and how nice the restaurant looked and how odd it was that we met over the phone. But after about five minutes of that, I'd had enough.

"You're white," I said, staring at his straight nose.

"And you're black," he said and smiled. He started snapping his fingers and swaying. *"Ebony and Ivory,"* he tried to sing without laughing.

"No, I've got a better one," I said and did my best Michael Jackson impersonation. *"I said, if you're thinking 'bout being my baby . . ."*

"It don't matter if you're black or white," he sang and joined me in impersonating Michael. He did everything except get up and do the moon walk, and afterward we had a good hearty laugh.

I'd never gone out with a white guy before and I could tell this was a first for Mitchell too. Still, I enjoyed his company and he was cute and his voice was so sexy. We had a good time talking and laughing, then one thing led to another, this turned into that, and at the end of the evening I found myself back at his apartment, lying in his bed and busting out of my blouse.

I have to admit, the only reason I was in Mitchell's bed was because I was curious. I wanted to know if there was a difference between the way black men performed and the way white men performed. And what I found out was that Mitch had it going on. He had no inhibitions whatsoever, and what amazed me most of all was that he liked to do it with the lights on. I'd never done it like that. Well, I've done it in the daytime, but never with a lightbulb. To tell the truth there was no difference between Mitch and all the black guys I'd been with except that Mitch's lips were smaller and I found that my big soup coolers nearly swallowed up his whole face. At one point he got up from the bed and did a little striptease act for me as he came out of his clothes piece by piece until he was wearing nothing but a pair of BVDs. I was impressed. His body was tight and the bulge in those shorts was a pretty good size, especially considering he was wearing boxers. He came back to bed and undressed me slowly as he planted soft kisses over every inch of my body. I was so turned on that I didn't want to close my eyes. This was a new experience for me and I didn't want to miss a minute of the action.

"Madison. You feel so good," Mitchell said as he grinded on top of me. "You're so beautiful. So soft," he said as I stretched my hand down his thighs. I let my hand slide between his legs and . . . It really is big, I thought and smiled with delight. Then he raised off me just enough so I could get a peek at his jewels and . . .

"Aaggh!" I screamed and sprung straight up in bed.

"What, what?" he asked as his eyes bulged out of his head.

"Your dick is pink," I wanted to scream, but the stupidity of that statement hit me just before I blurted it out. "Nothing's wrong, Mitchell," I said and pulled the covers over me. "I just can't go through with this."

"Huh?"

"I can't do this. It's too soon. We barely know each other." *And your dick is pink.*

"You've got to be kidding," he said, running his hand through his hair. "You want to stop now?"

"Yes," I said, wincing as I caught another glimpse of his pink penis.

He stared at me for a while, then got out of bed and slid on his pants. "I'm sorry," I said, feeling really stupid. What color had I expected his penis to be? I mean, it never gets any sunlight, so of course it was going to be pink. I felt bad for him and for some reason I felt sort of, I don't know, prejudiced. But it was all for the best that Mitchell and I didn't have sex. He was a nice guy, but we just didn't know one another. I got dressed quickly when Mitchell left the room, presumably to take a cold shower, but I couldn't be sure. When he came back to the bedroom, I was standing in front of his dresser mirror. He walked behind me and put his hands around my waist.

"I know I don't know you. But I really like you."

"I like you too," I said and leaned my head back onto his chest.

He laughed and stared at my image in the mirror. "I've never been with a black girl before," he said seriously. "Not because I'm racist or anything," he assured me. "It's just that I never considered black women as an option for me."

"I understand what you're saying. I know a lot of white guys, but I've never even remotely considered going out with one of them," I said and smiled. "And I'm the first one to speak out against color lines and breaking down walls and living as one. It's not that I don't like white guys; it's just like you say, I never considered you an option."

"What about now?"

"Now?" I said and looked up at the ceiling. "Now I don't think anything's changed. I mean if you call and ask me out again, I'll definitely go, because I like you as a person. But I don't think I'll be crossing over the line on a regular basis."

"But why?"

"My point exactly," I said and raised an eyebrow. "Why? I love my black men. I'm not running from them."

"Not even for me?"

"Well," I said and turned around to face him. "You're another story."

"So we can we do this again?"

"Anytime."

"Promise?"

"Promise," I said and swallowed him up.

I didn't care if Mitchell was white, Jewish, Indian—hell, he could have been Martian. I liked him. As a person. For who he was. That was all there was to it. Period. Nothing else need be said.

■

"Madison," a voice called out behind me.

I turned around to find Leonard. He looked good. Suit by Hugo Boss, shoes by Bruno Magli, scent by Opium *pour homme*. He had it going on.

"I'm sorry I'm so late," he said as I eased myself off the bar stool and gave him a hug. "Please forgive me," he said and complimented me on my simple Isaac Mizrahi black dress. "Come on," he said and held out his hand in the direction of the dining area. "Our table's waiting."

I walked in the direction he led me in, but when I got to the aisle, I turned toward the exit.

"Madison," he said, looking stunned. "It's this way."

"No," I said, and checked my watch to be sure. Eight-fourteen. "It's my way or the highway," I said and waved. "Have a good dinner, Leonard. Good-bye."

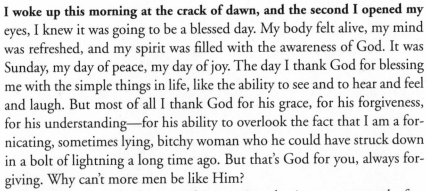

4

I woke up this morning at the crack of dawn, and the second I opened my eyes, I knew it was going to be a blessed day. My body felt alive, my mind was refreshed, and my spirit was filled with the awareness of God. It was Sunday, my day of peace, my day of joy. The day I thank God for blessing me with the simple things in life, like the ability to see and to hear and feel and laugh. But most of all I thank God for his grace, for his forgiveness, for his understanding—for his ability to overlook the fact that I am a fornicating, sometimes lying, bitchy woman who he could have struck down in a bolt of lightning a long time ago. But that's God for you, always forgiving. Why can't more men be like Him?

I was feeling peculiarly peppy this morning, due in most part to the fact that I was in before nine o'clock last night and got some well-deserved sleep thanks to Leonard's tardiness and my unwillingness to break my dating rules. I figured I'd start out my morn with a cup of hot coffee and a browse through the Sunday *Times,* so I stretched myself out and got up from bed. But before I could even get my robe on good, the phone rang out, and I knew it could only be one person. The only person brave enough to dial my phone number at six o'clock in the morning— Mother.

"Top of the day to you, Mom," I said without even asking who was calling.

"You up?"

"No, Mother. I'm sleep-talking," I said, shaking my head at the ceiling.

"Don't be so smart so early in the morning."

Don't be asking dumb questions so early in the morning. "Yes, dear Mother. I am up, I haven't forgotten about church, and I will be at your house to pick you up at seven-forty-five."

"What are you going to wear?"

"Leopard skin pants and tennis shoes."

"Don't be so smart."

"Why you want to know what I'm wearing?"

"I'm just asking."

"A suit."

"What color?"

"Why?"

"I like that cream-color suit on you," she said and paused. "And wear your hair up."

"What are you up to, Mother?"

"Nothing," she said too quick to sound truthful.

"Don't get any ideas about trying to fix me up with a churchman."

"I ain't got no ideas about nothing. I just want you to look nice."

"I mean it, Mother. Don't come dragging any men in my face, 'cause I'm not interested. Do you hear me, Mother? I am not interested."

"I hear you."

No she doesn't. "I'll honk when I get outside your house."

"Are you wearing the cream suit?"

"Good-bye, *Mother*," I said and hung up the phone.

If Mother thinks she's going to set me up with another one of her sanctified church friends, she'd better think again because a few things have changed since the last time I went to church with her. Namely, rule number twenty-one: Never pick up men in church. They may act like saints in the sanctuary, but get them out on a date and they turn into bargain basement Don Juans. I had to find that out the hard way last year when I got swept into a date with the notorious Deacon Jenkins, man of God by day, Super Freak by night. Whoever said the best place to find a decent man was in church must have been working for the devil.

Mother introduced the deacon to me last Easter after service had let out, and all I did was say hello to the man, shake his hand, and walk off to my car. That's it. I got into my car and waited for Mother to join me, and when she did . . .

"That Deacon Jenkins is something special, isn't he?" she said as I started up my car and pulled out of the parking lot.

"I guess," I said, barely paying Mother any attention.

"He's got nice teeth," she said, looking at me as I drove down the street. "Straight and nice. White."

"You wanna get something to eat?"

"What are you doing tomorrow?"

"Working," I said as I felt my stomach growl. "Want some chicken?"

"Deacon Jenkins wanted me to give this to you," she said as I stopped at a red light. She pushed a white scrap of paper into my hand, then quickly turned to look out the window.

"What in the world?" I said, caught completely off guard. I only said two words to the man and already he's writing me letters? I unfolded the paper and read: *Monday, eight o'clock, 252 Rodale Way. See you then and God bless.*

Excuse me? "What's this, Mother?" I asked as the light turned green again. She played like she didn't hear me and continued staring out the window and I knew then that something was up. *"Mother."*

"Deacon Jenkins is cooking dinner Monday night."

"Oh," I said, eyeing her suspiciously. "Is this some kind of church potluck?"

"No," she said hesitantly. "It's a date."

"A who?"

"The deacon invited you to his home for dinner. A date," she said and fiddled with the Bible that sat on her lap. "I told him it was okay."

"You told him it was who?"

"I told him you'd come, and before you get upset I just want you to know that I was only trying to help."

"You accepted a date for me?" I said, staring at her so hard that I almost swerved into another lane. "Are you crazy?"

"Only a little bit."

"I don't believe this shit."

"Watch your damn mouth. You just got out of church."

"How dare you make a date for me?"

"What?" she said, like a child who'd been caught getting into something she had no business getting into.

"Dammit, Mother."

"What?" she said, frowning and refusing to even look at me.

"I don't need you to fix me up. I do just fine meeting men on my own. I don't even know this Deacon Jenkins," I said, banging my hand on the steering wheel.

"I was just trying to be helpful."

"No," I said, pointing at her. "You were meddling in my business and you know I don't like that shit."

"You watch your mouth, Miss Grownie," she said, trying to get tough. "It ain't gonna hurt none for you to have dinner with the man. Ain't nothing wrong with breaking bread with a man of God."

I could break your neck, I thought to myself as I sped down the street. I wanted so badly to tell Mother off, but I had to hold my tongue. I just shut my mouth and drove, hoping Mother wouldn't say another word to me, but my luck soon wore out.

"A nice, good-looking, Christian man wants to cook you dinner and all you wanna do is act like you got a bar stuck up your butt."

Shut up, I thought to myself as I peeled down the street.

"Ought to be happy someone like Deacon Jenkins wants to look your way."

Shut up!

"Nice Christian man."

Why won't she shut up?

"Christian man. Nice."

Please.

"Deacon Jenkins is the kind of man you could marry."

I knew that was coming, and though I tried to keep myself calm, I couldn't keep myself quiet. "How many times do I have to tell you I'm not, never, ever getting married? So if you're thinking—"

"Silly girl," she said as she looked out the window and mumbled. "Never heard such a thing. Don't wanna be married. Don't wanna be happy. Silly, just silly. Don't know a good thing when you see it. Don't know where you get that silly mess."

I turned on the radio and tuned Mother out as I blazed down the street toward her house. She finally shut up when she realized I wasn't paying her any attention, but as I pulled to a stop in front of her house she gave me a look and I knew our conversation wasn't yet over.

"Look, Li'l Mama," she said, trying to take a softer approach. "Don't you want to be happy?"

"I am happy," I said quickly.

She paused and took a deep breath. "Don't you wanna settle down with one man? Have a wedding? A big, huge ceremony with flowers and food and music and—"

"I can always throw a party at my condo."

That was it, she'd had enough. "Silly girl. Just plain silly. All I want is for you to be happy, don't you understand that?"

"I am happy."

"You're not happy. You're alone."

"By choice."

"You need to see a doctor."

"Mother," I said softly and smiled her way. "Don't take this the wrong way," I said and patted her shoulder.

"What is it, baby?" she said, probably thinking I'd given in and broken down.

"Would you please get the hell out of my car now?" I said, rubbing her back. *"Please."*

"Silly girl," she mumbled, and fumbled around with the door handle. "Never knew someone so silly. Gonna be alone forever. Need to see a doctor. Get your head examined."

"Good-bye, Mother," I said as she finally got out the car.

I had every intention of calling Deacon Jenkins and turning down his dinner offer, but when I got home and looked at the scrap piece of paper I'd stuffed into my purse I realized he'd only written down his address, which meant the only way I could contact him was by going to his house. I thought about standing him up, but I decided it wouldn't be prudent to flake out on a man of God. So I went on the date the next night.

Big mistake.

That's when I found out that Deacon Jenkins would be better off named Freakin' Jenkins. The man was all over me from the minute I stepped through his door. Rubbing my back, squeezing my shoulders, stroking my face, and the killer came after dinner when we sat down on his sofa and the man licked my face. Licked my face. No, I need to repeat this one more time—he *licked* my face. Needless to say that was my cue to exit, which I did quick, fast, and in a hurry.

The first thing I did when I got home was call Mother and tell her about my date from hell, but she swore up and down that I wasn't telling the truth.

"Deacon Jenkins is a Christian man."

"Deacon Jenkins is a *man*."

"But he'd never."

"But he did."

"Well did you wear something low cut? Did you tempt the man?"

"Are you saying this is all my fault?"

"I know how you are, Li'l Mama."

No you don't. "Good-bye, Mother," I said and hung up the phone.

■

I hope Deacon Jenkins won't be in church this morning, I thought to myself as I walked into the kitchen and started a pot of coffee. I searched through a couple of drawers for a pair of scissors. It was coupon-clipping time. I headed to the front door to bring in the Sunday paper and when I opened it, I almost popped with surprise. Sitting on the floor in front of my door was a huge red basket, and attached to the handle was a bouquet of red and silver balloons. "Secret admirer strikes again," I said and put my hand over my mouth. I stepped around the basket into the hallway and looked for a sign of something, anybody, anything, but I saw nothing, so I picked up the basket, kicked the paper through the door and went back inside. I sat the basket down on the coffee table and looked inside it for a card, but all I could see was an array of muffins and cookies and miniature pound cakes. Then I looked up at the balloons and attached to one of the ribbons was a red envelope. I snatched it quickly and tore it open, and saw that for the first time, my secret admirer had written a message. "Today's the day," the note read in a handwriting that was barely legible. I fell down onto the sofa wondering what the hell that meant. Today's the day for what? Will I meet him today? Will he call? What? "Damn," I mumbled and closed my eyes. "What does all this mean?"

I grabbed a muffin from the basket and went back into the kitchen for a cup of coffee. Who is this secret admirer? Do I even want to meet him at all? Do I know him already? Then it struck me. The man knows where I live. Until then, all my gifts had been sent to my office at school, but now . . . He knows where I live. "Oh my God," I mumbled as I stood over the sink, thinking and chewing and sipping on coffee, trying to make sense of all this mess. He knows where I live, where I work. He knows everything about me and I don't know jack. What if this guy is crazy? What if he shows up at my door with a knife? "Oh shit," I said and threw my muffin in the trash. What if he's psychotic and he's been slowly poisoning me with all this food he's been sending? Maybe I should call Malik and tell him not to eat all those chocolate turtles. What if Malik is dead already? What if . . . what if . . . What if I just shut the hell up? Ain't no man worth all this anxiety. If he was going to do something to me, he would have done it by now. I am not going to let myself be worried about this secret admirer. If I meet him today, I meet him. If I don't, I don't. He's just a man, and there were plenty before him and there will be plenty after him, so fuck it. It's time for church.

When I got to Mother's house to pick her up, I found her and Serena standing out front on the curb waiting for me. Serena looked especially sweet this morning as she fiddled with the hem of the white skirt I'd picked up for her last month at the mall. And much to my surprise, Mother looked sorta cute too. Since she doesn't get out too much, Mother can sometimes overdo it when it comes to getting dressed up. She sees going to church as her one and only opportunity to *style,* which to her means donning anything fluorescent, sequined, laced, or rhinestoned. But today Mother was rather conservative. She wore all black except for the white gloves on her hands. Her skin was shiny and flawless and just a tad lighter than her outfit. Mother wasn't pretty per se, but she had a certain something about her. A distinguished type of look that made you want to bow down before her or kiss her hand. Mother looked like a queen this morning as she stepped off the curb and headed toward the passenger door. But for the life of me, I could not figure out why she was carrying this huge bowl of flowers and fruit.

"Hey," I said as they got into the car.

"You're tardy," Mother said, closing her door and setting her bowl down on her lap. I peeped at the clock and saw it was ten to eight and sighed.

"We got time."

"We late," she said and shook her head. "You can be late for the Lord, but I bet you're never late for your job."

Shut up, I thought and tried to block her out as she pulled down the sun visor on her side of the car and continued to mumble. She flipped open the mirror and ran a hand over her hair, then reached for her bowl. Oh my God, I thought as she maneuvered the huge contraption onto her head. The bowl wasn't a bowl—it was a hat. So much for conservative, I thought as I peeped at her out the corner of my eye. She flipped up the visor after a while of primping, then turned to me as if to say, "How do I look?" But since it was Sunday and my heart was filled with glee, I decided to keep my sarcasm to myself. I ignored Mother and looked over my shoulder at Serena. "What up?" I said and gave her a wink.

"Hi," she said softly as she sat looking straight ahead with her mouth stuck out.

"What's wrong with you?"

"Ain't nothing wrong with her," Mother butted in and turned around to give Serena the old evil eye. "She just lazy, that's all."

"I don't feel good," Serena whined back.

"You never feel good when it's time to go to church," Mother said and turned back around.

I peeped at Serena in my rearview mirror as she mumbled backtalk at Mother.

"And shut up," Mother said so loud that I jumped.

I peeped at Serena again. Poor child. I guess she was learning the hard way that playing sick to get out of going to church won't work on Mother. I know. I used to try it myself.

When we got inside the church, we found the place was so packed that we couldn't even find a spot where we could all sit together. Mother pulled Serena by the arm and squeezed into an already overcrowded pew in the front of the church. The only other place I could find was a spot next to mean old Sister Bertha in the back of the church near the exit.

"Morning, Sister," I said as I nudged myself into the pew beside her.

"Ssh," she said and frowned as she fanned herself with a dirty white handkerchief.

Bitch, I thought, then shrieked as I remembered where I was. I crossed my legs so I wouldn't rub up against Sister Bertha, and got comfortable. Sister Bertha hasn't changed a bit. She's still as mean as she was when I was a little girl. I used to be so afraid of her because whenever I used to cut up in church she would always give me a mean old look and shake her finger in my face. I could never seem to behave myself in church when I was a child. I don't know if it was because I was bored or because the preacher was talking so loud that I thought I could talk loud too. But whenever I got too unruly Mother would take off her shoe and threaten to smack me with it. She never actually hit me with the shoe, but she threatened to a million times. "Don't make me have to take off my shoe," she'd whisper, and the threat alone would usually get me to sit quietly. Usually. There was that one time when the preacher's sermon got so good that a bunch of women caught the Holy Ghost and started shouting and dancing around the church. I didn't know what was going on, but it looked like they were having fun, so I started shouting and jumping around with them. Mother tried to get me to sit down and shut up, but what was a kid to do? I thought the women had started up a game of hopscotch, and since no one at my elementary school could beat me in hopscotch, or tetherball either, for that matter, I joined in with the ladies and started jumping down the aisle toward the pulpit. Until, that is, mean old Sister Bertha caught me by the arm and whacked me on my behind. "Don't play around with the Holy Spirit, little girl," she told me and sent me back to my mother in tears.

"Sang, choir," Sister Bertha shouted out and waved her hand in the air as the choir stood to their feet and sang "Leaning on the Everlasting Arm." As they sang I could swear I heard someone calling my name, but when I turned around all I saw were a bunch of unknown faces. I faced forward again and tried to get into the choir's song, but as soon as I did, I heard my name being called again. The voice was deep and sounded familiar, but when I turned I saw no one I knew. What was going on? I wondered and scanned through the sea of faces until Sister Bertha gave me an ugly look that forced me to turn around and stop fidgeting. I felt like giving her the finger and shouting, "I'm grown now. You can't tell me what to do." But instead I decided to respect her and myself and just be quiet. Still, I couldn't help wondering who had called my name.

When the choir completed its song, the Reverend Marshall took to the pulpit and gave a sermon about faith and the power of prayer. Before long the entire church was calling out, "Well," and, "Preach, preacher." He was preaching so good that even I had to shout out a couple of times, which wasn't very like me. Usually I don't say much during church, but today I couldn't help myself. Soon I found myself on my feet, clapping my hands and shouting out, "Thank you, Jesus. Thank you." As I sat back down, I saw Mother stand up in the front of the church and wave her hand and throw her head back. "Yes, Lord," she said and stood with her arms outstretched. I closed my eyes and began silently thanking God for all he's done in my life as Reverend Marshall brought his sermon to a close.

"Let's take a moment of silence and give Him his due," the reverend said as a hush fell over the crowd. I was so into praising the Lord that I didn't even budge when I heard someone shout out again though we were supposed to be in silent prayer. This voice was much different than the voice that had called me earlier, so I didn't bother turning around. I continued praying until I heard the voice again. It was coming from the front of the church. The words were inaudible, but the voice was definitely familiar. I opened my eyes but kept my head bowed as I listened hard and the voice became more recognizable.

"Bit . . . bit. Bitch!"

Oh my goodness, I thought and kept my head bowed. I stared down at the floor in disbelief. I knew I had just heard what I had just heard, but I refused to look up because I didn't want to know who said it. But I knew.

"Bitch!" the voice said again and this time I looked up. "Bitch . . . bit . . . augh . . . bitch."

"Serena," I said and jumped up from my seat. I ran down the aisle of the church to the pew where she was sitting. She was the center of attention as she sat, grunting and ticcing her head from side to side. Her knee kept jerking up and down and banging on the pew in front of her. Mother just sat there staring at her.

I pushed my way down the pew, stepping on several feet as I went along. I grabbed Serena by the hand and pulled her up. Her arm violently swung out and caught me on the side of my head, but I didn't let her go. The only way to get her out without hurting her was to pick her up. I shot Mother a look that asked for help, but she just sat there like she was glued to her seat. As if she didn't know that Serena was having an attack. Like she didn't even know who Serena was. I strained myself getting Serena out the pew and into the aisle, and not once did anyone offer to help me. The few faces that I did catch a glimpse of only stared at me with frowns and shame. "What the hell are y'all looking at?" I wanted to shout. "It's called coprolalia. It's Tourette's syndrome. She's having an attack. What the fuck are you guys looking at? She's not crazy."

I carried Serena out the church into the foyer, then down the hall to the rest room, where I practically fell to the ground in exhaustion with her in my arms.

"Bitch," she repeated over and over again as she jerked her head and blinked her eyes uncontrollably.

"Where's your meds, Serena?" I asked and grabbed her pink purse with a picture of black Barbie on the flap. I pulled it open and flipped it over and let everything fall to the floor. I grabbed her white bottle of haloperidol and fumbled around with the safety cap until I forced it open. I poured the bottle into my hand and when I did, I saw that all the pills were cut in half. I picked up two pills and stuck them into Serena's mouth. "Swallow, baby," I said and pulled her over to the sink. I turned on the water and cupped my hands underneath the faucet. "Bend over, Serena," I said and lifted my hand to her face, but she jerked her head against my hand and sent the water spilling out. "Here," I said, trying again, and this time she was able to sip the water, but that didn't stop her body from jerking. I stood her in the middle of the rest room away from the walls and the sink and just let her move. Whenever she got close to knocking herself into something, I stepped in and pushed her back into the open area. It took about five minutes for Serena to calm down, and once she did, she was exhausted. She looked at me for a split second, then ran into one of the stalls, locked the door, and started to cry.

"It's okay, Serena," I said and leaned against the door. "Come on out. Let's go home."

"I'm not coming out."

"Come on, baby," I pleaded, knowing she must be embarrassed beyond belief. Serena had never had a spell like that before, but her doctor had warned us it could happen. "Coprolalia is a normal progression of Tourette's syndrome. The child will curse. Do not be alarmed." I can remember her doctor saying that as if it were yesterday, but I never dreamed it would happen. I bet Serena didn't either.

"They were all looking at me," she whined and coughed. "Everybody was looking."

"It's okay," I said and walked into the stall beside her. I climbed on top of the toilet and looked over the wall into her stall. "There's no need to be shamed, Serena," I said, looking down on her as she cupped her face in her hands. When she looked up at me, I smiled, trying to ease her pain, but it didn't work. Then I heard the rest room door swing open and turned to see who was there.

"I have never been so embarrassed in all my days," Mother said slowly and intently as she walked past the sink. I climbed down from the toilet and walked out the stall. I stared at Mother as she put her hands on her hips and seemed to boil over with anger. "Serena," she yelled and banged on the closed stall door. "You bring me your tail right now."

I could hear Serena start to cry harder as Mother continued to bang on her door. "Do you hear me, girl? I said get out here now."

"Hold on, Mother," I said and grabbed her hand. "What's your problem?"

"My problem? This child sits in church and yells out b-i-t-c-h." She spelled it out in a whisper.

"Mother, you know Serena was just having a spell."

"She's not going to blame this on Tourette's," she said and banged on the door. "Do you hear me, Serena? You're on punishment. And when we get home you go straight to your room and lay across the bed and wait for me and my belt."

"You can't punish her because she has a disease, Mother. The doctor told you Serena could have spells like this. It's called coprolalia, Mother, or have you forgotten?" I asked sarcastically.

"I don't give a damn what it's called or what the doctor says. Serena can control this disease if she wants to. She hasn't had a spell in months and suddenly today she starts jerking and swearing in church? She's doing this on purpose. She always does it on purpose," Mother said, practically screaming. She balled her fist and swung so hard at the door that I thought she was going to break it down. "She does this just to embarrass me. She can control it. She's not some kinda freak," she said and began kicking the door.

"Mother," I said and grabbed her from behind. "Stop it," I said and pulled her away from the door. She was swinging and kicking so wildly that for a second there I thought she had Tourette's syndrome too. "I said stop it, Mother," I said, pinning her against the wall until she calmed down.

"You get the hell off of me," she said and pushed me away so hard that her hat came swinging off her head. "Don't you ever grab on me like that again. I am still the mother," she said, straightening out her dress until she felt dignified again. "Don't you forget. I am still the mother."

"Then act like one," I said and stared her dead in the eye. "If it's so embarrassing to you, then how do you think your daughter feels?" I said and watched Mother struggle to find the words to answer me. She couldn't.

"I'm going to wait in the car," she said as she picked up her hat and hesitantly walked toward the door.

"You do that," I said and watched her disappear.

I closed my eyes and shook my head. Mother just didn't get it at all. She never really understood what was going on with Serena. Tourette's syndrome was not something Serena could control or make go away. Over time her symptoms will lessen, but Serena's at that adolescent age when the disease is at its most difficult to predict. When she was younger the tics and the jerks and sound making was an everyday occurrence, but since she's gotten older the signs have decreased, which I guess is why Mother seems to think that somehow, magically, Serena can now control it. But she can't. She's just lucky. Most times she doesn't show signs, but then there are times like these when it all comes pouring out. If Mother is embarrassed, she should be embarrassed with herself. Who gives a damn if the whole church saw Serena go through a spell? Mother should be more concerned with whether her daughter is alright than with her holy public image.

"Li'l Ma," Serena called and sniffled.

"What, baby?" I said and walked closer to the door.

"I promise. I tried to control it," she said softly. "I feel it when it's inside of me. It's like tension, you know. My eyes get tense and before I can do anything, they start blinking real fast. Then my neck gets tight and I know it's about to jerk, so I try to fight it, but it won't listen to me. And in my gut," she said as she slowly opened the stall door and stood facing me. She put her hand over her stomach like it was aching and stared at me. "I feel it in my gut. I know I'm about to make a noise, so I try to swallow and make it go away, but it comes out anyway."

"I know, Serena," I said, walking to her. I pulled her to me and held her tightly. "I know it's not your fault."

She stood back and looked up at me with tears in her eyes. "I'm sorry for being so unladylike, Li'l Ma. I'm sorry if I embarrassed you."

"You didn't, baby," I said and grabbed her by the hand. "I love you."

"Does Big Mama?"

"Yeah, Big Mama loves you too," I said and squeezed her as tight as I could.

Mother didn't say a word as I drove them back home. Serena was quiet too. I kept trying to talk to her so she'd know that everything was okay, but I knew she was still embarrassed. When I pulled in front of their house, I wondered if I should go inside with them, but Serena looked tired and I thought the best medicine would be for her to just get some rest. I got out the car and opened the door for Serena and gave her a big hug. "Call me before you go to bed, okay?" I said as she nodded her head and walked off toward the house.

When I turned to get back in the car, Mother was standing next to my door. Her lips were squeezed together like she was trying to keep herself from saying something. I stopped in front of her and waited for her to say whatever she was going to say.

"I'm sorry," she said and looked down at the ground. "I lost it back there at the church and I just wanna apologize."

"I'm not the one you should be apologizing to, Mother," I said, looking away down the street. "She's only fourteen. And she's got a disease that no one understands, not even her. She needs your love, Mother."

"I know. I just . . . She never showed that part of the disease before. You know, the cursing."

"I know, but you're gonna have to be patient with her. Serena does best when she's not around exciting events, so for a while I don't think you should take her to church with you."

"You're right."

"And another thing, Mother," I said and frowned as the thought came into my mind. "When I gave Serena her pills, they were all cut in half."

Mother rubbed her hands together like she was nervous. "I know," she said, embarrassed. "Her prescriptions are so expensive that I told her she had to cut back—"

"Dammit, Mother," I said and turned my back to her. "That's the reason she's tripping out. She can't cut back on her medication now. Not when she's in the critical stages of her disease."

"I know, but it's so expensive."

"Why didn't you just ask me for the money?" I said and turned back to her. "I would've taken care of everything."

"I don't need you to take care of me," she said and finally looked me in the eyes. "I am still the mother. I can take care of me and my daughter just fine."

"This isn't a question of pride, Mother. This is about Serena's health," I said, staring at her. "If you won't take the money from me, why don't you call up her sorry-ass father and tell that broke motherfucker to chip in for the medication?"

Dammit. She started crying. Well, fuck that. Fuck her tears. Mother can't be this irresponsible and put Serena's health in jeopardy. "Go inside, Mother," I told her and turned away. "I'll call you later."

She slowly walked away with her head hanging low and I got in my car and drove off. "Damn," I said as I peeled down the street. I'm so tired of being the mother of this family. Why do I have to be the responsible one? I thought as I drove like a maniac toward my home.

A red light caught me at the corner of Overhill and Slauson, so I turned up the volume on the stereo and tried to drown out my thoughts. It worked. Instead of focusing on Mother, my thoughts went back to church and that annoying but familiar-sounding voice that kept nagging me throughout service. It was probably nasty old Deacon Jenkins, I thought and cringed. He was probably sitting behind me the whole time, watching me, salivating, undressing me with his eyes . . . "Ick!" I screamed as the grossest thought ever imagined popped into my brain. I turned off the radio and sat motionless, thinking. Could it be? Is it possible? Deacon Jenkins . . . my secret admirer? "Oh my God." But wait. Wait, wait, wait. The gifts? They were all sent to my office. How would Deacon Jenkins know where I worked? . . . "Mother!"

HONK!!!

"Fuck off," I screamed and threw up the finger to the man driving the car behind me. The light had been green for I don't know how long, but I sat an extra second or so just to piss him off. "Damn it," I moaned as I sped off down the street, cursing Mother over and over in my head. So that's why she called this morning worrying about what I'd be wearing to church. She was sticking her nose in my business again, I thought and banged my hand against the steering wheel. "I am so sick of her," I mumbled as I came to a complete stop in the middle of the street. I gave a quick glance in both directions, then busted a U. Mother was getting too beside herself and it was about time I told her so. Within minutes, I was back outside her house. I jumped out my car and raced to her front door. "Mother," I yelled as I stuck my spare key in the lock and opened the door.

I stormed through the front room just in time to see her stepping out of Serena's room and closing the door behind her. When she saw me the huge grin that was spread across her face vanished. "What are you doing back here?" she asked nervously.

"Surprised you, did I?" I said and strolled closer to her. I felt like we were in one of those black-and-white Westerns and this was the final showdown. The point where we both take ten spaces and draw.

"Is there something wrong?" she asked as she scratched the back of her neck, looking guilty as sin.

"You didn't think I'd figure it out?"

"Figure what out?"

"Don't play goofy with me," I said and waited for her to say something. In the midst of our silence I could hear Serena laughing inside her room. At least somebody in this house is happy, I thought and redirected my attention back to Mother. "How many times do I have to tell you to stay out of my personal life?"

"But this is different, Li'l Mama," she said, shaking.

"I should have known," I said and threw up my hands.

"Just let me explain," she said as I turned away from her, leaving her talking to my back.

As she took her time gathering her thoughts, I could hear Serena laughing again, but this time I could also hear another voice. A deeper voice. Who is in the room with Serena? I thought as Mother began her explanation.

"Listen, Li'l Mama. It's not that I was meddling. *He* came to me first. I couldn't turn him away. Besides, you know how much he loves you."

"What?" I said and snapped my head over my shoulder. "He loves me? Deacon Jenkins doesn't love me, he just wants to . . ." "Fuck me" was what I wanted say, but being that it was Sunday and I *was* talking to Mother . . . "All Deacon Jenkins wants to do is get me into bed, Mother. I told you that before. I can't believe you're trying to set me up with a man like that."

"What?" Mother exclaimed and contorted her face like she'd just sipped sour milk.

"Don't play dumb with me, Mother," I warned and turned around. "I know you've been conspiring to hook me up with that freak."

"Huh?"

Okay. Now she's gonna play the old senile role, right? Oh poor Mother. She's getting old, she can't think straight, she didn't know what she was doing. Bullshit, I thought as I lifted a finger in preparation to really tell her off. But before I could open my mouth I heard the laughing coming from Serena's room again. She sure sounds happy for a girl who just had one of the worst spells of her life, I thought as I looked at Mother. By the look on her face I could tell she'd heard the laughing too.

"Who's in there with her?"

"Nobody," she said quickly, and cautiously moved toward Serena's door.

How obvious can you be? I thought as I watched her nervously block the doorway.

"Who's in there?" I repeated and slowly walked toward her as she stood stiffly shaking her head from side to side. As I closed in on Mother I listened as Serena and the deep voice laughed again. That's when it hit me. It was the same voice from church.

"What's he doing here?"

"It's not who you think."

"Yeah right," I said and tried to calm myself down. "You know what, Mama? Thank you," I said and clasped my hands together in front of me. "Thank you for inviting the deacon over, because now that I've got the both of you together I'm gonna give you a piece of my mind."

I tussled with Mother until I could safely get her away from the door without breaking any of her bones.

"Wait a minute, Madison," she said, panting as if she'd been in a two-hour bout with Tyson. "You've got it all wrong."

Yeah right, I said to myself as I twisted the knob and threw the door open.

I couldn't believe who I saw.

"Li'l Ma," Serena shouted, half shocked to see me and half unable to control her laughter. She sat giggling at me from the foot of her bed as she quickly glanced back and forth between me and a photo she held in her hand. To her right were more snapshots that she'd sprawled across her bed, and to her left sat the owner of those snapshots. I took one look at him and froze. It wasn't Deacon Jenkins. Not by a long shot.

"Now take it easy," Mother whispered in my ear as she lightly stroked my back. "This isn't the way you two were supposed to meet." She stared at me for a minute, then took her hand from my back and threw it across her mouth. "Oh," she said and shook her head. "It wasn't supposed to be like this."

"Like what?" Serena asked and stopped laughing.

"Come on," Mother said and grabbed Serena and pulled her off the bed. "Let's leave these two alone to talk."

"Wait!" Serena screamed as Mother pulled her past me. "You okay?" she asked me. But I was too much in shock to respond. All I could do was stare at the figure that sat before me. Serena followed my stare with her own eyes until they landed on him. "You're gonna show me the rest of the pictures later, aren't you?" she asked him.

He smiled and nodded her way, though his eyes never left mine. I could hear Serena giggle, and before she left the room she whispered to me. "He's sooo cute."

I hadn't noticed, though I'd been staring at him now for minutes. When you're in shock nothing seems to register. All I knew was that I was looking at a man I hadn't seen in eight years.

"You look exquisite," he said, dazed. But when I didn't respond he got nervous. "You must be in shock," he stammered and waited for me to say something. Anything. "Are you alright?" he asked cautiously.

"You're the one?" I asked, staring. "You're my secret admirer?"

The smile that sprang to his face confirmed my question.

"You're the one who's been sending me the plants, the cookies, the candy?"

"Guilty as charged," he said and seemed to lighten up. "I take it you got my gift this morning?" he asked, practically glowing with pride. "We were actually supposed to meet at church, but after Serena had her spell . . . well, everything sorta went haywire," he said, then stopped to examine me. "I tried calling out your name, but . . ." he paused and looked at me sideways. "Are you sure you're alright?"

I didn't know the answer to that question. What I did know was that he was beautiful, that he hadn't changed a bit, and that looking at him was making me weak. I could not believe it. After eight years, Christopher, my first love, my *only* love, was back.

"Madison," he said as he slowly rose from the bed and walked over to me. He put his finger beneath my chin and lifted my face to his. "It's been so long," he said as he wrapped me in his arms and held me tight. And as he did my mind slipped back eight years. I remembered the first time I'd met him, the first time I kissed him, hugged him. The night he proposed to me . . . The night he broke my heart.

"Get out of my face," I said slowly and pushed him away.

He stood before me, eyeing me, as if my actions had confused him.

"I can't believe you have the nerve to show your face here," I said as my eyes began to water. "You are not welcome here."

"But, Madi," he said as I stormed out the room.

As I raced toward the front door I saw Mother hurrying out of the kitchen to find out what all the commotion was about.

"What's going on?" she yelled as Chris came running behind me.

"Wait a minute, Madison," he pleaded. "Let me talk to you."

"No!" I screamed as I stopped dead in my tracks and turned around. I held in my stomach, straightened out my shoulders, and stared directly into Chris's eyes. "It has been eight long years, Christopher," I said, and paused so that my voice would stop cracking. "I don't care why you're back in town, I don't care how long you're staying, I don't care where you're staying. I don't care for you," I said and watched as he backed away from me. "You are not to call me. You are not to come to my home. You are not to send another gift to my place of employment. You are not to even think about me. It's been over since you left for Chicago and it isn't going to start up again now."

I turned toward the door and bolted outside to my car. I drove. I got out of my car, walked to my door, opened my door, closed my door, then slowly walked into my bedroom, where I proceeded to undress and laid down across my bed. I frowned. I stared up at the ceiling. I wondered why. Then, I cried myself to sleep.

Bastard. Who the hell does he think he is? Just out the blue—bam!—he shows up. Acting like everything is peachy keen. Hunky-dory. Well, bullshit. It's been eight years, almost a decade. I never expected my secret admirer to be some knight in shining armor, but I sure as hell didn't expect him to be a stupefied fool, which is exactly what Christopher is if he thinks he can just traipse back into my life like some curly-headed cupid and start up some kind of relationship with me again. How dare he think that he could simply bombard me with a slew of gifts and suddenly I'd forget about all the pain he caused in my life? It'll take more than a box of chocolates or a stack of CDs or an ugly fern to make me forget how badly Chris hurt me. I loved that man. He was the only man I ever loved. And what did he do? He left me. Adios, arrivederci, bon soir. He flew off to Chicago leaving me and our love behind. And now he's back. Eight years later. Just like that. What? Am I supposed to be happy now? Am I supposed to start break-dancing and doing the cabbage patch? Hell no. What's he doing back here anyway? What happened to his mission of mercy, his great big charity clinic for the underprivileged kids of Chicago? What's he doing in L.A. when he should be off saving lives somewhere in the Amazon ghetto?

To tell the truth, I don't really give a damn why Christopher is back. I don't care in the least. Okay, okay. If I'm honest with myself, which I'm not, I'll have to admit that seeing him yesterday was a shock. It threw me off balance. For a split second there, when he looked me in the eye, I could have melted. Chris hadn't changed a bit. Even though he wore an over-sized Tommy Hilfiger sweater, I could still make out that chiseled chest as it thumped underneath all that cotton. His face was smooth, hair nicely faded, eyes shielded coolly behind a pair of tortoiseshell Armanis, and his mouth was puckered out like a baby who needed attention. Chris was definitely looking good. Okay, he looked great. Alright already, he was knockout, drop-dead, Lord-have-mercy fine. But what else is new? Christopher has always looked good, but that handsome exterior didn't faze me. That beautiful smile didn't make me blink twice, and the gentleness of his hand on my face couldn't take away the pain that still lingered in every inch of my body from the love that I'd lost when Chris announced that he'd been unfaithful to me. And now he was back. But why? Chris can't possibly believe that after eight years I'd still be here waiting for him, wanting him. He knows me too well. I don't wait for any man. I don't need any man. I don't want any man. Chris has got to know that, yet he's still here. He's been secretly romancing me for weeks even though he knows that when he moved to Chicago, I'd totally given up on him. Doesn't he get the picture? It's over. Why can't he just take rejection and move on with some dignity? Why can't he just give up?

I know why. Because Chris is one of those go-getters. A successful man. He never loses. He succeeded through college, he succeeded through med school, through his residency, and though we haven't spoken since he left me, I'm sure he's succeeded with his dream of opening a clinic in Chicago. Christopher always wins and he probably thinks that he can win me again. But guess what, Chris? The buck stops here, baby. You will not succeed at capturing my heart. You will never get my love again and I will never accept yours. Never. I will never lay my heart on the line like I did for you eight years ago. I will never fall in love like that again. It doesn't matter how many ferns you send me, the *Closed* sign on my heart has been up ever since you left, and I don't believe it will ever come down again.

"Ms. McGuire," little Sandy Johnson called to me. I snapped out of the daze I was in and looked over at her as she flung her arm wildly above her head.

"Yes, Sandra," I said and looked around the classroom at all the bored little faces. I realized then that I'd let my mind drift away right in the middle of our vocabulary test.

"What's the next word?" Sandy asked, then quickly covered up her test paper as Todd Mayfield tried to lean over and sneak a peek.

"Oh yes," I said and cleared my throat. "The next word is 'mortified,'" I said slowly, enunciating each syllable as the class dropped their heads and began writing.

Mortified, I thought to myself as I rose up from my seat at the head of the room and walked around. Let's see if I can use that word in a sentence. Oh yes. I'm *mortified* by Chris. I can't believe him. After all these years, he shows up unannounced. Unbelievable. Simply unbelievable. I'm *mortified*.

The end-of-school bell rang just as I was about to allow my mind to drift deeper into hideous thoughts of Chris. Immediately the class began mumbling and getting restless as they all stared at me, waiting for me to give them their cue to leave.

"Alright, you little ragamuffins. We'll finish this test tomor—" I couldn't even finish my sentence before they were up and heading for the door.

I muddled around the classroom for a bit, then decided to head over to my office before I left for home. As I walked across campus, guess what thought kept pouncing through my mind? Chris.

Eight years. Eight years come and gone and he decides to start playing Romeo. What does he expect to accomplish? In all those years, hadn't he met someone else? Hadn't he asked another woman to marry him by now? He couldn't still be single. Could he? But he had to be. Otherwise he wouldn't have been sending me all those gifts in a futile attempt to get me interested in him again. If he was romancing me, he had to be single and available. But that doesn't make me none. I don't care. Chris could be single all he wanted to. I'm still not interested. I'm not. Chris hurt me bad and I'll never forget that. I never want to forget that, because that would mean that I'd forgiven. And forgiveness is something Chris will never get from me.

When I reached the third floor, I could hear the phone ringing off the hook, and though Thompson had told me I was only in charge of phones during the morning, I decided to go on ahead and answer it anyway. I picked up the phone and pushed line one, wondering who it could be, but when I put the phone to my ear I instantly wanted to hang up.

"You are the silliest woman I've ever heard of," Mother's voice rang through the receiver. "I can't believe you. I really can not believe you."

Damn, I thought and rolled my eyes. For just a split second I thought her anger could be due to the fact that I forgot to tell James to go over and fix her car. But the more she went on, the more I knew it was something else. Someone else. Chris.

"I swear, I could live my life the whole way through and I'd never be able to figure out why you do the silly things you do."

"What are you talking about, Mother?" I asked and sighed.

"You know what I'm talking about."

Damn. Here we go.

"That man has come all the way back from Chicago to see you and you shoo him away like he's some stray off the street? Are you sick?"

I really didn't feel like talking to Mother about this, but I needed to make myself understood. "I don't care why Chris is back in town, Mother. He's not my man anymore. It's been over between us for years and I don't have any intentions or any desire to see him again."

"You are out of your damn mind," she said, believing that fully. "He told me about all the gifts he sent you and how nice he tried to be yesterday. What is your problem, girl?"

"I don't have a problem. Chris does. If he thinks sending me gifts can make me forget about all the pain . . ." I wasn't going to have this conversation with Mother. I wasn't in the mood and I wasn't about to explain myself any further.

"Pain? What about the pain you caused him? That man wanted to marry you. You're the one that said no. Not him."

I didn't say a word, though Mother paused long enough for my response.

"Madison?"

"What?" Damn.

"You broke that man's heart. All he was trying to do was make a life for himself and you, and all you had to do was marry him."

"And move to Chicago and put up with his infidelity."

"What was wrong with that? A lot of men cheat, but not a lot of men come clean about it."

"I don't believe you just said that. It's not okay for a man to cheat on his woman, Mother. I don't care how many men do it. It's wrong. And it makes no difference that Chris came clean before the wedding. He still cheated on me."

"Do you hear how silly you sound?" she asked calmly. So calmly that I had to take a second to replay my words in my mind. What had I said that was so silly? Why couldn't she understand that I was the victim in this relationship? I was the one who was hurt. Chris broke my heart, not the other way around.

"Look, Mother," I said and closed my eyes tightly to ease the throbbing in my head that had started since I picked up the phone. "Chris is probably just in town for a few weeks for some doctors' convention or some medical retreat. He'll be gone again as soon as he came. I am not about to let myself lose it because he sent me a few gifts and showed me a smile. It's over between us. Understand that, Mother. It's over."

"Chris is back in L.A to stay."

"Excuse me?"

"You heard me right."

At first I wanted to ask why, but I didn't. I didn't care. If Chris was back in L.A to stay, then good for him. As long as he stayed away from me I had no problem sharing a city with him. "I've got to go, Mother. I've got to get home."

"Wait a minute," she said in a rush as if she expected to get a dial tone any second. "I want you to talk to Chris."

"I don't give a damn what you want. This is my life. I have nothing to say to Chris and I told him that yesterday."

"No, you acted a fool yesterday," she snapped in a no-nonsense tone. "The man is still in love with you. He told me so. You know Chris is just like a son to me. He tells me everything. He still loves you and I want you to talk to him."

"I'll say it again, Mother. I don't want anything to do with Chris. I've moved on with my life. I have other men in my life and—"

"Oh please. You ain't got nobody. You're just a silly little girl trying to act grown-up. And I know why you're doing it. I know why it hurts you to love."

"Stop it, Mother," I said, but Mother just kept talking like she didn't hear me.

"I know why you won't let anyone close to you anymore. I know what your problem is, Madison, and it has nothing to do with Christopher."

"Oh yeah, Mother. And why don't you let me in on what my problem is?"

"It's your father."

I hung up on her.

Listening to Mother whine about my relationship with Chris was one thing, but I was not about to sit and listen to her go on and on about what she calls my "poor Papa complex." Mother is always telling me that I let my feelings for my father shape the way I deal with all the other men in my life. She claims that I'm scared to commit to men because I'm afraid they'll hurt me like my father did, and if I'm honest with myself, which I'm not, I'll have to admit that she's right. But whether she's right or wrong is beside the point where Chris is concerned. I opened my heart to that man. Hell, I was ready to marry that man, and what did he do? He cheated on me. Well, that hurt. What Chris did to me has nothing to do with my father. Chris broke my heart all by himself.

I felt myself getting weak and though I promised myself that I wasn't going to cry over Chris again like I did last night, I felt the tears welling up in my eyes anyway. Damn, I thought and closed my eyes to fight off the flood I knew would begin in a minute. I can't let Chris get to me. I will not cry. I will not cry. "Damn," I said as a tear fell down to my cheek. "Here I go again."

"Madison," Malik yelled as he stepped through my office door and closed it behind him. I quickly wiped the tears from my eyes and straightened up in my seat.

"What's up?" I said and opened the middle drawer on my desk, pretending like I was looking for something.

"We're getting married."

"Huh?"

"You heard me," Malik said as he pranced in front of my desk with a smile so bright I almost had to squint. "Tyrone and I are getting married."

I stared up at Malik as he bent over my desk waiting for my response, and all I could recognize at that moment was how handsome he was. He was so handsome that I felt proud to be his friend. He was a beautiful shade of cocoa and his height was perfect. Not too tall that looking up at him was uncomfortable and not so short that one would feel sorry for him. Though he hardly ever worked out, his body was well shaped, chest just right for laying a lazy head against, and his butt was well placed. Just high enough to provide a resting place if you were to hug him around the waist. I know many a woman who'd act a fool if Malik were to wink her way, including myself. Though the no-dating-coworkers rule was well in effect by the time Malik started working with me, I often allowed myself to daydream about him during long, lonely hours when I had nothing better to do. I used to daydream about him a lot, especially before he confided in me that he was gay. But even after I knew the truth, I still daydreamed, wondering how it would be to love him. Wondering if he'd ever thought about being with me. If somehow I could change him. Make him straight. But I knew I couldn't. Malik was gay and that was all there was to it. He was born that way, he says, and I believe him. Unless you're a glutton for punishment, ridicule, and hate, I can't see why anyone would choose to be gay. Still, I wonder what a night with Malik would be like. But that's something I don't think I'll ever discover.

"*Hello,*" Malik said, pulling me back into the present. "I said I'm getting married. Now I know that may not seem like big news to you, but you could at least try to fake a bit of surprise."

"You're getting married?"

"Well, sorta. Actually it's called a dedication ceremony. It's the closest to a real wedding that I could get."

"Oh."

"Oh?" he repeated and frowned his face at me. "What about 'congratulations,' or, 'Oh Malik, that's wonderful,' or, 'Gee, I hope you'll be happy.'"

"I'm sorry, Malik," I said, but in an unapologetic tone. "It's not every day that a gay man walks into my office and tells me he's getting married. So you'll have to excuse me if I want to find out all the facts before I go jumping for joy and dancing a jig."

"Well, who or what has fucked up your day?" he asked, stepping away from my desk and taking a seat.

I rubbed the side of my temples and tried to ignore that question. "So you and Tyrone are having a dedication ceremony, huh? Are you sure you want to do that? Are you sure you want to make that kind of commitment?"

"You know I'm in love with Tyrone. And we're gonna do things the right way," he said defensively. "Tyrone and I want to be partners for life. We're serious. What is your problem?" he said, leaning forward in his seat. "I know you're in shock, but I've been telling you for the longest that this is what I wanted to do. You could at least be happy for me."

"Be happy for what? Because you're in love? Well, goody-goody," I said and stood up. "What the fuck is love?" I said and threw up my hands. "Next week you'll be in here telling me that Tyrone's cheating on you."

"Okay," Malik said, looking around the room as if to look at me would piss him off. "Do you want to talk about it?"

"Talk about what?"

"Whatever or whomever has got you acting like a bitch," Malik said, too through with my attitude. When I didn't respond, he got up and walked toward the door, then turned around. "Call me when you stop tripping," he said and gave me a good looking over, then walked out the door.

I sat back down and rested my head against the cushion of my chair. "Sorry, Malik," I whispered, though he was already long gone. I am definitely tripping. I thought all the hurt I'd felt over breaking up with Chris was gone. After he left and I moved on with my life, I never so much as thought of Chris—well, not often anyway. But now, in one day, the pain has come back. Christopher's presence has robbed me of my power. Seeing him brought back too many old memories. It's pathetic for one man to hold so much power over a woman.

I got up from my desk and went to my door and closed it. I just wanted to put my head down on my desk and chill out for a while. I thought maybe the silence would keep my mind off Chris and help me get myself together. But just as I'd closed the door and put my hand on the knob to lock it, it came nudging back at me so hard that I had to step out of the way before I got smashed into the wall.

"Afternoon, Madison," Tommy said as he walked into my office and shut the door behind him.

No . . . please. Go away. I do not have the energy to deal with Tommy right now.

"So glad I caught you before you left," he said as he strolled to my desk and sat down behind it.

I wanted so badly to tell him to get the fuck out of my chair, but I didn't have the fire inside me at the time. Besides, Tommy loves to get under my skin and that's exactly what he was doing, but I wasn't going to let him know he was succeeding. The less fuss I make, the sooner he'll be out the door. I took one of the seats in front of my desk as Tommy made himself at home by turning on the computer and opening my games file. He sat there playing solitaire for a good ten minutes before he even looked my way, and for some reason I didn't mind. I usually never let Tommy into my office for more than a hot second before I throw him out or, worse, curse him out. But today, his presence didn't rile me up at all. In fact it felt sorta like old times, when we used to be lovers and enjoyed sitting with each other for long periods of time doing and saying nothing. But as usual, Tommy had to go messing it up and reminding me of the reason why I now hate him.

"*So,*" he said as he turned off the game and leaned back in his, I mean my, chair. "Bet you're wondering what I'm doing here?"

"Getting on my nerves?"

"Good guess, but not quite," he said as he clasped his hands together under his chin. "I need a date tonight."

"Get the fuck out my office, Tommy," I said as I suddenly remembered that I couldn't stand the sight of him. But Tommy didn't budge an inch. He kept right on talking as if he didn't even notice that I was sitting in front of him with a snarl on my face.

"It's a business dinner for charity," he said, as cool as he could. "I'd ask my wife, but since she's filed for divorce, moved out the house, and threatened to kill me on numerous occasions, I don't think she'd be too interested. So," he said with a whirl of enthusiasm, "how 'bout it? Tonight, Century Plaza, seven o'clock?"

"So you really are getting a divorce?" I asked, trying to hide my curiosity.

"Yeah," he said solemnly. "It's over and I can't blame her. She always came last. This school has always been the priority in my life. I guess she finally got fed up," he said with a sigh. "I am gonna miss her, though."

I almost felt sorry for Tommy. On the outside he seems indestructible, but I know deep down inside he's just a scared little boy. I was feeling for him so much that for a second there I was actually considering going out with him, but as usual Tommy's mouth always ruins it for me.

"Anyway," he said, popping out of his somber disposition. "I'll pick you up at seven," he said matter-of-factly. "Oh, and, uh, wear something nice . . . something tight . . . something, oh . . . see-through."

"How do you do it?"

"What?" he said and ran a hand over his face. "Manage to look so good?"

"No," I said, feeling my blood pressure rise. "Manage to make me hate you more and more each day."

"So will you go with me or not?"

"Not."

"Fine," he said and put his hands on the desk to pull himself up. "I figured you'd say that," he said and walked from behind my desk until he was standing right in front of me. He stood there a long time, just looking at me as I eyed the zipper on his pants. If Tommy made one move toward me, I'd picked out the perfect spot to let him have it. But surprisingly, he was able to keep his hands to himself. Unfortunately he wasn't able to keep his mouth closed. "When's the last time you read the school's policy on teacher conduct?"

"Excuse me?" I said, trying to figure out what Tommy was getting at.

"I think you should read it again," he said, stuffing his hands into his pockets. "Actually it's not you. It's your *friend*, Mr. Tate. Why don't you have him read it as well?" he said and leaned back on my desk and crossed his ankles.

Oh shit, I thought and eyed him with suspicion. What the hell does he know? And why won't he just come right on out and say what's on his mind? "What are you getting at, Tommy?"

"Nothing," he said with too much coolness. "Just thought maybe you and your friend should read it. But anyway," he said and clasped his hands together, "are you sure I can't bend your arm to go out with me tonight?"

"Stop playing games, Tommy," I said and stood up straight in front of him. "Why is it so important that I read the school policy on teacher conduct? What's going on?"

"Ssh," he said and put a finger to my lips. "We can talk all this over tonight on our date."

I was two seconds away from knocking the shit out of Tommy, but I was smart enough to play it cool. I sat back down in my seat and laughed so long that Tommy had to join me. "You're something else, Tommy. You know that?"

"I've been told," he said, still laughing.

"I'm not going out with you."

"Come on now, Madi," he whined.

"Nope."

"You know I can't stand to go to these functions alone. Just do me this one favor," he said and winced as if he knew my answer would break his heart.

I folded my arms across my chest and boldly said, "No."

"No?"

"No."

"So, in other words, no?"

"No."

"So what you're really trying to say is—"

"No!"

"Alright," he said, defeated.

"But I'll definitely read the teacher conduct policy."

He laughed, then walked to the door. "Don't forget to have Malik read it as well."

"I'll do that."

"You do. And have a nice day," he said and walked out the door.

Son of a bitch. So that's his game. He knows that Malik and I have been sneaking behind his back and trying to change his precious school. One of the parents must have dropped a dime. If I know Tommy he's probably going to milk this situation for all it's worth. But he's not going to get to me. Malik and I are going to win this battle. We've got the support of the parents, and if Tommy thinks he can scare me by dropping these stupid innuendos, he's got another thing coming.

I opened the file cabinet in the corner of my office and searched for a copy of the school policy. I sat back down at my desk and read and reread the thick file from top to bottom, but I could find nothing in it that said what Malik and I were doing was wrong. In fact, section sixteen, paragraph four, clearly states that when a teacher has a suggestion affecting the general course of curriculum he or she may put the suggestion in writing and submit it to the principal for consideration. Well, that's all Malik and I are doing. We have a suggestion and we're putting it in writing. What more does Thompson want?

When I finally finished reading and looked up at the clock, I found it was five-forty-five. I'd been reading so hard that I didn't have a chance to think about anything other than the pages in front of my face, which was good, and now that I was finished and had allowed myself to relax a bit, I found that I was feeling better. I wasn't even tripping off of Chris anymore. As far as I'm concerned, I handled him yesterday. I don't care that he's back or that he's here to stay. All that matters is that Chris and I have an understanding. He leaves me alone, I leave him alone, and we'll live happily ever after, alone. Period. End of report. And as for Tommy Thompson, well, he can just kiss my ass.

"Now," I said and swiveled around in my chair to put the file back in the cabinet, "it's time to go home."

I stopped for a second when I saw the lights in the receptionist area come on. It scared me for a moment, then I thought it must be the cleaning crew and grabbed my purse. I bundled my car keys in my hand, threw my purse over my shoulder, and scooted my chair back so I could get up. But when I looked in front of me, I froze. I was still as a rock. I peered at the body standing in my doorway as my heart began to race, my head began to pound. What does he want with me? I wondered and squinted my eyes in his direction. I told him no. It was over. And once again, he was back.

"Bastard," I said and stood to my feet.

"Sit down," he said, with authority.

Who the hell did he think he was talking to? I didn't move.

"Alright then," he said, stepping through the door and closing it behind him. "Stand if you want to, but you're not leaving this room until we get a few things straight."

"Fuck you, Christopher."

"Shut up," he said forcefully and moved to the front of my desk and stared at me. His eyes were strong. Stronger than I'd ever remembered. He was almost scary. He *was* scary. But I wasn't fazed by his anger. He couldn't have been more angry than me. I'd told him to leave me alone and still he was in my face. Insubordination. Didn't he hear my words yesterday? How plainly can I say leave me the fuck alone?

"What do you—"

"I said shut up, Madison," he said and pointed toward me.

I hesitated to move and he saw in my eyes what I was planning to do.

"Don't even think about it," he said and moved to the side of my desk, blocking off my escape route. "I'll put my hands on you if I have to."

I took a step back and bobbed my head. "You bet not touch me."

"Don't make me have to," he said too seriously.

I weighed my options. Chris was just under six feet, one hundred and ninety pounds, big arms, long legs . . . I could take him if I wanted to, but lucky for him, I didn't feel like kicking a man's ass at that very moment. "What the hell do you want with me?"

"I want you to shut up and listen. Can you do that? Will it kill you to just give me five minutes to say what I have to say?"

I folded my arms across my chest and plopped myself back down in my seat. Five minutes? I've heard that line before. "What?"

Silence.

I stared up at Chris as he fiddled around in front of me. Now that he had the chance to talk, the fool couldn't get himself together. I raised my eyebrows and I wanted to say, "Well, start talking." But I didn't. I was having too much fun watching Chris squirm. Besides, I didn't care what he had to say. It wouldn't make any difference to me. I'd sit, I'd listen, then I'd tell him exactly what I told him yesterday, what I'd told Mother. It's over.

"I just don't understand you," Chris started, slowly. "What is your problem?"

Was I supposed to answer that? I thought I was supposed to just shut up and listen. When I opened my mouth to tell him that *he* was the problem and that I never wanted to see him again, he raised his hand in front of his face.

"I don't want you to say a word. I wanna talk."

Then talk, asshole. I don't have all night.

"I don't know what I'm doing, Madison. I don't know why I started sending you gifts . . . I don't know why I'm here right now. Uh, I, I've been back in L.A. for over a month."

You're rambling, I wanted to say, but didn't.

"The clinic in Chicago went bust about a year ago. It was broken into so many times that we finally had to shut it down. We started out with over a million dollars' worth of equipment and by the end all we had left was a stethoscope and a box of needles."

Why did that make me want to smile?

"So I took a job at Chicago Hope. Head of Pediatrics. Good job. Everything was going fine, but there was still so much more I wanted to do."

What a saint.

"I'd thought about opening up another clinic on the South Side, but I didn't have enough cash to do it by myself," he said as he began pacing the floor in front of me. "Then I got a call from one of the guys who I'd taken my residency with at Loyola."

Oh really. Could it be the med student with the jet black hair who you cheated on me with? I thought as a frown crept over my face.

"Dr. Fitzsimmons. Remember him?"

No, but anyway.

"Fitz said he was leaving Cedars Sinai to do his own thing. Open up a small clinic in Watts. And he asked if I was down to go into business with him. Hell yeah."

Can you please talk in full sentences? I'm getting lost.

"So I came back. I left my job in Chicago and was on the next flight to L.A. Just like that. I left behind a hundred and seventy-five thousand a year."

Idiot.

"I came back for two reasons, Madison. One, because I wanted to do something for my people and this clinic sounded like just the thing. I want to make a difference. I'll say this till my dying day. You shouldn't have to be rich to get quality health care. That's not right."

And two . . .

"And two," he said and stopped pacing. He stood in front of me and kept opening his mouth, but nothing was coming out. Then he took a deep breath and stared at me. "The second reason I came back is because of you."

Idiot.

"I never got over you, Madison. It's never been over for me. You broke my heart, girl."

I broke *your* heart? No. "*I* broke *your* heart?"

"Please," he said and held up his hand again. "Let me finish."

Go head.

"I know what I did was wrong. I should have never cheated on you. But I thought I was doing the right thing by telling you before we got married. I loved you. I wanted to spend the rest of my life with you. And I wanted to be open and honest with you. Why can't you see that? I could have lied to you. Never told you. But I couldn't do that. Not to you. Not to the woman I loved and wanted to be with forever. I know I screwed up, but how many men haven't? No, better yet, how many men come clean and tell their women when they fuck up? I tried to be a true man to you, Madison. So I told you that I did wrong and hoped you'd see that I was sincere. I hoped you'd see that though I'd done wrong, I was still a good person, a good man. A man worth marrying."

This conversation was useless. The more I sat there in silence listening to him rehash the past, the more disgusted I became until finally I could take it no more.

"I'm leaving," I said and stood up.

"No you're not," he said like he was king and this was his castle.

"Christopher," I said emphatically, "this conversation does not interest me. I do not feel inclined to sit here and listen to you talk about old news. It's over. What happened, happened. We can't go back and fix it."

"I just need to talk to you, Madi. I just need you to listen," he whined.

"Look, little boy. I am not your mama. If you need a shoulder to cry on I suggest you fly back to Chicago and run to Mommy. Maybe she can kiss your boo-boo and make it all better," I said as nasty as I could. And it worked. I broke him. Chris hung his head and sighed. Now, I thought to myself and perked up, I think I'll be going. I pushed in my chair and slowly walked around my desk. When I got close enough to Chris I snuck a peek at him and realized that my scathing remarks had really gotten to him. He was crying.

Poor baby, I thought and rolled my eyes. What? Am I supposed to feel sorry for him now? Am I supposed to pat his back, offer him a Kleenex? Oh damn, I thought as he really began to break down. I put my hand on my hip. "Chris," I moaned, uninterested. "You okay?"

No answer.

I sucked my teeth and shifted my weight to one side. "I'm sorry for being so crass," I said like a child being forced to say sorry.

"It's not your fault," he said as his voice crackled. He dabbed at his eyes and turned to face me. "It's just that I wish I could go running home to Chicago. I wish I could run to my mother and tell her all my problems. But I can't," he said as the tears continued to fall from his slanted eyes. "She died, Madison. Two months ago, Mom died."

"What?" I asked and stared at him, wanting him to repeat the news, but it was too painful to say twice. "Oh my God," I said and threw my hand over my mouth. I slowly turned to walk around my desk and plopped down in my seat, amazed. "I am so sorry," I said, feeling like the biggest jackass to ever breathe. "What, I mean, why . . . how did she die?"

Chris looked up at the ceiling. I could tell it was taking all his strength just to speak. "Mom died of a broken heart," he said, then looked straight at me. "She died because she loved my father too much." He gritted his teeth. "Mom and Dad celebrated their fifty-ninth anniversary this year. The next day, he had a stroke. In another day he was dead." His voice quivered as he spoke but he did not stop. For some reason I felt he needed to tell this story. "After Dad died, Mom just wasn't the same. She . . . she just stopped, you know? She couldn't live without him," he said and shook his head. "We see it all the time in medicine. An old couple, been together for years. One dies and within a year the other one's gone too. I tried to stop it. I, I took care of her, I . . . was there every day. I fed her, bathed her. I, I did everything." He paused to stop himself from crying but it was no use. "I tried to help her, Madison," he said softly. "But she just loved him too much."

"It's okay, Chris," I said as he stumbled backward into one of the chairs in front of my desk. I leaned forward, not knowing what to say or do. Part of me wanted to run over and hug him. The other felt awkward. Almost as if Chris was a stranger.

When he finally quieted down, he looked exhausted. He ran his hand over his head, reminding me of the many nights I'd met him in his dorm after he'd put in sixteen hours at the university Medical Center. That was so long ago, I thought. Too long.

"I'm sorry, Madison," he said and wiped his eyes a final time.

"Don't be," I said and for the first time that night I smiled. I reached my hand across the desk and waited for his to join mine. When it did, I stroked his hand, remembering all the times I'd done this in the past. "I know what you must be going through," I said and curled my hand against his palm. My touch seemed to soothe him. He closed his eyes and blushed. "Everything's going to be alright."

"Is it?" he asked sincerely.

"It's got to be."

I rested my hand against Chris's and relaxed. But before long uneasiness seemed to greet me. Chris grasped my hand so tightly that it began to sweat. His eyes peered at me without blinking. I knew the tides were turning.

"I love you so much, Madison," he said as if he were going to cry again.

"Come on, Chris. Don't go there."

"I have always loved you. Why can't you understand that?"

"Chris, please," I said and yanked my hand away from him. Why was he doing this? Why was he spoiling the moment? We were bonding as friends and he had to go blow it with this *love* crap.

"It's been eight long years, Madison, and I swear, I've loved you every day."

"And I guess you're going to tell me there haven't been any women in your life since me."

"I've dated a bit, here and there, but—"

"Now why doesn't that surprise me?"

"I even had a steady girlfriend for a couple years, but that didn't last. I knew it never would."

"Do I really need to hear this?"

"We had a big argument over you," he said and leaned forward in his seat. "I'd never mentioned your name to her, never even told her a thing about you. But she knew there was someone else. Someone who I always silently compared her to. She couldn't fight against your ghost, Madison. And even if she could, she would have never won. She knew it and she walked out on me."

"Are you finished?"

"I love you, Madison," he said and stood to his feet. "I stand here before you, the man that I am, and I tell you now, I have never loved anyone as much as I love you."

Where's my violin? Where's my tissue? This is so touching I could vomit, I thought and rolled my eyes. "I'm out of here," I said and slid my chair backward.

"You act like you don't even care."

"I don't," I said as I repositioned my purse on my shoulder. I stood up behind my desk, pausing for just a moment to decide if I should say something else. But no. I didn't want to talk. I'd said everything I wanted to say, and this little speech of Chris's hadn't shifted my position. I gripped my keys in my hand and took off toward the door.

"So you're just going to leave?" he asked as he caught me by the arm as I passed him. "You have nothing else to say?"

"Get your hands off of me," I told him. But Chris wouldn't let me go. I wiggled my arm and squirmed, but he just pulled me tighter and closer to him. There was no way I could get out of his grip, so I gave up and started talking. "How long has it been, Chris? Eight years?" I said, practically yelling. "Eight years, and you expect me to still be holding a torch for you? Well, just because you still love me doesn't mean I still love you. How dare you be so egotistical that you'd believe I'd still give a damn after all these years? This is Madison you're talking to, not some naive, insecure girl with a crush. And that's where you make your mistake, Christopher. You underestimate me. When you asked me to marry you, you'd thought I'd give up everything for you, but it's not like that. You wanted a baby doll for a wife. Someone you could lead and who'd follow you without a word of protest. But that's not me. This is Madison. I don't need you. I didn't then and I sure as hell don't now."

"I don't believe you."

"Bastard. Who do you think you're dealing with?"

"Can you look me in the eyes and tell me you don't love me, you don't need me, that you never want to get back what we had together?"

"I don't love you," I said, slowly and surely, staring directly into his eyes. "I don't need you and I never, ever want to get back what we had together."

"Liar," he said and pulled me even closer to him. "You are a liar," he said and kissed me on the mouth. I pulled my head back, but I couldn't escape him. "Madison, please. Don't lie to me," he whispered as he kissed my neck and behind my ears.

"I'm not," I wanted to say, but didn't. Instead, I let myself be kissed. I stood there quietly and stiffly while Chris kissed me everywhere. My eyes, my nose, my hair, everywhere. It felt lusciously soft, being kissed and held by this man I once loved. He'd always been so gentle with me, so caressing and warm, and nothing had changed. His touch was still the same. It lifted me and calmed me at the same time. My body began to ease and so did my mind. I felt myself drifting back to the way things once were. I let my purse and keys drop to the floor and I placed my hands on both sides of Chris's face and kissed him so deeply that I forgot where I was. I pushed him back into one of the chairs that sat in front of my desk and stood before him as eight years melted away and once again I was seeing the man I once loved so deeply. The only man I'd ever allowed myself to love that way. I thought I saw a tear in his eye as I lifted my skirt and climbed on top of him. I could see how badly he wanted me, how much he'd missed me. Chris hadn't been lying to me. The love he felt for me was present all over his body. I felt it as I sat on top of him, loving him hard, the way he had loved me for the past eight years. He held on to me tightly as I rocked slowly back and forth for what seemed like hours. Chris was a master at controlling himself. He could make love last longer than any man I'd ever known. He hadn't lost his touch. Even after we'd both reached our peaks, Chris held on to me. He relaxed his head onto my chest as I stroked the back of his head. I looked down into his face and saw that his eyes were closed as if he were caught up in a wonderful fantasy that he never wanted to end. I kissed the top of his head and slowly guided myself up until I was back on my feet in front of him. My skirt came tumbling back down to the middle of my thigh as Chris sat smiling and staring at me like I was a wonder girl.

I smiled briefly, then straightened out my clothes, picked up my purse and keys from the floor, and headed toward the office door.

"Wha . . . What? Madison?" Chris said as he stood up and turned around with his pants still around his ankles. "What's going on?" he asked as if he'd suddenly awakened from a bad dream.

"Good-bye, Chris," I said and opened the door quickly. "It's been real, but I gotta go."

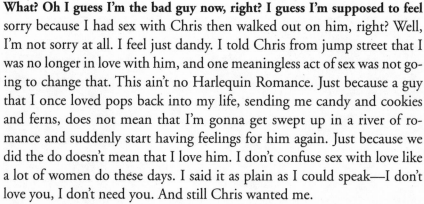

6

What? Oh I guess I'm the bad guy now, right? I guess I'm supposed to feel sorry because I had sex with Chris then walked out on him, right? Well, I'm not sorry at all. I feel just dandy. I told Chris from jump street that I was no longer in love with him, and one meaningless act of sex was not going to change that. This ain't no Harlequin Romance. Just because a guy that I once loved pops back into my life, sending me candy and cookies and ferns, does not mean that I'm gonna get swept up in a river of romance and suddenly start having feelings for him again. Just because we did the do doesn't mean that I love him. I don't confuse sex with love like a lot of women do these days. I said it as plain as I could speak—I don't love you, I don't need you. And still Chris wanted me.

By the time I got home, I had five messages on my machine. All from Chris. "Don't you have any feelings? What kind of woman are you? I love you. I want you. Need you. Please take me back." Oh puleeze! He sounded just like a bitch. I wanted to barf. Now I know how men feel when a woman keeps riding their ass. Calling day and night asking for another chance when they know the man doesn't want them to begin with. That's how Chris sounded. Like a scorned woman. It was sickening. But yet and still, after I told him I wasn't in love with him, that I didn't want him back, that I had no feelings for him, and even after I left him in a stupor, half dressed with his dick hanging out in the middle of my office, he still wanted me. Idiot. In his final message he said that no matter what, he still loved me, would always love me, and hoped that one day soon I'd realize that I loved him too and would stop playing games and admit it. Games? He thinks I'm playing games? It wasn't a game when he cheated on me eight years ago and left me high and dry. It wasn't a game when he broke my heart. It wasn't a game when I realized that I'd never be able to completely trust a man again. And it's not a game now. Was he really that stupid to think he still had a chance with me? Why doesn't he just accept the fact that I'm too through with him and get on with his life? I've said it before and I'll say it again—it's over. O-v-e-r, over.

I called in sick to work this morning. I was way overdue for a mental health day. But I wasn't sick or even tired. I just needed a day to rest my mind. To regroup, to chill out. When I called in to the administration office, Malik answered the phone and I could tell by the snip in his voice that he still had an attitude with me about the way I talked to him yesterday. I told him that I was sorry for not being more enthused about his upcoming dedication ceremony and asked him to stop by my house after work so we could talk. But he wouldn't agree to come by until I told him what had me in such a bad mood the day before. "My secret admirer is an asshole," I told him. "It's Chris."

I bitched and whined for nearly thirty minutes about what had happened the night before, and when I was done, Malik had but one question for me.

"Do you still love him?"

"Hell the fuck no, I don't still love that no good son of a bitch."

"Then why are you still so upset?"

"Because I resent like hell that that bastard thinks he can just bust back in my life and expect me to forgive and forget. I'm not some stupid teenager anymore. I'm grown. And I'm far from a fool."

"That's right. Both of you are grown now. And from what you've told me, it sounds like the brother has grown enough to realize he messed up. He was just a kid back then."

"Whose side are you on?"

"I'm on the side of love," Malik said blissfully. "You think Tyrone has never done me wrong? Shit. We've broken up so many times that I've lost count. But I tell you one thing, Madison. Love always wins in the end. Love always wins."

Well wasn't that a beautiful story? "I gotta go," I said as I felt my stomach turn.

"Alright. See you around six."

"Peace," I said and hung up the phone, hoping Malik would get over his sappy sentimental bullshit by the time he showed up at my door.

I moseyed around the house in my pajamas for most of the morning. The phone kept ringing, and since I knew it was probably Chris, I turned down the volume on the answering machine and let it pick up all my calls. I didn't even open the door to get the morning paper till after eleven o'-clock, but before I read it, I remembered Mother's car and called up James and asked him to meet me at Mom's around two to see if there was anything he could do to salvage the old woman's hooptie. I'd offer to put a down payment on a new one for her, but Miss I Can Do All Things On My Own wouldn't hear of that. It's already going to be hard enough to get Mother to accept a check from me to help her out with Serena's medication. I was still pissed off that she would let Serena cut back on her meds instead of coming to me for some help. But Mother was like that. Always trying to make it on her own. Still, I was going to help out. If she wouldn't take the money from me, I'd just give it to Serena. What's important here is that Serena is well and has her medication, not Mother's stupid pride. If she's too stubborn to accept money from me she should at least call up good old Cleophus McGuire and ask him for it. But that will be the day.

Speaking of the sorry son of a bitch better known as my daddy, I thought to myself as I opened up my morning paper and turned to the obituaries. Maybe today is my lucky day. Maybe his name will be listed among the dead, where it rightfully belongs. I scanned the obits as I mumbled his name, "Cleophus McGuire, Cleophus McGuire." A no-show as usual, but what else is new? I sat down on the sofa with my paper and scanned the obits again, just to make sure I hadn't overlooked my daddy's name, and my eyes kept coming back to one name in particular. Ronald Olbright. *Ronald Olbright.* Where did I know that name? *Ronald Olbright.* I put the paper on my lap and tried to remember why that name sounded so familiar. But nothing came to me. I picked up the paper again and read the lines that appeared under his name. Age, thirty-five. Survived by his mother and sister and a host of nieces and nephews. Ronald Olbright was an ex–running back for the Los Angeles Vipers . . . A running back for the Los Angeles Vipers? *Ronald Olbright, thirty-five, running back, L.A. Vipers?* "Oh my God," I whispered and put the paper down again. I know him. I sort of dated him. Ronald Olbright. He's dead? Damn.

It was about four or five years ago when I first met Ronald, and I must admit, looking back on our one and only date now brings a slight taste of shame to my mouth. I'm not proud of the way I met Ronald or of the way I acted on our date. I guess that's why I've sorta blocked his name from my mind. I wish that night had never happened, but it did, and it's something I have to live with for the rest of my life.

I've always been a big sports fan. Football is my favorite. Most women can't stand the stuff, but I don't think they know what they're missing. I could sit for hours in front of the TV watching those big, burly men in those tight pants, bending over and rolling around on the grass. Woo, I just love it. So five years ago, when Malik called me up and told me he had an extra ticket to go see the L.A. Vipers, I jumped to attention. Back then Vipers tickets were hard to come by. They were the hottest football team on the West Coast, due in no small part to the expertise of Ronald Olbright, or Ronnie-O, as everyone called him at the time. He was the Vipers' star player and as a matter of fact, he scored three touchdowns that night Malik and I attended the game. I sat in awe as I watched him strut across the playing field. I was oblivious to everything and everybody except Ronnie-O. I knew all about him. He was the league's leader in touchdowns that year. He'd led the Vipers to two previous Super Bowl victories. He was last year's *Sports Illustrated* Man of the Year, and best of all, he was single and made over one and a half million dollars a year, and that wasn't including the money he made off those Nike and Gatorade commercials. Ronnie-O was the man.

Malik was well aware of my passion for football and also my crush on Ronnie-O. That's all I talked about during the game, and after it was over, Malik surprised me and pulled out two locker room passes from his pocket and told me we had permission to go meet the players. I almost passed out. I don't know how he got those passes, who he bribed or begged or killed. I was too excited to ask. I just kissed Malik and shouted, "Thank you, thank you, thank you." After all those years of watching and lusting after Ronnie-O through my TV, I was on my way to meet him.

But when we got outside the locker room, I came to find that I wasn't the only one interested in getting an up-close and personal glance at Mr. Olbright. Not only was the corridor filled with a slew of reporters, but everywhere I turned there were women. Women, women, everywhere women. Women of all shapes, sizes, and ages. Most of them looked like they'd just stepped off the pages of *Playboy*. I could tell just by the volumes of cleavage that they were all looking to nab a rich, professional football player. They were groupies. Women who did nothing all day but get their hair and nails done so they could come out to the games, stand around in their tight skirts, and hope to catch the eye of one of the L.A. Vipers. I was disgusted. Didn't these women have any dignity? Didn't they know that even if they did grab one of the players' attention, all he'd do is take her home, fuck her brains out, then kick her to the curb? I swear, women can be so stupid sometimes.

I'd soon grown tired of the freak show and asked Malik, the only male in the bunch besides the reporters, if we could please go home. But just as we were about to depart, the locker room doors came flying open and out stepped the man of the hour—Ronnie-O. The corridor went crazy. The reporters began shouting out questions and the girls began bumping into one another as they vied for the perfect spot to position themselves in order to show off their best sides, usually their behinds, to the players. I had the best position, though. Malik and I stood right next to the exit, just left of the locker room doors, and after signing a couple autographs and answering a few media questions, Ronnie-O was headed straight in my direction. When he stopped in front of me I thought I was going to die. There was no way he could get out the door unless he picked me up and threw me to the side. He was all mine, but all I could do was smile and gaze at his sculpted body and perfect face. The same face that I'd watched for years on my TV screen. Then Malik nudged me and snapped me out of my daze and I finally opened my mouth. "Oh Mr., I mean, Ronald. Uh, Ronnie," I said like a blubbering idiot. "May I have an autograph?"

"Yeah. No problem," he said, looking around at the crowd of people behind him. "Where's your paper?" he asked and eyed me.

Paper? Damn. I shot Malik a look and he patted his pockets, but all he came up with was a pen. I took it and handed it to Ronnie, who stood watching me like he was both bored and embarrassed. He sighed as I fidgeted around as if a piece of paper was going to magically fall from the sky. Then he said something that I wasn't prepared for. "What's your name?" he asked and stared at me as if suddenly he was seeing me in a new light.

Damn. What was my name? "Madison," I finally shot out. "Madison McGuire."

"You like to party, Madison?"

Huh? Party? Me? "Oh yeah," I said, trying to be cool. "I like to get my boogie on."

"Well, look here. Me and some of the fellas are getting together back at my place. I got plenty of paper there."

"Huh?"

"The autograph?"

"Oh yeah. Yeah. Party at your place?"

"You down?"

"Down to the ground," I said, trying to sound as hip as possible.

"Cool. You'll ride with me."

Cool. I'll ride with you. "Sure. That's fine," I said, but I don't think he was asking a question.

I was all set to walk out the door and follow Ronald wherever he'd lead, until, that is, Malik caught me by the arm and raised his eyebrow. "Are you sure about this?" he tried to whisper. "You don't even know this guy."

"Say, man," Ronnie-O stepped in like he was my big brother. "Why you trying to cock-block?"

Cock-block? I really needed to bone up on my slang.

Malik stared at me for another second, then threw his hand into the air and backed off. And I, Madison McGuire, ran off with Ronald Olbright, a man I didn't even know. As soon as we got into the car I knew I'd made a mistake. Big mistake. It was as if being away from the crowd brought Ronald into a whole new light. He was just a man. Nothing special about him. He was sorta plain, actually. Yet there I sat riding in his black Ferrari as the music blasted all around me and Ronald ignored me. There I was going to the home of a man I barely knew. I'd been picked up like a prostitute. Like a horny tramp. Minutes ago I'd found myself disgusted by the women who fell all over themselves to get a look at Ronnie-O. Now, I was one of those women. A tramp. A hoochie.

By the time we made it to his home in the hills, which was the size of a castle, I was completely through with myself. What was I doing there? I kept asking. This wasn't my scene. When he opened the front door, I found the entire bottom floor packed with people as if they'd been there all night long. The music was pumping, drinks were exchanging hands, and the smell of marijuana filled every breatheable inch of air. This was definitely not my scene, but though I wanted to go home, I didn't want to make a fuss. I figured I'd just find myself a quiet corner, sit for an hour, then ask Ronald to take me home. When I turned to Ronald to tell him I couldn't stay very long, he was gone. I didn't see him again until I was in the corner of the television room, where I'd found a semiquiet spot to sit. Ronald was dancing in the middle of the room with some blond chick. Guess I wasn't his only date for the night. I sat back and tried to relax, but the smell of all the weed was giving me a contact buzz, and before long I found myself dozing off in my quiet little corner. But when I woke up the party was still going strong. I checked my watch and found it was one in the morning, long past my time to go. I got up from my seat and searched through the crowd for Ronnie, but he was nowhere to be found. So I searched for a phone instead so I could call a cab. But when I picked it up I could barely hear the dial tone for all the music. I had to find another phone. I tapped a guy who stood behind me and asked him if he knew where I could find another phone, but he couldn't hear me the first time. "A phone. Do you know where I can find a phone? . . . A PHONE."

"Right behind you," he said, pointing to the phone I'd just put down. Idiot.

Just as I was about to scream for holy mercy, another guy called over my shoulder. "Up the stairs, baby," he said and pointed me in the right direction. I thanked him and pushed my way back through the crowd toward the spiral staircase.

When I got upstairs it was like I'd entered another world. It was peaceful, and the smell of marijuana was far gone. I checked the corridor for a phone extension but couldn't find one, so I opened a huge door that I figured was the master suite and spotted a phone laying on a sofa in the sitting area of the room. I headed directly to it, but this time, before I could even dial . . .

"Millicent," Ronnie called to me.

"It's Madison, " I said and spun around. But when I did, I noticed that Ronnie didn't quite look the same. He was as high as a kite. I looked him over, trying to estimate how many drinks and joints he'd taken to get to the degree of ugliness he had achieved. He eyed me lovingly. Like a pet. A dog. A bitch. I felt like one. And as he approached me I felt like covering myself even though I was fully clothed.

"I've been looking all over for you," he said coming closer and closer.

"I was just about to call a cab, " I said uneasily, but for some reason I had the strangest feeling that I wasn't going anywhere. It was the strangest and saddest feeling I'd ever felt. There I was in this stranger's bedroom. He was high. I knew what he wanted from me. If I was honest with myself I'd have to admit that I'd known it ever since I was outside that locker room.

I wasn't different from any of those other girls who stood out there, and Ronald didn't see me any differently. For that night I was a two-bit whore. A groupie. A slut. That's the way Ronald saw me. That's the way I felt. I didn't even put up a fight when Ronald grabbed me by the waist and cupped my breast in his hand. He was rough with me. He didn't care. And I deserved everything I was about to get. He treated me like the whore I'd allowed myself to be. I didn't deserve better. A respectable woman does not wind up in the bedroom of a complete stranger at one o'clock in the morning. What was I supposed to do now? Scream "no"? I should have done that a long time ago. But I was too intrigued by this man who meant nothing to me. Now I had to take my punishment. I felt like a prisoner on death row. A dead woman walking. I knew I'd committed a crime just by being there, and now I had to pay the price. He laid me facedown on the bed and ripped off my clothes and entered me through my rear. He came in two minutes, then rolled over and passed out. My punishment was quick; still, it was painful. When I got up to go to the bathroom, I found I was bleeding. I was in so much pain that I wanted to cry, but I didn't. Whores don't cry. I just stuffed my panties with tissue, then washed my face with cold water. When I came out the bathroom, Ronald was up again, hunched over the side of the bed and leaning on the nightstand. When he heard me he paused a second, looked over his shoulder, then went back to his business. As I walked to the bedroom door I saw him stick a needle in his left arm. I watched as he injected himself, heaved, then rolled his head back and fell down across the bed. I didn't call a cab, I just got out. I walked from the hills of Hollywood to Pico and Fairfax and never once did I look back. I'd have to live with the memory of that night forever. The lowest night of my life.

The next year, I heard on the news that Ronald had been suspended from the Vipers after failing a routine drug examination. He never played pro ball again. As I sat on the sofa, suffocating myself in old memories, I read Ronald's obituary once more. No cause of death was listed, but that must be normal with drug overdoses. The funeral was to be held today at four o'clock at a church in Inglewood. I put down the paper and decided I had to be there. I don't know why. I just had to go to that funeral.

Though I knew he was in class, I picked up the phone and called Malik on his pager. He called me back during the noon lunch break and I asked him to meet me at the church around a quarter to four. Malik agreed immediately. Though I never told him what had happened that night after I left with Ronald, I knew he suspected. I'd seen the look in his eyes that next day at work. He knew I'd been a tramp, but he never asked for the details.

I hung up the phone with Malik and got up to get dressed. I had just enough time to stop by Mom's and meet James before I went off to the funeral. As I drove to Mom's I kept asking myself why it was so important for me to attend this funeral. I'd met the man one time. One sleazy, unforgivable time, yet I still wanted to go to his funeral. Why? All I could figure was that maybe I felt the need to be at his funeral so I could put closure on that one night. The one night that even to this day still brings shame to me when I think of it.

■

I pulled in front of my mother's house at the same time as James. He was driving one of those gigantic Suburban trucks that took up at least three normal car lengths in front of the house, so I had to park across the street. The side doors of James's truck were painted white and had the words *James Taylor Auto Mechanic* stenciled in black. When he got out the truck I noticed he wasn't wearing his blue overalls that he usually wore whenever he was about to work on a car. Instead, he was decked out in a pair of brown slacks and a matching long-sleeve polo shirt, and I knew from the second I laid eyes on him that he had more on his mind than just fixing Mother's car. I smiled and waved as I crossed the street, and when I got in front of him he wrapped me up in his arms and kissed me softly on the cheek. Yep, I thought as I pulled myself out of his strong grip. James thinks he's gonna get some tonight, I thought as he eyed me with sweet anticipation. James is a nice guy but I'm really not in the mood for any dates tonight, so if that's what's behind those fancy pants, the shirt, and that bear hug he just gave me, he can forget it. I hate to be that way with James since he's always been so nice to me. Whenever I need my car fixed he's right there. But dating James is another matter. Whenever we go out, I start to feel sorry for him. That big-ass truck he drives is not only his work vehicle, it's his house. James has been living out of that truck ever since his mechanic business started to take a fall a couple years ago. Now, don't get me wrong, I'm not some snooty, stuck-up wench who only dates men with money. I knew James was living out of his truck before I ever went out with him. It's just that whenever we date I find myself feeling sorry for him, and since I'm making pretty good money I always try to pick up the check, which always turns into a big argument between us. I call myself being nice, but James calls it being indignant. "I wouldn't have asked you out if I couldn't pay for the date," he always says. And I think, "But you can't even pay rent. How can you afford steak and lobster?"

Even when he comes over to tune up my car, he refuses to accept money from me. I tell James he's just being silly and that he should at least charge me half price or something. But James won't hear of it. That's why I don't like to date him anymore. Not because I don't like him, but because I know he can't afford me. If James had it his way, he'd take me out every night of the week. He'd work on a car or two during the day, then take every dime he made and spend it on me that night. I can't let James do that. I can't use people like that.

"You're looking mighty fine in that black outfit," James said as we walked to Mother's front door.

"You don't look so bad yourself," I said as I took out my spare key. "I hope you don't get oil and grease all over yourself."

"Oh I ain't worried about that," he said and stopped me just as I was about to unlock the door. "Say," he whispered as if we were in a crowded room. "How 'bout we go get a bite to eat after I finish with your mother's car?"

I hated to hurt his feelings, but . . . "Sorry, James," I said in a squeaky, apologetic tone. "I've got a funeral to go to later."

"Oh, oh," he said and backed away from me. "I understand," he said quickly, trying to regain his composure, but I could tell his feelings were hurt. James had probably been anticipating this moment ever since I rang him up this morning.

"How about sometime next week?" I asked, hoping to take the sting out of turning him down.

"Sure," he said weakly, then cleared his throat. "Next week."

I smiled and patted his shoulder, wishing I'd agreed to go out with him anyway. Life was already hard enough on the man without me coming along and breaking his spirit. I unlocked the front door and held it open for James as my way of apologizing for stomping all over his hopes of having a date with me, but James was too much of a gentleman to let me pacify him.

"After you, lady," he said and showed me a smile to let me know his heart wasn't completely broken.

"Thanks," I said as I walked into Mother's living room. I took only two steps before I paused in the middle of the floor and peered into the kitchen. "What the hell?" I said and squinted at my mother as she sat at the dinette table across from—whom else?—Chris. "Mother," I yelled as she looked up from her coffee cup.

"What are you doing here?" she said and stood up. When she saw James behind me she found the answer to her question. Chris said nothing as he sat at the table peering in my direction. What was he doing here again? Crying on my mother's shoulder? Telling her all his problems in the hope that maybe she'd be able to talk me into getting back together with him?

"What the hell is he doing here?" I asked and pointed a stiff finger in Chris's direction.

"Madison," mother scolded as she walked to the living room and smiled a quick hello to James. Her smile vanished when she turned to me again. "Chris is fixing my car."

"No, Mother. I told you I was having James take a look at your car."

"Well Chris—"

"Chris has no business being here."

"Hey, this is my house," Mother said forcefully. "Chris is welcome in my home anytime."

"Maybe I should go," James said, realizing there was more going on here than what was actually going on.

"No," I said and turned to him.

"Well," Chris butted in as he stood up from the table. "I checked out the car. All it needs is a new fuel pump," he said as he completely ignored me and walked over to James. He put his arm around James's shoulder and ever so gently eased him toward the door. "I've taken care of everything around here," he said as he patted James's back and opened the door.

"James," I said and ran to the door. "You don't have to leave."

"No, it's okay. I've got a carburetor to go fix," he lied as he put on a smile and waved good-bye to my mother.

"Bastard," I said and turned around to face Chris.

"Watch your mouth," Mother jumped in, but I paid her no attention.

"Who are you to get rid of my company?" I asked, staring at him with my hands on my hips. "Why are you hanging around here? Don't you have a job?"

He took too long to answer me. "For your information, I don't start work at the free clinic until next month. In the meantime, I'm trying to buy a house and—"

"Just get out, Chris."

"You hold on," Mother said as she got closer to Chris and me. "This is my house," she said and took a place next to Chris. Somehow I felt they were ganging up on me. "Chris is staying here for a while."

"What?"

"That's right," Mother said unapologetically. "I told Chris there was no need for him to pay that high price for that hotel he was staying in when there was a decent bed right here for him to lay his head on."

Chris smiled at me victoriously. This was all a part of his master plan. He didn't give up. "It's just for a while until the deal closes in on my new house," he said with a grin. "Looks like we are going to be seeing a lot of each other, Madison."

I couldn't believe it. I couldn't stand for this. "As long as he's here, Mother," I said, peeling my eyes off Chris and turning to her. "As long as he's here, you don't have a daughter." I whipped myself around and raced for the front door.

"Hold it, Madison," Chris said. "Let me talk to you."

I flung open the door and walked out. I think I heard Mother say, "Just let her go," but I couldn't be sure. Chris flew by me and beat me to my car. He stood in front of my door and I didn't hesitate to swing my purse at his head. He ducked just in time and grabbed my purse by the strap and held on to it as we proceeded to play tug-of-war until finally the strap broke. Chris laughed. "I'm sorry," he said, holding my purse in his hand while I gripped the broken strap.

"What the fuck are you snickering about?" I said and kicked my foot toward his knee. He moved out the way and my foot went ramming into the side of my car. *Shiit*, I screamed silently, though I felt like yelling out in agony.

"I'll buy you a new one," he said, still snickering.

"I don't want you buying me shit," I told him as my foot throbbed. "I just want you to leave me and my family alone. How many times do I have to say that?"

"I know you still love me."

"No, Chris. I don't. I really don't."

"What about last night?" he asked childishly. "Was that revenge sex?"

"Call it what you want."

"You're kidding yourself."

"No, you're kidding yourself. I do not love you, Chris. Leave me alone, leave my family alone. Just *leave*."

"I can't!"

"Why?"

" 'Cause this is the only family I've got!"

He stood still as a rock. As if he couldn't believe he'd just admitted that. At that moment, I could feel Chris's pain so deeply that it frightened me. I . . . we were all he had now. That's why he's here. That's why he can't let go. Instantly I started to cry. I don't know what came over me, but I was crying like a baby. Chris stared at me in shock, but no one was more shocked than I. Where were these tears coming from? Maybe I had too much on my mind with Chris, the funeral, the old memories. Or maybe it was PMS. Whatever it was, it had me tripping. Chris was so shocked that he started apologizing, though I could tell he didn't know what he was apologizing for.

"I'm sorry. Can I get you anything? Are you hurt?"

Well, my foot was killing me, but other than that . . . "Just let me go," I said as I took what was left of my purse out of his hand and opened my car door. I got in and sat for a moment, then rolled down my window and looked up at Chris as he stood in the middle of the street.

"If you really love me, you'll back off."

I could see in his eyes that he wanted to protest, but he let me finish what I had to say.

"Eight years ago may have been just a childhood fling to you, but for me it was real. I loved you with all my heart and you abused that love. Yeah, we were both young, but that doesn't mean it wasn't painful. But I'm gonna be honest with myself right now—for once," I said and paused, trying to find the right words. "I'll admit that somewhere deep inside, somewhere lodged between my rib cage and pancreas, is a small spot that still has your name on it."

Now I saw hope in his eyes, but I didn't want him to get carried away.

"It's a very tiny spot, Chris. And it's covered up with years of tough, concrete layers. I need you to back the fuck off. I need you to respect me and the words I say. Give me some time."

He nodded his head obediently and for the first time I was certain that he understood what I was saying. I started my engine and slowly rolled my window back up.

"I'll call you," he said and waved.

"No, Chris. *I'll* call *you*—when or if I'm ready."

"Right," he said and backed his way to the curb as I drove off.

■

The outside of the church looked deserted. I'd expected it to be packed with media, fans, old players from the Vipers, but there was hardly anyone present. There was one reporter, but he didn't even go inside. Just scribbled words on a pad and soon walked off. I guess no one cared about Ronald after he got kicked off the Vipers. Fame is fleeting, or so they say.

"Hey, Madi," Malik called and I turned around to find him walking up behind me. He was frowning like the world had come to an end. "You'll never guess what happened at work."

Oh shit, I thought to myself and put my hands on my hips. "What?" I asked, not wanting to hear anything about whatever had gone wrong. All I wanted to do was focus on this funeral, not stress myself any further over the minutiae of work.

"Thompson definitely knows what's up. For real this time," he said anxiously. "He showed up at my office after school, talking some bullshit about reading the school policy on teacher conduct. When I asked him why, all he said was, 'You know why,'" Malik said, mimicking Tommy's deep voice.

I squeezed my forehead with my fingers and tried to figure out what Tommy was up to.

"Madison," Malik called, noticing my mind had drifted off.

"Yeah, yeah," I said and sighed. "He told me the same thing. I think you're right. He knows something."

"So what do we do?"

"How many parents' names do we have so far?"

"A hundred and forty-eight."

"Alright," I said and gritted my teeth. "We'll take our proposal to him tomorrow. The shit's about to hit the fan."

"And what if he goes off?"

"We'll deal with that when it happens. Remember, we've got the support of over a hundred tuition-paying parents."

"Alright then," he said and grabbed my hand. "We'll deal with this tomorrow."

"You know, Malik," I said and paused. "On second thought I think you should let me talk to Thompson alone."

"I can't do that, Madi. If he goes off, I want to be there to back you up."

"Trust me, Malik. I know Tommy. Let me do this by myself. I'll be alright."

He shook his head no, but I shook mine right back.

"I'll handle Tommy," I said and pulled Malik up the front of the church steps. "Trust me on this. I can handle Tommy Thompson."

It was quiet inside the church and besides the two of us, there were only five other people present. One lady I assumed was Ronald's mother stood over the closed casket, crying a river. She looked like an older, female version of Ronald except for the fact that her hair was completely gray. In the front pew sat another couple and behind them two more. Neither of them were crying. They just sat quietly with their heads bowed. Malik and I took seats in the third row.

"I expected more people," Malik whispered and leaned toward me.

"So did I," I said and stared as Ronald's mother tried to compose herself enough to sit down.

One more person came in after Malik and me, and she sat down next to me. She barely looked up at anyone. Just sat there shaking her head and gripping a Bible between her knees. Just as the reverend took to the podium she began howling like a wolf. I searched my purse for a tissue, but all I could find was my silk Anne Klein II scarf. I handed it to the woman and she took it and blotted her eyes, but continued to cry. Loudly. So loudly that I could barely hear the reverend's eulogy. For a second there I thought the poor woman was having some sort of attack by the way she cried and lifted her hands in the air. "Why, Lord?" she said and shook her head. "I told that boy. I told him, I told him, I told him."

Was this Ronald's girlfriend? Wife? Sister? Had she warned him about the dangers of drugs?

The woman began to rock back and forth in her seat and finally she just gave up and ran out the church. I don't know why I followed her. Maybe it was because I felt for her. Maybe it was because I wanted to soothe her. Or maybe it was because I didn't want her to run off with my fifty-dollar AK II scarf. Whatever the reason, I went after her and found her kneeling in the hallway just outside the double doors. I stood watching her as she heaved up and down. When she saw that she wasn't alone, she tried to stifle her tears, but they were just too overpowering.

"You knew my cousin?" she asked as she stood to her feet.

I nodded and closed the distance between us.

"I tried to tell that boy," she said again as she looked at me through watered eyes. "Over and over," she said, and blotted with my scarf. "Leave them drugs alone. Leave 'em alone."

"I know," I said and reached out for her hand and suddenly found my own self in tears. She grabbed me by the neck and pulled me to her and held on to me like she'd known me for years.

I rubbed her back and kept telling her everything was going to be alright, but that was a lie. Ronald was dead at the age of thirty-five. Nothing was right about that.

I saw Malik step out the double doors and look in my direction as if to say, "Is everything alright?" I nodded as he came closer to us, then pulled away from Ronald's cousin and looked her in the eyes.

"You think you're ready to go back in now?" I asked as she trembled in my grasp. "I know it must be hard. Having someone you love die of a drug overdose at such a young age. But I promise, Ronald's in a better place now."

She looked at me curiously and shook her head slowly. "Drug overdose?" she said, questioning me with her eyes. "Don't you know? Ronald didn't OD," she said as tears rolled down her cheeks.

I gave Malik a curious look and he shrugged his shoulders. I looked back at Ronald's cousin and asked, "How did he die?"

She shut her eyes as if the words were just too painful for her. "AIDS," she said, then opened her eyes toward the ceiling. "My cousin died of AIDS."

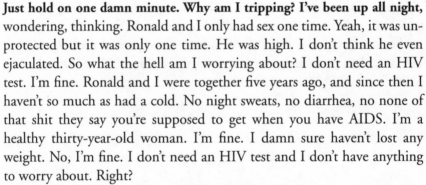

7

Just hold on one damn minute. Why am I tripping? I've been up all night, wondering, thinking. Ronald and I only had sex one time. Yeah, it was un-protected but it was only one time. He was high. I don't think he even ejaculated. So what the hell am I worrying about? I don't need an HIV test. I'm fine. Ronald and I were together five years ago, and since then I haven't so much as had a cold. No night sweats, no diarrhea, no none of that shit they say you're supposed to get when you have AIDS. I'm a healthy thirty-year-old woman. I'm fine. I damn sure haven't lost any weight. No, I'm fine. I don't need an HIV test and I don't have anything to worry about. Right?

Since I could hardly sleep anyway, I got up early this morning and came into work. Being out the day before, I wanted to get in early so I could go over my substitute teacher's notes and prepare for class, but more impor-tant, I wanted to be here bright and early, waiting on that asshole Tommy Thompson and looking for an explanation as to why he was suddenly so interested in how Malik and I were conducting ourselves.

I sat outside in the reception area of Tommy's office, waiting and seething and trying to keep my mind off yesterday's funeral. Trying not to think about Ronald, that night we spent together, his cousin, her words— AIDS. I never suspected. I knew Ronald's drug use would be the end of him, and though he didn't die of an overdose, drugs were the real culprit behind his early demise. How could he be so stupid to share needles? Hell, the guy was a millionaire. Couldn't he afford to get his own syringes? Probably, but I guess when you're high and out of your mind, you tend to fuck up.

Speaking of fuckups . . . "I want to talk to you right now," I said and caught Tommy just as he stepped off the elevator on his way to his office.

"Madison," he said, without stopping. "I always love to see your beautiful face first thing in the morning."

I followed him into his office and slammed the door behind me. "Playtime is over, Tommy."

"What are you talking about?" he said, placing his briefcase atop his desk and sitting down. I didn't answer that question. Instead I just stared in his direction until he became so self-conscious that he had to straighten out his tie. "Games?" he said and cleared his throat. "The only game I play with you is the game of love," he said as he tried to make himself comfortable, but the anger in my eyes kept him off guard. "So," he said, finally relaxing enough to put on a fake grin. "How was your day off yesterday?"

"I know you know, Tommy."

"Excuse me?" he said, leaning over his desk. "You know I know what?"

"Look," I said and walked closer to his desk, knowing I had only one shot to get out everything I wanted to say before I caught major hell. "I've read the school policy on teacher conduct and there is nothing in there that states that what Malik and I have done is wrong. As a matter of fact, we followed the rules to the tee. Not only have we put our proposal for adding sex education to the students' curriculum in writing, we've also garnered the names of one hundred and forty-eight parents who agree with us." I pulled my attaché from my shoulder and opened it up. "Here," I said and plopped the proposal down on the middle of his desk. "Read it for yourself," I said and put my hands on my hips as Tommy cautiously picked it up. "Our position is this, Tommy. We are not trying to drastically change this school's curriculum. However, due to recent events it has become obvious to us that our students are missing out on a very fundamental aspect of their education. We feel a course in sex education will help us groom our students into socially responsible beings. Beings who are aware of their sexuality and the consequences of their sexuality. We need to teach these kids that it's okay to say no to sex, and if they don't, we need to teach them to be responsible with themselves. I know you feel that sex education has nothing to do with these students' academic futures, but it has everything to do with forming well-rounded, socially aware young adults. And in conclusion," I said, pausing to catch my breath. "The bottom line is the parents are behind this proposal. So before you dismiss this, remember, the parents and their fat pocketbooks are the ones that keep this school going."

Woo, I thought to myself as I leaned over Tommy's desk. I had been talking so fast that I could barely remember what I'd said, and by the confused look on Tommy's face you would have thought I had been speaking in another language. I pushed back off his desk and waited anxiously for his response. Finally he tilted back in his chair and slowly, deliberately clapped his hands. After he was done mocking me, however, he picked up the proposal once again and flipped through the pages.

"I had no idea," he said, then slid the proposal across his desk. "No idea at all."

"Yeah right, Tommy," I said and sucked my teeth.

"No, Madison," he said sincerely. "I had no idea about any of this. But after listening to your *long* speech," he said and raised a brow, "I guess I'll have to take this under serious consideration."

Huh, I thought and watched Tommy like an eagle. If he had no idea about any of this, then why all the innuendos? Why was he hinting around that Malik and I weren't conducting ourselves properly? What kind of game was Tommy playing now?

"Well, Madison," he said and stood up behind his desk. "If that is all . . ."

"You don't have any questions for me?"

"No. Your speech said it all. By the look of this proposal you've done your homework. I'll let you know my decision soon."

And that's it, I thought. Too easy. Too strange. I turned around and headed for the door, but as usual, Tommy had one more thing to say. "Oh, Madison," he called to me as I stopped in the middle of the room.

"Tommy?"

"How's Malik?"

I paused for a second and thought what a strange question that was. Since when was he the least bit concerned about the welfare of Malik? "What?" I asked and turned back around to face him.

"I said, how's Malik? You know, your gay friend?"

I ran a hand over my braids and paused again. "Gay friend?" I said, trying to play it off. "What do you mean, my gay friend?"

"Come, come now, Madison," Tommy said and sat back down in his chair. "Don't you know by now that I know everything about my employees?"

"I don't know what you're talking about, Tommy. But since you asked, Malik is fine. Now why don't you tell me what you're really getting at."

"Nothing," he said, too quickly. "I just like to know how all my employees are doing. It's nothing."

Nothing? It was obviously something, but I didn't know what to say or what to even make of Tommy's comments, so I just shut my mouth and went to the door.

"You know, I'd be able to come to a decision about this proposal much faster if you'd just agree to have dinner with me," he said, adding his final comments as I opened his office door. I hate him, I thought and gave him my response—a stiff middle finger.

I decided my next stop had to be Malik's office. I didn't know exactly what Tommy was getting at with all his questions about Malik, but I knew I had to let my friend in on what was said. When I got to Malik's office, I found him swamped with calls. We still had no receptionist and since I was off with Tommy, Malik had to put in work. Every line on his phone was lit up, so I sat down and waited for him to finish. It took him a good ten minutes to clear all his lines, and when he finished his last call, he slammed down the phone and said, "Well?"

"I told him."

"And?"

"He said he'd take the proposal under consideration and get back with me soon."

"And?"

"And nothing."

"That's it."

"It."

"No tirades, no 'How dare you plot to change my school behind my back'?"

"Not a thing. I don't think he even saw it coming."

Malik frowned, obviously not believing that statement.

"I'm serious. He looked shocked when I told him about it."

"Then what was up with all the 'Have you read the teachers' policy' bullshit?" he asked, faking Thompson's voice.

"I haven't the slightest idea," I said as the phone rang out and Malik snatched it up.

As I waited for him to finish, my mind kept going back to Tommy, and I had to let Malik know that his secret was out. Still, I didn't quite know how to approach the subject. Malik had tried so hard to be discreet about his lifestyle, and now that Tommy of all people was nosing into his business, I knew he'd be plenty pissed. But before I could get into his personal business, he jumped into mine.

"Are you okay?" he asked as he hung up the phone. He asked the question with so much concern that for a second there I thought I was sick or something.

"Yeah," I said and gave him a smile. "I'm fine."

"You didn't look fine after the funeral yesterday."

"I was just in shock. It was bad enough knowing Ronald was dead, but to find out he died of AIDS? That blew my mind."

Malik got really quiet for a second there, and I knew my friend was about to get serious with me. "So," he said, obviously not sure how to ask his next question. "What are you going to do?"

"Do about what?"

"Well," he said as nonchalantly as he could muster. "Ronald died of AIDS . . ."

"Yeah. And?"

"Okay, look," he said and put all bullshitting aside. "I know we never talked about it, but . . . well . . . I mean, you two did do the do. Didn't you?"

"Yeah. Once. And?"

"Well, I'm just saying. You don't get AIDS on Monday and die on Tuesday," he said, waving his hand around for emphasis. "The brother was probably infected for a while. Years, even. Five years, even."

"You think I got AIDS?"

"No," he said, sternly. "No, no, no, no, no. I'm just saying that if you wanted to . . . I mean if you felt like it was necessary . . . I mean—"

"You think I should get tested?"

"No," he said and shook his head hard. "I mean, we both know you don't have it."

"I don't have it."

"Hell no, you don't have it," he said, still shaking his head. "Not in a million years do you have it."

"That's right."

"Absolutely right. I'm just saying, if you wanted to, if you felt up to it, you might just wanna go take the test."

"You think?"

"Maybe. I don't know."

"Maybe I should. I mean, just to be sure."

"If you wanted to. Of course, we already know what the results are going to be."

"Negative."

"Positively negative."

"Should I do it?"

"If you want."

"How long will I have to wait for the results?"

"Three, four days."

"Three, four days? Why does it take so long?"

"Hell, I don't know. Just because I'm gay doesn't mean I've got the inside track on AIDS info."

"Have you ever been tested?"

"Five times."

"Five?"

"Yeah. Twice before I got with Tyrone. Then when we got serious we went for tests together every six months until we were sure both of us were negative. Now that we've been together for three years we don't get tested anymore."

"Will I need to get tested that much?"

"Girl, I don't know. How much unprotected sex have you been having?"

"Ronald was the only time . . . Oh wait a minute. There was that time with Benson—it was a spontaneous thing, you know. And there was Terrence, just recently and—"

"Damn, girl. Don't you know you always got to put on the jimmy?"

"I know, Malik. But sometimes you forget about that step, you know?" The look Malik gave me after I said that left me feeling rather stupid. "Then other times, it's just too awkward asking a guy if he has a condom. They always give you that look, like, I ain't got no disease. Then you feel sorry for questioning them so you just give in and go with the flow," I said, trying to explain, but Malik wasn't taken in by my excuses. I felt like I was sitting there with a big floppy hat on my head with the word "Duh" plastered across the brim. "But what the hell does it matter? I don't have anything anyway. Never even had a yeast infection," I said, trying to regain my dignity.

"It doesn't matter what you have. The point is you don't know what *they* have. Did Ronald look like he had AIDS? Hell no. Does Magic Johnson look like he's about to keel over?"

"So you're telling me you use a condom each and every time you have sex."

"Not now that I've been in a committed relationship for the past three years. But when Tyrone and I first got together, hell yeah, I put that jimmy on. I wore one every time until we took our third test and it came back negative. And before Tyrone, girl, you best believe I was packing protection. Shit, condoms are like American Express cards. I never leave home without 'em." Malik looked at me like I was crazy to even think for a second that he would not use a condom. And I sat across from him feeling like a stupid child. There I was, a grown woman, smart, on the ball, but too dumb to protect herself from disease.

"So you think I should be tested?"

"I don't think you're HIV positive, girl. You know that."

"So why get tested?"

"You don't have to."

"But I should, huh?"

"If you want to."

"I think I will. Just, you know, to be sure. Not 'cause I think I got something or nothing. I mean, I know I don't."

"Of course you don't."

"I'm negative."

"Of course you are."

"Right."

"Damn right."

"Then maybe I just don't need to be tested. It'll just be a waste of time, right?"

Malik didn't answer, but I'd made my decision anyway. I knew I'd been fucking up by not wearing a condom each and every time I had sex. I know it's stupid and a woman of my intelligence should know better. But from now on, I'll wear one. I'll even carry them around in my purse, you know, just in case I want a little spontaneity. But as far as getting tested? Please. I'm fine. I know it. Now . . . "Let's change the subject."

"Subject changed. Next topic."

"You and Tommy."

"Me and Tommy?" Malik said and cringed.

"When I talked to him this morning, he said something that sorta threw me off guard."

"Yeah," Malik said as I hesitated to continue.

"I think Tommy may know that you're gay," I said and frowned.

"Oh yeah," he said calmly without the least hint that he was upset that the secret he'd tried to shelter for so long was out.

"I don't know who told him or how he got a clue, but . . . Malik?" I said staring at him. "Aren't you upset?"

He sighed, then spun around in his seat to unlock the file cabinet behind him. He pulled out a stack of cards, searched through them, then pulled out one with my name on it and handed it to me. It was an invitation to his dedication ceremony. It was beautiful and elegant, just like a wedding invitation. It had a picture of him and Tyrone on the front in an embrace, and under their picture was the inscription, "When two are in love, they become one."

"I started passing them out yesterday," Malik said as he watched me read the card he'd given me. "I wanted you to be the first to have one, but what with the funeral and all . . ."

"You passed these out at work?"

He nodded. "I even took one up to Thompson's office personally," he said and smiled when I looked at him in dismay. "I'm thirty-four years old, Madison. I'm tired of hiding. Tyrone and I are tying the knot. We're doing the right thing. I'm not ashamed of that and I'm not ashamed of myself. I don't care who knows anymore. I'm gay and I'm proud. I'm coming out the closet."

Whoa. "Malik, I, I . . ." I didn't know what to say. For so long he'd been adamant about keeping his life private, and now this? "Are you sure you want to do this?"

"I'm doing it, baby," he said firmly without a shadow of doubt.

"You know I'm down for you, don't you?"

"I know."

I put the card on my lap and took a deep breath. "I didn't mean all that shit I said the other day in my office. I'm really happy for you, Malik. It's not every day we find someone we love and want to spend the rest of our lives with. And I just want you to know that I think you're doing the right thing," I said, staring at my friend and hoping he knew how deeply I meant my words. "I'm truly happy for you."

"I know you are," he said and flashed me a smile.

"So what can I do to help? I see you've already got the invitations."

Malik's face lit up. "Everything's pretty much set. We've got the reverend from the Everyone Is Loved Church to preside over the nuptials."

"Everyone Is Loved Church?"

"Yeah, that's the gay parish out in the San Gabriel Valley. The only damn place gay people can go worship without feeling like black sheep," he said and paused for a frown, then quickly perked up. "Anyway, the reception is being catered by Mo Better Greens."

"Oh shit. Hot water, corn bread, and collard greens."

"You better believe it, honey. Only the best. Only the best."

"Well, since you said that, you know I'm gonna be there, bright and early, with my knife and fork in hand."

"Oh you'll be there alright," Malik said and grinned. "I want you to stand up for me," he said seriously.

Huh? "You mean like a bridesmaid sorta thing?" I said, wincing.

"Sorta," he said and stood up to walk around his desk. "I don't care what you call it. I just want you to be there by my side. You're my best friend, Madi. I love you."

"Malik," I said and stood up, finding myself fully caught in his sentimental shit again. But I couldn't help myself. I was truly touched. "I'd be proud to be your matron of . . . your bride's m—"

"My best girl."

"Your best woman," I said and hugged him tightly. We were both so overwhelmed that we had to blot at our eyes when we released each other. But before we could be even more sappy, the phones took flight again.

Malik rolled his eyes back in his head. "I quit," he said as he rushed back to his desk and snatched up line one. I blew him a kiss as I left him to his phones and trudged down the hallway to my own office, where I figured my phones were probably just as bad. And as I approached my doorway it was just as I'd suspected. My phone was ringing off the hook.

"Mighty Avalon, Madison McGuire, may I help you?"

"Good morning, Madison."

"Mother?"

"Yes, dear. How are you this morning?"

Uh-oh. She's trying to sound pleasant. Something's up. "What you want?"

"Just to talk to my daughter."

"Serena will be home at the usual time."

"I want to talk to *you*."

"About . . ."

"How are you?"

"What do you want?"

"Nothing," she snapped, losing the concerned mother act. "You seen Christopher?"

I knew it. "No, Mother," I said and sighed. "He's your houseguest. Don't you see him every day?"

"Not since you came over here and scared the man off. He moved back to that high-priced hotel yesterday after you left, and I haven't seen him since. What the hell did you say to that man?"

So Chris moved out, I thought to myself and bit my bottom lip. He really did take my words seriously yesterday.

"What did you do to him, Madison?"

"Why?"

"Why? 'Cause he was paying rent, that's why. Three hundred dollars, dammit!"

"So you want him back for the money?"

"No, I don't, and don't you insult me like that. You know I love me some Chris. That boy is like my boy. It's just that I was planning on using that extra money to help with Serena's medication."

"I'll give you the money for Serena's medication."

"No, thank you."

"Excuse me?"

"I don't accept charity."

"But you'll take it from Chris?"

"I was providing a service for Chris," she said proudly. "Until you scared him away," she barked. "What did you do to him?"

"I asked him to respect my time and space."

"What? What kind of bourgie talk is that? Respect your time and space? You better respect a good man when you see one and get with the program. He ain't gonna wait around for you forever and a day. Why don't you call the man? Talk to him?"

"Mind your own business, Mother."

"Your business is my business. Now I'm telling you—"

"Good-bye, Mother," I said and pulled the phone away from my ear until I heard her scream out for me to wait. The threat of the impending dial tone always gets Mother to change her tune.

"I need you to pick up Serena from school today."

"Chris didn't fix your car?"

"You scared him off before he had a chance to finish. Once he got through talking with you, he came back inside, packed his bag, gave me a kiss on the forehead, and was out the door. You ought to be shame for breaking that man's heart."

Oh shut up. "I will pick up Serena and I will call James and ask him to come see about your car again. *Okay?*"

"Okay," she said and paused. Then, "Eight-five-three, three-thousand, penthouse number one," she said quickly.

"What?"

"That's the number to the Bonaventure Hotel. Chris is staying in penthouse number one. Call him," she said, and this time, she beat me to the dial tone.

I pulled the dead phone away from my ear and placed it back on the hook. I didn't realize I'd drifted into a daze until I caught myself tapping out an annoying beat on my desk with my fingers. I took my hands away from my desk, but I couldn't take my thoughts away from Chris, and here, once again, was my dilemma: Chris did me wrong. I don't care how you look at it, or how much you blame what happened to our relationship on the fact that we were both young. The man still hurt me. And yet, I can't get him off my mind. After all the pain he caused me, I still find myself wanting him. But why? Why do we women allow this? Why are we always attracted to the men that do us wrong? Men we know we shouldn't accept into our lives. I'd always prided myself on being a tough cookie. A woman who wouldn't take no shit from nobody, especially a two-timing man. Yet Chris was still on my mind. He was in my heart. Why? What was it about the bad guys that always makes us want them? Is it the challenge? The allure of danger? What? How could Chris do what he did to me and still be in my heart? Maybe it's because I'm just a fool. Or maybe it's because Chris isn't really one of the bad guys. Am I being stupid to believe that he was only trying to do what was right when he told me that he'd cheated on me before our marriage? Is it stupid to believe that he has never given up on me after eight years? Or am I just falling for the hype? Believing because I want to believe. Believing because somewhere deep inside of me is a needy damsel in distress. A fairy-tale princess who, though she talks a big game about never needing a man in her life, is really just waiting for her prince to return and sweep her off her feet and take her to a better world. Do I believe Chris and give him another chance? Or do I close the door and walk on with life the way I've been doing for the past eight years? Playing the field, dating whom I want, never letting anyone get too close, never feeling the love, the true love of a real man who really loves me and whom I really love back. What do I do? Decisions, decisions . . .

■

I was in my car waiting on Serena at three-thirty on the dot. I was in a rush to pick her up and get her home because, since I was out the day before, I had a ton of papers to grade and a slew of book reports that I had yet to read. Of course, Serena was only prolonging everything by not being out front like she was supposed to be. I got out the car and stood next to my door, wondering if Mother had told her I'd be taking her home today. Maybe the girl decided to go ahead and take the bus home, I thought to myself as I crossed over the school's front lawn and made my way back through the iron gates. I didn't have to go very far before I spotted Miss Serena, and just like last time the big-head boy was all up in her face. And just like last time, I played detective and watched on as my little sister went through the first rounds of her dating dance. I felt like Ace Ventura as I hid myself on the side of the administration building and peeked around the corner as Serena and big-head stood next to a tree in the middle of the playground making goo-goo eyes at each other. I guess big-head called himself being inventive as he pulled out a pen and started carving something into the tree. Probably a heart with both their names in it. How cute, but I'd have to confer with Serena about that. It's a big no-no to plaster the fact that you belong to a guy for everyone to see. Discretion is an important rule. I'd have to lecture her on that later. Though time was passing and I knew I needed to get home, I didn't break up Serena's magical moment. She looked so pleased at whatever big-head was carving into the tree and besides, I had a feeling I knew how this little meeting would end and I wanted to have a front row seat for the festivities. When big-head finally put down his pen and showed off his work to Serena she smiled gloriously and he, just as I figured, licked his lips, blew out a handful of breath, and smelled it, smiled at the odor, then moved in closer to

Serena. He put his arm around her shoulder, said a few words in her ear, then placed a finger on her cheek and turned her face to his. It was time for the big kiss. Someone had taught that boy well, I thought as I watched on gleefully. Serena looked nervous, which was to be expected. I told her even if she wasn't nervous to play like she was. Boys always like to think they know how to get a girl all riled up. Big-head took one final look into Serena's eyes, then moved in for the kill. Don't let him put his tongue in on the first kiss, I said to myself, hoping Serena would remember my advice. She leaned her head to the side just a taste like I'd showed her on numerous occasions, and just as their lips were about to touch—what? The girl pushed him away. No, no, no, Serena, I thought, shaking my head. Don't you remember the rules? You can't be a tease. If you didn't want to kiss the boy you should have never let it go that far. What was she thinking? I looked on as big-head took a step back and threw his hands up in the air. Serena didn't seem to move at all. She just stood there looking at big-head as if she was frozen. Poor big-head. He'd done all the right moves and still came up empty. Bet it would take months for him to ever try to kiss a girl again . . . No. Looks like I'm wrong. Looks like he's gonna try again right now. Did Serena say it was okay? Did she want to try again? I guess so, 'cause the girl didn't protest as he moved toward her again. She stood there in a puckered position and waited for the contact. Okay, I thought and crossed my fingers. Serena's first kiss . . . Oh my God—no. "Damn it," I said as I pushed off the building and ran across the playground. She's having a spell. "Oh God," I mumbled and ran like a bolt of fire toward my sister. I could see her head begin to quiver, her arms begin to shake. She was trying to hold back the tics and jerks, but just as I reached her, she spun out of control.

"Serena," I screamed and caught her by the arm.

"Ms. McGuire," big-head said and pulled me away.

Huh? I thought losing control of Serena's arm. "You better move, little boy," I said and snatched my arm away from him. Little motherfucker. Who does he think he is, pulling on me? When I turned back to Serena I saw her stumble against the tree and fall to the ground. I bent over to rescue her, but big-head was faster than me.

"Renie," he said and grabbed her by the neck as her head jerked to the side and knocked against the tree. "You okay, baby?"

"Get your little tail out the way, boy," I said, trying to get to my sister. But big-head pushed me back.

"This is my lady," he said, hugging Serena's ticcing body to his chest.

"That's my sister, you little punk," I said and reached out for Serena. "You don't know what's going on here."

"I do too know what's going on here," he said, soothing Serena with gentle strokes over her head. "Just relax, Renie," he said to her, then stroked her face. "Just take it easy."

"Why, you little asshole," I wanted to say. That was my sister. I was supposed to be soothing her. Big-head didn't know what was going on. How dare he push me aside like I was nobody? I'm her sister, dammit!

Once he had her calm enough, he reached into Serena's backpack that had fallen to the ground and got out her meds and pushed one into her mouth. Within minutes, Serena was calm enough to sit up on her own, and when she did I saw the side of her head was cut. I pushed big-head out the way with as much strength as I could muster up. I didn't want to hurt the boy, but someone had told him he was Superman for a day, and he wasn't going to give up Serena without a fight. But neither was I, so I strong-armed him out the way and took Serena by the hand. "I'm taking you to the hospital," I told her, and for the first time she looked at me. I don't believe she even knew I had been there all along.

"Yeah, we gotta get you to the hospital for your head," big-head said and picked up Serena's backpack as I helped her to her feet.

We? Little boy, please. "I can handle it from here," I said to him and snatched Serena's backpack from his hand and pulled Serena along with me.

"But Anthony," Serena called as I hurried her along. "Wait, Li'l Ma," she said and pulled back.

"Girl, your head is cut. I'm taking you to—"

"Anthony," she said and pulled out my grip. She slowly walked back to him and into his outstretched arms. "Thank you," she said as I stood watching like a scorned lover. He held her so long that I had to go pull her away.

"Time to go," I said and led her to my car as she looked back over her shoulder the whole time.

■

We sat for over an hour in the emergency room at Kaiser. I held my just-cleaned AK II scarf to Serena's head as she leaned over into my lap.

"You know, Serena," I said after a long period of silence. "You don't have to be embarrassed about what happened today."

"I'm not," she said and sat up, taking the scarf with her. "Anthony knows. I told him everything."

"But I thought you didn't want anyone at school to know your business."

"Yeah. At first I wanted to keep everything on the down-low, but I started to really like Anthony and I didn't want there to be any secrets between us."

Is this my sister talking, or a thirty-year-old woman?

"I explained everything to Anthony. Me, him, and Dr. Chris—"

"Who?"

"You heard me," she said arrogantly. "Me, Anthony, and Dr. Chris had a big talk about Tourette's and what it does. And you know what? Anthony wasn't scared at all, especially not after Dr. Chris told us that the symptoms start to go away as I get older. That way by the time we get married, I won't have any symptoms at all."

"Excuse me? Married? Girl, you're only fourteen years old."

"Anthony and I aren't getting married till after we both finish college and get jobs. You taught me that, remember?"

"Girl, do you know how many other men you're going to meet by the time you've finished college? You won't hardly be thinking about big-h— I mean Anthony—by then."

"Yes I will," Serena quickly corrected me. "Anthony is down for me. I can trust him. He don't care that I have this illness. He just likes me for me. Didn't you tell me that I should marry a man who likes me for me?"

Damn. Do you have to remember every little thing I say?

"But you know why I'm gonna marry Anthony?"

"No, Serena. Why?"

"Because I told him about Tourette's and he didn't break up with me. When a guy likes you even though you're sick, that means he's special. Even though I got a disease, Anthony still thinks I'm the bomb."

"The bomb?"

"Cute, fine—the bomb."

"Oh," I said and pulled Serena toward me. I gave her a kiss then laid her head back in my lap. Smart girl, I thought to myself and wiped blood away from her face with the scarf. She's happy, she's found a little big-head boy who thinks she's the *bomb* . . . What else could a girl ask for?

"Li'l Ma," she said and tapped my knee.

"Uh-huh?"

"How come you being so mean to Dr. Chris?"

"I'm not."

"You are," she snapped. "I like him."

"You barely know him."

"For your information, Dr. Chris is one of my honorary homeboys. Plus I remember him from when I was little."

"Girl, please. You were just a baby."

"Uh-uh. I do too remember," she said and paused. "Rainbow sherbet."

"What?"

"Rain—bow—sher—bet," she said as if she were talking to a dunce. "From Thrifty's. Double scoop. Dr. Chris would always bring me ice cream when he came over to visit you."

So she does remember, I thought and smiled as I remembered myself.

"I like having him around the house. He's nice," she said and turned her head slightly to look up at me. "He's cute too."

"How many times do I have to tell you that just because a guy is cute doesn't mean he's the right man for you?"

"But Dr. Chris says he loves you. I heard him telling Big Mama. He was sounding like he was gonna cry. Then Mama said that you was too silly to appreciate a man like him."

"Then what did he say?"

"Then he said that he still loved you. And that if you would just give him another chance, he'd spend the rest of his life showing you that. Then Mama said you was silly again."

Thanks a lot, Mama.

"I like Dr. Chris, Li'l Ma. I think you should marry him."

"Marry him? Why are you so stuck on marriage all of a sudden?"

"Because I don't wanna end up like Big Mama," she said, just as a nurse stepped out from behind a door and called Serena's name.

I helped her up and walked her over to the nurse and showed her the big gash on Serena's head. The nurse told me she would take it from there and said that it would be at least another hour's wait.

So much for getting any work done tonight, I thought as I took a seat and checked my watch. Serena was becoming quite the little lady, I thought to myself and smiled, knowing I was partly responsible for her outcome. She was just as much my daughter as she was anybody else's. But today she seemed more like my friend, and I couldn't forget what she'd said about Chris. It was like hearing it from her, an innocent bystander, put everything into perspective. Chris was indeed a good guy. He was nice, sincere, and he loved me. That's more than I could say for any of the other men I've dated. So why not give him a chance? A date. One date. I mean, what could it hurt?

I leaned my head back against the wall, trying to make myself comfortable since I knew I had another hour to be there. But when I pulled my hands up to cross them over my chest, I gasped. I looked down at my hands and noticed that they were covered in Serena's blood. I looked around and spotted the sign for the ladies' room and jumped up. I raced to the sink, turned on the water and rinsed my hands till all the blood was gone. Then after I dried my hands, I found myself checking them. Did I have any cuts on me, I wondered as I examined my hands on all sides. Then I stopped myself and looked in the mirror. What was I checking for? What? Did I think I might have been cut too? Was I concerned that maybe some of my blood may have mixed with Serena's? Why would that concern me? Why was I being so stupid? So overprotective? And who was I protecting? Me or Serena? I thought back to my conversation with Malik as I looked at myself in the mirror. I didn't have anything. I was fine. There was no need for me to get an HIV test and there was no need for me to be concerned about whether or not I was cut. What did it matter? I didn't have anything. I was fine. "Shit," I said to myself as I left the bathroom. "Why am I tripping?"

I sat back down in my seat for a second and before I knew it I was back up and walking over to the nurses' station. If I don't have anything, then I don't need to trip, and if I don't need to trip, then I shouldn't be worried about taking a stupid HIV test. Right?

"Excuse me," I called to a nurse and waited for her to come over to me. "Is it possible for me to take an HIV test here?"

"What?" she asked and leaned toward me.

That's when I realized I'd been whispering. "I need to take an HIV test," I said, louder.

"May I have your Kaiser card?" she said and pulled out a form and handed it to me. "Fill this out and a nurse will call you in a minute to draw blood."

That's it? I just fill this out and give up some blood? Cool. No problem, I thought and pulled out a pen and started filling out the form. But if it was no problem, I thought as I wrote down my name on the paper, then why in the world was my hand shaking?

8

I'd never been good at waiting. Never. The nurse said it would take three or four days for the results of my HIV test to come in, and even though I was sure what the results would be, I still didn't like the waiting part. It was now day four and no one had phoned me to let me know anything, which to me was a good sign. Of course, it was Sunday, which meant that even if the tests had come back I probably wouldn't hear anything till Monday. But you know what? Fuck it. I've had enough of waiting and pondering. I know the tests are negative. They have to be. So I say forget about it. No more waiting. Today I'm going out. Today I'm throwing caution to the wind and letting my heart lead the way. Today I'm going to see him. I'm going to see Chris. Don't ask me why, I just feel it's time.

I didn't bother getting all dressed up. I just threw on a pair of jeans and a T-shirt and hit the road. I didn't even call first. I just went. I didn't want to think about it, because if I did I probably would never have gone. I just jumped in my car and drove and when I showed up at his door . . .

"Madison," he said, nervously and stared at me like I was a ghost. He stood in the crack of his doorway, gawking, as if he'd never seen my face before in his life. At first I thought he may have had someone in there with him, but my thoughts were erased when he cracked a smile and stepped back to let me in. "I'm so glad to see you," he said as I walked through the door and waited for him to close it behind me. "This is fate, a miracle, an astounding twist of cosmic energy."

"Cut the bullshit, Chris," I said and walked through the front room of his penthouse suite. "It's just me. I don't even know if I should be here, but I am. So just chill out, okay?"

"You don't understand," he said, walking to my side, still gawking. "I knew you'd be here today. I'd been thinking about you ever since I woke up this morning."

So what else is new?

"I just had this feeling. This overwhelming notion. This psychic intuition."

"Chris," I said and put up my hand.

"Sorry," he said and held out a hand toward the sofa. "Have a seat."

"Thank you."

"Want something to drink? Beet juice, V-8, Natural Springs mineral water?"

"Got some vodka?"

"Let me check the bar," he said and swiftly moved to the back of the room. He returned with a miniature vodka sampler and a glass. I took the vodka, not the glass, turned it up, and downed it. There, I said to myself and handed Chris the empty bottle. That ought to help me relax, or at least help me deal with Chris's sappy optimistic spirit.

"So," he said and sat down next to me. He patted his hands on his knees and didn't say another word. He just stared. Stared so hard that I thought I may have had something on my face. I wiped my hand over myself, feeling the most awkward I'd ever felt in my entire life. I'd known Chris for years, yet I felt uncomfortable with him. I didn't know how I was supposed to act, and by the cheesy grin on his face I could tell he didn't have a clue either. "So," he said again, then nodded his head. "Want something to eat?"

"Not hungry."

"You sure? 'Cause I could order something from room service. Or they have a terrific restaurant on the top level where we—"

"No, Chris. I said I'm not hungry."

"Okay," he said and crossed his legs, and once again, "*Sooo.*"

"Maybe I should go," I said and stood up.

"No, Madison," Chris said and jumped up with me. "Let's talk," he said and put his hand on my shoulder to guide me back down to my seat.

"Talk about what?"

"About us."

"Oh no," I said and jumped up again, only to be tugged back down by Chris's strong hand.

"Okay, let's not talk," he said, quickly searching around the room for a distraction. "Music," he said so loud that I jumped. "Let's listen to music."

"Okay," I said and thought really hard. "You got some Chanté Moore? No, some Rachelle Ferrelle?"

"Sorry. All my CDs are in storage. But ninety-two point three, the Beat, ought to be jamming," he said and jumped up to turn on the radio. Some rap singer came growling through the speakers and I shook my head indicating to Chris that I was not in the mood. He flipped through the stations until he came across a jazz tune. I smiled and he turned it up just a taste, then came back to the sofa.

"I like this song," I lied, not even knowing who it was.

"Me too," he said, obviously lying too because when he tried to hum the melody, he was all off.

"What were you doing before I came over?" I asked for no other reason than I couldn't find anything better to say.

"Praying."

"For what?"

"For you to come over."

"Stop the drama."

"It's not drama."

"Anyway," I said and rolled my eyes. It was now my turn. *"Sooo,"* I said and nodded my head, racking my brain for something interesting to say, but coming up with nothing.

"Quick," Chris said and turned his body toward me. "Name one R-and-B song that doesn't have the word 'baby' in it."

Good. Trivia. "Let me see," I said and thought. And thought. And thought. "I don't know. You name one."

"I don't know either."

Okay, I thought and drummed my fingers on my knees. So much for trivia. Now what?

"Well, why don't we talk about what we've been doing for the past eight years?" he said, clasping his hands together in his lap. "What's been going on in your world?"

"Work," I said, feeling comfortable with this topic of conversation. "As you know, I went to work for Mighty Avalon right after college like I'd planned. The rest is history."

"Right, right," he said, glad to have finally found something we could talk about. "I take it you enjoy your work."

"It's what I've always wanted to do."

"Right, right," he said, after noticing I was all talked out about work. "Well, how about your family? I see Big Mama is still the same."

"Yep. Still a pain in the ass."

"And Serena," he said, astounded. "The last time I'd seen her she couldn't have been more than three or four. She sure has grown."

"Yes. Too fast if you ask me."

He paused and got serious for a moment. "I had a little talk with her and her boyfriend the other day."

"She told me," I said, then stuck up a finger. "By the way, that's her *friend*, not boyfriend."

He smiled and sighed. "Anyway, she was feeling a little scared about telling him about her disease so I helped her out. I'd treated a couple Tourette's cases when I was in Chicago so I let loose with some of my *expertise*."

"Expertise," I said, mimicking him while he beamed with pride. "That was sweet of you."

He blew off my compliment with a wave of his hand, then shrugged his shoulders. "I just talked to them. It was nothing."

"It meant a lot to Serena," I stressed. "I appreciate it too."

He fidgeted around with his hands and looked away. "Actually, it meant a lot to me too. It sorta made me feel . . . like . . . like . . ."

"Like you were a part of the family?"

"Yeah," he said and dropped his head. He seemed almost embarrassed. "Oh," he said and turned back to me. "I slipped Big Mama some money too. I know how expensive Serena's haloperidol pills can be."

"Now wait a minute, Chris. You don't have to do that. I told Mother I'd give her the money for Serena's medication."

"I know I don't have to do it. I want to," he said slowly, then paused. I could tell his thoughts had left the room. Somehow I sensed they'd gone all the way back to Chicago. To his mother. I wanted to protest more, but I didn't. Helping out Serena and my mother was something Chris needed to do right now. He needed to feel a part of something.

"You okay?" I asked and placed my hand on his thigh.

"Fine," he said as he stared down at my hand. But as he reached his hand to mine, I moved away. I wasn't ready for that just yet. All I wanted to do right then was be Chris's friend.

We sat silently for an awkward minute, neither of us knowing what to say or do. We'd talked about work and family. Now what? I thought as I shifted around on the sofa. Maybe I should go. Why did I come here?

"So what about your love life?" he asked clear out of the blue.

Now I know I should go.

"Big Mama says you're not seeing anyone seriously."

"I'm sure Mother told you a lot of things about me."

"Well, you know how she loves to talk."

Don't I?

"Why?"

"Why what?" I asked, frowning.

"Why haven't you settled down yet?"

"Me? What about you?"

"I told you my story the other night in your office."

Please don't remind me of that night.

"Now, what about you. In eight years you haven't been able to find that one special man?"

"I haven't been looking for him," I said, feeling slightly offended by that question, though I didn't know exactly why. "It's not like I've been a hermit. I mean, I get out. I date. I do my thing. I just don't feel a need to be married. I don't believe in fairy tales."

"I do."

He got that look in his eye like he was about to start talking that cosmic, optimistic, this-is-fate bullshit, so I decided to change the subject before he could get started.

"So tell me about this clinic you're going to be working at. Where did you say it was located? Watts?"

Chris's eyes lit up as he turned to me and smiled, showing all his sturdy white teeth. "Got wheels?"

"Huh?"

"You drove here?"

"Yeah," I said and shrugged.

"Then let's go," he said and pulled me clean out of my seat.

In no time we were standing outside the Bonaventure Hotel waiting for the valet to pull my car forward. Chris could barely contain his excitement. He snatched my keys from me when he saw my car rolling our way. And before the driver could even come to a complete stop he was opening the passenger door and pushing me in. He then jumped into the driver's side and we were off.

"You're gonna love this place," he said as he fled down Figueroa and hopped on the 110. "It opens up on the first of the month," he said as he tapped his fingers against the steering wheel. "I swear, I cannot wait."

I braced myself by placing a hand on the dashboard as he swerved in and out of traffic, and hoped we wouldn't get stopped by the police. But nothing seemed to faze Chris. He just kept right on talking.

"I'm going to be handling all the emergency care patients, which is going to be tough. I'll probably be on call twenty-four hours a day. But hey, this is what I wanted to do. If I wanted a cheesy bullshit job, I would have stayed in Chicago."

"Well, Chicago couldn't have been that bad. You wouldn't be able to afford that penthouse if you hadn't gone."

"True," he said, trying to watch me and the road at the same time. "I made some dollars when I went to work at Chicago Hope. But that's not what it's all about. A brother can't hold his head up high until he knows he's done all he can to help his people. What good does it do me to make a lot of dough if I don't try and give back to the community? All my work will be in vain. Now, don't get me wrong. In five or ten years, this clinic will start to turn a nice little profit. But that's not why I'm in it. I'm in it to help my people. To give back and do good. Ain't that what it's all about?"

Damn, I thought as we exited the freeway and stopped at a red light. Most women are into looks, some are into money, but me, I'm into a man who is about something. And that is exactly what Chris is. I just love it when he talks about his work. He gets so passionate. So intense. That's the reason why I fell in love with him eight years ago. Because he was a believer. A believer in doing the right thing. The honorable thing. Chris was pumped. And as we took off again down Imperial, I thought, How nice it is to have a job that you really love. Most people can't claim that.

We drove for another ten minutes or so, then slowed down just as we passed the corner of Grape Street. Chris grinned from ear to ear as he jumped out the car and ran around to my door. "This is it," he said as he opened my door and grabbed my hand.

"Nice," I said as I looked cautiously down the street. I was impressed.

When Chris told me the clinic was in Watts I pictured a gray slum area with winos hanging out on the street corner. But this was actually nice. The street was clean, the few faces that passed us wore smiles, and the clinic itself was larger and nicer than I'd expected. This was not the vision of Watts that I'd held in my mind. Guess I'd looked at one too many riot documentaries over the years.

I peeped through the windows at the inside while Chris unlocked the sliding iron gate, then the front door. He held out his hand for me to go in first, and as he followed behind me, he flipped on the lights. They fluttered a few seconds, then brightened the room to a piercing white.

"This is the reception slash waiting area," he said as he stood in the middle of the floor with his hands stretched out. "And this," he said as he beckoned me to follow him down the hallway, "this is the room where we'll be giving out free immunization shots."

"Mmm-hmm," I moaned as I nodded and peered around the room. Seconds later, Chris had me by the arm, pulling me back down the hall.

"Now this," he said, opening a squeaky blue door. "This is my examining room," he said with pride. He took a deep breath and looked around the room with satisfaction. "Across the hall is Fitz's exam room, and," he said, pulling me again, "down here is X ray, and the business office is in the back." Chris couldn't stop himself from grinning. I couldn't tell which of us was more impressed. "Oh," he said, once again yanking me by the arm. He pulled me all the way back to the front of the clinic and opened another blue door. "This is the teen center," he said and flipped on the lights.

"Teen center?" I said and peered around at what looked like an empty classroom.

"That's right," he said as his energy finally seemed to wane and he sat down in one of the chairs against the wall. "Once a week we'll hold counseling sessions here."

"What kind of counseling sessions?" I asked and took a seat next to him.

"Well, the topics will change every week. One week we'll tackle teen pregnancy; the next, drug addiction; the next—"

"Sexually transmitted diseases," I blurted out almost unconsciously.

"Hell, we could have a whole clinic devoted to that topic."

"I'll bet," I mumbled as a quick thought of Ronald Olbright popped into my head. I quickly dismissed it and turned to face Chris. "This is sort of a coincidence," I said and crossed my legs.

"What is?" he asked and rested his head against the wall behind him.

"Well, for the past month or so, I've been trying to get a proposal together so that we could start teaching sex education at my school."

"What?" he said and lifted his head from the wall. "A proposal? You mean you guys don't already have a sex ed course?"

The smirk on my face answered his question.

"Damn. Are these the nineties, or what?"

"I know, I know," I said and shook my head. "But Malik and I are sure we'll get things going. We've got support for the proposal. Now it's just a matter of doing it."

"Malik?" Chris said and raised a brow.

"Oh that's my best friend. He and I have been working on this sex thing together."

"Uh-huh," he said and eyed me.

"What?" I said and curled my lip.

"Best *friend?*"

"Yeah."

"He?"

"Yes, and?"

"Nothing," he said and folded his arms across his chest.

I decided to ignore this little fit of jealousy, though Chris was making it quite clear that he did not approve. Tough, I thought and rolled my eyes. "Anyway," I said and flipped my braids over my shoulder, "it is a coincidence that you and I are sort of working on the same goals. You with this teen center and me with the sex ed class. It's like we're on the same wavelength, you know."

"Now you're talking," he said, nodding slowly. "We think alike, we have the same goals, same wavelength—we're meant for each other."

"Hold on, partner. I didn't mean it like that," I said, putting my hand in Chris's face.

He grabbed it and laughed. "So what do you mean?"

"I mean I'm proud of you. This place is great, Chris. I'm really happy for you."

"Not as happy as I am," he said and sighed. "I can't tell you how thrilled I was to get that call from Fitz asking me to come back to L.A. and help him run this clinic. I was at a point in my life where I was really beginning to question myself. When my clinic closed down, I took it really hard. I started to question whether I was doing the right thing, you know. Then Fitz calls and it's like . . . like *fate*. Like my prayers had been answered. I knew then that my vision was right. I knew I had to come back to L.A."

Damn, I thought as I stared at him. I was really getting turned on by all his talk. It was as if he was in another zone. All he could think about was his work and his vision of helping the underprivileged. The way his eyes lit up when he spoke about helping others was unbelievable. And once again I was seeing the man I fell in love with. The real man. The man with goals and dreams. The man who cared outside himself and taught me to do the same. Was it possible that I could still love him? After all that had happened between us? I always knew that I still had a tiny spot left for him in my heart, but now if I'm honest with myself, which I think I should be, I'll have to admit that the tiny spot has grown. If I'm all the way honest with myself, I'll have to admit that, yes, I do still love Chris. That's a fact that I don't think I can deny myself any longer.

"You know what else is fate, Madison?" he asked, looking at me with dreamy eyes. "The fact that you are here with me now. Everything happens for a reason. We met for a reason, we broke up for a reason, and after eight years, we're sitting here talking for a reason."

"And the reason is?"

"Because we love each other."

"Oh my God," I said and rolled my eyes. I knew it was coming.

"We're supposed to spend the rest of our lives together."

"Don't start, Chris."

"No, I'm going to start, Madison. I'm going to start because I can't let this go on and on when I know we were meant to be together."

"Chris."

"Listen to me. I'm talking knowledge here. You can deny it all you want, but I know the reason why you never got close to a man in all these years is because you have never gotten over me."

"Don't flatter yourself."

"I know I'm right. It's been the same for me. That's why I'm not waiting anymore. This is all a part of the master plan of our lives," he said and paused.

"Toward the end I had a serious talk with my mother. She told me that there was nothing more important in life than finding someone you loved to share it with. I told her I had already found that person, but I'd lost her. And you know what she told me?"

"No Chris. What?"

"She told me to do whatever it takes to find her again," he said and slid off his chair to the floor. He propped himself up on one knee and slowly said, "Madison. Will you marry me?"

"Fool, are you crazy?" I laughed, until I realized I was laughing alone. Chris, on the other hand, was as serious as a heart attack.

"No. Marry me."

"I'm leaving," I said and stood up. "You have lost your mind."

"Madison," he said and reached out for my hand as he fell on his face. He got up wincing as if he'd pulled a muscle, but that was the least of his concerns. "Am I not an intelligent man? Am I not sane?"

"Have you not been calling too many psychic hot lines?"

"Trust me. Marry me. You know me. I'm no fool. I wouldn't be asking you this if I didn't truly believe this is the way our lives were supposed to turn out."

"You've flipped," I said, pulling away from him and heading down the hallway.

"Look, look, look, look, look," he said, breezing past me to get to the front door. He blocked it and held out his hand so I wouldn't get too close. "Just think about it. Just think. Search your heart, search your soul."

This is just too fucking dramatic for me. Are we on *Candid Camera*?

"Please, Madison. I felt it ever since I came back to L.A. I'm here for a reason."

"Yeah. To help children. To provide them with quality health care."

"And for you. My mission is twofold. You're the other half. Together we are whole. Apart, we die."

Lord have mercy on this poor fool's soul.

"Please, Madison. Promise me you'll think about it."

"Sure," I lied and put on a stern face so he'd believe me. "I'll think long and hard about this, Chris."

"Promise?"

"What did I just say? I'll give it some thought. Lots of thought. It'll be the only thing I think about," I said and curled my eyes back in my head.

"Okay," he said and eased away from the door. He gave me a kiss on the cheek, then opened the door for me, and as I stepped outside he started to sing, *"If you look into your heart . . . with a positive mind . . ."*

Oh—my—God. I walked slowly towards my car and waited for him to join me. But when I turned around he was still standing in the doorway of the clinic, staring at me like the fool he was.

"You go on without me," he said and tossed me my keys.

I pulled my keys from the air and shook my head. "And how do you plan on getting back to the hotel?"

"I'll get there," he said and waved to me. "I think you need some time to be alone. To *think*."

Fine, I thought and said no more. If he wanted to stay like a goofball, then let him. I hopped in my car and took off. That boy needs rest, I thought as I shook my head. Chris is definitely out of his mind. He ought to be lucky that I even came to see him after all these years. But no, Chris always has to take things a step too far. Will I marry him? Please. This is the third time I've seen his face in eight years, and he comes at me like that? Crazy, just crazy . . . Isn't he?

My first thought was to go home and forget about the fact that I ever went to see Chris. But the more I drove, the darker it became, and the closer I found myself to West Hollywood. I was headed for Malik's.

Driving through West Hollywood always gave me the feeling of being at Mardi Gras. The streets were always packed, especially during the evening. Pedestrians don't believe much in obeying the traffic laws out here. They just walk out in the street whenever they feel like it. And don't even think about honking your horn at them. Please. They'll curse you out in a minute. Malik calls this place Fag Town, but that always makes me wince. Just because the residents are predominantly gay doesn't mean it's okay to refer to the city like that. I mean, when I go to South Central, I don't call it Nigger Town. When I ride through Beverly Hills, I don't call it White Bitch Wonderland. But Malik says I need to lighten up. It's only a joke. Yeah right. I can find better things to joke about.

I drove up Sunset and turned off onto a quiet cul-de-sac that looked like it came straight out of Mayberry. Malik's house was right in the center of the street, and as I pulled into his driveway and brought my car to a stop, I noticed no lights were on in the house. Be here, Malik, I thought to myself as I walked up to his door and rang the bell. I don't know why I felt this overwhelming need to talk to him. Maybe I was just feeling lonely and needed a friend. Or maybe it was because my conversation with Chris was eating away at my brain and I needed to vent.

"I just had to stop by," I said as I breezed through Malik's doorway. I didn't even give him a chance to say hello, let alone invite me in. "I'm so glad you're here," I said as I walked into the front room and stopped. The place looked wonderful. The dining room table was set for two and candles were burning all around the room. "Oops," I said and turned around to Malik. "Am I interrupting something?"

"Hell no," Malik said and flipped on the lights. He had a frown on his face and I knew I must have come at the worst possible time.

"I'm sorry," I said and backed my way to the door. "I should have called first. I'll see you tomorrow at school."

"Sit down," Malik said as he walked over to the dining room table and blew out the candles.

"But I can see you were planning a romantic—"

"I said sit," he barked and grabbed the bottle of wine from the table. He snatched up two glasses and filled them up. One he held out for me, the other he downed in one quick gulp.

"What's up?" I said and took the glass and sat down at the table.

"Working late. Again," he said, obviously referring to Tyrone.

"Well, at least you know where he is."

"Bullshit. It ain't that much overtime in the world," Malik said as he went into the kitchen and came back out with an enchilada casserole. "I think he's getting cold feet about the dedication ceremony."

"No, Malik," I said as he sat the casserole in front of me and handed me a fork. "You guys have been together too long for that. He probably really is working late." I dug into the casserole as Malik poured himself another drink.

"No," he said and sat down next to me. "It's more than that. I can't believe him. This whole dedication ceremony was his idea in the first place. Now he wants to trip?"

"Working late is not tripping. *Damn*," I said and reached for my glass of wine. "This casserole is hot."

"That's how he likes it. Or used to," Malik said and turned up his glass. "I don't know anymore. Since we got serious about this dedication ceremony, everything about him has changed. He won't come home on time. Suddenly his friends are taking up more of his time. Shit, Tyrone don't even like to fuck no more. Just comes home, gets in bed, and starts snoring."

"Hey, hey, hey now," I said, smacking on another bite of casserole. "What happened to all that talk about love winning out in the end?"

"Fuck love."

"Come on, Malik. You're starting to sound like me. This is probably just a phase Tyrone is going through. You know, all men get cold feet before their weddings—I mean dedication ceremonies."

"I don't have cold feet. I know what I want. I'm just not sure Tyrone knows what he wants anymore," he said, slamming his glass down on the table. "Well, I tell you one thing. If that fucker wants to back out he better let me know now. I ain't trying to have none of that melodramatic shit in my life. If he wants out he better tell me before the ceremony 'cause if that motherfucker leaves me standing at the altar all by myself I swear I'll hunt his ass down with a vengeance. You hear me?" he said and picked up a crystal knife. "I'll slice and dice his ass, Madison. I ain't no joke."

"Do you hear yourself? You're blowing this all out of proportion. You and Tyrone are in love. This is just a phase. If Tyrone wanted out of the relationship, he would have been gone years ago. Why would he wait till the last?" I said as I stared at the casserole dish and noticed I'd eaten damn near a third of it already. I put my fork down and pushed the dish to the side. "Everything's gonna work out fine. Trust me. It's like you said, love always wins."

"What the fuck has gotten into you?" Malik said and leaned back into his seat. "What's with the bliss? What's with the love? What's with all the mushy talk?"

"Not a damn thing. I'm just tripping off of Chris."

"You saw Chris? Now that must have been interesting."

"Very. I decided to give the brother a chance, you know. Nothing serious. I stopped by his hotel suite just to feel him out, right? Then he takes me down to his clinic, and what does he do next?"

"What?" Malik said as his eyes nearly popped out of his head.

"He got down on his knee and made a fool out of himself."

"He proposed?"

"Like a damn fool. Can you believe that? After eight years? As if I would be stupid enough to say yes. All I wanted to do was talk to the man, and he comes up with some crazy shit like that. I mean, please."

"You wanna do it, don't you? You wanna say yes?" Malik asked and gave me a knowing grin.

"Is you lost in space or something? This is Madison you're talking to. I ain't hardly trying to think about no marriage. Shit. Not this black woman and not in this lifetime."

"Ah," he said and leaned toward me. "I see it in your eyes. You're thinking about it."

"The hell I am. I'm thinking about how ridiculous it is."

"Nope. I can see it. You love Chris. You want to marry him. I can see it, Madison. I can feel it. It's, it's—fate."

"Oh damn. Now you sound just like Chris. Both of you must be high on something."

"Okay," Malik said seriously. "Tell me truthfully. Have you ever really gotten over Chris?"

"Boy, please."

"Aha. You haven't."

"I'll put it this way. Chris was my one and only love, so of course I still have feelings for the man. I finally admitted that to myself. But I ain't trying to hear nothing about marriage. Please. What? So I can end up like Michael Jackson and Lisa Marie, Prince Charles and Di, Roseanne and Tom Arnold?"

"You can't compare yourself to them."

"And why not?"

"None of those people are black."

He had a point there.

"Besides, none of those people have been in love with the same person for eight years. You can't tell me you'd rather continue dating dork after dork like you've been doing."

"Hey. I date some really nice guys."

"They may be nice, but they aren't *the one*. I think Chris may be the one for you. It ain't too many men who'd put their pride on the line like he's done for you. The brother is sprung."

"No. I can't get serious with Chris. I'd lose all my freedom. The freedom to date whoever I want whenever I want."

"The burden of changing one condom after another."

"I took an HIV test, if that's what you're getting at. Four days ago."

"And . . ."

"What else? I'm still alive and kicking," I said and held up my glass for a toast.

"Yes," he said and clicked his glass against mine. "Praise the Lord. Now maybe if you settle your ass down you won't have to worry about ever taking the test again."

I drank the rest of my wine and stood up. "I'm outta here," I said and headed for the door. "Enough foolish talk for one evening. There will be no marriage," I said and laughed. "That's the most stupidest thing I'd ever heard of. Me. Married? Please."

As I waited for Malik to join me at the door and walk me out to my car, the front door came bursting open. It was Tyrone, complete with flowers, more wine, and a quart of vanilla ice cream. I shot Malik a look that said, "Told you you had nothing to worry about." Then I turned to Tyrone and gave him a kiss on the cheek.

"Hey, Madi," he said almost dropping his bag of ice cream. "I hear you're going to be a part of the dedication ceremony."

"Yeah. You're looking at the best woman," I said, but somehow I don't believe Tyrone was paying me any attention. His eyes were focused on Malik as he silently apologized for whatever he'd done wrong. I knew that was my cue to make myself scarce.

"I'll see you tomorrow," I said to Malik, but he, like Tyrone, barely glanced my way. As I walked out the door, I saw Tyrone pass Malik the flowers and as I took care to close the door behind me I saw them embrace. How cute. Guess love does win in the end. Sometimes.

Must be nice, having someone to care for, I thought as I made my way home. Having someone to depend on, to love, someone who you know loves you back. I never had that with a man. Not really, not completely. And until now, I never thought it was something that I had the right to expect. But now, Chris has got me thinking. Malik and Tyrone have got me thinking. Serena and Mother have got me thinking. Why shouldn't I expect to be loved? Am I not a good person? Am I not halfway decent looking? Don't I have good qualities? Hell yes, I do. So why don't I want love? Why don't I want to give love?

I know why, I thought as I made it to my front door and walked in. I went straight to the kitchen table and picked up the Sunday morning paper where I'd left it. I turned to the obituaries and began my ritual search. "Cleophus McGuire," I mumbled as I looked for my father's name. Nothing. "Bastard," I said and threw the paper down. He's the reason. Because of him, I've never felt worthy. I never felt completely free to love or receive love. I loved him. I loved my father. And what did he do? The bastard turned his back on me. He was the first man to ever walk out of my life, the first man to instill that hurting feeling in me. That love-lost feeling. That painful, disgusting heartbreak that one feels when she's been abandoned. And because of him, I swore that no man would ever hurt me like that again. Daddy's the reason, I thought as I picked up the phone. That motherfucker is the root of all my evil.

"Where's Daddy?" I asked when Mother picked up my call. "Where is he?"

"Madison," she squeaked. "Girl, what are you talking about?"

"Where's my daddy?"

"I don't know, child. I haven't spoken to him in two, three years."

"You don't have a number for him? The father of your children and you don't know how to get in contact with him?"

"What's wrong with you, Madison?" she asked. "You okay, baby?"

"No, Mother. I'm not okay. I want to know where my daddy is. I want to talk to him. I need answers."

"Answers? Madison, calm down," she said, confused. "What kind of answers do you need?"

"I need to know why my daddy didn't want me. I need to know why he left me. I need to know why he would lie to me," I said as tears ran down my face. "I just need to know what I did, Mommy. What did I do to scare my daddy away from me?"

"Oh Madison," she said and paused. I could hear her sniffling. "It wasn't about you. You didn't do a thing. You were just a baby."

"I had to have done something. Maybe I cried too much as a baby. Did I cry a lot, Mommy? Maybe he couldn't take all the noise. Did I have colic? Or, or maybe I was costing too much money. Babies can be expensive. Do you remember how much Pampers were back then? Did I tear up the house? Was I always getting into things? What, Mommy? Tell me what I did that was so wrong. Tell me why Daddy didn't love me."

"He did love you."

"No, Mommy. You're lying. I need to talk to my daddy. I need to understand why. Everything I do and everything I don't do is all tied in to him. He controls every part of me, Mommy. I can't go on like this."

"What you mean you can't go on like this? I don't like the way you sounding, girl."

"I just want to see my daddy. That's all. If I could just see him face-to-face . . ."

I couldn't talk anymore. It was no use. Mother didn't know where Daddy was or how I could find him. There was nothing she could say that could take my hurt away. Only Daddy could do that, and he was nowhere to be found.

Before I got off the phone, mother made me promise to take two Tylenols and get in bed, but when I hung up with her all I could do was sit and think. And the more I sat, the more I thought, the more my hurt returned to its normal position of hatred. I hated that man. And the more I thought, the more I began to hate myself. Here I was a grown woman, allowing her punk papa to control her life. After all these years, he was still over me. Why couldn't I shake him? Why couldn't I just forget that I had a father and move on with my life? Move on with love.

When my doorbell rang, I could have sworn it was Mother. She sounded on the phone as if she thought I was gonna do something stupid like kill myself. This was probably her, coming to check on me and tuck me into bed, I thought as I sloughed my way to the door and opened it up. "Chris," I said and took a step back. He was the last person I expected to see, and though I wanted and needed to be alone with my thoughts, I didn't shoo him away. "What are you doing here?" I said and held back the door so he could come in.

"Something inside me told me you needed me, Madison. That's why I'm here. And here is where I want to be for the rest of my life. With you."

And before I could even get control of myself, he grabbed me and pulled me into his arms. He held me with a force that convinced me he would never let me go, unless I wanted him to. I didn't want him to. Right then, I needed to be held. I needed someone to tell me he loved me and I needed that person to mean it. Chris did. I held on to his neck as he picked me up and carried me to my bedroom. He laid me across the bed and slowly began undressing me. I closed my eyes and enjoyed just being there. I barely moved at all as Chris slid my T-shirt over my head and tugged at my jeans. I just laid there like a stretched-out zombie. I couldn't see a thing, but I could feel, and what I felt, I have to admit, was love.

"Chris," I moaned as I felt his naked body fall over mine.

"Madison," he panted and delved into my neck.

"Chris," I said again and patted his back to get his attention.

"Oh, Madi," he said and grabbed a handful of my braids and pulled them.

He wasn't quite getting it. "Chris, honey. *Hello*. Chris," I said and popped open one of my eyes.

"Huh, oh, what?" he said and finally stopped kissing me long enough to listen.

"Do you have a condom?" I asked.

"A, uh, a condom," he muttered, trying to catch his breath.

"Safety, safety," I said, feeling just a tinge of awkwardness. But Chris didn't trip. Well, actually he did trip, but it was only because the sheet had gotten wrapped around his ankle and when he got up from the bed he fell to the floor. But that was okay. He got right back up, but after a couple of seconds of fidgeting around he realized his dilemma.

"I don't have a condom," he said as if he was embarrassed.

"Check the medicine cabinet," I said, and watched as his naked body bolted to the bathroom. In seconds he returned to the bedroom, fully strapped, and jumped into bed. I never knew it could be so easy to get a man to put on a condom. But I guess when they love you, they'll do anything for you. We made love for real this time. It wasn't an act on my part like it had been that night in my office. I loved him right and he loved me back. And it was real. It was as if I was a virgin all over again. As if I were being loved and touched and soothed for the very first time. And when it was over, Chris held my head against his chest and ran his hands through my braids and then . . .

"Will you marry me?" he asked and lifted my chin until our eyes met.

I thought for a second, knowing what I had to do. I couldn't let my daddy continue to run my life. I had to be my own woman. If not now, when?

"Yes, Chris," I said, staring clear through him. "I will marry you."

■

We made love all night long and by the time I opened my eyes and looked at the clock, it was eight o'clock Monday morning. I sprang up in bed and shouted to Chris, "The time," but all he did was pull me back to him and begin making love to me all over again. We could have gone on for hours, but I had to get to work and Chris was dying to get out to the jeweler's. He vowed to surprise me later that evening with the biggest rock I'd ever seen.

We took our shower together and got dressed, though the whole process took longer than it should have, considering we had to stop every two to three seconds for a kissy break. We were both all set to step out the door when the phone rang out. I gave Chris one last kiss and told him to go on without me. It was probably the school calling to see where the hell I was. "I love you," I said and kissed his neck. I closed the door and ran back to the phone and swooped it up.

"I'm on my way," I said, practically out of breath.

"Ms. McGuire?" a voice asked. "Ms. Madison McGuire?"

"Speaking."

"This is Dr. Rosalind Baker from Kaiser calling."

"Morning, Doct—" I stopped before I could finish. What was Dr. Baker calling me for so early?

"I need to see you in my office as soon as possible."

"In your office? Why?"

"Can you be here in thirty minutes?"

"No. I'm on my way to work."

"Please, Ms. McGuire. It's pertinent that I see you."

"What is it, Doctor? Tell me now."

"We need to talk about your test results."

"My HIV test? What?" I found myself screaming. "What is it that you want with me?"

"Calm yourself, Ms. McGuire."

"Tell me, dammit."

"This is not the sort of thing I get into over the phone."

"You'd better speak to me and you'd better speak now. What about my HIV results?"

"They're positive, Ms. McGuire. Your HIV test came back positive."

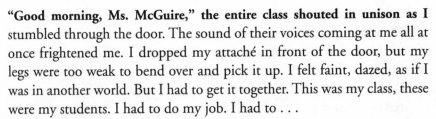

$$9$$

"Good morning, Ms. McGuire," the entire class shouted in unison as I stumbled through the door. The sound of their voices coming at me all at once frightened me. I dropped my attaché in front of the door, but my legs were too weak to bend over and pick it up. I felt faint, dazed, as if I was in another world. But I had to get it together. This was my class, these were my students. I had to do my job. I had to . . .

"Ms. McGuire. *Ms. McGuire.*"

"Just put it on my desk," I said as I finally noticed that little Mike Taylor was standing before me holding my attaché.

I was able to get my legs to move just enough to get me to my desk, and when I was there I plopped myself down and stared straight ahead. *Breathe,* I kept saying to myself as I looked over the classroom. All eyes were on me, listening, waiting, as if they knew instinctively that something was off about me. I tried to focus and pull myself together, but I couldn't think straight. I felt like a zombie. Like . . . *Breathe, Madison, breathe.*

"Ms. McGuire? What's wrong with you?" Sandy asked as she waved her hand as if her arm was out of its socket.

Wrong? "Nothing. Nothing is wrong," I said and sat up straighter. "Michael," I said, searching around the room.

"Yes ma'am," he said and nearly scared me to death. He was sitting right in front of me, and as he stood up to come over, I grabbed my empty coffee cup and handed it to him. "Run down to the faucet and get me a drink."

"'Kay," he said and bolted out the door while the rest of the class began to mumble.

"Why he get to go?" I could hear them saying. "He always get to go."

"Quiet!" I screamed as I stood to my feet, but the movement was too quick and I fell right back down. I grabbed the sides of my temples and closed my eyes. "The rest of you take out your books," I said as I found enough strength to reach into my attaché and pull out Richard Wright's *Black Boy*. "Sandy, you start us off," I said and opened my book to where we'd left off last time. I knew I'd have time to relax while Sandy read. She was a ham. Always trying to read two and three pages even though I only asked for one paragraph. She liked being the center of attention, which was just fine with me now. I didn't want the children focusing on me. I needed time. Time to get my head together, time to think about . . . No . . . No, no. I can't think. I can't . . . Huh?

"Here you go, Ms. McGuire," Michael said, appearing out of nowhere and setting my cup of water in front of me. I swear that boy needs a bell around his neck.

I picked up my cup and gulped down my water while Sandy continued to read and little Janet Matthews stared at me as if to ask, "Can I have a turn now?"

"Thank you, Sandy," I said and flipped forward five pages in my book to find where she'd left off. "Janet, you take it from here," I said as she broke out in a grin.

I rolled my eyes back in my head and tried to follow along. Only, when I looked down at the black-and-white page before me, I couldn't see the text. All I saw staring back at me were those words. Words that had no business being there. POSITIVE, HIV, AIDS, SEX, POSITIVE, NASTY.

I looked away quickly and jumped up from my seat. No, no, I thought as I walked to the back of the classroom. Nope, nope, uh-uh. *Breathe*, I kept telling myself as I stared out the window onto the school lawn and tried to calm down. Only, the words were there too. They were every-fucking-where.

I turned around quickly and saw Janet staring at me as if she'd already asked a question and was waiting for my response. "What did you say?" I asked and slowly made my way to her desk.

"What's this word?" she asked and held up her book and pointed.

I squinted down at the word next to her finger. It was . . . It was . . . POSITIVE. No, it was . . . HIV . . . AIDS.

"Sound it out," I said and backed away from the book as if it was a monster.

"I know what it is," Sandy shouted out and flung her arm in the air. "That's the word we talked about last week. It's 'nigger,'" she said, pleased with her memory.

"And what did I tell you about that word?"

"I know, I know," Timothy Wiggings shouted, cutting Sandy off. "You said 'nigger' was a bad word that people use to put African-American people down."

"Yeah, yeah," Sandy broke in, trying to regain her crown as Miss Know It All. "And you told us we should never, ever use it to describe ourselves. And that when we see the word we should replace it with 'queen.'"

"Or 'king,'" Timmy added just as the bell for recess sounded.

I nodded my head to give them permission to leave the room, and as they hustled out past me, I leaned over onto one of the tables and tried to catch my breath. But I couldn't. I closed my eyes to calm my racing heart, but when I did all I saw were the words again. AIDS, DIE, POSITIVE, VIRUS, HIV.

"No," I screamed into the empty classroom. This is some kind of nightmare? A crazy dream? What's wrong with me? This is just some kinda mistake, that's all. Some crazy foul-up.

Yeah, that's it. A mistake. Big mistake. Happens all the time. I've seen it on TV before. There was a mix-up in the lab. A terrible mix-up. The, the blood samples got switched. Yeah. It's happened before, this type of thing. Dumb doctors. Stupid doctors. Can't even take blood right. How dare Dr. Baker call me talking nonsense? HIV positive? Please. Not me. Hell no. Not me. No . . . Uh-uh. I'm too, I'm too, I'm intelligent. I got a job. I got a home. A car. A life. Friends. Family. Serena—Chris. No, no. I'm getting married. Settling down. Future. I've got plans. I found love—Chris.

No, no, no. Somebody goofed. It's all a big mistake. I just, I just need to get this all straightened out. I gotta, I gotta call the hospital. Tell 'em they made a mistake. I'm gonna sue that fucking hospital. Stupid motherfuckers. Calling me, telling me I'm HIV positive when I know good and well I'm not. Johnny Cochran. No, Marcia Clark. Call her. I'm gonna sue. They made a mistake. They can't do this to me.

"Gotta call Dr. Baker back," I said as I raced out the class and straight to the administration building. I've got to tell her about her mistake, I thought as I reached my office and snatched up the phone. Gotta call Dr. Baker. Number? "What's the fucking phone number?" *Think*. Breathe, *breathe* . . . Dial . . .

"Kaiser, West L.A."

"Hello, hello?"

"If you know the extension of the department you are calling, please enter now."

"Extension? What's the extension?"

"If you need the assistance of an operator, press zero now."

Zero. Press zero.

"Please hold for the next available operator."

"Hurry up, dammit!" *Breathe*. Wait. Breathe. Music? "*Love lift us up where we belong. Where the eagles fly . . .*"

"Kaiser, West L.A. How may I direct your call?"

"I gotta speak to Dr. Rosalind Baker."

"Please hold."

"No!" Music. "*And it's me you need to show. How deep is your love . . .*" Bee Gees. *Saturday Night Fever*. Travolta . . . "Hurry up!"

"Internal Medicine, Dr. Baker's office. How may I help you?"

"I need to talk to the doctor."

"Who's calling?"

"Madison McGuire."

"Are you a patient?"

"What the fuck do you think?"

"Please hold."

Stupid bitch. Is every-fucking-body down there retarded? Fucking *music*. "*And I-ey-I-ey-I will always love you . . .*"

"Ms. McGuire."

"Dr. Baker."

"I'm so glad you called back. I've been trying to contact you ever since we got disconnected this morning."

"You made a mistake, Doctor. A huge mistake."

"Ms. Mc—"

"No. What you would want to do now is shut up and listen, okay? . . . I said, okay?"

"Yes, Ms. McGuire."

"Now. My first inclination was to sue your ass, but I thought about it and all I want to do now is get this whole mess cleared up. So, I need you to redo my blood work and retest me. Is that clear?"

"Ms. McGuire. It is our customary practice to draw enough blood in order that we may retest any queries that return positive."

Huh?

"Your HIV test has already been tested and retested. The results are conclusive. You have tested positive for HIV."

"Are you deaf? Either I'm not hearing you or you're not hearing me. I think it's the latter. Now, like I said. There has been a mistake. A big, fucking mistake. Now, I want to be retested. Do you hear me? *Retested.*"

"I understand your pain, Ms. McGuire, but I need you to remain calm."

"Bitch. Fucking bitch. You're wrong."

"Ms. McGuire, I need you to come to my office. It is imperative that you get here so that we can talk and get you started on some type of preventative treatment program. You are HIV positive, but the sooner we can get you on an AIDS prevention program, the longer we can preserve your life . . . Ms. McGuire? Do you hear what I'm saying? I need you to come into my office . . . Ms. McGuire?"

"I don't wanna die. I don't wanna . . . This can't be happening to me. This can't. I'm not positive. I can't. You're lying."

"Please, Ms. McGuire. When can I expect you in my office?"

"Never! If I ever see you again, I swear, I'm gonna hurt you. You're a lie. You are a fucking liar."

"But Ms.—"

Damn her. She don't know. She's a lie. Bitch. "No!"

■

"Sit down, shut up, take out your math books, and get at it," I said as the class filed back into the room. "The first person who opens their mouth gets a hundred and fifty standards," I said as I sat down behind my desk and shut my eyes.

Ronald Olbright. Motherfucking asshole. Better be glad your ass is already dead or I'd hunt you down and kill you all over again. Motherfucker! You had everything. Fame, money, the good life. Did you have to do drugs? For what? What could have been so bad in your life that you had to do drugs? You had it all. Why'd you have to shoot up? Couldn't you have just taken pills, snorted? Idiot. No, you had to shoot the shit in your veins. Got a better high that way, didn't you? A quick, easy escape. Well I hope it was good for you. Hope you got good and high and crazy and stupid. Didn't you watch who used your needles? I mean, who'd you do drugs with? Any- and everybody? Sharing needles, shooting up, getting good and high. Not thinking, just getting high, just whatever, whomever. You just didn't care, did you? And Malik. Oh Malik. Ain't none of my friend. "Got tickets to the game. We can go meet the players." Dammit. Why'd you let me leave with Ronnie? A true friend would have stopped me. A true friend would have said, "No Madison. We came together, we leave together." You ain't no friend, Malik. I hate you. Never shoulda gone to that game. Never shoulda gone to that house. Stupid. Stupid. Stupid! God, that was stupid . . . God. God? Shit. Ain't no such thing. What kinda God lets this happen to people? To me? Huh? What kinda God? Oh I know. Yeah. It's the same kinda God that kills babies. The God that lets little innocent kids get caught in drive-by shootings. The God that lets little babies be born without hearts or lungs or kidneys. The same God that lets innocent people go to a Social Security building in Oklahoma when he knows the place is gonna get bombed. That same God that lets old ladies get run over by cars, that makes people suffer with leukemia, cancer, strokes. Whatever happened to the God that was supposed to watch over his children, keep them safe from evil? Where he at? Why didn't he protect me? I ain't no bad person. I go to church. I pray. I give money to the needy. I'm good, dammit. Why me? Why couldn't Jeffrey Dahmer get AIDS? Charles Manson? Hitler? The drug dealer who sells crack to fourteen-year-olds? Why did I get it when so many other people deserve it? I don't deserve this. Why me? This is fucked up. This is way fucked . . .

Breathe, dammit, breathe.

I can't keep still. I've got too much energy. I feel . . . I feel . . . I gotta get out of here.

I jumped out of my seat and bolted out the door. I ran all the way to the end of the hallway before my legs refused to move any further. *Breathe, breathe.* I bent over and put my head between my knees. What do I do now? How do I live? How much longer do I have to live? I'm going to die. Right here. DIE, POSITIVE, AIDS, SICK, NASTY, PAIN.

"Shit!"

What's my life going to be like now? Am I going to get sick? Am I sick right now? Will I suffer? I'm already suffering. I'm scared. Real scared. Deep, down, pitiful scared. What do I do now? . . .

"Oh shit." I . . . I've got to . . . vomit.

I couldn't get to the girls' bathroom fast enough. Vomit was everywhere. On the floor, my shoes, my jacket. When I finally made it to the bathroom, I ran into a stall and fell to my knees. I stayed there until nothing else would come up. I was a mess. A filthy mess. I sat on the floor after it was over, again trying to catch my breath. Just let me sit here, I thought and pulled my knees to my chest. Let me think . . . HIV positive. Me? What's gonna happen to my life? No one lives. No one makes it through. There is no cure. I'm dying. I've been sentenced to death. Can I eat? Can I exercise? Can I go out in the rain? Can I . . . can I have sex ever again? Oh my God—Chris. What about Chris? How am I supposed to tell him? What do I say? And Mother. Serena. *Everybody.* How can I tell them? What will I say? What will they say? What will they think? NASTY, FILTH, POSITIVE, STUPID, AIDS, DIE. They'll say it all. Especially Mother. I'm so scared. So, so scared. How do I cope with this? How do I deal with the fact that I know I'm going to die? Soon. Not at eighty, ninety, but quickly. "Why? Oh God, why?" Please, God, let me live. I'm so sorry. I tried to be good. I thought I was being good. I don't *understand*, God. I, I, I can't breathe. I gotta get out this bathroom. I, I . . . I gotta get back to class.

I went to the sink and rinsed my mouth out with water and tried my best to get the vomit stains off me. Then I slowly walked back to class, and when I walked through the door all eyes turned on me.

"Oooh, Ms. McGuire," the kids said in unison and giggled. I ran a hand over my face and tried to walk to my desk like nothing had happened. When I looked around the class, I saw nothing but smiling faces and I wondered why. What were they thinking? I tried to figure as I made my way to my desk, faking an air of confidence. But when I got to my desk, I saw a little black box sitting on top of my attaché.

The kids snickered as I picked it up and when I opened it . . . "Oh my God," I said as I stared down at the biggest diamond my eyes had ever seen. I looked over the class in amazement. "Hello, Mrs. Anzel," a voice shouted out, and when I looked up I saw him. There he was, hunched down between Janet and Andrew at the back of the class.

"Chris?" I said as my eyes instantly welled up.

"Ms. McGuire got a boyfriend," a few of the kids whispered and laughed.

"No, boys and girls," Chris said and stood up. "Ms. McGuire has got a husband. Isn't that right?" he said and stared at me.

My mind went blank. I felt faint. "Oh my God," I said as the tears began to fall. I snatched up my attaché, unaware that I'd let the ring drop to the floor. "I gotta get out of here," I said and ran. "I've got to get out of here."

■

I scraped the entire passenger side of my car as I blazed into my parking spot at home. I ran up the stairs and into my condo, but when I was inside I felt like running some more. I felt, I felt like . . . like . . . like ripping shit up. "Fuck this shit!" I yelled and rammed my fist into the wall again and again. I turned over the table, threw the chair, another chair, another, and another. Television—smashed it. Stereo—knocked it to the floor. Curtains—ripped 'em down. I couldn't control myself. I ran into the bathroom. Soap, towels, toothpaste, perfume, everything—smashed. I ran into the bedroom and tore everything I saw to pieces. Everything my hands touched was destroyed. When I was too exhausted to go on, my eyes fell upon my bed and the only thing I could think about was Chris.

We made love, I thought as I fell to the floor. *Breathe. Breathe.* "Chris!" I yelled. We made love that night in my office. And it wasn't just him. There was Terrence. And Benson. I may have killed them all. Just like Ronnie killed me. No, no. Gotta get up. I can't sit still. I ran to the mirror and bashed it till it cracked. "Murderer!" I screamed as I slumped down to the floor again. *Breathe. Breathe.*

"I'm sorry. I'm so sorry, Chris. Oh God. All of you. I'm so very sorry."

Oh shit, I thought and held my breath as I listened to the knocking at my front door. I knew it was Chris, but I couldn't face him now. I crept into the front room, holding my breath and hoping Chris would just go away. He knocked for a good two minutes, but when I didn't answer, the knocking stopped. He's gone, I thought and thanked God. Still, I'm going to have to face him soon. I've got to tell Chris. I gotta tell him and everybody else. Every man since Ronnie who I had unprotected sex with. I gotta tell 'em. But how can I? How do I tell Chris, the man I'm supposed to marry, that I'm HIV positive? How do I tell him that he may be infected too? That because of me, he could be dying. I could have killed him already. Oh God. How do I tell him? . . . Oh shit. He's back. Knocking.

"Madison. I know you're in there," he yelled and pounded against the door. "Madi. I see your car downstairs. Open this door. *Madi?*"

Ssh. Just be very still. He'll go away. Don't make a sound, I thought as I tried to move away from the door. But when I took a step, I tripped over one of the chairs I'd thrown earlier. "Shit," I whimpered, then quickly held my breath.

"Madi? Is that you? Open up."

He heard me. Oh Lord. What now? I can't face him. Not now.

"Open up. What's wrong with you?"

Breathe. Breathe. "Wh-who is it?"

"What are you doing in there? Open this damn door."

I'm so sorry, Chris. So sorry that you picked a nasty, trampy slut like me for a wife. You deserve so much better. I've got to say something. He's waiting. I'm so scared. "Go away."

"Girl, you better hurry up and open this door."

"I said go away, Chris. Get the hell away from my door and don't come back."

"Madison?"

"I, I . . . I had time to think." *Don't cry. Don't cry.* Breathe. "I can't marry you, Chris. I don't love you. I don't want to see you anymore."

"What are you talking about, Madison?"

"Get away! Go! Just go!"

"Madison—"

"Go!"

He hit the door so hard that the walls shook. "What the fuck is your problem?"

Breathe, breathe.

Hits the door again. Hard. Wall shakes. "I'm tired of this shit, Madison. I'm tired of you tripping."

I'm so sorry.

"You know what?" he said slamming against the door. "Fuck it. I'm through with this shit, Madison. Do you hear me? I'm through."

"Then go. Leave," I screamed, hating every inch of sound those words made. "Disappear just like you did before. Consider me dead. Just like your mother."

Oh—my—God. I could not believe I said that. What is wrong with me?

I could hear nothing on the other side of the door. I wondered what Chris was thinking as I stood clutching the doorknob in my hand. I wanted so badly to open the door. To tell Chris the truth. But I couldn't. I just couldn't do it.

I bent over as I heard the sound of Chris's shoes moving away from my door. *Breathe, breathe*, I kept telling myself. But I could take in no air. "Oh God," I said and covered my mouth with my hand. I gotta throw up again.

10

Her receptionist wasn't at her desk, so I went right on in. When she saw me
standing in the doorway she gasped. She was pretty, and for some reason
that pissed me off. I hate it when I come into contact with beautiful
women when I look like shit. I did at least wash myself this morning—
sorta. I turned on the water in the shower and just stood there. Didn't have
the energy to lather up and all that. No, letting the water flush over me
was enough, all I deserved. What was the point in getting extra clean?
HIV don't wipe away. Once you catch it, you've caught it. Ain't no giving
it back.

I had gotten out the shower and threw on a long, loose-fitting dress that
I usually save for days after I've eaten a large heavy meal or gained a couple of pounds. I slid into some flip-flops, shook out my braids, and headed
for the door, cautiously. Nothing seemed real this morning. As I stepped
out the door, it was as if I hadn't been outside in months. I walked lightly,
almost sneaking across the ground. I was waiting for something to happen. Something bad. Maybe I'd fall, trip, squash a snail, get melted by the
sun. But nothing went wrong, not even a car crash. Guess the worst has
already happened. I'd been diagnosed HIV positive, sentenced to death.
What could be worse?

And now I'm here, staring at this beautiful, obviously intelligent
woman. A woman with a future, a woman with the rest of her life to live.
Suddenly, I felt so small.

"Ms. McGuire," she said, giving me the eye as if she didn't know whether to smile or pick up the phone and call security. I couldn't blame her. I looked scary. Plus I'd already threatened her life and called her out of her name on several occasions. But I hadn't come to her office today to do her harm. Today I just needed to talk, and she was the only person I knew who'd listen.

"Dr. Baker," I said as I closed her office door behind me. "I know I don't have an appointment, but . . ." I couldn't bear to look her in the face. She was too pretty and I was too filthy. I wondered what she thought of me as words seemed to dance in front of my face. POSITIVE, AIDS, DEATH, NASTY, FILTHY.

"Please," she said with a smile that I didn't deserve. She motioned for me to come closer. "Have a seat."

I didn't. I couldn't move. It had taken all my will just to make it to her office, and now that I was there I wasn't sure why I'd come. What was the point? I already knew my status. There was nothing she could say to me that I'd want to hear except that the last two days had been a dream. But I knew she wasn't about to tell me that, and there was nothing that I could say to her now, except, "I apologize." I was shaking, so I put my arms across my chest in a futile attempt to calm myself. "I didn't mean to curse you out yesterday."

She smiled, I guess to make me feel comfortable, but I didn't want to be smiled at. "It's no problem, Ms. McGuire."

"Madison," I said and squeezed myself. "You can call me Madison." Ms. McGuire was who I used to be. A respected teacher at one of the finest private schools in L.A. That was then. Now that I knew the real me and what was inside me, there was no need for formalities. I might as well be called Jane Doe.

"I'm glad you came," she said, clasping her fingers beneath her chin. "There's much we need to discuss."

"Yeah. My death," I said, finally able to get my feet to move so I could take one of the seats in front of her desk. As I did, I noticed another smile creeping across her face. Was this funny to her? Was I funny? Suddenly I found myself getting angry with her again. Was she mocking me? Was I going to have to kick her fucking ass after all?

She caught a glimpse of the tension on my face and quickly wiped off what was left of her grin, but I wasn't satisfied with that. "What's with the hee-hee and the ha-ha?" I asked, feeling as if I could reach out and slap her silly. "Is it your customary practice to giggle at all your dying patients? Is it okay to make fun of the terminally ill? I'm HIV positive, Dr. Baker. I don't see a damn thing funny about that."

"Well, preach on, sister."

"I ain't none of your sister, okay?"

"That's right. Let it out. Let it all out."

"Let what out? Are you enjoying this?"

"Sort of," she said and twisted around in her seat. "You know, Madison—"

"It's Ms. McGuire," I said, trying to regain a bit of my respect.

"Your anger is normal. I expect it from you at this point. I bet you're not only angry but confused, in shock, scared. And all those emotions are okay. Let it out."

"Let it out?" I said and squinted toward the doctor. "Let it out? You say that as if all I have to do is scream and everything will be okay. Well, I've done that already. I've screamed, I've cursed, I've thrown things, I got drunk, I've done it all. And still I sit here HIV positive. Nothing's gonna change that, Doctor. I'm going to die. That's all I know. I'm going to die. Aren't I?" I asked, hoping for a second that she'd say, "Naw, you're gonna live forever." But I knew better than that. Death was coming, that was a fact.

"Ms. McGuire—"

"Call me Madison," I said, realizing that no amount of respect would be able to bring me up from the valley I'd allowed myself to fall into.

"I asked you to come to my office for one reason and that is to help you."

"To help me die," I said, rolling my eyes as the doctor reached inside her desk and pulled out a stack of pamphlets. She pushed the stack in my direction, then leaned back into her seat.

"Those will help you understand what you're dealing with."

I looked at that woman like she was out of her mind. "Do you think I'm stupid?" The tone of my voice put her on alert. "I know about HIV and AIDS, okay? I'm not some dummy off the streets, alright? I am thirty years old. I'm a teacher. I finished at the top of my class at Loyola Marymount University. I am not stupid and there is nothing in those pamphlets that I don't already know. Don't you understand, Doctor? That's why I'm so pissed. I know about AIDS. I know about condoms and all that other bullshit. And still, I fucked up. I was ignorant. I took chances. Oh, it's okay if I don't use a condom this one time. Nothing will happen. Oh, I don't feel comfortable asking this man if he has a condom. He might think I don't trust him. That was me, Doctor. Madison McGuire. I said those things. And I *knew*. I knew what I was doing. Fucking around, fucking anybody, just because I was a woman and it was my right. And now look at me. Do you see me, Doctor? I'm HIV positive, my life is ruined. Future? What future? It's all fucked. Everything is fucked. And here you are, passing me a pamphlet. Fuck that," I said and swiped the pamphlets to the floor. "I'm dying, Doctor. I don't need a pamphlet to tell me that."

Breathe, I silently told myself as the doctor sat before me, watching me as if she was seeing me for the very first time. I kept waiting for her to say something, but she just kept watching me. She was waiting on me. "Let it out," her eyes told me. "Let it all out."

"The night before you called me, I did something I said I'd never do. I told the man I loved that I would marry him. I'd swore I'd never get married, that I'd never let myself get caught onto one man. But I said yes, and I meant yes. I love him. My life was set to move in a whole new direction, Doctor. Then you called and, and . . ."

"It's okay, Madison. Let it out. It's okay."

"No, it's not okay, Doctor," I said and jumped up from my seat. "How am I supposed to tell him that I'm HIV positive? That I'm going to die? How do you tell anybody that? Huh? Doctor? Say something, dammit!"

"It won't be easy, but it's got to be done. It's very important that you contact anyone that you may have had unprotected sex with and let them know. They may be infected themselves and they could be out there infecting others."

"Don't you think I know that?" I yelled and banged my fist on her desk. "That's what's killing me. The thought that I may have sentenced someone else to death. I don't think I could go on if I've passed this virus on to someone else. I just—aaggh!" I screamed and beat both fists against her desk. I pounded like a madwoman. I *was* a madwoman. The doctor kept calling my name, but I couldn't stop what I was doing. At that moment there was nothing more important to me than beating the hell out of that desk.

"Dr. Baker," a voice called from the doorway. "Is everything alright?"

The sound of the voice shocked me enough that I stopped and turned around. It was the receptionist, I presume. She was staring at me like I was crazy. But not the doctor. I got the feeling she'd been through scenes like this hundreds of times, which only added to my frustration. There was nothing special about me anymore. I was just another arrogant fool who thought it could never happen to me. And now look at me. PITIFUL, EMBARRASSING, DERELICT. I was all those things. This was the new me.

I ran out the doctor's office as she called for me to stay. "We're not finished. I need to run some tests on you," she said as she chased me out her door, but I was too quick for her. I had to get out of there. I had to go somewhere, anywhere, but where I ended up was back at home. There was nowhere else for me. When I walked into the mess I'd created the day before I felt relieved. This is where I belonged now. In this mess. I sat down on the sofa and kicked off my flip-flops and before I knew it, I was lost in tears. I hadn't allowed myself to cry much yesterday, but now I'd given myself permission and it seemed I couldn't stop myself.

The sun was still out when I took my first sob, and by the time I heaved for the final time, it was dark. I could have cried on for hours, but I guess there was only so much water in my eyes. When I stopped and rose up from the sofa for the first time, the first place I headed was the bathroom. I peeled out of my dress, turned on the shower, and got in. This time I used soap. When I got out, I went to my bedroom and found a clean T-shirt and a pair of shorts. The next stop was the bathroom mirror. I brushed my teeth, rinsed my mouth, then looked at myself for a very long time. It was so difficult, standing there, seeing me, and knowing what I knew about myself. I guess I thought I'd look different now, but what I saw staring back at me was—me. Same complexion, same eyes, same little brown spot on my cheek where that pimple had been, same braids, same everything. The only thing that was different was the way I felt about myself. Usually when I see myself in the mirror, I get this satisfied feeling. A feeling like, yeah, it's me, Ms. Madison McGuire. But looking at myself now, all I felt was emptiness. Like, like I might as well be dead. But I was too scared to die.

I'd never thought about death much. Well, at least not for myself. Death was something that was way off. Now it was right upon me. Oh sure, they say HIV positive people can live for years now. Ten, fifteen years, they say, as if that's supposed to be some sort of consolation. Even if I live fifteen years, I'll be dead before I'm fifty. Probably before I reach menopause. "Breathe, Madison, breathe," I whispered to myself, but my knees gave out on me and I found myself sinking to the floor. Oh God. Why is this happening to me? If everything happens for a reason, then why? I just don't understand. I sat on the bathroom floor as the tears rushed through me again. Why now, when everything seemed like it was going my way? Chris was back. I was going to be married. Life was turning for me. And now . . . I've got to tell Chris. There's no way around it. He has to know. Benson and Terrence have to know too. Being HIV positive is one thing, being a silent murderer is another.

I pulled myself up from the floor and went into my bedroom. I searched through the mess of clothes and shoes and hangers and toiletries until I found it. My little pink book. They were all in here. Every man I'd dated. And in the back was the list. My dating rules. Seeing the book made me cry all over again. It used to be my prize possession, now it was like a poisonous snake.

I took the book into the living room and plugged in the phone, which had been disconnected ever since Dr. Baker called Monday morning. I picked up a chair and set it next to the phone and took a deep breath. "Benson Geoffrey," I said as I thumbed through the book. I figured I'd start with Benson because he was the most laid-back of the group. I'd dated him about four times, which was a lot for me. I enjoyed his company, but if I remember correctly, Benson is responsible for rule number eleven: Never date a man who works night shifts. Benson is a security guard at the Regency Suites Hotel, by the airport. I met him there one night when Thompson held the annual Thanksgiving feast for all the staff. Benson was a cool guy, but since he worked nights, we could never get our schedules to mesh. But I liked him enough to meet him for lunch on a few occasions, one of which turned into an afternoon rendezvous in one of the top-floor suites. That was an incredible afternoon. I almost smiled as I thought about it, but my smile was quickly erased as I picked up the phone and dialed his number. I didn't know what I was going to say, not even after he picked up the line.

"Hello," he rushed out, and as I sat in my darkened living room I realized he must have been getting ready to go to work. I almost hung up the phone, but I knew I couldn't put this off any longer. I had to speak to him now.

"Hi, Benson," I said, shutting my eyes tightly.

"Is this? Naw. Madison? Is that you?"

Oh God. "Yes. How are you?"

"Fine, just fine. Damn, girl. I haven't heard your voice in a while. What's been up?"

"Oh, nothing. Same old thing, you know." *Don't cry, please don't cry.* Just breathe. "Guess you're getting ready to head out for work, huh?"

"Gotta make them dollars," he said and laughed. "Say, why don't you stop by the hotel tonight? I can meet you in the restaurant in the lobby on my first break."

Lord, give me strength. "No, Benson. I, I can't tonight. I, um, I'm calling because I need to talk to . . . to tell you something. And, uh . . . it's very hard for me to say these words, but, uh, I've got to tell you . . ." I couldn't stop the tears. I wanted to hang up that phone so badly.

"Madison. Are you crying? Tell me. What's up? What's the problem?"

"I, I." I paused to take a deep breath. "Benson, you are such a good friend."

"Tell me what's wrong, Madison."

"I've tested positive for HIV, the virus that causes AIDS."

Silence. Dead silence.

"Um. I think I contracted it five years ago, and . . . I think you should be tested to make sure, to see if you have . . . I'm so sorry, Benson. I don't know what else to say. Benson? . . . Benson?"

"I gotta go, Madison. My shift starts in twenty minutes."

"Benson, you've got to get tested. I know we only had sex once, but you've got to go get tested."

"I ain't sick or nothing like that."

"Neither am I, but I'm still infected."

"Well, that's you. That ain't me. Hey, I feel for you, you know. I'm sorry you're going through what you're going through. But hey, I ain't got that shit. Naw. I'm perfectly healthy. Ain't a damn thing wrong with me."

"Benson, please. You've got to get this checked out."

"I don't have to do nothing but get off this phone and get my ass to work. Look, I'll talk to you later. I gotta go."

"Wait," I called out, but I was too late. He'd hung up the phone. I thought about calling him right back and pleading with him to go to a clinic, but I thought I'd give him some time. He was in shock, just like I'd been yesterday, but Benson was a smart guy. He'd do the right thing—I hoped. I'll give him two days, I thought and took another deep breath. Two days before I call and beg him again to be tested.

And now it was time to phone Terrence. I didn't even think. I just picked up the phone and dialed. If I'd given myself any chance to gather my thoughts, I probably wouldn't have gone through with calling him. It seemed so unfair. Terrence and I had just been together for the first time less than two weeks ago. I hadn't even liked Terrence. Thought he was too pretty. Didn't even want him in my home, and still, I had sex with him. This is what makes me so mad. I knew better, and still, I acted a fool. I couldn't say no to Terrence. Just because he gave me some line about a five-minute orgasm, I gave in to him. Gave in to the thrill of it all. Never once did I think. Condom. No, I just wanted to see what it would be like. I wanted to live a little, and now I had to call him, after two weeks have passed and tell him that I may have infected him with a deadly disease. I never really liked Terrence, but I never wanted to kill the man. Again, I didn't know what I was going to say as I dialed his number and waited for him to pick up. All I knew was that I had to get this over with, I had to let him know.

"Hey, this is Terrence." Dammit. An answering machine. Of course, my first inclination was to just spit out what I had to say at the beep, but I knew I couldn't go out like that. Terrence deserved more. "I'm not in right now, so you know what to do."

"Uh, hi, Terrence. This is Madison. I need to speak with you as soon as you get in. So please, give me a call when you get this message. Thanks. Bye."

Damn, I wish he'd been home. I wanted so badly for this whole ordeal to be over. Now I had to wait for him to return my call, and who knew when that would be? What if he's out on a date right now? What if he's with another woman, in her bed, making love to her, giving her the five-minute fantasy? What if he's killing her, just like I may have already killed him?

There was still one more person I had to contact, the most important person—Chris. I swear, the thought of calling him up and telling him I am HIV positive was enough to turn my stomach. I didn't want to think about it. I unplugged the phone and began pacing the floor. I couldn't move more than three spaces in any direction because of all the junk that still remained on the floor, so I decided to clean up. I knew all I was doing was putting off the inevitable, but calling Chris was more than I could handle at the time. I began cleaning everything in sight. I picked up the television and stereo, brought all the chairs to their upright position, I wiped and dusted and picked, and when I was through in the living room, I moved on to the kitchen. I picked up broken glass, wiped up spilled alcohol, cleaned off the counters, mopped. Before I knew it, three hours had passed, and my entire home was spotless. And still there was one task left undone. And still I couldn't bring myself to plug in the phone.

How could I call Chris and tell him I was HIV positive, just like that? With the snap of a finger. I kept trying to reverse the tables, to imagine how I'd feel if Chris came to me now, after all we'd been through—a broken engagement, eight years apart, denied feelings, a renewed marriage proposal. After all this, how would I feel if he came to me and said, "Madison, I'm HIV positive"? I think I would die. I would never instantly turn my back on him, but inside I'd look at him differently. My view of him would be forever changed. And no, I wouldn't want to continue in a relationship with him. What would be the point in having a relationship with a man that was soon going to die? No matter how much I loved him, things could never be the same between us again.

And after I tell Chris what I have to say, I know everything will change. But I'm prepared for that. I don't expect Chris to want to have anything to do with me anymore, especially not after the way I've treated him recently. Still, I love Chris and I feel he deserves more from me than a simple call on the phone. I needed to see him in person. I needed to handle this the right way with him. It's the least I can do. I've got to see him in person.

I grabbed my car keys from the coffee table and headed toward the door, but as soon as I opened it . . .

"Terrence," I gasped and had to take a step backward to keep myself from falling over.

"Got your message, baby," he said, flashing an unstoppable grin at me. "I knew you'd be calling soon. I see you're one of those women who likes to play hard to get. Don't call a brother for weeks. But I knew you'd come around sooner or later," he said, putting one hand on the wall and leaning into the doorway. "You glad to see me?"

"I wasn't expecting you, Terrence," I stuttered. I began to sweat, my hands became slick.

"So what's up? Dinner, dancing, movies? Or," he said, with a sly grin, "do you wanna stay in tonight?"

"I've got to tell you something, Terrence," I said. I should have invited him in, but I felt I had to tell him right then and there, while I had the nerve. A second later, I wouldn't have been able to speak. "I called you for a reason."

"I know your reason. That's why I didn't bother calling. Here I am, baby. Take what you want," he said and reached out for my face. I turned away.

"Just listen to me, Terrence," I said as my throat began to choke up. "I, I have to tell you and I don't know how to say this, but you've got to know. I'm, uh, yesterday, I received a call from a doctor at Kaiser."

"Ah naw," he said, nervously. "You pregnant? Hell naw. Don't even try to come at me like that. I know better. You ain't dealing with no fool."

"Terrence, please let me finish."

"What, you, you got something? You think I gave you something? I ain't got no STDs, sweetheart. My shit is correct. I'm clean."

"Listen to me!" I shouted, then put my hand over my mouth. "Just listen," I said and tried to remain calm, though Terrence's fidgeting wasn't making this any easier for me. "I took a blood test, Terrence. An HIV test. And the results came back positive."

He shook his head like he hadn't heard me.

"I'm not saying I got it from you. I think I may have been infected five years ago. But you need to—"

"You bitch!" he said and beat his hand against the door jamb. "You HIV positive?"

I began to tremble. For the first time I really realized how much bigger Terrence was compared to me, as his face turned red and his eyes glazed. He looked at me as if he could kill me. I'd never been afraid of a man before, but now I feared for my life.

"You scandalous ho. You gave me AIDS?"

"No, no. You don't know that. You need to be tested. You may be fine."

I saw it coming. I knew he was about to go off. I moved out the way just as he lunged for me. I took off. I ran through the hallway and jumped down the staircase. I could hear Terrence behind me. He was calling me every name he could think of. I ran to the garage gate, but I couldn't get my keys situated in my hand fast enough to open it. So I kept running. Terrence wasn't giving up. He wanted me. I turned around for a brief second and sure enough he was still coming. He was too fast. I started to scream for help. I was too nervous to keep running. I felt like one of those silly girls in a horror movie, and before I knew it I was acting like one. I tripped and fell and before I could get up, Terrence was standing over me. He kicked me in the stomach, then bent over to pick me up. I was hollering, "Please, Terrence, please. I'm sorry," but that didn't satisfy him. He slapped me back down to the ground.

"You gave me AIDS, bitch? I'm gonna *kill* your ass," he said as he reached for me again, but this time, something stopped him. I couldn't see what was happening. My eye was swollen and the pain in my stomach was so intense that I couldn't stand up. I felt like I was going to pass out. I'd never been hit like that before. I was on my hands and knees, scrambling to get away, then out of nowhere a hand grabbed me around my waist. It was a gentle touch, yet strong. I was lifted to my feet, but I was so weak that I slumped back down to my knees. I was losing it. Barely conscious. Then I heard his voice.

"Madison. You all right, baby? Please be all right."

I fought to get my eyes open, but it was no use. I was a goner. The last thing I remember was mumbling, "Please don't hurt me." Then I passed out.

11

I had a dream, but the damn thing turned into a nightmare. Hate it when that happens. Anyway, it was sorta animated, you know. Like a fairy tale, almost. I was dressed up in this frilly Victorian dress with rhinestone slippers, and my hair was braided down to my ankles. I lived in a forest with beautiful trees and a lake and waterfalls. I guess I was some kind of princess or something. I don't know, it was weird. It was like I was Cinderella, Alice in Wonderland, Little Red Riding Hood, and Sleeping Beauty all rolled into one. It was fabulous, until, that is, one day I took a dip in the lake and got poisoned. Seven little dwarfs rescued me from the water and laid me on the grass. They couldn't revive me though they tried everything. Mouth-to-mouth resuscitation, the Heimlich maneuver, covering my body with some type of secret powder. But nothing worked. Then a man came riding through the forest on a horse. I know he was fine, though I can't really remember how he looked. It was one of those dreams where nobody has faces. Anyway, he was there, of course, to save the day. The seven dwarfs told him that he was the only one who could save me, and the only way he could save me was to give me a kiss. That's when things got a little ugly. The man came and knelt by my side. He looked at me, ran his hands over my face, then kissed me . . . But nothing happened. Every time it seemed as though I was about to wake up, my body would give out and I'd just lay there. My mind was telling my body to move, but it wouldn't obey. And the more I tried to force my arms and legs to come to life, the deeper I would fall into sleep. I wanted to scream, but nothing would come out except tiny little murmurs. Then everything got black. I couldn't feel my body. I was slipping further and further into sleep and I couldn't stop myself from slipping away into more and more blackness . . . "Aaggh!"

"Madison? Madi," he said and patted the sides of my cheeks. "It's okay. I'm here. Wake up, baby. It's okay."

My eyes slowly opened and slowly everything came into focus. "Chris," I said and tried to sit up straight in bed, but the slightest movement sent a sharp pain up my side. Not only was I in pain, I was confused. I was in my bed, in my home, but I had no idea how I'd gotten there. My mind was playing tricks on me. I got scared. I wanted out. *Terrence!* "No, no, no," I said and shook my head. I forced myself to try to get up though the pain in my body was excruciating.

"It's alright, Madison," Chris said. Or at least I think it was Chris. Everything was a blur. I pulled away from the man that sat on the side of my bed and balled myself up in a knot, where I stayed, shaking, until things finally began to come clear for me. I remembered what happened the night before. Terrence, the fight—no, the beating. It was Chris who came to my rescue—I guess. It had to have been him. I must have passed out on him, right?

"What happened?" I asked as I stared at Chris. He looked scared too. No, concerned would be a better way of putting it. He didn't look himself. He just sat there looking back at me as if he had a lot on his mind.

"Who was that guy?" he said almost as if he was jealous.

The question swarmed over me. I was afraid to say. If I told Chris who he was, I'd have to tell him everything. This wasn't how I wanted to do this. I wanted to go to Chris and talk to him rationally. Like an adult. It would probably be one of our last conversations together. I didn't want it to end like this. But I had to tell him. "His name is Terrence," I said and winced from a bolt of pain that tapped my back.

"Are you okay?" he asked, but made no move to comfort me. It was as if he knew I was okay, or maybe he didn't care. There was no expression on Chris's face. He just stared at me, blankly. He was upset. But why? I hadn't even told him the whole story yet.

I nodded that I was alright, then asked, "What happened to Terrence? I can't remember a thing."

"I kicked his fucking ass and sent him home," he said and clutched his fist. "I swear I could have killed that motherfucker with my bare hands for what he did to you."

I'd never heard Chris talk like that before. He pounded his fist onto the mattress, then stood up and began pacing the floor. He was on fire. He was frightening me. I didn't know if I should tell him the whole story or if I should wait until he calmed down. He stood still for a moment and put his hands on his waist. "Is it true?" he asked and slowly turned to me.

True? Is what true? "What are you talking about?"

"Is it true?" he said louder. So loud that I jumped and felt a tingle of agony zip down my back.

"I don't know what you're talking about, Chris," I said and began to shiver. The same look that I'd seen on Terrence's face was now present on Chris's. I wanted to run again, but there was nowhere to go.

"Do you or don't you have AIDS?"

Oh God. "Terrence told you that?"

"Answer the question!"

"No, no. I mean. I, I'm. Chris, please," I said and held up a hand toward him. "This isn't how I wanted you to find out. I was on my way to your hotel last night. I wanted to sit down and tell you in person." The words were coming out so fast that I couldn't think straight. I had to pause and catch my breath before I could say another word. "No, I don't have AIDS—yet. I'm HIV positive."

Chris threw his hands to his face, then ran them over his head as it shook ever so slightly. He was trying his best to remain calm, but I could see it. The pain, the devastation, the "goddammit, why me?"

"I found out two days ago. The morning after you proposed," I said and stopped talking to fight off the tears that were sneaking up on me. But I couldn't. I began sobbing for what seemed an eternity. I could barely control myself. At one point, I expected Chris to reach out for me. To try and soothe me. But he never moved an inch in my direction. This was it. I had to finish talking to Chris. I wanted to make him understand. If this would be our last conversation, I had to tell him everything. "I never meant for this to happen, Chris. I love you. I have all along. It was just my stupid pride that kept getting in the way. I didn't want to be hurt. But now it seems I may have hurt you. You could be infected, Chris," I said remembering that night he came to my office. I watched Chris as he took a deep breath, and at that very moment I hated myself. "You do not know and I cannot fully express to you how sorry I am that I put you in this predicament. Christopher, I am so sorry. I know that you may not ever want to see me again after today, but I want you to know—I love you with all my heart, Chris. I swear. It took me a long time to admit that to myself, but I swear to God it's true. If I could give my life for you right now I would," I said, desperately trying to hold back the tears. "Oh God, Chris. You don't know how this hurts me. After all we've been through, to know that I may have wrecked your life . . . I'm so sorry."

That was it. I couldn't say another word. I couldn't hold back the tears another second. They came over me like a flood. My eyes filled so much that I couldn't see anymore. I closed my eyes and cried, wildly. I was ashamed. I wanted to be dead.

When I opened my eyes again, Chris was still standing beside my bed. He was watching me, but he didn't try to comfort me. I could tell he wanted to say something and I was prepared for it. I knew he couldn't leave without giving me a piece of his mind. Not after all I'd put him through. I stared up at him, waiting for my punishment. I was ready to take it. I deserved it. "Go ahead, Chris," I said and braced myself. "Say it."

"Say what?"

"Say whatever. That you hate me. That I disgust you. That you never want to see my face again. Say it."

"Shut up, Madison," he said and pointed his finger toward me. "Just *shut up*." He took his finger away and sat down on the edge of the bed. "What kind of man do you think I am?" he said, staring at me through glazed-over eyes. "I love you. Do you hear me? *Love you*. Nothing is going to change that." He turned away from me for a moment to calm himself, then turned back. "Last night, I came here for a reason. Fate brought me here, Madison. No matter what, I want to be with you."

"Chris, no. You don't know what you're saying."

"I know exactly what I'm saying."

"Chris, I'm going to die. You may be infected too. This isn't fate. This is crazy."

"Madison, you listen to me. I am going to get tested, alright? I'm no fool. But whatever those test results may be, doesn't matter to me. Us, *we*, matter. I'm not leaving you. I don't care. I love you. If I'm negative, thank God, hallelujah. If I'm not . . . Whatever the results, Madison, we'll deal with it. We're gonna deal with this together."

"Chris, you're talking crazy."

"No, Madison," he said, pulling out a small box from his shirt pocket.

"We're in this together," he said and opened the box to expose the brilliant diamond ring.

"I can't accept that, Chris. I can't."

He took the ring out the box and grabbed my left hand.

"No, Chris. Please."

"Are you saying you don't love me?"

"Chris, I love you, but I'm HIV positive. Do you hear me? I'm going to die."

He slid the ring onto my finger. "You've already said yes, Madison. Don't go back on your word now."

And here is my dilemma: I love Chris with all my heart, but love can't save us now. There is no escaping the fact that I am dying. I can't let Chris marry me. I know he loves me, but he's not thinking clearly now. He's trying to do the right thing. I should have known that Chris was too much of a man to walk out on me now. Still, I can't let him marry me. I can't do this. I can't let Chris do this . . .

"Madison," he said, holding my hand to his face. "Please say you'll be my wife."

"No," I said and pulled my hand away from him. I slid off the ring and held it out. "I can't say that. I can't."

He wouldn't take the ring so I stuffed it into his pocket myself.

"I'm never leaving your side, Madison. I'm gonna see you through this. I don't care what you say," he said as he rose from the bed and went to my closet. He pulled out a pair of shoes and brought them back over to the bed. Then he pulled back the covers and grabbed my feet.

"What are you doing?"

"We're going out."

"What?"

"You're going to the hospital to get your eye and back checked, and I'm going to get my HIV test."

"What?"

"And by the way, didn't your doctor tell you that you needed to get started on an AIDS prevention program?" he said as he slid on my shoes. "I'm sure she did, but you were probably too stubborn to listen. Well, guess what? While I'm getting tested, you can see your doctor and get yourself all checked out. Maybe she'll start you on some AZT. I don't know. We'll see. I'll have to talk to her."

"Hold on a minute," I said and put on the brakes.

"No. You hold on," Chris snapped and jumped in my face. "I said I was not leaving you. I am going to help you through this. So you won't marry me. Fine. But you sure as hell aren't getting rid of me. You're going to let me help. So shut up and let's go to the fucking hospital. Okay?"

Was this Chris talking?

"I said, okay?" he said loud enough to make me jump, and all I could do was nod my head. Chris was in control now.

12

One thing is for sure. Chris is no liar. He's been playing me closer than butter plays toast. By my side every step of the way. Of course, it's only been three days since I told him about my test results, but Chris has shown no signs of letting up. He says I shouldn't have to go through this alone, and as usual, he's been putting a cosmic spin on things. "Keep your head up," he's always telling me. "You're gonna live forever. Don't see this as a death sentence, see it as an opportunity to grow. God is trying to tell you something." And on and on and on. I have to admit, having Chris by my side has lifted me up. Still, sometimes when Chris is talking all that faith and spiritual shit, I want to tell him to shut the fuck up. I don't care how optimistic I get, the fact remains that my life is coming to an end, more sooner than later. Oh, excuse me. I'm not supposed to talk about death anymore, according to Chris. I'm supposed to focus on the here and now, the living, on making my way in the world one day at a time. And I've been trying to do that, but sometimes it's hard. It's really hard. Everything is still so new to me. I'm thirty years old and HIV positive. How can I put a happy face on that? I can't just smile and accept it. But Chris says I have to live with it and deal with it, and as long as he's breathing he's going to help me through.

Still, I can't help thinking that Chris's attitude may change, sooner than he thinks. His HIV test results should be back any day now, and what then? What if he's positive too? He'll hate me. I know it. Oh sure, Chris will put a positive spin on it and say some bullshit like, "God must have a plan for me." But I know, deep down inside, he'll hate me. How could he not? He keeps saying that if he comes up positive, he'll be just as responsible as me. That night in my offic he made a choice to have sex with me without using a condom, so he's just as much to blame. But no. I don't follow that logic. That night in my office, I was the aggressor. I jumped on him. This is all my fault and if I've infected him . . . I can't deal with that thought. I just can't. I really mean it when I say I'd give my life right now to save Chris.

To be honest what I'm really hoping is that Chris's test results will come back negative, everything will be okay with him, he'll come to his senses, and finally, he'll leave me. Yes. I want Chris to leave me. Why should he stay with me when I'll only become a burden to him, especially after a few years when the virus starts to take me over? Right now I'm healthy. There is nothing wrong with me. Unless I tell people I'm HIV positive, no one would ever know. Not just by looking at me, anyway. But I've had the virus now for five years. That's a long time. There will come a time, be it five years or ten years from now, when I will start to deteriorate. When my body will not be able to ward off opportunistic infections. Chris is a doctor. He knows this and he has to know that one day I'll become a burden. He looks at me now and sees the same old Madison. The healthy Madison. But in a few years all that will change. No one should have to watch someone they love die. It's not fair to him. But every time I bring up the subject, Chris tells me to shut my mouth. He's been quite forceful with me lately. Whenever I say something negative, he quickly turns on me. "We'll have none of that talk," he says and if I persist, he simply tells me to shut up. But I'm only being realistic. Though I don't know what I would do without Chris in my life, one day, soon, I'm going to have to let him go. I don't know how I'm going to do it, but for Chris's sake, I'm going to have to end it.

"Madison," Chris said and put his hand on my shoulder. I was so deep in my own thoughts that I didn't even notice him walk into the room. I still haven't gotten used to him being here all the time. I never thought the independent, need-my-own-space Madison would ever be shacking up with a man, but that's the way it's been lately. "Have you meditated this morning?" he asked and sat down next to me on the sofa.

"Yes, Chris," I answered and took the cup of tea he was offering me. "I've prayed and meditated, just like you told me."

"Good," he said and took a sip of his own tea. "Have you been thinking about what I asked you last night?"

There were so many things that Chris talked to me about that I didn't know what he meant. It seems that's all Chris has been doing lately—talking. It's his way of keeping me focused on positive thoughts, but sometimes it gets boring as hell. "What are you talking about?"

"I asked you to do some thinking. You know, about why this has happened to you. What you're supposed to learn from it. What's the purpose of it all. What you want to do with your life now."

Damn. I didn't want to think about that right now. I didn't care why this had happened to me. All I know is that it's fucked up. But I couldn't let Chris hear me talking like that. But what my mouth didn't say came out in the expression on my face.

"Madison," he sighed and set his cup down. "I'm serious about this. You need to find the answers for yourself. Everything happens for a reason. You've got to search yourself and find the reasons. God is using you, you know that, don't you?"

"God needs to pick on someone his own size."

"Stop it," he said and held up a finger. "Get serious. If you dig deep and find out what it is you're supposed to be learning from all this you'll be better able to deal with your situation."

I was not in the mood for this right now. "Can we change the subject, please?"

"No. It's about time you put some thought into this."

"I don't want to think about that now. I'm not psychic. I don't know what God is trying to teach me. I don't know, Chris."

"You're being negative again. Think about what you want to do now. Where's your light at the end of the tunnel?"

"There is no fucking light at the end of the tunnel. I don't want to do shit now. I just want this to be over."

"That attitude will get you nowhere. You've got to make sense out of this for your own sake."

"Well there's not a whole hell of a lot about this that makes sense."

"You can feel sorry for yourself if you want, but—"

"Fuck you, Chris, alright? Of course I feel sorry for myself. Aren't I allowed that? I sure as hell ain't happy. What? You want me to give myself a pat on the back because I'm HIV positive? You want me to jump up and down because I'm going to die? Fuck that. There is no bright side to this, Chris. I might as well go on ahead and die right now."

"Shut up, Madison. Just shut the hell up. I won't listen to you talk like that. Do you hear me?" The authority in Chris's voice almost scared me. Every day I was becoming more and more intimidated by him. That was new for me. No man has ever been able to do that to me. Not even Chris, until lately. But as I stared at him, frowning as he sipped his tea, I realized it wasn't quite intimidation I was feeling. It was respect. I'd been a bitch for years, used to having my own way or no way at all. Only, Chris wasn't having that anymore. When he said he wouldn't tolerate any negative thinking, he meant it. And as a man, he put his foot down and demanded it. Wow, I thought as I stared at him. No other man had ever been able to tame me. Guess there's a first time for everything. "I don't mean to yell," he said and looked at me out the corner of his eye. "But as long as I'm living with you—"

"Um, excuse me? Living with me?"

"That's right. I'm not going anywhere. I'm staying right here for the duration. You got a problem with that?"

Hell yeah, I had a problem with that, but at the moment I couldn't get into it. There was a knock at the door. I turned to Chris. "The first of our guests is here," I said and took a deep breath.

"I'll get it," he said and got up from the sofa. Chris had convinced me that the time had come for me to let a few people in on my little secret. I didn't want to at first, and I'm still not sure if I'm doing the right thing. But Chris convinced me that I needed support from people who loved me. That, he was right about. I couldn't keep this a secret forever. I had to let the people I loved into my new world.

Chris opened the door to reveal Malik. My heart shook as he and Chris introduced themselves and exchanged hellos. When Malik walked through the door and saw me, he immediately stuck a finger at me. "You've got some explaining to do, Miss Thang," he said and cracked a smile. "How dare you take a vacation from work? For a whole week, no less. You know Thompson has been bitching," he said, faking a frown.

"How are my students?" I asked and stood up to greet him.

"Confused, like we all are," he said and wrapped me up in his arms. "I want to know what the hell is going on. And why haven't you been answering your phone? Every time I call I get the damn machine. Are you okay?"

I looked behind Malik to Chris and took another deep breath. "I'll tell you all about it, but we have to wait for our other guests."

"Other guests?" Malik questioned just as another knock came at the door.

Malik took a seat in the recliner as Chris answered the door. It was Mother and Serena. They must have come directly from church. Mother grinned like a Cheshire cat when she saw Chris, and Serena ran right over to me and gripped me around the waist.

"Where you been?" she asked, burying her head in my chest. "Why haven't you been at school or come by the house to see me?" she asked, then kissed my cheek. "Why haven't you been answering your phone?"

"I think I know why," Mother said as she walked through the door, eyeing Chris and me like she knew the answer to the million-dollar question. She patted my shoulder, then pulled Serena over to the sofa and sat down. "So," she said, still grinning. "What's this news you have to tell us?"

"You've met Malik, haven't you, Mother?"

"Oh yes," she said and waved.

Serena's eyes lit up when she noticed her teacher sitting in the corner. "Hi, Mr. Tate," she said as she shyly batted her eyes and smiled.

"Can I get anyone a drink? Soda, water, juice?" I asked nervously.

"Why don't we just get down to the reason we're all here?" Mother said, forever grinning.

I began trembling noticeably. Chris came to my side and put his arm around my shoulder to calm me down, but it didn't help much. We'd talked the night before about how I would handle telling everyone. That I should just be calm and say what I had to say. But now that they were all here, I didn't know what to do. I was scared. What would they think of me once I told them? Would they still love me? Or would they run from me?

"I can't tell them," I whispered to Chris and turned away.

"Oh," Mother said, overcome with joy. "She's shy. It's okay, baby. I know. We know. You two are getting married."

"Uh, no," Chris said to Mother, then squeezed my shoulders. "It's okay, Madi. I'm here for you. You've got to tell them."

"You're pregnant," Mother said as her mouth dropped wide open. "You two are having a baby."

"Mother, please," I said and rubbed my hands together.

Chris pulled over one of the kitchen chairs and set it in the middle of the room. I sat down as he stood behind me and placed both his hands on my shoulders. I looked into each face for as long as I could, then lowered my head.

"Madison?" Chris said.

"No. I'm alright. I'm alright," I said and lifted my head again. "I am alright," I said to everyone. "Remember that." I folded my hands in my lap, then looked up at the ceiling to keep the tears that were boiling in my eyes in their place. "I asked you all here today because I love you. But more importantly, I need you. More than I ever have before." I reached up to feel Chris's hand on my shoulder. I found strength in his touch. "I am, uh . . . My life has, uh, gone through a bit of a change this past week. I don't know how to say this, but I've got to . . ." I sighed. "I have found out that I am HIV positive."

Confusion was on every face.

"I have the virus that causes AIDS."

Confusion and silence . . . Mother didn't blink. Serena sat straight, and Malik was the first to speak up.

"But last week you said—"

"I know. When no one from the hospital called I just assumed . . . But now the results are in and, and I'm positive."

"AIDS," Mother whispered and bowed her head.

Serena raised her hand like she was in class.

"Yes, Serena." There was pain on her young face.

"Does this mean you're gonna die?"

I gripped Chris's hand. "I don't have AIDS yet. But when I get it . . ."

She lowered her hand and put it in her lap. Her eyes filled with tears.

"Don't you cry," I told her. "I'm alive. I'm gonna be here for a long time. So don't you cry."

Mother didn't listen to that advice. She burst out in tears. "Oh God," she screamed. "Oh God." She sprang up from the sofa and ran into the bathroom and shut the door behind her. We could all hear her.

Malik dropped his head and leaned over in his seat. Then before I knew it, he was kneeling before me and clutching me in his arms. The only word he could say was my name. Then I felt another pair of arms around me. It was Serena. I lifted my head just barely to catch a glimpse of her. The tears were still bottled up in her eyes, but when she shut them, the tears oozed out onto her face. "I don't want you to die, Li'l Mama," she said over and over again.

The three of us stayed locked together for quite some time as Chris went off to the bathroom to check on Mother. I was getting concerned about her too, but I didn't want to leave the loving embrace of Malik and Serena. It was so warm there, so filling. Though everyone was in tears, I knew they loved me. They cared. And most important, they wouldn't leave me.

"Let's go, Serena," I heard Mother's voice say out of nowhere. "We've got to go."

I looked up at Mother and wiped my eyes. She stood behind our huddle with her hands wrapped across her chest. We were the only breathing things in the room, yet she couldn't bring her eyes to focus on us. She looked everywhere. At the sofa, the floor, the window. Everywhere but at us, at me. Her face was blank, her stance firm, her eyes red, and her mouth quivering. I couldn't read her. I couldn't figure her out. Once again she gripped her purse in her hand and stared down at the floor. "Serena, I said let's go."

"I don't wanna go," Serena whined and hugged me around my neck. "I don't wanna leave Li'l Mama."

"What did I say?" she asked, finally turning to look in our direction, but only at Serena.

"No," Serena cried and gripped my neck. "I don't wanna go, I don't wanna go."

"Bring me your tail," Mother said and stomped her foot. When Serena didn't move, Mother whipped over to us and grabbed her by the back of her dress. "Girl, you better hear what I say."

"Mother," I yelled and rose to my feet. But when she didn't look my way, I quieted down. "Mother?"

I got no response. Malik moved to my side and put his arm around me, but I shook him off. "Mother?"

Chris was the next to come to my side. He too reached out for me, but I didn't want his comfort either. I wanted my mom. "Mother? Talk to me. Say something."

"I've gotta go," she said, pushing Serena toward the door.

"Mommy, please."

"Just let her go," Malik whispered.

"No," I said, following her to the door. "Mommy, please don't leave now. Please," I begged.

She stopped, facing the door, and put her hand on the knob. Her whole body seemed to quiver, and as I stood behind her I wanted so badly to reach out for her, but something kept me away. I was standing right on her heels, but the distance between us seemed like miles.

"Miss Mavis," Chris said as he walked over to us. "Are you okay?"

Silence.

"Let me drive you home," Chris said, cutting between my mom and me. Mother nodded her head slowly, then opened the door and walked out without looking back.

"I'll talk to her," Chris said as he followed her out.

As the door closed I could hear Serena. "I love you, Li'l Ma."

"I love you too, baby," I whispered.

They'd been gone for ten minutes before I was able to pull myself away from the door. As I stood there I wondered. Does Mother still love me? Will she be there for me? Will she talk to me? It was strange. Those were the same things I used to wonder about my father, and as I stood next to the door, wondering and thinking, I couldn't help but feel as if I'd lost her too.

"Malik," I said as I turned away from the door. I'd almost forgotten he was there. He must think I'm crazy, the way I'd been just standing there, staring at a closed door. Either that, or he understood me and knew that what I needed was time to think. Good friends are funny like that. They always know what you need and when you need it, when to step in and when to walk away. By the look on Malik's face, I could tell he knew what I needed. Honest conversation. "I don't look different, do I?"

"Still beautiful."

"I've lost five pounds. I'm not sick, just stress," I said, turning around. "Can you tell?"

"Everything looks good to me," he said and motioned for me to come sit next to him on the sofa. "You okay?"

"Fine."

"I'm here for you."

"I know."

"Are you scared?"

"Yep," I said and paused. "You know what I'm scared of the most?"

"What?"

"Getting ugly." I laughed.

"Figures."

"No, I'm serious."

"I know you are."

"I'm scared of getting skinny and fragile and getting bumps on my face, and lesions. What if my hair falls out? You think I should get my braids taken out?"

"You look fine."

"Do I really?"

"Really."

"I'm scared of dying, too. Real scared. But let's not talk about that."

"We won't."

"Chris says I've got to stay positive. Focus on the fact that I'm still healthy, you know. I've still got a lot of years ahead of me. I start AZT in a couple weeks. That oughta help a lot. I saw the doctor the other day and all she talked about was AZT, T cells, vitamins—I hate talking about all that stuff . . . Oh shit, I'm rambling."

"It's okay. I can keep up."

"I mean I feel fine. I'm depressed a lot, but Chris helps with that."

"He seems to be a good man."

"He is. That scares me too. He hasn't gotten his test results back yet. He may be infected. I called the two other people I had sex with too. Without protection. I don't know if they're infected either." I almost lost it for a second, but Malik grabbed my hand and steadied me. "I'm sorry," I said and took a deep breath. "I just need to talk."

"Talk on."

"I don't know what I'm going to do if they're infected too."

"You can't beat yourself up about that. You've told them, now it's up to them to get tested. Remember, they didn't use condoms either."

"Yeah. That's what Chris keeps telling me, but it doesn't make how I feel any better. Oh, shit. Your dedication ceremony."

"Next weekend."

"I've got to get a dress. What color should I wear?"

"Whatever you want."

"You hungry? You want something to drink?"

"I'm fine."

"We could order some pizza, or Chinese."

"I'm fine."

"Am I talking too much?"

"You're fine."

"I'm glad you're here."

"Me too."

"Can I tell you something?"

"What?"

"I know it sounds sorta weird considering everything I'm going through right now, but . . . I mean I can't help but think about it. I mean, I just wonder you know . . ."

"What?"

"I mean, you've known people with AIDS and HIV, right?"

"Yeah."

"Well I'm just wondering . . ."

"What?"

"What about sex?"

"Sex?"

"I know, I know. That's how I got in this fucked up situation to begin with. But I don't know, I . . . So much of who I am has always been about my sexuality, you know. It's like my whole identity is sexualized. Does that sound awful?"

"Nope."

"Out of all the things I should be worrying about, all I can think of is what am I going to do without sex?"

"Who says you have to do without?"

"I know what you're thinking. Condoms. Believe me, I love Chris a lot, but to make love to him with a condom every single time seems so, I don't know . . . It would just remind me that I have a deadly disease, you know. Plus, I'd always think, you know, it would be in the back of my mind— What if the condom breaks? What if Chris didn't put it on right? What if I'm infecting him."

"Have you talked to Chris about this?"

"No. No. He's been great. He hasn't left my side, Malik. Day and night he's been with me. It's like he's not afraid of me at all. He gets into bed with me at night and holds me. Like I said, I've been pretty depressed so by the time bed time rolls around I'm usually in tears. But Chris just gets in there with me and holds me till I fall asleep."

"You should talk to him about it."

"I can't. No. Not right now."

"You know, Madison," he said and leaned closer to me. "I'm not afraid of you either. And I'm here for you. For whatever."

"I'm hungry," I said and made a move to get up. "Let's order pizza."

"I'm serious, Madison," he said and gripped my hand in his. "I'm here for you. I'm your friend."

"My best friend."

"And I know you."

"And?"

"And I know you have needs."

"Yeah?"

"And I'm here for you. For whatever you want to do. If you're scared about having sex . . ."

"Malik."

"I'm not afraid of you."

Was Malik offering to have sex with me?

"I'm here for you. For whatever."

"Let's change the subject."

"For *whatever*."

"I'm hungry."

"Subject changed."

"How's work?"

"Next subject."

"It's that bad, huh?"

"Worse. But you don't need to worry yourself about that."

"I'm coming back tomorrow. I've got to. Chris says I need to get back in the swing of things. He's right. I want to go back. Do I look okay? Do you think anyone will know?"

"You look fine, Madison. But since you're thinking about coming back to work I'd better fill you in on a few things."

"Like?"

"I've been suspended."

"What?"

"I got the news on Friday."

"No, Malik. You have got to be kidding."

He shook his head. "Thompson sent a memo to me at the end of the day. Suspended indefinitely without pay. Motherfucker wouldn't even accept my calls. I went up to see him personally and he was conveniently in a conference."

"Oh, hell no. This is bullshit."

"Don't worry about it, Madison. It's cool. I can handle the loss of money. It's just that the bastard didn't have the decency to tell me to my face."

"No, Malik. Thompson is up to something else. I know he is," I said and got up from the sofa. "This has nothing to do with our proposal. We followed all the rules of proper teacher conduct. There's got to be something more. I know him."

"Look," Malik said calmly, "just let it ride. Don't get yourself all worked up over this shit. You've got more important things to worry about. I don't even think you should be coming back to work so soon. You've got the time. Take another week off if you have to."

"No," I said and sat back down. "I've got to get my life back on track. All I do around here is sit and mope and think about dying. I'm not going to do that anymore. I'm HIV positive, but I'm still alive, Malik. I've still got a life. And I'm going to live it. To the fullest."

"I love you. You know that, don't you?"

"I know," I said and reached out for my friend.

We held each other until the front door opened and Chris came in.

"I'm going to leave you two alone," Malik said and squeezed me one last time, then got up from the sofa. He stood in front of Chris and held out his hand. "Take care of my friend," he said as he gripped Chris's palm.

"Always," Chris said and patted Malik's shoulder.

"I'll call you tomorrow," Malik said over his shoulder as he walked out the door.

"During lunch break," I yelled to him just before the door closed.

"Lunch break?" Chris said and turned to me.

"I'm going back to work," I said and stood up. "I'm getting my life back in order. I'm going to live, Chris. Not wait around here to die."

"If that's what you want to do," he said and ran his hand across my face.

"That's what I want to do," I said and took a deep breath. "It's what I've got to do."

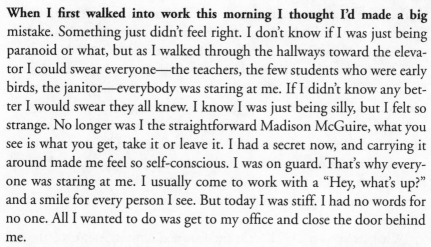

13

When I first walked into work this morning I thought I'd made a big mistake. Something just didn't feel right. I don't know if I was just being paranoid or what, but as I walked through the hallways toward the elevator I could swear everyone—the teachers, the few students who were early birds, the janitor—everybody was staring at me. If I didn't know any better I would swear they all knew. I know I was just being silly, but I felt so strange. No longer was I the straightforward Madison McGuire, what you see is what you get, take it or leave it. I had a secret now, and carrying it around made me feel so self-conscious. I was on guard. That's why everyone was staring at me. I usually come to work with a "Hey, what's up?" and a smile for every person I see. But today I was stiff. I had no words for no one. All I wanted to do was get to my office and close the door behind me.

I had really believed that I was ready to return to work. Ready to get on with my life and get things back to normal. But now that I was here, I felt out of place. I watched all the people as they hustled and bustled down the halls with their briefcases and files and cups of coffee, making small talk about this, that, and the other, and as I watched them all, a single thought kept running through my mind. Well, it wasn't really a thought, it was more like an image, a question mark, a big fat *"why?"* Why are we all here? Why am I here? What is the purpose of all this? Why? Why, why, why?

As I stood in front of the elevator, waiting for it to arrive, I thought about Chris. He was the reason I had this big, fat question mark floating through my head. He had started in on me this morning while I was getting dressed for work.

"Did you say your prayers, did you meditate?" he asked as he stood watching me slip on my stockings in the bathroom.

I had been too rushed for meditation and prayer this morning, but I lied and told him yes anyway, just so I wouldn't have to hear his mouth. But my lie didn't keep Chris quiet.

"So have you done any more soul searching?" he asked as I squeezed past him in the doorway and searched around the floor for my brown pumps. I pretended like I didn't hear his question as I rumbled through my closet, hoping Chris would see that I had too much on my mind to contend with his constant nagging about soul searching and finding the *reasons*. My mind was on getting back to work, but as usual Chris was there pushing me to dig deeper. "You can't keep putting this off, Madison. You've got to find the meaning in all of this. You can't be at peace until you figure out why all this has happened to you," he said as I continued to ignore him and busied myself with getting dressed. "Madison, do you hear me?" he asked as I brushed past him to get back to the bathroom. "I know I may sound like a broken record," he went on as I fought the urge to agree with him, "but I'm saying this for your own good."

"Can you pass me my brown belt?" I asked him, trying to change the subject, but Chris wasn't having it. "Fine. I'll get it myself," I said and tried to make my way past him again, only this time he stopped me. He took hold of my arm and held me to his chest.

"I'm not so sure you should go back to work today," he said like a fretful parent.

"What are you saying?" I asked and frowned at him. "Aren't you the one who said I can't let this disease stop me from living? That I can't just sit around this house being depressed?"

"Yes," he said, loosening his grip on me. "But you can't run from reality either."

"I'm not running from shit. I'm going to work."

"It's only been a week, Madison. You need more time. More time for this to sink in. More time to understand it all."

"Man, please," I said and yanked my arm away from him. "I'm not in any kind of denial, Chris. I know I'm HIV positive. I know what that means. I've had a whole week to do nothing but think about that. What more do you want me to do?"

"Feel."

"Fa-uh-*feel*? You are just about getting on my last nerve. One minute you say move on with life, go to work, don't think negatively. And the next minute you're talking this feeling shit. Like all you want me to do is sit around here and brood over the fact that I've got this terrible terminal disease."

"All I want you to do is be real with yourself. Don't cover up your feelings."

"Chris, please," I said as I slumped down onto the bed. "Would you just shut the hell up? *Damn*," I said as I dropped my head into the palms of my hands. "I'm doing the best I can. I'm trying to survive. Don't you understand that?"

He leaned against the bedroom door and crossed his arms over his chest. "I'm sorry," he said as he stared up at the ceiling. "It's just that I love you so much and I want what's best for you."

"The best I can do is try to get my life back to normal, and I can't do that with you here."

He immediately opened his mouth to protest, but I held up my hand and shook my head.

"I know you're trying to help, Chris, and I thank you. I love you. But I need some time to myself. Just a day or two, so I can get my head together."

"But, Madison—," he started to say. I shook my head again.

"Listen to me. One day. Just *one* day to be by myself and get it together. Can you give me that?"

"Don't shut me out."

"I'm not. I swear. I just need some time by myself. I'm not used to having someone around all day, every day. And you need some time too. You've put a lot of things on hold for me, to be here for me and help me through this. But I know you could use some time to yourself. You need a break."

He slowly nodded his head as he thought about everything I was saying. "I do need to take care of some things down at the clinic. It opens up next week."

"Next week?" I said, like I was astonished to hear it was so soon. But I already knew the clinic's opening date. And I knew unless I pushed Chris, he'd never leave my side for long enough to take care of the business in his own life. "You've got to get down to the clinic, Chris. You can't put your life on hold for me."

He looked like he wanted to protest again, but I simply closed my eyes and shook my head. I didn't want to hear it. "I'll be alright for a couple of days," I said and stood up. "And maybe tonight, while I'm alone, I can do some of that soul searching you've been talking about."

"Are you sure?"

"Yes, I'm sure."

"Alright," he said, grudgingly. "But I'm gonna call."

"I know you will," I said and huddled myself against his chest.

He squeezed me tightly and whispered, "I love you."

I lifted my face to his and gave him a quick peck on the mouth, but that tiny gesture left me wanting more. I hesitated a bit, then I closed my eyes and kissed him deeply, and for the first time in a long while I felt romantic—lustful, even. But it was over too soon. I don't know who pulled away first, him or me, but we stopped. Just stopped. Like we both knew we'd caught ourselves doing something wrong. Like we were two kids making out in the bushes and heard the grown-ups coming. I didn't say anything to Chris after that. I just backed away, grabbed my purse, and headed for the door. I knew I should have said something. I wanted to say something. I wanted to ask, "Do you still want me? Do you still like holding me, touching me?" No, what I really wanted to ask was, "When are we going to have sex again?" But I was too scared of what his reaction would be. The fact that I was even thinking about having sex again bothered me. In my condition sex should be the furthest thing from my mind. But I can't help the way I feel. HIV or no HIV, I still love Chris. I still want him. The question is, does he still feel the same about me?

■

"Hey, girl," a voice called from behind me just as the elevator doors opened up. I turned around to find Cynthia, Tommy Thompson's secretary.

"Morning," I said as we both walked onto the elevator.

"Look at you," she said and eyed me from head to toe.

I freaked. *Look at me? Look at what? Can you tell? Do I look different? What do you know?*

"You look great," she said and smiled. "Between you and me," she said, whispering, "I know you weren't off because of the stomach flu. You've been working here nine years straight, girl. Even the best of us need a vacation every now and then."

"Yeah," I said and faked a smile as I pressed the button for my floor. I could feel myself stiffening again as Cynthia stared at me. I felt like she was expecting something from me. A joke, a grin, a rundown of my week away from work, but I was too self-conscious to speak. Too paranoid that my secret would somehow mysteriously slip out. I got the feeling that Cynthia could sense I wasn't in the mood for small talk, so she dropped the girlfriend routine and opted for a more professional chat.

"In case you haven't heard, there's a mandatory staff meeting this morning in Thompson's conference room."

I thought and rolled my eyes. Just the asshole I wanted to see. He had a lot of explaining to do, starting with why the hell he suspended Malik. I hated to have to act ugly on my first day back to work, but I was damn sure going to get to the bottom of this. "So what's the topic of this mandatory meeting?" I asked as Cynthia's face lit up.

"Your proposal," she said, smiling. "It's going to happen. Mighty Avalon is stepping into the nineties."

"Thompson gave the okay for the sex ed course?"

"Thanks to you and that list of parents who demanded it."

"Really," I said as my curiosity began to peak.

"Yes, really. He's going to make the announcement this morning," she said and looked down at the floor. "Too bad Mr. Tate won't be here to witness this."

"What happened with Malik?" I asked and moved closer to Cynthia. "Why'd he get suspended?" I asked just as the elevator stopped at the third floor.

"I don't know nothing," she said defensively. "I don't know a thing."

"Cynthia," I said and held the doors back.

"I don't know, Madison. Please."

"Alright," I said as I stepped off the elevator, realizing I wouldn't get any more out of her.

"Where are you going? The meeting starts in five minutes."

"I'll be there," I said as the elevator doors closed behind me.

When I reached my office door, everything started to feel like old times.

The phone was ringing off the hook and a stack of mail was piled high on the floor. I scooped up the mail, opened the door, and ran over to my phone and picked it up.

"Mighty Avalon, Ms. McGuire speaking," I said as the phone slipped out my hand and landed on top of my desk along with the armful of mail I'd been holding. I scrambled around for the phone and sat down, but when I put the phone back to my ear all I heard was the dial tone.

I put the phone back down and slumped into my chair. Though I knew I had to hurry to get to Tommy's conference room, I also knew that I had to take a moment to get myself together. My mind was too full. I guess Chris's nagging about soul searching had really gotten to me. The big, fat question mark in my head was all I could focus on. Why? I thought as I sat and stared straight ahead. Why? Maybe Chris was right. I shouldn't have come back to work so soon. My brain wasn't ready for this yet. So many other things were on my mind, consuming my thoughts, and none of it had to do with this school. Damn. I need to go home, I thought as my phone rang out again.

"This is Madison."

"Hi," a familiar voice said, and instantly I began to shiver. "It's me. Benson," he said as if he wasn't sure he should have called me.

"Hi," I said through trembling lips as my mind replayed our last conversation together, when I told him I was HIV positive and that he may well be infected too. I couldn't believe he was calling me. What more could he have to say, unless . . .

"I got tested," he said and paused. My shaking became so uncontrollable that the phone almost slipped out of my grip. I switched hands and waited for him to continue. I could feel sweat beading under my armpits.

"And?" I asked and closed my eyes.

"I'm negative."

"Negative?"

"Yes, Madison."

"Benson," I said as my eyes filled with water, "you don't know how happy I am to hear you say that. I've been praying and praying and . . . I'm just so happy for you."

"You? Ain't nobody happier than me. I was so scared that I almost didn't go take the test. But I did and I got the results this morning. *Shit*. Girl, I tell you, I'm so relieved I feel like going to Disney World," he said, then quickly stopped himself. "Oh. I'm sorry," he said and got really quiet.

"It's okay, Benson. I know you must be relieved."

"But what about you? I mean, you okay and everything?"

"I'm doing fine. Really. I'm doing even better now that I know I didn't infect you. I'm really sorry I had to put you through this, Benson."

"Yeah. It's cool, though. You know it takes two to tango," he said and paused again. "I'm real sorry for you, Madison. If there's anything I can do or anything you need, you know where I'm at."

"I know. You take care, okay?"

"No, girl. You take care."

I was motionless for a long time after I hung up the phone. Hearing Benson tell me that he was not infected both made my day and wrecked it. While I was thrilled he was okay, his call forced me to think about the other men I'd been with. Terrence and, most important, Chris. If Chris is infected I think I might die. And although Terrence nearly beat the shit out of me, I still had every hope that he too would test negative. I don't condone what Terrence did to me after I told him I was HIV positive, but I can certainly understand it. Hell, when I put myself in his shoes, I can see myself reacting just as he had. If Ronald Olbright were still alive, believe you me, I'd be on his ass like white on rice. How else could I expect Terrence to react? I told him to his face that I may have ended his life sooner than he'd expected. That's enough to make anybody go crazy. Anybody but Saint Christopher. He's the only one who seems to be okay with all of this, and under any other circumstance I could really appreciate that. But Christopher is being a bit too cool about it all. Since he got tested he hasn't said a word about how he hopes the results will turn out. And he talks about me covering up my feelings? I know he has to be afraid for himself. I know he does. But Chris has been too concerned with me to think about himself. I love him for that, but still, I wonder. Is he negative or positive? And what then? How will he react when he finds out the news? How will I react? "Dammit," I said as the phone rang out again. Does everybody and their mother know that I'm back at work today?

"Madison McGuire, may I help you?"

"It's me," Malik said. "Just calling to see how you're doing."

"I'm fine, Malik," I said, cuddling the phone between my neck and shoulder. "What about you?"

"Just lounging. Wondering if I should call Thompson and beg for my job or just ride this thing out."

"Don't you worry about a thing," I said and pointed a finger as if Malik was standing right in front of me. "We have a meeting this morning, and after it's over I'm going to have a little talk with Mr. Thompson."

"Hold on, Madi. I don't need you risking your neck to go to bat for me. This is my problem."

"No, Malik. You're my friend. It's my problem too."

"Madison."

"Look, I can't talk now. I've got to get to the meeting. I'll call you at recess."

"Wait a minute."

"Gotta go."

"You okay?"

"Yeah, I guess," I said and slowed down. "I guess I know what it's like to be in the closet now, though."

"You mean keeping it a secret about . . . about, you know."

"Keeping it a secret about being HIV positive. Yeah."

"Hey. You do what you have to do. You know what's best for you."

"Yeah. Still feels strange, though."

"I love you."

"Oh shut up."

"What?"

"You don't have to baby me, Malik. I'm fine. I'm dealing."

"Alright, then. Call me. I ain't going nowhere," he said sarcastically.

"I love you too," I said and hung up the phone.

"Do I need to be jealous?"

I almost jumped out of my skin, until I looked in the doorway and saw Chris standing there.

"What are you doing here?" I said when I finally caught my breath enough to speak.

"Just checking on you."

"I've only been gone for an hour," I said as he walked in and sat down in front of my desk. "I thought we agreed to give each other the day off. You should be down at the clinic, handling your business."

"I was just worried about you."

"I'm gonna tell you like I just told Malik. I'm fine. Don't worry about me. Now go," I said and pointed to the door.

"Okay, okay," he said and leaned forward in his seat. "But I've got something else to tell you first."

"I love you too. Now go."

He smiled and took out a piece of paper from his shirt pocket and handed it to me. It was his test results. Chris, too, was negative.

"Since it hadn't been that long since we made love, I have to have another test taken in six months. But so far, everything looks good."

My reaction was not as it should have been. I should have screamed hallelujah and jumped up for joy, danced a jig. Instead I just sat there, staring at the paper he'd handed me, with barely any reaction at all.

Chris stood up and walked around my desk. He stood behind me and leaned over to kiss my cheek. "I've got to go. I just wanted you to see my results," he said and rubbed the side of my face. "I'll call you later, okay?"

I nodded my head as he walked out my office. I was too stunned to move. I read and reread the paper over and over again before I put it down, then I rose up from my seat and went to my door and closed it. Before I knew it I was in tears, but I couldn't understand why. This was good news. Preliminary, but good. And yet I was crying. I leaned myself against the door and slid down to the floor in a stupor. Chris was negative, Benson was negative. And me? I was positive. "Why?" I mumbled as I cried uncontrollably. Why me? Why was I the only one? This wasn't fair. I felt like a freak. It wasn't that I wanted Benson and Chris to be infected too, but, but—why was I the only one? What did I do that was so bad? I had sex. So what? Everybody has sex. Unprotected sex. Why was I the only one who had to die from it? The more I thought about it, the angrier I became with myself. There I was, crying and whining, when what I should have been doing was rejoicing. What? Did I want Chris to die? Did I want someone to share in my despair? Would that make it easier for me? What kind of person was I to be having these types of thoughts? A decent person would be overjoyed that she didn't inflict this deadly virus on someone else. Maybe I wasn't decent. Maybe I deserved this disease. Maybe God knew something about me that I didn't know. Maybe, just maybe, I was meant to die young.

I don't remember how long I stayed on the floor, slumped against the door, but when I got up all I knew was that I had to get out of there. I was tripping. Hard. And I knew I had to get home, back to the place I felt the most safe. I scrambled up from the floor and went to my desk to grab my purse and attaché. In no time I was out the door and at the elevator, and when the doors opened I rushed on and smack-dab into Cynthia.

"Madison," she nearly screamed. "I told you the meeting was before class. Where've you been?" she asked as she pressed the button for the fifth floor. "Thompson sent me down here for you. The meeting is halfway over by now."

She held her hands at her hips as I stood, dazed, staring at her back. I just wanna go home, I kept saying to myself. I didn't think I could stomach a meeting and I surely couldn't stomach seeing Thomas Thompson right now. But soon the elevator doors opened up and it was too late to run. Cynthia had to take me by the arm for me to step out. I didn't know what I was doing. I couldn't think straight. I was a walking zombie, going wherever Cynthia led.

When we walked into the conference room of Tommy's office, everyone turned to look at us. Cynthia went directly to her seat next to Tommy, but I couldn't move. Everyone was looking at me. Why? Did they know? *I want to go home!* was all I could think.

"So nice of you to join us, Madison," Tommy said as I stood in the back of the room clutching my attaché against my chest. "Don't be shy. Have a seat," he said as I finally found movement in my legs and pulled out the chair nearest to me. When I was in my seat, Tommy began speaking again. All around me people were taking notes and nodding their heads, but my mind was so far away that all I could do was keep my head in an upright position and fake like I was listening. Then it happened. The words came back. All around me were words. On the walls, on the table, the ceiling. AIDS, DIE, POSITIVE, PAIN, FILTH, HIV. It was all I could do to keep myself from jumping up and running out the room. I shook my head and closed my eyes, hoping that the words would disappear. But when I opened my eyes they were still there. Larger than ever. Mocking me, parading in front of me. And just when I thought I could take no more, I heard my name called. For a second there I thought the words had learned how to speak, but when I heard my name again, I realized it was being spoken by a human. Well, it was being spoken by Tommy.

"Do you have anything to add to that?" he asked as everyone turned their eyes on me.

Add to what? What are we talking about? "No," I mumbled and shook my head, but my answer didn't stop everyone from looking at me. "Stop it," I wanted to yell. "Look somewhere else." But all eyes were on me, until, that is, Tommy spoke up again.

"Alright, people. I think that's enough for today," he said and stood up from his seat. "I think we should all give Ms. McGuire a round of applause. It was she who got the ball rolling on this and I must say I couldn't have come up with a better plan to teach our students how to be socially and sexually responsible. Thank you, Ms. McGuire," he said as the entire room began clapping. "Meeting adjourned."

Everyone was quick to jump up from their seats and crowd themselves toward the door, but no one wanted out more badly than me. I pushed my seat backward and into someone behind me. I didn't bother with apologies, I just wanted to be gone. But when I rose up from my chair, I heard my name called once again.

"I need to speak with you for a moment," Tommy said and paused to examine me. "In private," he said as he whispered a final few words to Cynthia and sent her on her way.

"Oh God," I mumbled as I froze behind my chair and watched everyone file out the door.

Tommy kept quiet until everyone was gone, then he went to the conference room door and shut it. I tried to get my head together. I had to. I needed every ounce of Madison to deal with Thomas Thompson. I walked away from my seat toward the huge window that overlooked the parking lot, and stared outside. I could feel myself regaining strength as I thought about Malik and his suspension. Though I would have preferred to run out the door and go home, I knew I had to stay. I had to find out what Tommy was doing to Malik and why. By the time Tommy finally spoke up, I was in control of myself enough to face him.

"So," he said, walking over to the window beside me, "how was your spontaneous vacation?"

"What do you want with me?"

"Just to know how you are."

"I didn't stick around here to shoot the breeze with you, Tommy. I want to know what's going on with Malik. Why did you suspend him?"

"Who were you with?"

"What?"

"Who did you take your vacation with? Got a new beau?"

"At first I thought you may have suspended Malik because he and I had gone behind your back to petition the parents about this sex ed class. But I know it's not that. You suspended Malik for another reason. What is it?"

"You know, I've got some vacation time coming up too. I've been think-ing about the south of France. Join me?"

"I ain't got time for your bullshit, Tommy," I yelled and turned to face him. My professional charisma had given way to the homegirl in me, and I wasn't about to put up with none of Tommy's shit. "Now, tell me. Why did you suspend Malik?"

"Malik had better be glad I didn't fire his ass," Tommy said, going on the defensive.

"What are you talking about? Malik is an outstanding teacher. His kids love him, the parents respect him."

"He's gay."

"What?"

"You did read the school's policy on teacher conduct, didn't you? Sec-tion eight, paragraph five. No employee will conduct themselves in a man-ner unbecoming to the professional image of this school," he said and began walking around the room. "That means I expect all my employees to represent Mighty Avalon to the fullest. That means men in suits, women in stockings. I don't want any men walking around here with half-grown beards or earrings, no jeans, none of that feminist bullshit with women dressed in suits with ties. I want my people to be professionals. We have an image to uphold around here. We owe it to our students. Every-body knows that. Everybody signed the employee conduct contract when they got hired, so I expect everybody to live up to their end of the agree-ment."

"What the hell does that have to do with Malik being gay?"

"Like I said, I expect all my employees to present themselves in a man-ner becoming to this school. I can't have one of my teachers parading around like some damn faggot."

"You make me sick," I said, barely separating my teeth as I spoke. "Ma-lik has been working here for six years. You wouldn't have even known he was gay if he hadn't given you that invitation to his dedication ceremony. He doesn't parade around. Hell, according to the gossip mill, half the school thinks he's screwing me."

"Well, that's a very lovely thought. However, Malik should have kept himself in the closet if he wanted to keep his job. I tried to cut the brother a break. I've known for years that Malik was gay. A thirty-five-year-old sin-gle man who never talks about women? I knew, Madison. But I was willing to let it slide until he started broadcasting his business. This school has a reputation to uphold. Next thing you know he'll be showing up to work in a dress and high heels."

I couldn't believe my ears. Tommy was really serious about this. I stood there staring at him, unable to believe what I was hearing. And the more I looked at Tommy, the more I realized how much I hated him. How could I have ever been involved with him? This man was a true-to-life ass, but he wasn't going to get away with this one. "You can't do this, Tommy," I said, pointing a finger at him. "This is unethical."

"This is in every teacher's contract."

"I'm going to tell Malik to sue. You cannot do this and get away with it."

"Now, Madison," he said coming closer to me. "I am the owner, founder, and principal of this school. I am fully within my rights. If Malik doesn't like his suspension, he can go teach in public school. Matter of fact, that's a good idea."

"Aaggh!" I yelled and turned away from him. "I can't believe this. I cannot believe this. So . . . What? Is this suspension temporary? What? Are you suspending Malik until he magically stops being gay? What, Tommy? What?"

"Take it easy, Madison," he said and came up behind me to put his hands on my shoulders.

"Get off of me," I snapped and jerked away from him.

"I haven't decided on Malik's fate yet, but you can help me figure all this out over lunch."

"What? Fool, are you crazy?"

He paused like he had to think about that one, then shook his head. "What happened to us, Madison? We used to be so good together. Now you act as if you don't even like me. Like you hate me."

"I do hate you. I could kill you."

"I remember a time when you used to love me."

"Get over it."

"I can't get over you, Madison," he said, staring at me seriously. "It's been a long time and I still can't get you out of my system," he said and reached out for my face, but got his hand slapped away. "You know," he said, putting his hands behind his back and coming closer. "Things could be so different if you would just act right."

"What?"

"I wouldn't have to do all these things to get your attention if you would just go back to being the Madison I once knew."

"The young, dumb Madison who thought the sun rose and set with you? The idiot Madison who you screwed on top of your desk before you went home to your wife?" I said and squinted my eyes toward him. "Are you saying that if I go back to being that Madison, things would go back to normal? You'd stopping fucking with me? Malik could have his job back? Is that what you're saying?" I asked and stared at him, hating every second of what I saw.

"I'm saying I want things to be like this," he said as he leaned over to me and kissed my neck. I slapped his face and backed away from him, but he just kept getting closer and closer. I shook my head trying to deny the things I found myself thinking. I hated the thoughts that were running through my head. For an instant, when he was near me, I wanted him. I wanted him to touch me. I hated and wanted him at the same time. Since I'd been diagnosed, the thought of having someone to want me, to love me erotically, was something I thought I'd only be able to fantasize about from now on. I hated Tommy and wanted him nowhere near me. But when I looked at him, I knew he could tell I had mixed feelings. What he didn't know was that I was HIV positive. He reached out for me again and I pushed him away.

"Don't come near me," I warned him. But it was a weak warning. He could tell that. He smiled and closed the distance between us again. "I mean it, Tommy. Don't touch me," I said, backing away from him, but he wouldn't listen to me. I'd given him a sign. A sign that maybe, just maybe, I wanted him too. But as I looked at him, I realized I hated him more and more every second. Maybe, just maybe, Tommy deserved to have sex with me. It was people like him who deserved to be HIV positive. People like him who should die, not me. I didn't deserve this. Tommy did. "What, Tommy?" I snapped and held out my arms. "Is this what you want? You want me? You want all of me, just like old times?"

His response was a kiss. This time I didn't pull away. I let him have me. It's what he wanted. It's what he deserved. And it was just like old times. His tongue was everywhere, hands everywhere. He lifted me on top of the table and positioned himself between my legs. Go on and take it, I thought as I let him do to me whatever he pleased. I even helped him. I reached under my skirt and pulled down my panties. I unbuckled his pants and felt my way around. I even kissed him back. I pulled him close to me, unbuttoned my blouse. I rubbed against him. I gave myself to him. Just like he wanted. Just like old times. I think I was even enjoying myself. Tommy was giving me what I'd wanted from Chris but couldn't ask for. Passion. I closed my eyes and leaned myself back onto the table and pulled Tommy with me. But as I laid there spread-eagle, waiting for Tommy to come inside, they came back. The words. They filled my head. HIV, AIDS, NASTY, DIE, PAIN, HURT.

"Stop!" I screamed and opened my eyes. Tommy hovered over me and put his finger over my mouth.

"Just relax, Madison. We've got time."

I shook my head vigorously and tried to scream, but Tommy covered me with his mouth. I kicked, I scratched, but nothing worked. Tommy wanted what he wanted and I had led him to believe he could have it. There was no turning back now. Was I about to kill him? Was I going to put another man's life in jeopardy?

"No," I screamed and jerked my body to the side just as Tommy was about to enter me. "I can't do this. Not even to you," I said as I jumped down from the table. Tommy caught me by the arm and pulled me to him.

"I like it when you tease me, baby."

"Stop!" I screamed as I began to shake. I pulled my panties back up and ran my hand over my face. Still, Tommy wouldn't give up. He pulled me to him again and put his hand underneath my skirt. I could barely feel his hand groping me as my mind focused on what I was doing. I was disgusted with myself. There I was, fully prepared to have sex with a man with no condom. Fully ready to potentially take this man's life. My body gave out on me. I felt like I was going to pass out. I stumbled out of Tommy's grip and fell backward against the table as tears pushed out my eyes. "What am I doing?" I cried and looked around the room. "What am I doing?"

Tommy took a step back and eyed me with confusion. His whole demeanor softened. I looked at him through watery eyes and for the first time in a long while, I saw the man who I had a relationship with so long ago, and I remembered why I had fallen for him. He was my father figure. That's why I'd been so attracted to him when I first started work here. He was older, established, and I was but a young naive girl whose heart had been broken. A girl who was looking for someone to step up and be the father I never had. Tommy was concerned for me now as he stared at me, wondering what was the matter. "Are you okay?" he asked like the man I once knew. He'd dropped the asshole routine and now he was just a man, and I felt like running to him and crying on his shoulder. "I'm sorry," he said as he pulled up his pants and buttoned them. "What did I do? What can I do? Tell me, Madison. What's the matter?"

"I'm HIV positive." The words slipped out before I could stop them. It wasn't until I looked into Tommy's eyes that I realized I'd let my secret out. He looked down at himself and backed away from me. I panicked. What had I just done? What had I just said? I flew toward the back of the room, scooped up my purse and attaché, and ran out the door. I couldn't wait for the elevator. I took the stairs and ran all the way out the building into the parking lot and jumped in my car. I couldn't believe myself. I told him my secret. "Why?" I screamed at myself as I sat behind the steering wheel. "Why, why, why?" I'd made a big mistake.

14

I figured it out! I know what's going on. I know why all of this is happening to me. It didn't take me long to figure everything out. Once I stopped at the liquor store and picked up a pint of vodka, everything became clear. And that's why I'm home now, in my kitchen, with my vodka, my Bible, and my razor blade.

See, I get it now. I understand. Gone is the question mark that had been floating through my head. *I can see clearly now the rain is gone. I can see all la, la, la, la, la, la.* It's amazing how much better I feel now that I've figured everything out. Chris was right. I only needed to dig deeper, to find out the reasons. And now that I have, I can do what I've got to do. But first, I need another drink. Excuse me . . .

Okay, now. The way I figure it, this is all a part of God's plan for me. I didn't realize that at first, but now that I've put two and two together, it's plain to see. See, God wanted this to happened to me. He wants me to die. Okay, okay, I know that may sound strange, but I've done my research on this. Those pamphlets on AIDS that Dr. Baker gave me? Well, I finally read them and they say . . . hold on, let me find the page. Wait, hold on again, let me get another drink . . . Okay, now. It says, women are twelve times more likely to get the virus from men than the other way around—I'm paraphrasing. See, that's why Chris and Benson have tested negative, because it's harder for a man to get the virus from a woman than it is for a woman to get it from a man—or something like that. Now, that doesn't mean a woman can't give the virus to a man. No, no, no. That can happen. Wait, I need another drink . . . Okay, the point of all this is that . . . that . . . Fuck it. I don't know what the point is, except that it was meant to be that I get infected with this virus. That's what God wanted. For me to die. So I figure, hey, ain't no sense in prolonging the inevitable, right? Oh, oh, oh. I also read that for some reason women are more likely to pick up HIV from IV-drug users. Don't ask me why, the people who wrote the pamphlet didn't even know. So you see . . . you see . . . Well, I don't know what you see, but as for me all this means is that what is happening to me is what God wanted to happen to me.

See, I checked it out with the Bible too. I read about Jezebel, then the Ten Commandments, and God says over and over again, don't be fornicating. But did I listen? Hell no. God wasn't playing around when he said that stuff. He was trying to tell me something, only I didn't listen, so now I'm paying the price. And now I know that this is all a part of God's plan for me. He wants me to die. Really, he does. And this time, I'm gonna listen to him. I'm gonna do what he wants. I'm gonna take that razor blade and . . . Damn, I need another drink. Excuse me . . .

See, I've been doing a lot of thinking. Lotsa, lotsa thinking. And I know now that God doesn't want me to suffer. See, I thought he was just fucking with me at first. I thought that maybe he didn't like me and was putting all this gloom and doom in my life to punish me. But as I read the Bible, I found out that God doesn't want any of his children to suffer. He wants us all to prosper. And that's why I figure I might as well go on ahead and use that razor blade and get everything over with. 'Cause if I continue living like this, all that's left ahead for me is suffering. I may be healthy now, but AIDS is on its way. I know that, ain't no dodging that truth. Four, five, ten years from now, all I'm going to be doing is suffering. I'll get sick, I'll become a burden to everyone, and my life will be miserable. God doesn't want that for me. That's why I'm going to handle my business right now. Get it over with. Ain't nothing left for me on this earth anyway. I'm probably out of a job by now. Ain't no way Thompson is going to keep me on after what I told him today. Especially not after I almost had sex with him. That's attempted murder, ain't it? He could have me put away for that. But I'm not going to give Thompson the chance. I'm gonna put my own self away.

You know, maybe I should leave a note behind. Yeah. Where's a pen and paper? Oh shit, almost knocked over my vodka. Excuse me . . . Okay. Got the pen, but where's the paper? Fuck it, I'll use a napkin. Now, let me see. What do I want to write? Uh-oh. I can't write anything. Can't even get my hand steady enough to write my name. Fuck it. I'll just write "Bye-bye." There. That's good enough. No need to get all sappy. That's not my style. Just say "Bye-bye" and leave it at that. They'll know what I really mean.

And now . . . one last drink . . . and the razor blade. "Dammit!" Never fails. The phone always rings at the wrong time. Should I answer it? Excuse me . . .

"Hello."

"Madison?"

"Hey, Mama. What's up? How ya doing?"

"Uh, fine. Have you seen Serena? She hasn't made it home from school yet."

"Nope."

"She hasn't called you?"

"I love you, Mama."

"Has she called you? I've been sitting here waiting for her for over an hour."

"Tell Serena I love her too. Y'all take care of yourselves."

"Madison? Have you been drinking?"

"Yep. But that's besides the point. Excuse me a second, Mama . . . Okay, now. Did I tell you I love you?"

"Madison, are you alright?"

"You know, Mama. I know you love me too. I know you're having a hard time dealing with—"

"I don't want to talk about that right now."

"Okay, okay. It's cool. I'm understanding. Excuse me . . . Don't forget to tell Serena I love her when you see her. Okay? I gotta go."

"Wait—"

"Tell Chris I love him too. Bye, Mommy."

I feel much better now. Now I can handle my business. Razor blade? Here we go . . . Wait! I need another drink . . . Okay. I'm ready. Razor blade? Wrist. Here we go . . . "Ouch!" *Shit.* Was this supposed to hurt? "Shit!" *Breathe, breathe.* Other wrist. Here we go . . . "Oh fuck!" It doesn't happen like this in the movies. The girl always cuts her wrists then slips off into some fantastic oblivion and passes out. Well, I'm here to tell you, this shit hurts. I need another fucking drink. Yeah, good vodka, bloody good vodka. Where's my oblivion? Where is it? This is taking too long. Messy too. Blood's everywhere. Glad I won't be around to have to clean it all up. *"Woo."* Feeling a little weak now. Needta sit down. Take my bottle with me to the sofa. Needta stretch out . . .

Yeah. I can feel it. The fantastic oblivion. It's coming. Blood all over the sofa. It's coming. Soon I won't have to suffer anymore. I'll be gone, just the way He wanted it. Just the way God wanted it. Gone. Adios, arrivederci, bon soir, hasta la vista—Baby . . . Huh? What? Not the door. No, go away. Whoever you are. Can't you see I'm trying to die here? You can't stop me. You can't stop God's plan. I'm outta here. Gone. Bye-bye.

"Li'l Mama! No!"

Don't touch me, don't touch me. Mind your own business, little girl.

"What? Madison? Oh my God!"

It's too late, baby. I'm outta here. See ya. Wish I had the strength to take another drink. Damn. Just let me lie here, stretched out. Just let me go.

"Nine-one-one?"

Don't do that, baby. Don't call them. There's no need for that. I'm already gone. Serena?

"Yes. It's my sister. She slit her wrists. I need an ambulance. Quick!"

Okay. Have it your way. I'll be gone by the time they get here. Damn, I wish I could talk to you. Look at you. My little sister. So pretty. I'm gonna miss you.

"Dammit, I don't know. Just get the fucking ambulance over here now."

Girl. What did I tell you about cursing?

"Madison. Madison. Talk to me."

Sorry. Can't. You be a good girl now. And stop crying.

"I can't believe this. I can't believe you."

Huh.

"How could you do this? How could you leave me this way? I need you."

You'll be alright. Just chill out, girl. Have some vodka.

"Mama was right. You are a bitch. All you do is think about yourself. Well, what about me? Who's gonna be my Li'l Ma now? Who's gonna teach me things, keep me out of trouble? Who's gonna replace you?"

I, I'm sorry.

"I don't believe you, Madison. You bet not die. I swear, you bet not die."

I'm sorry, Serena. I wish I could tell you . . . I wish . . . I . . .

"Madison. Madison! Noooo!"

15

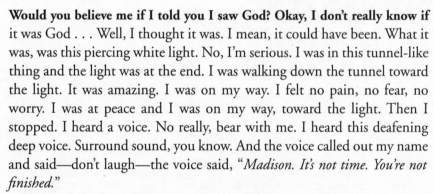

Would you believe me if I told you I saw God? Okay, I don't really know if it was God . . . Well, I thought it was. I mean, it could have been. What it was, was this piercing white light. No, I'm serious. I was in this tunnel-like thing and the light was at the end. I was walking down the tunnel toward the light. It was amazing. I was on my way. I felt no pain, no fear, no worry. I was at peace and I was on my way, toward the light. Then I stopped. I heard a voice. No really, bear with me. I heard this deafening deep voice. Surround sound, you know. And the voice called out my name and said—don't laugh—the voice said, "*Madison. It's not time. You're not finished.*"

So I said, "*Okay.* Who am I talking to?" 'Cause I didn't believe it myself.

Then the voice said, "*Don't ask stupid questions.*"

And that's when I knew I was talking to the Man. Then his voice got even louder, almost like he was upset, and he said, "*No one decides when it's time except me. And I say it's not time.*"

That's what happened. I swear. I know how it sounds, but that's really what happened. No joke. So I turned around in the tunnel and started walking back the other way, and when I got as far as I could get . . .

"Madison," I heard a voice call out to me.

I couldn't open my eyes at first, but I could hear them. "She's coming out of it," they said. "She's coming back."

For a while, I thought I was dreaming. Then I slowly opened my eyes, and even slower, everything came into focus. I was in the hospital and they were all there. Serena, Mama, Malik, Chris, and some goofy-looking guy who stood over me flashing a light in my eye. "Do you know your name?" Goofy asked and put away his light.

"Do I look stupid to you?" I said and rolled my eyes at him.

"She's definitely back," Malik said and dabbed at his eyes with a handkerchief.

"Why don't you tell me your name anyway?" Goofy asked again.

"Ms. Madison McGuire," I snapped. "Now, if you don't mind, I'd like to get out of here and go home."

"Not yet," Goofy said and took out his light again. "Can you spell your name for me?"

"Yeah. Fuck-U," I said and prepared myself to get out of bed.

"Hold on," Chris said and moved to the side of my bed. "I don't think you'll be going anywhere too soon."

"Chris," I said and turned to him, "you don't understand. I had a talk with God. He gave me another chance."

Goofy gave me a strange look, but Chris didn't even wince. Somehow I knew he thought I was telling the truth, though everyone else in the room seemed a bit skeptical.

"That's really swell," Goofy said and scribbled something down on a piece of paper.

"You've got to get me out of here, Chris. God gave me another chance and I don't want to waste any time."

Goofy cut me another look and scribbled some more on his paper. "Hey," I said and caught his attention. "I'm not crazy. This is for real. I had a talk with God. I saw him. Really."

"Calm down," Chris said and leaned over me. "They're gonna need to check you out some more. Run a few more tests before they just let you walk out of here."

I grabbed Chris by his shirt and for the first time, I noticed my wrists. They were all bandaged up. It was shocking, seeing and knowing what I'd done to myself. I let Chris go and turned to the others in the room. "I'm sorry," I said and motioned for them to come closer. Serena was the first to get to me. She wrapped her arms around me and held on tight.

"Don't leave me, Li'l Ma," she begged and cried.

"I won't," I said and pulled her away so I could look her in the eyes. "I won't leave you."

I hugged her close to me as I closed my eyes and thanked God that I was still alive. Then I looked over to Chris. "Can I go home now?"

"I don't think so," Dr. Goofy butted in.

"Get out," I said and pointed to the door. "Bye-bye. Leave," I said and kept pointing until Goofy got the message and turned away. I followed him with my eyes until he was completely gone, and as I turned back around I found Mother moving toward me. I don't know what came over her, but all of a sudden she came to my bedside and hugged me. Then the next thing I knew she was out the door.

"I know, I know," I said as Chris came to me and squeezed my shoulder. "She's having a hard time with this. We all are," I said and turned to Serena. The look on her face told me that she was having the hardest time. I ached for the pain I'd put her through. To walk in and see her sister dying in a pool of blood . . . "I'm sorry, baby," I said again and reached out for her. "I'm so sorry. I don't know what I can do to make it up to you."

"Just stay here as long as possible," she said and buried her head into my neck.

I held on to her for dear life, hoping she could feel the love I had for her. Hoping that she could forgive me for making her into an adult before her time.

When we finally let each other go, I kissed her on the cheek and turned around to talk to Chris. "Chris, you've got to get me out of here," I said, but before I could finish my sentence, the door opened behind him. Serena gasped. I stared. Chris turned around to see who was behind him, and when he didn't recognize the man he went over to him and put a hand up in front of the man's chest.

"You've got the wrong room, buddy," Chris said, trying to protect me and my privacy.

"No," the man said and brushed away Chris's hand. "I've got the right room," he said, looking past Chris to me. "Madison is my daughter."

16

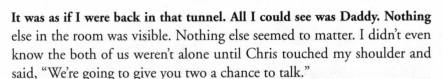

It was as if I were back in that tunnel. All I could see was Daddy. Nothing else in the room was visible. Nothing else seemed to matter. I didn't even know the both of us weren't alone until Chris touched my shoulder and said, "We're going to give you two a chance to talk."

I didn't respond to him because that would mean taking my eyes off Daddy, and I didn't want to do that. I didn't want to miss a second of him. I couldn't remember the last time I'd seen him or spoken to him, I thought as I watched him standing at the end of my hospital bed with his hands folded on top of the little movable food tray. I felt like asking him to pinch me, just to make sure one of us was real. But this wasn't a joke, this was my daddy, Cleophus McGuire. Suddenly, my mind filled with everything from hate to curiosity to a faint feeling of love and respect. But mostly there was hate, and to go along with that hate were a bunch of things I wanted to say to this man. But my mouth wouldn't move. I was too stunned to speak. I just kept focusing in on his beard. Where did that come from? I never remembered Daddy having a beard, but then again I never remembered much about Daddy at all except the fact that he was never around, and now that he was here, his presence was rocking my world. I had resigned myself to the fact that I'd never see him again, or at least if I did, it would be at his funeral. But here he was. Looking better than I'd expected, and for some reason that pissed me off. Daddy was in a suit and tie, looking almost like he just stepped off the pages of a magazine. My eyes swept across his face, down his body, then back to his face, or more specifically his ears. Those were my ears, I thought, then glided my eyes toward his mouth. I examined his thick lips, noticing how the top one stuck out more than the bottom. Overbite, I suspected. Just like mine. This was indeed my daddy. Except for his beard, his face was clear, hair nicely cut and brushed to the back, and if I wasn't mistaken, I could swear that was a coat of clear polish on his nails. Daddy was manicured from head to toe. He wasn't supposed to look this good. He was supposed to look like he had been suffering. He was supposed to be in dirty jeans and a ripped T-shirt. His hair was supposed to be matted and his eyes were supposed to be filled with years of remorse. His posture should have been bent. Bent and begging like a homeless man on the streets. The years of pain he'd given to me was supposed to show all over his body. Daddy was supposed to look helpless and sad. Like he'd been suffering all these years he'd been out of my life. Instead, he stood before me erect. Like he had the confidence of Muhammad Ali. Like at any moment he was going to say, "I am the greatest. Float like a butterfly," and all that other shit. This was not a man who looked like he was sorry for stepping out on his children. For leaving us daddyless. For making us grow up without a man at the head of the dinner table. This man that stood before me looked like he owned the world, and that pissed me off. There were so many questions and comments and curses that I wanted to get out of me, but when I opened my mouth all I could say was, "Get the hell out of here."

"I don't think so," was all he said. He didn't stutter, he didn't frown or even raise his voice. He just looked at me and stood still.

If my hands weren't bandaged up, I swear I would have reached out and slapped the shit out of him. Who the hell did he think he was? He didn't think so? What? Does he think he has some kind of authority around here because he laid down with my mother and gave her a shot of sperm? Well, he didn't. Daddy wasn't running things anymore. I was. And I said, dammit, "Get the hell out of here."

When he didn't move, I flipped. I almost turned myself over, looking around my bed, searching for the nurse call button. I wanted him out of this room and out of my life, and if security had to come and take his ass out, that would be just fine by me. But when I found the control button for the nurse, Daddy quickly swiped it out of my hand. He moved to me quicker than a ghost, snatched the remote away from me, and took it back with him to the foot of the bed and placed it on the portable food tray.

"I'm not going anywhere," he said, regaining his composure. "I came here to see you, and dammit, that's what I'm going to do."

"Well, take a good look, Mr. McGuire, 'cause in about two seconds I'm gonna scream for security."

"Do what you gotta do, but I'm not going anywhere."

"What the hell are you doing here?" I asked and propped myself high upon my pillow. I wanted to look as in control as I possibly could. Daddy had gotten the best of me over the years, but today it was my turn to be on top.

"Your mother tracked me down," he said, staring at me with so much confidence that for a second there I was almost intimidated. Almost.

"It's a sad day when a mother has to *track down* the father of her children, Mr. McGuire."

He winced at the sound of his name.

"Oh excuse me if I don't call you Daddy or Father, Mr. McGuire. But you see, you've never been one to me," I said and watched as a smile crept onto his face. What? Was this funny to him? I thought as I began to seethe. Or maybe he was smiling out of embarrassment. Out of shame. When a tiny dot of perspiration beaded on his forehead, I realized I was right and I loved it. I wanted him to be embarrassed, shamed. I wanted him to feel low, to experience the same kind of pain I'd experienced when I realized that I didn't have a father. "So, Mr. McGuire. I'll ask again. What the hell are you doing here?"

"I had to see you."

"You had to see me?" I said and stared at this man. He showed no signs of remorse. He acted as if he'd never done anything wrong. Like he'd been the perfect father. And now he was here to see me. As if he'd been gone on a long trip and just gotten back in town. His attitude was unbelievable. It was as if he took pride in the fact that he'd never been a father to me. "So why did you *have* to see me?"

"Your mother told me everything," he said and took his eyes off me for a second. That was the first sign of nervousness I'd seen in him, but he quickly recovered. "She told me that you'd been asking about me and I figured I should come see you now."

"You figured? After all these years, you're just now figuring out that maybe you should come see your daughter? Your own flesh and blood? One of your daughters has to be dying for you to show your face?"

"If that's what you think, then I've got a lot of explaining to do."

"There's no need to explain, Cleophus. There is nothing you can say to me now."

"I know you're upset with me."

"Upset with you? No. Why should I be upset with you? You were only my father. A father that I haven't seen from or heard from in years. Why should I be upset?"

"Just let me say something."

"Say what? What are you going to tell me, Cleophus? That you've been on vacation in the Caribbean for the last decade and a half?"

"Madison, please. Let me talk," he said, exasperated. "I want to tell you where I've been. I want you to understand."

I folded my arms across my chest and said nothing. This I had to hear.

"I know you're wondering where I've been all these years. Why I haven't called, why I haven't been there for you or your sister," he said and took a deep breath. "I know I haven't been a father to the two of you, but it's not entirely my fault."

"Get out of here!" Mother screamed so loud that her voice was unrecognizable, but her presence could not be denied. She rushed into my father's face and pointed her finger. I'd seen Mother mad before, but what I was witnessing here was mad to the umpteenth power. "Get out," she yelled again as her rich black skin seemed to turn purple.

"Mother," I shouted. "What's wrong?"

"I have been listening from the doorway," she said, turning to me for a second then pointing back at my father. "I called you over here so you could support your daughter, Cleo. Not so you could come in here talking all kinds of mess. You're upsetting her. Can't you see that?"

"I'm upsetting her, Mavis?" he said, looking around Mother's pointed finger. "You the one coming in here whooping and hollering. All I'm trying to do is get a few things straight with my daughter. If she's upset, it's on the cause of you."

"Excuse me. I'm not upset," I said, but no one seemed to listen. Mother just kept shouting, "Get out," and Cleophus kept shouting, "Hell no."

"I shoulda never called you here in the first place," she huffed and put her hands on her hips.

"She's my daughter too."

"Since when?"

"Don't start no mess, woman."

"Just get out."

"I ain't going nowhere till I speaks my peace with my daughter."

"I said get out."

"You just don't want me to tell her," Daddy said vindictively and moved slightly closer to mother.

"I don't give a damn what you do," Mother said and stood her ground.

"Then why don't you leave so I can talk to my child?" he said and held his hand out toward the door.

Mother didn't budge.

"Umm . . . What's going on here?" I asked, wishing I had enough strength to get out of bed. I felt quite uneasy laying there. A better place for me would have been in the middle of those two. I could just feel it. Someone was gonna get hurt.

They stood, staring at each other and fuming, neither one willing to give the slightest hint of weakness.

"Hello," I called, waiting for one of them to acknowledge me, but neither would look away from the other. "Mother," I snapped, hoping a change in tone would jar her. *"Mother."*

"What?" she snapped back and continued glaring at Cleophus.

"Look, I don't know what's going on here, but I promise, Mother, I'm okay. Just give me a couple minutes alone with . . . with him," I said, jerking my head toward Cleophus.

"I want him gone."

"No, Mother. It's okay. I want to talk to him."

"No."

"Mother."

"What's the matter?" Cleophus asked as his eyes seemed to tear straight through Mother. "Are you afraid of what I might say?"

"Why don't you go jump in a lake?"

"After you."

"Hey now, dammit," I jumped in. "You don't talk to my mother like that."

"That's right," Mother said with pride and moved closer to me.

"You hold it too, Mother," I said as she came to my side. "I still need a few minutes alone with him," I said and eyed Cleophus. "Mr. McGuire was just about to fill me in on why he's been a deadbeat dad. Isn't that right, Mr. McGuire?"

"You're absolutely right," he said, unmoved by my sarcasm. "I was just about to tell you how your mother kept me away from you all those years."

"You lying son of a bitch," Mother screamed and raced toward him.

"Oh, I'm a liar, Mavis? I'm a liar?" Daddy spun halfway around and ran his hand over his head to keep calm. "You kept me away from my kids and you know that's right."

"That's a damn lie. Your drunk ass never wanted to have nothing to do with your girls."

"That's a gotdamn lie."

"No, you the gotdamn lie."

"Wait!" I yelled out in a voice deeper than usual. I looked up at the ceiling, trying to process everything I'd just heard. Still, it wasn't coming together. Cleophus wasn't making sense, but I wanted to hear what he had to say. "Mother, please leave," I said, still gazing upward.

"I will not—"

"Leave the room, Mother!" I said as she turned to me in shock as if I was betraying her by wanting to talk to my father alone. But I wasn't. I just wanted to hear him out. Give him one last chance to speak before I kicked him out of my life forever.

Slowly, Mother left the room, leaving Cleophus at the foot of my bed. He wasted no time returning to his speech. He was like a hyper child, waiting to tell it on his bad friend.

"It was all your mother's fault. She kept me away from you."

Oh—my—God. Was that his best line of defense?

"Please," I shouted and frowned. "How dare you try to blame your lack of responsibility on Mother, you sorry son of a bitch?" His eyes widened as my voice grew stronger. "Nothing is ever your fault, right? You're just a victim, huh? Bullshit. If you were a real man, there ain't nothing in this world that could have kept you from your kids. You knew where we lived, you knew our phone number."

"You're right," he said, becoming rattled. "And, and I *tried* to keep in contact with you. Remember how I used to call you and we'd talk on the phone?"

"Yeah. I remember. I remember how you'd lie and say you were coming to see me and never showed up."

"That was because of your mother," he said, pointing toward the door. "She said I couldn't come see you unless I was willing to stay, to be with her and work things out. She told me I couldn't have anything to do with my kids unless I wanted to be with her. She used you all against me," he said, lowering his voice, like what he was about to tell me was confidential. "I know you may not want to hear this, but I ain't gonna lie. I was never in love with your mother. We were never actually a couple, we just . . . just . . . you know," he said as his eyes quickly darted around the room. I guess he was looking for a hidden camera or a microphone, since what he just told me was top secret information. I swear, I could not believe this asshole. When he first walked into the room, he'd passed himself off as credible. But now I see the real him. He's the same stupid fool I always knew he was. "You've got to believe me when I say I wanted to be with you," he said, firmly. "But it was your mother. She kept you from me."

"Oh *please*," I said, wanting so badly to strangle him. "You could have seen us if you really wanted to. And why wouldn't you want Mother?" I asked and frowned. "You wanted her enough to screw around with her. If you didn't want to be with her, then you never would have made Serena."

"You don't understand," he said, flagging his arms through the air. "I tried. I said okay. If being with your mother was the only way I could be near my daughter, then I'd have to give it a try. And I did. Just to be with you, I tried to work things out with your mother. But it just didn't pan out. Before I knew it, she got pregnant again. I didn't know what to do. I didn't even have a job at the time. I could barely support myself, let alone two kids."

"So you ran out on us," I shouted. "How do you think Mother coped all these years? She wasn't rich. She didn't have nothing. You should have thought about the fact that your ass was broke before you got in bed with her."

"I know, Madison. And I know it's not right, but your mother was on welfare at the time and—"

Oh—my—God. Was he joking? "You'd rather have the state supporting your children than to have to go out and get a good job to do it yourself?"

"No, it's not like that," he said, exasperated. We weren't speaking the same language, and that frustrated him. Daddy just didn't get it. Somehow, somewhere in his brain he really believed he was justified. "I know there are no excuses, but I was young at the time," he continued. "I was stupid. But besides all that, I loved my two girls. I wanted to be with you. But your mother—

"There you go blaming again," I said, rolling my eyes. "This isn't Mother's fault. This is yours. And you still haven't explained why after all these years you haven't so much as called me. We live in the same city, Cleophus. I'm in the phone book. If you wanted to talk to me all you had to do was look me up."

"I was scared, Madison."

What?

"I was scared of this. Of confronting you after all these years. I know I did you wrong," he said, pounding his chest. "And I can't tell you how bad I hurt inside that I wasn't there to see my girls grow up. But as the years passed, I figured it would be best if I just stayed away. I figured you wouldn't want to see me."

"So, in other words, you gave up?"

"No. It's just that the more time passed, the more afraid I got."

"You gave up. You were not a man. You gave up."

"No," he snapped. "I could never give up on my children. I can't tell you how many times I wanted to show up at your door, or pick up the phone and call, but I was scared. Can't you see where I'm coming from?"

"No, I can't. I can't see at all," I said, shaking my head. "I don't understand how a man can walk out on his children. It's beyond me. And now you're here telling me all this crap like I'm supposed to understand. What? Am I supposed to forgive and forget now?"

"No. I don't want you to forgive and forget. I just want you to know that I care for you. I've always loved you."

"Care for me. How cute. All I know is that I used to cry myself to sleep, trying to figure out why my daddy didn't love me enough to be with me. I used to fret for days, trying to find you whenever my elementary school held the father-and-daughter banquet. I used to hurt to the bone when I'd sit in the living room waiting for you because you said you'd be coming over and I believed you. That's all I know, Daddy. All I know is the pain I felt and still feel to this day. I'm a grown woman, thirty years old. And you know what? I still ache for my daddy."

I saw a tear well up in his eye, but that wasn't good enough for me. I wanted Daddy to hurt. I wanted him to hurt really bad.

"You know what else, Mr. McGuire? Do you know why I'm really in this hospital. In this bed?" I said and raised both of my hands up so he could see my bandaged wrists. "It's not because I tried to commit suicide. It's not even because I'm HIV positive. It's because of you. You are the reason I'm here," I said as I stared him down. "See, I never knew what real love was. I never knew because there was never a father in my home to teach me. But I wanted it and I went out in search of it. Unconditional love. Fatherly love. I petitioned many a man on my quest for this love that I never got from you. Unfortunately, one of these men had a deadly virus. And now I've got it. And because of you, Mr. McGuire, I'm going to die."

He froze before me. I could see on his face that he was replaying my words in his mind. It wasn't long before he was in tears. He put both hands on the edge of my bed and leaned over. He cried for so long that I became uncomfortable. I wanted him to leave. There was no reason for him to be there. "I'm sorry, Madison," he said finally and looked up. "I'm so sorry."

"No need to be," I said, feeling a confidence I hadn't felt in weeks. "There's nothing you can do. I've got to live with this now. And you know what? I am. I'm not going to die in vain. I'm going to live and love and be happy. That's something I couldn't do before. I always had this missing link in my life. You. I thought because I never had a father to love me that I could never be loved and be happy. But I know better now. My life is not over, Cleophus McGuire. It's just getting better."

"You've got to believe me when I say I wanted to be there for you," he said, taking small steps to get closer to me. "I want to be here for you now. I don't want my daughter to leave this earth not knowing how much I love her."

"Your kind of love I don't need, sir." The tone of my voice stopped him in his tracks. "The fact of the matter is that you weren't there for me and we can't change that. And now I don't need you anymore," I said and bit my lip. "I'm not saying that out of hatred or because I want to hurt you. It's just the truth. It's too late to fix things," I said and looked away from him. "I want you to leave, Mr. McGuire. Go back to your life, whatever that may be, and let me continue on with mine."

"No," Serena said as she came busting through the door. "I don't want you to leave, Daddy," she said and ran into his arms. "I don't want you to go."

It was a *Brady Bunch* portrait. Father and daughter entwined, crying, rocking from side to side—how cute. Only, I felt out of place, like my name was Alice and maybe I should excuse myself and go make dinner. I watched them, feeling a tinge of jealousy, betrayal. Serena was supposed to be on my side. She was supposed to lick out her tongue and say, "Yeah, Daddy. Get the fuck on out of here." Instead, she stood gripping this man. A man who she barely knew. She held on to him as if to let him go would destroy everything she was. Didn't she know he was no good? Didn't she know he didn't care about her? Didn't she care that this man, who was supposed to be her father, had never been there for her?

No. She didn't care. Serena wasn't like me. All she saw was her daddy. All she knew was that she was a part of him and to let him go would be letting herself go. She was only fourteen. She hadn't lived long enough to know that she was supposed to hate him. But I knew. And I hated him enough for the both of us.

"Serena," I said, wanting so badly to break up this Kodak moment. But Serena was oblivious to me. She had her daddy and that's all that mattered. "Serena," I said louder two times more until she looked over at me with tear-filled eyes. "Daddy's got to go now," I said and watched as she shook her head and tightened her grip around his waist. "Isn't that right, Cleophus?" I said and gritted my teeth.

He shot me a look that begged me for time, but the look I gave him in return let him know that his time was up. He grabbed Serena's hands from around his waist and held them in front of him. "Daddy's got to go now," he said to Serena as she began to cry harder. "I gotta go, sweetheart. But I'll be back."

Yeah right, I thought as I watched him lie. How many times had he told me that in the past?

"I promise, baby. I'll be back."

"When, Daddy?" she whined, tilting her head to the side and hoping he'd say the right thing.

"Soon, baby. Real soon," he said and kissed her forehead. He looked over at me as if he were thinking about doing the same to me. But he knew better. "I will be back," he said, staring at me with a raised brow as if I still believed in fairy tales. He walked slowly to the door, leaving Serena crying. He didn't take his eyes off me. I guess his stare was supposed to make me believe. But I'd been fooled by him too many times. I knew this was good-bye, forever. And strangely enough, it didn't bother me.

"Why'd you let him go?" Serena asked after her father disappeared through the doors. "Why were you so mean to him? He's our father. You shouldn't have let him go like that."

"You can't hold on to a man that doesn't want to be held."

"Bullshit."

"What? Girl, I will knock you out."

"Sorry, but—"

"You best watch your mouth."

"No, you best watch your mouth," she said with so much authority that I thought I'd better shut the hell up. "He's still your daddy. I don't care what he's done, he's still your flesh and blood and you ought to respect that. You ought to respect him."

"Who do you think you're talking to?"

"You. You don't know everything, you know."

"Oh, is that right?"

"That's right. I mean, Daddy was trying to reach out to you. You may not know it, but you need him now."

"Don't tell me what I need. I know what I need, little girl."

"Well, what about what *I* need? I need my daddy. I'm already losing you, Li'l Ma, and, and . . ."

The tears came so fast that she couldn't finish her sentence, and I couldn't help but feel guilty. This was too much for this girl. Too much for any girl. She should be off doing homework, or talking to some boy on the phone, or watching videos. She shouldn't have to be here in a hospital crying over the sister she will lose someday, or the father she never had. I wished I could make it all better for her, but I knew I couldn't. I wanted to tell her everything was going to be alright, but I didn't want to lie to her. Still, I was the big sister and I had to start acting like one. For both our sakes. "Come here, Serena," I said and patted a place next to me on the mattress. She didn't want to come. She was like a stubborn baby whose feelings had been hurt. "Come here, Serena," I said again, and reluctantly she moved toward me. I patted the mattress again until she sat down, and when she did, she threw her hands over her face and began to heave up and down. There was no stopping her tears, so I waited while she cried them all out. And when she was done, I raised my bandaged hand to her face and turned her to me. "You're not losing me just yet, Serena," I said and soaked up some of her tears with my bandage. "I'm still here and I'm going to be here for a long time. I promise."

The words I thought would bring her comfort only started her crying again. She pushed my hand away from her. "I can't believe you did that," she said, pointing at my bandage. "You are so selfish," she said and squeezed her eyes together. "I can't believe you actually went through with it. I never did."

"You never did what?"

She stopped crying and vigorously wiped her eyes before she spoke. "You aren't the only one living with a disease, you know. You think I like being a part-time freak? You think I like not knowing if today is going to be the day I flip out? I thought about doing it once."

I turned away from her, not wanting to believe she was saying what she was saying.

"I had a real bad spell one day and I thought about it real hard. But I never, ever could have done it," she said as her tears came back. "You know why?" she said as her shoulders hunched up and down. "Because of you. And because of Mama. I thought about you and I knew I couldn't do it," she said as she pinned her sharp finger into my chest. "Did you think about us? Did you think how we would feel if you killed yourself?"

The room was silent except for Serena's sobs. There was nothing I could say. She had me. I couldn't justify what I'd done. Couldn't spin the situation around to benefit me. Serena was right. I was selfish. I caused the dearest people in my life needless pain. I didn't feel right saying these words, but what else could I say? "I'm sorry, Serena," I said and winced as I watched her cry.

"Don't say that. Just say it won't happen again."

"It won't happen again," I said dutifully. I reached out my hand for her again. "Hey," I said and wiped away more tears. "Do you hear what I'm telling you? I'm here. I'm not going anywhere."

"But you will."

She was right.

"And Daddy's gone again too."

Forget him, I thought, wanting to tell her she doesn't need him in her life. Wanting to tell her she can make it without a father, just like I did. But as I thought about that, I realized I hadn't made it at all. I survived, but I hadn't lived. I thought about all the emptiness I'd felt over the years, especially when I was Serena's age. How badly I'd wanted a father, needed a father. Needed the love only he could give. I knew Serena's pain too well. I'd been through it. But I also knew that waiting for love from a man like

Cleophus McGuire would be like waiting on snow in southern California. "I can't promise you anything where Daddy's concerned, Serena. I know you love him and you want him in your life, but you can't force him to be with you. Daddy's going to have to make that decision for himself."

"But why wouldn't he want to be with me? What did I do to make him not want me?"

I closed my eyes and remembered how often I'd asked myself the same question and how it felt to feel unwanted by the very person who was supposed to want you the most. I didn't have any answers for Serena. All I could do was pull her to me and hold her. "Daddy loves you," I told her. "He loves us both. Believe me," I said and rubbed my bandaged hand over her face. Was I lying? I wondered as I closed my eyes. Even if I was, it was a nice thought anyway.

17

What I could do is tie a bunch of sheets together, knock out the window with a chair, and shimmy down the side of the building. Or I could call for one of the nurses, wait behind the door for her to come in, knock her on the back of the head, steal her uniform, and walk out through the Emergency Room. I'm not sure what I'm going to do, but I do know this—one way or another, I'm getting out of this damn hospital. Today.

"We're keeping you here for observation," they keep saying, but I'm not trying to hear all that. What they don't understand is that I made a promise to Malik. His dedication ceremony is tonight and I've got to be there. I'm his best woman and I can't let my best friend down like that. He said he would understand if I couldn't make it, but what he doesn't understand is that I wouldn't miss this for the world. Malik is tying the knot—so to speak—and nothing, not even Dr. Goofy, is going to keep me away from that.

And furthermore, I've been in this hospital, under observation, for days now and all I've had time to do is think. Now call me crazy if you want to, but the fact of the matter is that ever since my near-death experience, I've been . . . well, I've been seeing God on a regular basis. No, this is not a Tale from the Darkside, or some kinda freaky Twilight Zone moment, it's the truth. God and I have gotten pretty tight over the last few days, and every time I see him, I'm convinced even more that I've got to get the hell out of this hospital. God has given me a mission. Really, he has. He hasn't come right out and told me exactly what it is he wants me to do, but he's made it clear that I've got to do something.

I thought maybe I could write a book about dealing with AIDS and HIV. Then I thought that wouldn't be such a good idea since I haven't actually dealt very well with being positive myself. Then I thought I might join this modeling agency I heard about awhile ago where all the models are HIV positive and do print ads and public service announcements to alert people to the disease. But I decided against that too. Modeling isn't my thing. I know it's for a good cause and all, but I can't see myself posing in front of a camera and all that. That just ain't me. Then I thought about calling up the AIDS L.A. Foundation and just being a volunteer, but I don't think that would suit me either. I'm just not the volunteer type. Any work I do has got to be paid. A sister still has to make money in the nineties.

The more I thought, the more it became clear to me that I was going to have to do something about my job. That is, if it hasn't already been done for me. I don't know if I'm employed or not right now. Who knows how Tommy reacted to the bomb I dropped on him? Hell, he wants to fire Malik because he's gay. No telling what the penalty is for being HIV positive. But to tell the truth, I really don't give a damn. As much as I love teaching, I've been seriously considering quitting. I can just imagine how the parents will react when they find out about me. Oh sure, they love me now. Their children love me. But I can just hear them when they find out the news. "What if she gets cut and touches my child? What if she breathes on my son the wrong way? What if she brushes past my daughter the wrong way?" Prejudice is thick, and the days of Ryan White are not so far behind. He was just a kid. Can you imagine what would happen to *me*? My face would be on every newspaper in the world because as far as I know I've never heard of another schoolteacher with HIV or AIDS. I'm sure they exist, they probably just keep their mouths shut. But it's too late for me to do that. I'd be the first grade-school teacher to ever admit that she's HIV positive. The publicity would be overwhelming. That's why, even though I'll hate it, I do believe I'm going to have to stop teaching.

When I first thought about it, I felt sorta bad. Like I'd be quitting, giving up. Maybe I wasn't brave enough to stand up and tell the world that I'm a schoolteacher with HIV. Maybe I was a coward? But the more I think about it, the more sure I become. I've got limited years left on this earth and I refuse to spend the majority of them stressing out. Let the high-profile celebrities teach the world about HIV and AIDS. I'm just Madison McGuire. My work has got to be on a smaller scale. Quitting teaching will not mean I'm giving up. It just means that I've opened the door to another hallway. What that hallway is—I don't know. But I'll come up with something. I've got to do something. That's why God let me live. I'm one of the chosen ones. I would have preferred to be chosen for something else, maybe president of the United States, but that's not how it turned out. God chose me for this and I'm not going to let him down. When I'm dead and gone, which will be in a few years, I want to stand before him and let him know that my life was not in vain. I want him to pat me on the head and say, "Job well done." But most of all, I want to do this for myself. I want my life to have been for something. I almost cut my life short, but now I want to live, and live for a purpose. Damn. I'm sounding pretty sappy, I know. But this is real. I've got HIV and there's no getting rid of it. All I can do now is live as long as possible, as well as possible, and with as much dignity as possible. But I can't do any of that in this damn hospital. They've got me on lockdown, but little do they know this sister is about to escape from Alcatraz.

I got out of bed, walked over to the closet, and pulled out the clothes that I'd been brought in with. They were completely covered in blood. Not a very discreet wardrobe for breaking out of a hospital. I put the outfit back and started pacing the floor. Suddenly, knocking a nurse over the head and stealing her uniform didn't seem like such a far-fetched idea. Or maybe I could throw myself into one of those towel carts, like they do in the movies, and let some orderly wheel me down to the laundry room. Or maybe I could close my eyes again and wait for God to make me magically disappear. Since he and I have gotten so close over the past two days, that shouldn't be a problem. Right?

I laid down on my bed and closed my eyes. I didn't do anything special. Just laid there like I usually do and waited for him to come to me. You can't rush him, you know. He's funny like that. Anyway, I laid and laid and laid, until . . .

"*Madison.*"

Oh my God . . . "*God?*" I'm getting really good at this.

"*Are you ready to break outta this joint?*"

Oooh. I didn't know God had a little street in him. "Hell yeah. Oops. I mean, yes, Lord."

"Madison?"

"Savior?"

"Madison!" the voice said again, and this time I could feel him. He put his hands on my shoulder and shook me so hard that I thought I was going to break. "What's up, God? I hear you. What's the problem?"

"Madison. Madi. Wake up. Wake up, baby."

Baby? This ain't my God. I opened up my eyes and realized I wasn't talking to God at all. It was Chris. He stood next to my bed, staring at me like I was losing my mind.

"Are you okay?" he asked and put his fingers on my eyelids and opened them even wider. "It's Chris," he said louder, as if I couldn't understand him.

"I know," I said and quickly slapped his hands away from me. I sat up straight in bed and blinked my eyes to take the strain away, then suddenly I was overcome with urgency. I grabbed Chris's collar and pulled him so close to me that our noses touched. "You gotta get me out of here," I said like a desperate prison inmate.

"Wait a minute," he said, pulling my hands from his neck. "Are you okay?"

"Yeah. I just thought you were God for a second there."

"Okay, Madison," he said, calmly putting his hand to my forehead. "Just relax. I'll go see if the nurse can give you some Valium—"

"Do you think I'm crazy?" I said and snatched him by the collar again. "I'm not crazy. I thought you believed me. I really did talk to God. Several times. I ain't out my mind, Chris."

"Okay," he said again, too smoothly. "Just take it easy."

"No, you take it easy. I did just like you told me to do. I've been searching."

"Okay . . ."

"Okay nothing. What did you come here for, Chris? To tell me I'm crazy?"

"No," he said and pulled himself out of my grasp. "I came here to get you out of here, but now—"

"See. See," I said and lifted my head to the ceiling. I said a quick "Thank you, Jesus," then turned back to Chris. "He sent you, Chris. God sent you. I asked Him to get me out of here, and he sent you to do just that. It's fate," I said and stopped cold. I'm starting to sound just like Chris, aren't I? Damn. "Come on now," I said and scrambled out of bed. "Let's be out."

"Wait a minute, Madison."

"Clothes. I need clothes. Did you bring me some clothes?"

"Yes, but wait."

"Wait, nothing."

"Hold on, Madison," he said and grabbed my arm. "There are a few things you need to understand first," he said and turned me around to face him so that he had my full attention. "Your doctor wanted you to stay a few more days, but I pulled a few strings and got him to release you on one condition."

"Yeah, and?"

"Your doctor has agreed to release you, but only into my care."

"Into your care?"

"Yes ma'am. My care. That means I'm responsible for you."

"Oh you are?"

"That's right," he said and smiled. "Us doctors got it like that."

"Oh, is that right?"

"But now I'm not so sure if you're ready to leave. Physically you seem fine, but mentally, I'm not so sure."

"Are you calling me crazy again?"

"No. I mean, I don't know."

"Chris, I promise you, I am not crazy. I've just been very prayerful lately. I've got a lot to be thankful for, you know."

"I know."

"You've been right all along. I've needed time to be still. I've needed time to think."

"Have you come up with any solutions?"

"I'm thinking about quitting my job."

"Quitting your job?" he said and frowned. "But you love teaching."

"How many HIV positive teachers do you know?"

"None, but so the hell what? If you want to teach you fight for that right. Don't give up just because you think they won't accept you."

"That's not it, Chris," I said and paused. "I don't want to fight. Time is too short."

"But think about what this could mean for other teachers. You can't get HIV from learning," he said and threw his hands in the air. "Maybe your coming out could break down some of that prejudice. Maybe you have an obligation here, Madison."

"My only obligation is to myself, Chris. I can't put the whole world on my shoulders. I have to do what's right for me. If I walk away from teaching, it will be on my own terms. Not because I'm afraid of the fallout, but because I want to do what's best for Madison."

"Hmm," he said and nodded his head. "I see what you're saying."

"Do you?"

"Most definitely. I'll back you whatever you decide."

"I'll remember that," I said, then clapped my hands together. "Let's get out of here!"

"Alright," Chris said reluctantly. He got up from the side of the bed and walked behind me to a chair and picked up a garment bag. "I bought you something to wear," he said and laid the bag out across the bed.

I walked over to the bed and opened the bag slowly to find a beautiful beaded dress. I looked at Chris, then back at the dress, then yanked it out the bag. "This is incredible. You picked this out?"

"Actually, Malik picked it out. It's your dedication ceremony dress."

"Oh my goodness," I said and held it up to me. "The ceremony." I looked inside the dress at the tag. Adrienne Vittadini. Yeah, Malik picked this out alright.

He checked his watch and said, "We've got about forty-five minutes."

"Oh shit," I said and froze in the middle of the floor. I picked up the garment bag. "I'll be ready in a second," I said and rushed into the bathroom.

When I came back out, Chris and Dr. Goofy were huddled together in front of the door. I heard Chris assure the doctor that he would take good care of me, then he signed a couple of papers and handed them to the man. When Dr. Goofy walked out the door, Chris turned around to me. For the first time I really looked at him. He was gorgeous. He was all suited up in what I concluded had to be Versace by the cleanness of the cut on the jacket. His hair was freshly faded, sideburns expertly clipped, eyebrows smoothed to perfection. Chris was looking good. But something had changed. I'd only been in the bathroom for ten minutes, but when I came out I detected a distinct change in Chris. He was nervous, almost fidgety. He kept checking his watch and pacing the floor. He didn't even know I was present until I cleared my throat.

"I'm just about ready," I said as I limped over to the bed and sat down. The shoes Chris had bought me to go with the dress were beautiful, but a half size too small. But I wasn't complaining. I was ready to get out of that place and would have walked out barefoot if I had to. "Okay," I said after I crumbled up my toes and stood back up. "Let's go."

"Wait," he said when I got to the door. He put his hand on my shoulder and turned me around to face him. He didn't say a word. The only sound that came between us was the ringing of his pager. He jerked when he heard the sound, as if he hadn't even been aware he was wearing it. He opened his jacket and looked down at his waist. "I gotta make a call," he said and looked back at me. "Give me a minute," he said and rushed over to the side of the bed and picked up the phone. He dialed a number, said, "Hello, yeah, alright," then hung up.

"Problem?" I asked when he turned back around to me.

"No," was all he said.

"Was that the clinic? Do you have an emergency?"

"No," he said and began fidgeting with the buttons on his suit. Something was up, but Chris wasn't saying. "Are you ready to go?"

"Sure," I said and turned around for the door.

"Um," he said and paused.

"Yes," I said as I quickly turned back to face him, waiting for him to tell me what was going on with him.

"Nothing," he said and reached around me to open the door. "We better get a move on."

∎

The drive to the dedication ceremony was silent and awkward. I kept getting the feeling that Chris wanted to say something to me but was just too scared. And as usual, in the absence of data, my mind starts to wander. I kept trying to think what it could be that Chris wanted to say to me, and the more we drove in silence, the more I began to see the clear picture. This was all getting to be too much for Chris. I knew there would come a day when he would realize that my burden was too overwhelming for him. He had a girlfriend who was HIV positive. A girlfriend who tried to commit suicide. What's next? Any other man would have left a long time ago. And now, I believe, Chris is reaching the point of exhaustion. It's so ironic. I know Chris is having second thoughts about me now, and I can't blame him for that. But now, at this very moment, I swear, I couldn't love Chris more. If only I could change things. If only I could turn back the hands of time. If only I could be a virgin. A pure, holy, untouched female. But I can't change the way things have turned out. I can only live with it all now. But the more I look at Chris, the more I realize that I've got to let him go. I can't allow him to live out my burdens with me. He deserves so much better.

When we pulled in front of the church, I reached over to Chris as he turned off the ignition. "We've got to talk," I said to him and took a deep breath. But before I could get the words out, Chris was out the car and walking around to the passenger side. He opened my door and took my hand.

"We'll talk later," he said and pulled me to my feet. He wouldn't look me in the eye. It was as if he knew what I was about to say and just wasn't ready to hear it yet.

We walked arm in arm up the steps to the church, and when we got inside he let my arm go and stood next to me. His posture was so erect. Like he had a gun stuck in the small of his back. Chris was definitely on edge. He ran his hand over his face and stood there like he was afraid to move. Something was definitely up. I had to talk to him. I had to find out what was wrong. If it was me, I wanted him to know that he didn't have to worry. I was fine and I'd be fine without him. If he wanted to leave, it was okay with me. I loved him, but I could let him go.

I turned to Chris and touched the side of his face. "Chris," I began, until a tiny little voice came screaming at me.

"Li'l Ma," Serena's voice yelled to me. I turned to find my sister running at me and wrapping her arms around my waist. I was shocked.

"What are you doing here?" I asked, not knowing that Malik had invited my family to his dedication ceremony.

"Big Mama's here too, and guess what?" she started to say, but when she looked over at Chris she stifled herself.

"What's wrong?" I said and cut my eyes back and forth between the two of them.

"Nothing," Chris said and looked away.

"Nothing," Serena repeated and turned her back to me. "I think I'm gonna go sit down now."

"I'll go with you," I said and began walking behind her, but Chris placed a firm hand on my shoulder and stopped me.

"I think you better go see Malik first," he said and smuggled me down the vestibule of the church to a private room.

"What is going on?" I whispered as he opened the door to the room. He practically shoved me through and sat me down in the first chair he saw. Seconds later, Malik came rushing through the door, and behind him was Mother and Serena. When they were all in the room and the door shut behind them, I was certain something had gone wrong. I panicked. "What, what? Somebody tell me something."

"You didn't tell her?" Mother said, looking at Chris.

"You didn't tell her?" Malik said and frowned.

"He didn't tell her?" Serena said and sat down next to me in a chair.

The rest of them stood staring at me as if they were all afraid, until finally I had to ask the obvious question. "Tell me what?"

Malik was the first to clear his throat. "Tyrone flaked on me," he said with little emotion.

"He what?"

"That's right. That no good son of a bitch—oh, excuse me Lord," he said and looked up at the ceiling. "Anyway, that, that, *man* decided that he didn't want to go through with the ceremony after all."

"Oh no, Malik," I said and stood up to embrace him. "I'm so sorry."

"No need to be sorry, honey," he said and pulled away from me. He did not want to be pacified. It was as if he'd gone through all his emotions already. He'd accepted it already. "I saw it coming," he said matter of factly. I knew he wasn't ready for this. I'd known for a long time, I just didn't want to admit it to myself. He left me last night. Or should I say, I threw his tired ass out last night?—oh, excuse me, Lord."

"This is terrible," I said and sat back down. "But why are we here?"

Silence fell over the room again. And this time it was Chris who cleared his throat. Malik made way as Chris came to stand before me. He was sweating now. His hands were shaking so hard that he had to stick them in his pockets to control them. For a second there, I thought he was going to have a breakdown. And then . . .

"Madison," he said, slowly and intently. He opened his mouth again to continue, but this time his face just shook and no words would come out.

"Go head, baby," Mother said and walked over to him to put her hand on his shoulder. "Do what you've got to do."

Chris took a deep breath, lowered himself to his knee, and grabbed my hand.

"Oh my God," I said as I looked down on the top of his head.

He raised his face to look in my eyes and I knew what was coming next.

"Madison," he said again. "I know marriage is a scary thing for you.

You swore to yourself that you'd never do it. But I love you. I love every-thing you are. Nothing has changed that, not even you being HIV posi-tive. *I love you.* I have for the past eight years and I will forever. And I know you love me too. I want to be there for you. Not because you need me, but because I need you. I have dedicated myself to you and I'm ask-ing you to dedicate yourself to me."

And here, once again, is my dilemma: I love Chris and I know he loves me. But can I do this? Can I let him do this? Doesn't he deserve to share his life with a woman who at least has a future? Doesn't he deserve at least that?

What about what you deserve?

God? Is that you for real this time?

I said, what about what you deserve?

I looked at everyone in the room and when I didn't see any of their lips moving, I figured either somebody has been taking ventriloquist lessons or I was indeed talking to God.

Think about what you deserve.

Think about what I deserve. Think about what I deserve . . . I deserve to be happy. I deserve real love. I deserve . . .

"Madison," Chris said and squeezed my hand to bring me back to the present. "Will you dedicate yourself to me?"

My mind went blank. I wanted so badly to say yes, but I just couldn't. Chris deserved so much better and I deserved . . . I deserved . . .

For crying out loud, would you just tell the man yes?

"Yes," I said and gripped Chris in my arms. "Yes, yes, yes, yes, yes."

18

When I said that I would never get married, I meant it. My word is bond—
sorta. Okay, so I'm getting dedicated. That sounds so nineties, so California. *Dedicated.* I don't even know what the ceremony consists of. I had
planned on asking Malik, but after I said yes, everybody cut out the room
so fast that I didn't have a chance to say anything. I guess they figured
they'd better get out to the church and get the ball rolling before I decided
to change my mind. But there was no chance of that. I was sure I was doing the right thing. Chris was the man I wanted, and although I didn't believe in marriage, the thought of dedicating myself to him sat well in my
mind. It fit me. "Marriage" was such a vulgar word to me. Such an old,
static institution. But dedicating myself to the man I loved was the best
thing I could ever do. And strangely enough, I didn't feel any apprehen-
sion. It was as if all my worries and concerns about Chris giving up his life
for me had all disappeared. When he told me he loved me, I felt his words
like never before. Chris knew what he was doing. And there was nothing
that I could say that would change his mind. He was dedicated to me, and
in a few minutes we'd be dedicated to each other.

When the door to the private room opened, my heart began to quiver.
I knew it was about that time. I opened my purse and pulled out a com-
pact and checked myself in the mirror. When I looked back toward the
door, I saw Mother. She stood in front of the door staring at me as if she
didn't know how to approach me. To be honest I didn't know how to ap-

proach her either. Today was the first day I'd seen Mother since my talk with Cleophus McGuire. I couldn't figure out if I was mad at her. I didn't know if she was mad at me. Besides that, I got the feeling that I had been such a disappointment to her. Ever since I told her that I was HIV positive, she'd backed off from me. No longer was she my mother. It didn't even feel like we were family, really. We were strangers. Two women who once knew each other but now didn't know what to expect.

We stared at each other for the longest time without saying a word. It felt awkward for a while, but soon the awkwardness disappeared. As I looked into my mother's eyes, I saw love. She didn't have to say it. She didn't have to rush over to me and wrap me in her arms. She just had to be there. And when the time is right, Mother will speak. She will reach out her hand to me and I will feel her love. But right now, no words need be said. I understand Mother. I understand her completely.

"Alright now," Malik said as he came bursting through the door. Mother jumped out the way and put her hand over her chest.

"Is everything set?" she asked Malik.

"Almost," he told her and nodded as Mother left the room.

"What do you mean, almost?" I said. "Chris isn't having second thoughts, is he?"

"No, girl. That man's nose is wide open for you. I hope you know how lucky you are."

"I do," I said and smiled. "I'm ready to do this."

"Good," he said and opened the door. "There's one more thing," he said and waved his hand out the door to someone. "I'll see you down the aisle," he said and walked out the door.

I stood in the middle of the room looking confused. What's going on? I thought, and soon I found out. He was here. Cleophus McGuire.

He walked into the room looking almost as nervous as Chris had looked earlier. His demeanor was totally different from the day he had come to the hospital. Today he looked humble, almost shy. He smiled at me, but his face was laced with fear. "I had to be here," he said and walked closer to me. Instinct made me take a step backward, but there was nowhere for me to hide. He held out his hand to me. "I'm here to walk my daughter down the aisle," he said as his outstretched arm began to shake. "Will you let me?"

This day has been full of dilemmas, and here was yet another one: Daddy has never been there for me. Ever. And now, here he stands, open arms, wanting to give me what he should have been giving me from the day I was born—love. It was too late for that, wasn't it? Or was it? I'd heard it said somewhere that things may not come when you want them, but the most valuable things come right in the nick of time. I may not have had my daddy's love when I was growing up, when I wanted it, but now he was here. And right now was the nick of time.

I reached out and took his hand. I didn't hold it tightly. I wasn't ready for that just yet. But I was ready to start, and as I looked at my father, I knew he was ready too.

"I love you," he said as we walked to the door.

I didn't say it back. I couldn't. But I squeezed his hand and for the first time in my life, I truly felt like I had a daddy.

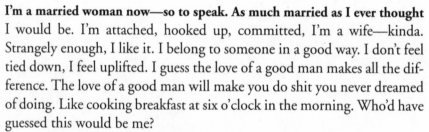

19

I'm a married woman now—so to speak. As much married as I ever thought I would be. I'm attached, hooked up, committed, I'm a wife—kinda. Strangely enough, I like it. I belong to someone in a good way. I don't feel tied down, I feel uplifted. I guess the love of a good man makes all the difference. The love of a good man will make you do shit you never dreamed of doing. Like cooking breakfast at six o'clock in the morning. Who'd have guessed this would be me?

And who would have guessed that last night would have happened? Who would have thought that Chris would have touched me like that? Who would have thought that he would carry me into the bedroom, undress me, and make love to me all night long? And who would have thought that when he pulled out a condom, neither of us would feel awkward or scared? Who would have thought that it could feel so right? Who would have thought that we would go through three condoms in one night? Who would have thought that I'd feel so good that I'd yell out his name? Who would have thought that he'd whisper, "I love you, Li'l Mama," or that the flow of those words would sound so good to my ears? I never did. I never thought that being HIV positive left room for me to be happy. But I am. I truly am. I'm satisfied in every way.

"Morning," Chris said as he walked into the kitchen. He grabbed me from behind and placed a kiss on my neck, but it didn't stop there. His hands were everywhere. He couldn't get enough of me. Ha! And to think

I thought Chris didn't want me anymore. I thought he was turned off by my disease. But Chris not only loves me. He adores me. And I adore him back.

"Isn't this a glorious day?" he said, reminding me of the first conversation we ever had, when we were in college. He still uses that word. Glorious. Damn. I do believe I's in love.

"Eat your breakfast," I told him and spun out of his grasp.

"If you insist," he said and snuck in one more kiss before he sat down at the table and began digging into his eggs.

I sat down next to him, but I didn't eat. I just watched him, thinking how lucky I was. How much I had to live for and look forward to. Last week I tried to bring on death. How stupid was I? Now I realize I have a future, and it's all because of Chris—my one-time secret admirer, now my dedicated partner for life. Amazing what the love of a good man can do.

"Aren't you excited?" I asked and propped my head up on my hand. "The clinic officially opens in one hour and fifty-two minutes."

"I can't wait," he said with a mouth full of eggs and toast. "It's gonna be hard work, but I'm ready."

"Well, don't you work too hard. We are supposed to be on a honeymoon, remember? Just because it wasn't a real wedding doesn't mean we can't have a real honeymoon."

"It was real to me," he said and paused.

I reached out for his face. "Me too," I said and kissed his cheek.

He reached out for his apple juice, then sat it right back down. "Speaking of honeymoons," he said and grinned. "I rolled over at about four o'clock and half of the honeymoon couple was gone."

"Oh I got up early this morning," I said and took his apple juice and sipped it. "I had some final decisions to make."

"Decisions?"

"Yeah," I said and sighed. "I was hoping I could run them by you before you left."

Chris picked up on the seriousness in my voice and swallowed hard. "Talk to me."

"I was just wondering . . . Well, I was thinking . . . You know, if I were to quit my job . . ."

"Madison, I told you. If that's what you want to do I'm behind you one hundred percent. We aren't broke, baby."

"I know, I know. But . . . Well, I sorta had an idea."

"Talk to me."

"I thought maybe I could come work at the clinic. With you."

Silence.

"I mean as a counselor. I think the Teen Center would be a great place for me. I really think I can be of help, you know. I just wanna do my part. It may not be much, but maybe I can help some of those kids. Maybe I can show them how not to end up like me. Mayb—"

Chris grabbed ahold of me so tight that it startled me. I hadn't seen it coming. "I love you," he whispered as he loosened his grip and looked into my face. "I love you."

"Does that mean you like my idea?"

"I like your idea."

"Good," I said and pushed him away from me. "There's more where that came from," I said and jumped up to go to the kitchen counter. I snatched up a piece of paper and handed it to Chris. "I jotted down a few ideas while I was up this morning," I said and sat back down. "See, I figure the clinic could work in conjunction with neighboring schools. Either the schools could arrange field trips to the clinic for counseling sessions or I could personally go to the schools on behalf of the clinic and give little mini seminars. And—"

"Uh, hold up a second," he said and put down the paper. "We've been dedicated less than twenty-four hours and already you're trying to change things."

"That's right, baby. You know what they say. Beside every good man," I said as I leaned over for a kiss, "is a woman with an idea on how to make him better."

"Oh is that right?" he said and gave me a peck.

"Absolutely."

"I love it," he said, skimming over the paper I'd handed him.

"Good," I said and snatched it away. "You, my dear Doctor, had better get a move on," I said and watched him quickly stick another forkful of eggs in his mouth.

"You're right," he said as he got up from the table and rushed off to the bedroom. When he came back he was wearing a white lab coat and carrying a leather briefcase.

"Oh look at my baby," I cooed and pinched his cheeks. "Off to heal the world."

"I'm gon' put a healing on you when I get back home, woman."

"Ah, watch it, now."

"I'll see you later, Mrs. Anzel."

"Okay," I said and walked him to the door.

"I love you."

"I know you do."

I stood in the doorway and watched Chris disappear down the hallway before I closed the door and took a deep breath. Today was the day, I thought as I stood in the middle of the living room. The rest of my life started now.

I went back to the kitchen and cleared away the table before I went to my room and got dressed. I searched around the condo for my car keys, then took a final deep breath before I left. As I drove, I tried to think of the best way to handle things, the right words to say, the right things to do. But when I finally reached my destination, I decided to just let things happen naturally.

I opened the door to his office and stood there until he noticed me, and when he did I almost thought he was going to jump up and run away. Instead, Tommy kept his cool. The only sign that he was ill at ease came from the steady drumming of his fingers against his desktop. I didn't show up here to torment Tommy. I just wanted to know one thing. "Am I fired?"

Tommy's only response was to stop drumming his fingers. He stared at me like I was some kind of ghost. Like he couldn't believe I was there. And finally he asked, "Is it true?"

"That I'm HIV positive?" I asked as he nodded his head. "Yes. I am."

Tommy dropped his head and stared down at the floor. When he looked back at me, tears were in his eyes. "Do you understand that I love you?" he asked clear out the blue.

"What? Why are you telling me this now?"

"Because it's the truth. I don't think you've ever truly understood that."

I dropped my head as I thought over what Tommy had just said, and for once I believed him. Tommy was a good man—sorta. He just didn't know how to show it.

"So am I fired?"

"No."

"Good, 'cause I quit!" I said, trying unsuccessfully to hold back a laugh. "I've always wanted to say that," I said, but my humor wasn't doing much for Tommy.

"You don't have to quit."

"Yes I do, Tommy."

"Look, if you're scared about what the fallout from all this will be, don't worry. I'll handle it. I don't know how yet, but I'll do whatever you need me to do, Madison."

"No," I said and shook my head. "I'm not quitting because I'm scared, I'm quitting because it's what's best for me now."

Tommy leaned back in his seat and scratched his head.

"Here," I said and reached into my purse and pulled out a paper. "You'll have to excuse the handwriting, but I didn't have time to put it into the computer."

"What's this?"

"An addendum to my proposal," I said and propped myself on the edge of his desk as he read.

"You want to lecture here?"

"Yeah," I said and crossed my legs. "As a part of the sex education program. Or you can arrange trips for classes to come down the Watts free clinic for counseling sessions," I said as I leaned over him and pointed out a sloppily written paragraph. "It's really up to you, or whomever you find to teach the sex ed course," I said as I stood up. "What do you think?"

He put down the paper and stared at me. "I think it's great, but you don't have to quit, Madison. We don't even have to tell anyone you're HIV positive."

"No, Tommy," I said and put up a hand. "I want to do this my way."

He sighed and massaged his forehead with his fingers. "Alright."

"As a matter of fact," I said hesitantly, "I was hoping I could say a few words to my class today before I left. If their teacher wouldn't mind, that is. You have replaced me by now, haven't you?"

"I've found a sub for your class, Madi. You could never be replaced."

I smiled as he looked away from me. I could tell he didn't quite know what to do with me.

"There is something I need you to do for me, Tommy," I said, breaking the silence that had fallen between us.

"What's that?"

"Give Malik his job back," I said and folded my arms across my chest. "I've never asked you for anything, Tommy. You owe me. And besides, you know you're wrong as the day is long."

Tommy dropped his head for a minute, then got up from his seat and walked close to me. He put his arm around my shoulders and gripped me tightly. I could feel the teardrops that fell from his eyes as they dropped down my neck. "I'm so sorry," he said and loosened his grip and looked me in the eyes.

"No, I'm sorry. The last time we were together was almost a disaster. You should hate me for that."

"You just don't get it, do you?" he asked, seriously. "I really love you, Madison. I just never showed you in the right way. I could never hate you," he said and backed away from me. "Whatever you want is yours. I'll reinstate Malik immediately. I'll do right by you," he said and leaned into me. He kissed me softly on my cheek and hugged me once more, then he slowly walked over to his window and looked outside. Nothing else needed to be said.

I walked to the door of his office, silently thanking him, but some things never change. Tommy always had to have the last word, and as soon as I was almost out the door he called my name.

"What?" I said not bothering to turn around.

"I hope you'll be able to stop hating me some day."

"Some day is today, Tommy."

■

I hadn't been in my classroom for so long that it felt strange. When I opened the door, I gasped. It was filled with smiling, surprised faces. I guess they'd expected to see another sub this morning, but I'd stopped her in the hall and asked her for a few minutes alone with my old crew. "Good morning, Ms. McGuire," they said in unison.

"Good morning, you little ragamuffins," I said as I walked over to my desk and put down my things. As usual, Sandy had her arm flying through the air. "Yes, Sandra," I said as I walked to the front of my desk.

"Where've you been?" she asked as a bunch of other students nodded their heads waiting to know the answer. "Were you sick?"

Was I sick? "Not really," I said as I propped myself against the desk, realizing it was time for me to give my first lesson on sex education. I may not have been qualified in the teaching sense, but I knew my life, and I had to let my class know. "How many of you have heard of AIDS?"

A few hands shot up.

"What about HIV?"

More hands.

"Well that's what I've got," I said as a hush fell over the room.

"Ms. McGuire," little Kevin Stock called to me. "My uncle had AIDS. He died."

There was an audible gasp, then silence as they all stared at me. They were too scared to ask any more questions. They were in shock, but that was okay. I had their full attention. Maybe now they'll listen good.

"You never forget the day that you find out you have a disease that one day will take your life before its time. You never forget the pain that sinks into your heart when you realize that you could have done something to prevent it from happening to you. When the power to control your life rests in your hands and you blow it, the pain that follows is a beast that you can never get off your mind. It lingers in your soul, forcing you to remember each and every day that you could have done something to prevent this. I am HIV positive and one day I am going to die."

Half the class stared at me with their mouths open. Some may have thought I was joking, but soon they'd realize.

"Life is not over for me yet, though. When my doctor called me to tell me the news, I figured heck, might as well go on ahead and kill myself. Might as well get it over with in a hurry. But thank God, I'm still here. You should thank God that I'm still here because I've got a message for you. A message that you've heard over and over again, on TV, in magazines, the radio, but most of you haven't listened. You probably thought you were too young to listen. But are you listening now? Are you seeing me? I am HIV positive. I am going to die. If I look healthy to you, it's because I am. Funny thing about being HIV positive. Nobody knows unless you tell them. That guy you meet at the arcade? The one with the big chest and the strong arms? The one you think you might want to take home and twist with on the sofa? He may have it. And that girl, Miss Thang? The one with the big butt and the smile? The one you've been trying to get with and get on for weeks? Does she look like me? Well, she may have it too. The point is, you never know and that's why you've got to arm yourself.

"I know you've heard this before, but I don't care. It's the same old lecture, the same old story, the same old yippity-yack smack that makes you bored, makes you sad, makes you want to turn away every time you hear it. But I'm going to say it and I don't care whether you want to hear it or not. Everyone's been telling you, but most people still don't get it. Magic told you. Arthur Ashe told you. Liz Taylor, Liberace, they've been telling you for years. But no one is listening. Well, guess what? I'm gonna say it again. There are certain rules that you must live by in the nineties. Rules that can save your life. And the most important rule of all is this," I said as I walked to the blackboard and picked up a piece of chalk. In huge letters I wrote the words, *Rule number one: Stroke the mind before the behind.*

"When you find that special someone, love them for who they are inside, for their minds, for their personality. Don't get caught up on the sexual. If you're thinking about having sex, don't. You're too damn young. I know you don't want to hear it, but you are. Look at me," I said and pounded my chest as I looked over at Sandy and saw a tear lingering in her eye. "Look at me and learn."

I stood before the class in silence, letting the words I'd spoken permeate every inch of the room. Some faces held concern. Some could not look in my direction. And others wiped away tears.

"Don't cry for me just yet," I said as I tried unsuccessfully to be perky. "I'm still here, you guys," I said as I cracked a smile. But no one would join me. It was okay, though, I thought as I looked into each one of their faces. I'm going to be just fine. They don't know it yet, but I do. I'm going to be alright. God will see to it. This is a fact.

About the Author

Sheneska Jackson was born in Los Angeles, California, where she grew up in South Central and West L.A. She teaches fiction writing at UCLA's Extension Program. She currently lives in Sherman Oaks, where she is fantasizing about her third novel.

3